Kale didn't so m
the heel of his
a solid, meat-a
from the out-thrust hand and Ben saw him stagger
backwards—

—and then he was looking up at the sky, and
feeling the rough concrete floor under his back.
The world tilted to one side as he tried to get his
feet under him. He nearly vomited and then Colin
was helping him up. His lower face was dark and
shiny with blood. 'Come on, let's go.' His voice
sounded wet and nasal.

'Where's my boy?'

Also by Simon Beckett

Fine Lines
Animals
Where There's Smoke

Owning Jacob

Simon Beckett

CORONET BOOKS
Hodder & Stoughton

First published in Great Britain in 1998
by Hodder and Stoughton
First published in paperback in 1999
by Hodder and Stoughton
A division of Hodder Headline PLC
A Coronet Paperback

10 9 8 7 6 5 4 3 2 1

A CIP catalogue record for this title is available
from the British Library

ISBN 0 340 68595 6

Typeset by Palimpsest Book Production Limited,
Polmont, Stirlingshire
Printed and bound in Great Britain by
Mackays of Chatham PLC, Chatham, Kent

Hodder and Stoughton
A division of Hodder Headline PLC
338 Euston Road
London NW1 3BH

ACKNOWLEDGEMENTS

Thanks to Peter Liver of South Yorkshire NSPCC and Sarah Pimlott for their guidance on legal aspects, Dick Bunting for background on firearms and police procedures, Rob Quayle of Rowan School for information on autism, and Carolyn Mays and Patrick Walsh for all their help and enthusiasm. Special thanks also to Sheila and Frank Beckett, my mom and dad, for all their support.

ACKNOWLEDGMENTS

Chapter One

———◆◇◆———

He found the locked box the day after the funeral.

It had been his worst day even before he opened it. Until then there had been an aim, something to focus on that filled the days with at least the illusion of purpose. The bureaucratic rituals of death and burial were details behind which he could hide, while the funeral itself was unreal, a pantomime which he watched with a numbed detachment. Afterwards, though, once he had closed the door on the last of the friends and mourners, there was nothing to occupy the space that Sarah's death had caused. He had put Jacob to bed, turned on the TV and quietly got drunk until the fact of tomorrow, and the tomorrows after that, was smudged by an alcoholic fog.

When he woke the next morning the day was as cold and bleak as the empty bed beside him. He got up and dressed, as though by moving he could keep one step ahead of the awareness that dogged his heels. Jacob was silent as Ben poured milk on his cereal, but his eyes darted about the kitchen as if he were looking for something. Ben wondered how much of what had happened the six-year-old was able to understand. He rested his hand on his stepson's head.

'Maggie's going to take you to school today, okay?'

Jacob gave no sign of having heard. He bent and held one ear close to the cereal, listening to the puffed rice crackling in the milk. Ben tried to think of something he could say, but the effort of words was like lifting a weight above his head. He gave the boy's hair a brief ruffle and moved away.

Maggie was on time, as usual. Her forced cheerfulness filled the kitchen like a clashing colour scheme. Ben suppressed his irritation as she greeted Jacob with an enthusiasm that was as grating as it was false. Jacob didn't acknowledge her. His attention was still fixed on his breakfast cereal, which by now had soaked itself into silence. He had eaten some of it and was arranging the rest in a neat line around the rim of the bowl.

Maggie looked at Ben, her expression becoming one of predictable concern. 'How are you?'

'Okay.' He turned away from her sympathy before she could offer it. 'Would you like a coffee?'

'No, if Jacob's ready we'd better get off. It said on the radio that there's roadworks on the way to the school, so there's bound to be jams.'

'You won't forget to take him the usual route, will you?'

Her smile twitched a little. 'Of course not.'

She had tried going another way to the school one morning and Jacob had thrown a tantrum in the car. Ben had apologised, explaining that he grew upset at any variation from his routine, without mentioning what they were both aware of; that she'd known that already. Maggie had expressed regret, but it was a little too saccharin to be sincere. And he thought there was a trace of mistrust in her eyes now whenever she looked at Jacob.

She kept up an aimless chatter as Ben helped him into his shoes and coat. 'Are you sure you don't want me to collect him as well?' she offered. 'It won't be any trouble.'

'No, it's all right, thanks.' He maintained the semblance of a smile until Maggie accepted this. She gave him a hug as she kissed his cheek. Her own was so over-powdered that it felt like suede. Her perfume had the same cloying pungency as the flowers on Sarah's coffin. 'If you want me to do anything, just give me a ring.'

Ben said he would and crouched down to give Jacob a kiss. 'See you later, Jake. Be a good boy for Maggie.'

The boy didn't answer. He had a puzzle game in his hand, a plastic maze with a tiny ball rolling loose in it. Whenever he succeeded in manipulating the ball into the centre he gave the puzzle a quick shake and began all over again. He didn't look up from it as he went out with Maggie. Ben watched from the doorway as the two of them got into the car where Scott and Andrew, Maggie's own two young sons, were waiting. He waved as they drove away.

He closed the door and went back into the house.

The lack of Sarah echoed from every room. It battered at him as he returned to the kitchen. He picked up his coffee, but it was cold. He put it down again. Even the sound of the mug touching the table seemed loud in the silence. The familiar ordinariness of their home had been subtly altered, shifted into a new perspective, a parallel dimension of loss. Ben closed his eyes against it and straightaway his imagination began to play its cruel tricks. He could see Sarah, thoughtlessly humming along to the radio as she moved around the kitchen, pausing to take a hurried drink from her mug of coffee. The blue one, that she liked. He could hear her voice, internally, but clearly nevertheless as she spoke to Jacob. 'Hurry up with your breakfast, Jake, there's a good boy.' She half turned to Ben as she fixed her light brown hair in the mirror. 'I forgot to tell you, I told Imogen that we might see her and Neil this weekend.'

'Aw, no, you're joking,' he heard himself say, mouth moving in silent unison to the remembered words. 'Neil's the most boring man in the world.'

Her reflection gave him an arch smile. 'Well, you'll just have to be extra interesting to make up for him, won't you?' She turned her head and quickly examined her hair from the side. 'Sod it. That'll have to do.'

She went to where her jacket hung on a hanger behind the door, short skirt whisking against her legs as she walked. 'Come on, Jake, time to go.' She squeezed her son's ribs from behind, making him squirm as she tickled him. Ben had smiled to see them both laughing. He smiled again now, replaying it.

Sarah planted a kiss on the top of Jacob's head and bent to tie his training shoe laces. 'Will you be working late tonight?'

'Don't think so. I should be back by seven, anyway.'

He watched her pull back the seat for Jacob to jump down. As she straightened she winced and rubbed at her temple. 'I think I must have had one glass too many last night,' she said. She looked trim and smart as she came towards him. He could see the exact pattern of freckling that spread faintly across her cheeks and the bridge of her nose, smell her perfume when she came close. 'See you later.' She smiled up at him, lifting her face for a kiss, and the image was so vivid that he swayed forward and opened his eyes.

The empty kitchen confronted him. The breakfast dishes still sat on the table. Two of them, his own and Jacob's. He wished now that he hadn't accepted Maggie's offer to take Jacob to school. For a moment he was tempted to go out, to escape to a more neutral environment that didn't resonate with Sarah's absence. But that would only be putting off what he knew had to be faced sooner or later. It was better sooner.

She wasn't coming back.

He took a roll of black plastic bin-liners and went upstairs to their bedroom. Her personality was almost tangible in here. Trying to close his mind to what he was doing he opened the wardrobe and took down an armful of her clothes. Her scent clung to them like a distillation of grief. He couldn't believe she was never going to wear any of them again. He got as far as the bed before he stopped, clutching the bundle to his chest as the sobs chopped into him.

The call had come through just over a week ago. He had

been at the studio in the middle of a shoot when Zoe, his assistant, told him that Colin was on the phone. Colin was Maggie's husband and his oldest friend, a solicitor at the same entertainment law firm where Sarah worked. Ben hadn't looked up from the camera as he told her to say he'd call back.

I think you'd better take it, Zoe had said. He was about to snap that he was busy when he saw the expression on her face.

The term the doctors used was aneurysm. It had been just another word to him before then. He hadn't even been sure what it was, but what it meant to him now was that a vein in Sarah's head had swollen and burst. A minuscule part of her, a fraction of the whole person that was his wife, had given way, and now she was in intensive care. There had been no warning, except for the casual mention of a headache that morning. Ben had felt a vast sense of wrongness as the doctor talked of CT scans, the possibility of emergency surgery.

They wouldn't let him see her at first. Intellectually he had realised it was serious, but emotionally it was too much to take in. The night before they had cooked a meal, put Jacob to bed, drunk a bottle of wine. It didn't seem possible that she could suddenly be desperately ill. Even when the doctor came to tell him that she was on a life support machine, and that they had done everything they could, Ben couldn't accept what was happening. It was only when he saw her lying still and unconscious in the hospital bed, with her head shaved and her face bruised and pale, that he understood she was dying.

The machines had kept her alive for three days. When they turned them off on the fourth, Ben had sat holding her hand, talking to her until she stopped breathing with a lack of fuss that was almost an anticlimax.

Maggie and Colin had taken him home. He'd known Colin since university, drunkenly tried to warn him out of marrying Maggie, reluctantly been best man at their wedding. But now neither he nor Maggie seemed completely real. They had waited with him until Jacob arrived back from school, and then left for Ben to try to explain to the boy that his mother was dead. Jacob had kept his eyes averted. Only the fact of him rocking backwards and forwards gave any indication that the news might, after all, have reached him.

Ben could have envied his stepson's autism right then.

He cried himself out and set the clothes gently on the bed before returning to the wardrobe for another armful. There were a lot of them. Sarah had been a hoarder, never throwing away anything unless she absolutely had to. He had often ribbed her about it, calling her a magpie. She countered by accusing him of having a consumer mentality.

The memory brought a short-lived smile. 'Don't worry, Oxfam won't throw them out either,' he said out loud, but the joking tone rang hollow.

He finished emptying her clothes from the wardrobe and moved on to her dressing table. He made a second pile next to the first, then a third. He tried not to look at what he was stacking, knowing if he weakened he'd never be able to get rid of anything. It was just pieces of fabric, not her favourite dress, the matching silk bra and pants he'd bought for her last birthday. He emptied another drawer, closed it and opened the one beneath. As he reached in to lift out the compressed clothes his fingers touched something cold and hard at the back. He carried the bundle of sweaters to the bed then went back and took it out.

It was a battered old strongbox. The black paint was chipped and faded to reveal the dull patina of brass. He couldn't remember seeing it before, but Sarah had been a compulsive wanderer of antique fairs and flea markets. He'd lost track of half of the things she'd bought. Even so, he thought, it was odd that it had been hidden.

There was a faint rustling from inside when he tilted it, but the lid was locked. He looked in the drawers for a key. There wasn't one. He thought for a moment, then went to the antique tea caddy where she'd kept her jewellery. She had been buried in her wedding and engagement rings, but there were other pieces, none particularly valuable in themselves, that he couldn't see himself casually discarding. He tried not to think about that as he poked among them for a key.

He found one under a nest of thin gold chains.

It fitted the lock of the strongbox. There was a click and the lid sprang open against the sudden lack of resistance. Ben laid it back against its hinges.

Inside was a cluster of yellowed newspaper cuttings, folded and paper-clipped together. A larger piece of paper lay at the bottom. Jacob's birth certificate, he saw when he took it out. Except for that the box was empty. He put the certificate down and unfolded the pieces of newspaper.

The headline of the top one was 'BABY STEVEN'S MOTHER IN TV APPEAL'. He looked to see what was on the other side, but there was only part of an advert. He flicked quickly through the rest. They weren't in any chronological order, but were all concerned with the same story, a baby abducted from a maternity hospital. All seemed to be from the *Daily Mail*, which surprised him a little because the only papers he'd known Sarah to read were the *Guardian* or the *Evening Standard*.

The thought *I'll ask her why she kept them* was followed by the gut punch of remembering that he couldn't. He put them down, his curiosity suddenly soured. They were just another loose end that would now never be tidied up. He would have left them on the dressing table, ready to be thrown out, except for a nagging feeling that he had missed something. He picked them up again. There were five of them, decreasing in size from the banner-headlined 'BABY STOLEN FROM MATERNITY UNIT' to a single-column filler as the story sank without development beneath the weight of fresher news. Only the one from the front page had a date on it, but as far as he could tell they spanned about a week, all from March, six years earlier. Something about that hovered, waiting to be recognised. He looked at Jacob's birth certificate, then at the date on the first cutting. March the third.

Jacob's birthday.

A sense of unease was building up in him like a trapped gas bubble. He read the reports again, paying more attention now. They dealt with the search for a newborn baby that had been taken from its hospital cot in central London. Its parents were a John and Jeanette Kale. The names didn't ring any bells. Kale was a Royal Engineer corporal, serving in Northern Ireland and described as a 'veteran' of the Gulf War. It was their first child, a boy, and there was editorial indignation that someone should have abducted the son of a soldier who was 'serving his country'. There were the predictable police appeals, both for witnesses and to whoever had taken the baby. One of the cuttings showed a photograph of the parents. It was a poor picture of the father, a youngish man with a cropped, military haircut, head half turned away as he emerged from the hospital. Next to him his wife looked older than her given age of twenty-three. But who wouldn't, Ben supposed, feeling uncharitable as he took in the anguish the shot had frozen.

The unease was expanding. All at once the touch of the desiccated scraps of paper repulsed him. He dropped them back on the dressing table, rubbing his hands on his jeans as he turned away. The sight of Sarah's heaped clothes on the bed struck him like a crack on the face. It shattered the last of his restraint. He rushed out of the bedroom, almost falling downstairs, and stood in the hallway at the bottom, gasping for breath. He felt himself beginning to hyperventilate and tried to fight the growing panic. *Stop it.*

He went into the kitchen and splashed cold water over his face, spilling it down his throat and chest. The shock was calming. He turned off the tap and braced his arms on the sink. Water dripped from his nose and chin as he looked out through the window. On the other side of the glass the street appeared the same as always. The houses were hard-edged in the bright afternoon sun. Parked cars lined both sides of the road, parallel lines facing in opposite directions. A man walked a dog, pausing to let it urinate against a lamppost before continuing beyond the edge of the window frame.

Normal.

Ben let his head hang, feeling limp with reaction. What in Christ's name was he thinking of? He felt ashamed of the suspicions that even now he couldn't fully acknowledge. Jacob was Sarah's son, for God's sake. He held on to that thought, building it up and strengthening it until the fear he'd felt in the bedroom seemed unreal and irrational.

Then he thought about the date on the newspaper cutting and a ghost of it returned.

Pushing himself away from both the sink and the fear, he dried his face and looked at his watch. It would soon be time for him to collect Jacob from school. He didn't want to have Sarah's clothes lying about in piles when he got home.

He went back upstairs to finish packing them away.

Chapter Two

He'd met Sarah through Colin. It was part of the folklore of their relationship that they might have been in the same room on several occasions before they finally spoke, but if they had neither of them could remember it. They didn't become aware of each other until they were thrown together, at a party to celebrate the signing of one of Colin's fledgling bands. Colin had negotiated the contract with a major record label and seemed to regard the deal as a personal coup. At times Ben thought he was more like a frustrated manager than a solicitor, and, like a convert to a new religion, he seemed to regard it as his duty to involve Ben in the heady world of the music industry.

'You've got to come, it'll be great!' he'd enthused. 'The record company's really pushing the boat out on this one. Should be a good night.'

Ben wasn't convinced. He'd been to signing parties before and not enjoyed them. Most of the bands he never heard of again, and he found their habitual mixture of naïveté and arrogance irritating. The whole idea bored him. But there had been nothing boring that night. Not after he broke his camera on the lead singer's head.

He'd been in a bad mood to begin with. He had recently split up with a girl he'd been seeing for the past six months, a model he had met on an advertising agency shoot. He was still smarting over the acrimonious end, which was probably why Colin had asked him along. And why, perhaps, he had accepted.

He had regretted it as soon as he walked into the club and felt the hammering music hit him. He had seen it all before, from the bottles of free champagne, tequila, imported beers and Jack Daniels, to the burning car suspended on chains from the ceiling. He would have turned around and left if Colin hadn't seen him and waved him over.

In his dark lawyer's suit his friend stood out from the clubbers like a crow among budgerigars. They'd shared a flat at university. The posing first-year fine art undergraduate and the ironed-jeaned third-year law student had regarded each other suspiciously to begin with, both convinced of a mistake by the accommodation department, but a mutual love of football and beer had soon overcome the less-important differences. After university they had kept in touch, despite Colin marrying Maggie against Ben's advice when she became pregnant, and the differences between them becoming more apparent. Ben's hair grew longer and Colin's suits more expensive. Maggie had once referred to them as the Odd Couple. Ben thought that was probably the closest to a joke she had ever come.

He sometimes wondered if Colin's decision to go into entertainment law, dealing with musicians and actors, was a reaction against the confines of his home life. He'd never risked their friendship by asking, though. He made himself smile as he reached Colin's table and was introduced to solicitors and sharkish executives from the record company. They acknowledged Ben with polite lack of interest, which mirrored the way he felt about them. He excused himself as soon as he could and wandered off to get a beer.

That was his first mistake. With no one to talk to, he drank more quickly than he should have done. The camera dragged around his neck. Against his better judgment he had taken it with him, at Colin's insistence.

'If you get some good shots of the night, you know, just snapping people, you might be able to get more work from the label,' Colin had said, despite the fact that Ben had repeatedly told him that he had no interest in working with bands. He liked working with either professional models or people who weren't aware they were being photographed, not four or five usually unphotogenic individuals, one of whom could always be guaranteed to blink as the shutter came down. Photographing live gigs was even worse. Ben had tried it for a while when he was scrabbling to find his feet after graduating, but soon gave up. When it came down to it, he wasn't interested enough in music for it to be worth the grind.

He was on his fourth or fifth beer when Colin materialised at his elbow. 'Come on, I'll introduce you to the band,' he shouted, leaning closer to be heard above the thumping beat. Doing his best to look enthusiastic, Ben followed him through the crush of people. Empty glasses and bottles were spilled over a pair of tables pushed together in a booth, where twice as many people as it could comfortably hold were clustered around the four budding celebrities at one end.

Colin greeted them familiarly. If he was aware of the condescending looks he received he gave no sign. He was still a few months shy of thirty, but his suit and neatly cut, already thinning sandy hair made him seem middle-aged even in comparison to Ben, who was only two years his junior. He reeled off their names, which Ben made no attempt to remember. 'They're going to be massive,' he enthused, aiming the comment at the band.

There were self-congratulatory smirks. 'Yeah, that's right,' one of the band said. 'Massive.'

Colin seemed not to notice the parody, or the sniggers it provoked. He clapped Ben on the shoulder. 'Ben's a photographer. He's here to take a few pictures.'

Ben was uncomfortably aware of becoming the focus of attention. He felt his anger rise as the patronising looks were switched to him. *You arrogant little pricks*, he thought, staring back with his own fuck-you smile. Then Colin said, 'I'll see you in a bit, Ben,' and with an encouraging squeeze on his arm left him standing there.

Ben silently cursed him. And himself, for not guessing that Colin would think he was doing him a favour. He would have left as well, but before he could one of the band spoke.

'So you want to take our pictures, then?'

It was the same one who had ridiculed Colin. He had been introduced as the singer. Even slouched back in his seat he was obviously tall, good-looking in a gangly sort of way, with a tight black T-shirt and mop of thick, dark hair. Despite the club's dim lighting his pupils were shrunk to pinpricks, a sign that he had been celebrating with more than alcohol.

'Not really,' Ben answered.

The singer pointed at the camera hanging on its strap. 'So why the fuck have you got that round your neck? Is it a necklace, or what?'

There were laughs from around the table. 'Yeah, that's right,' Ben said, turning to go.

'Hey, come on, man, you're here to take some photos, aren't you? How about this?' The singer sprawled back in an exaggerated model's pose, pursing his lips.

Ordinarily Ben would have grinned and walked away. But the beers he had drunk had added to his already bad temper. And he had drunk them on an empty stomach.

'Get fucked,' he said.

The mood around the table instantly changed. The singer sat up, no longer smiling. 'Don't tell me to get fucked, arsehole. Who the fuck invited you, anyway? You just come here to scrounge free drinks, or what?'

Ben carefully placed his beer on the table. 'Fuck you, and fuck your drinks,' he said, which would have been a fine exit line if the singer hadn't picked up a glass and thrown its contents in his face before he could move.

The table erupted with laughter, but his first concern was for his camera. It wasn't in a case, and liquid was dripping from it. Whatever had been in the glass smelled of blackcurrant, and if there was one thing worse than getting a camera wet, it was getting it wet with something sweet and sticky.

'You stupid bastard!' he snapped, taking it from around his neck, and as he did the singer snatched it from him. The strap snagged on Ben's head, only briefly, but enough to jerk the camera from the singer's grip. Ben tried to catch it but missed. It struck the edge of the table and then bounced to the floor with a terminal crash.

'Oops,' the singer said as Ben bent to pick it up. The lens came away in his hand, sprinkling glass. There were one or two giggles, but most people seemed to realise that what had happened wasn't funny. The singer wasn't one of them.

'You weren't going to use it anyway,' he jeered, and the last of Ben's restraint disappeared. He flung the broken camera across at him, more of a reflexive gesture than anything else. He expected the singer to block it, but he had taken that moment to turn and laugh with the girl sitting next to him. He was still grinning when the camera struck him in the face.

The singer cried out and fell back as blood spurted from a gash on his forehead. Ben had time to realise that things had got a little out of hand before another member of the band sprang up and swung at him. He ducked and felt the punch land on the top of his skull. His vision burst into popping lights and he flailed out himself as he stumbled and fell. The next seconds were a vague impression of bodies, shrieks and breaking glass. He felt himself hit several more times and covered his head, then he was being hauled to his feet by a burly pair of arms. He looked out through the eye that didn't hurt to see Colin's anxious face as he tried to calm everyone down, including the door staff, who seemed inclined to join in themselves. Beyond him, the singer's face was slick with blood as he pressed both hands to the cut on his forehead, while the musician who had thrown the first punch was cradling one of his hands to his chest and moaning.

'Okay, it's cool, it's cool,' Colin was assuring everyone, his anxious expression belying the words. He shot Ben a look that was part concern, part anger, then spoke to someone at Ben's side. 'Take him outside. I'll be along when I've sorted out this mess.'

Ben thought he was talking to the bouncer who had helped him up, but it was a young woman whom he had seen at Colin's table earlier. 'Come on,' she said. 'Can you walk?'

They made their way through the club to the exit.

'Do you want to clean yourself up?' the young woman asked. She was wearing a matching dark jacket and skirt, the businesswoman's equivalent of Colin's suit. Ben shook his head. He still hadn't spoken to her yet. The adrenalin was draining out of him now, and mortification was flooding in to fill the gap. It was only just beginning to dawn on him what a fool he had made of himself.

They went outside and waited by the club's entrance. The night air tasted like oxygen after the smoky atmosphere of the club. It was September, still warm but with enough of a cool edge to feel like a sobering flannel on his face. Ben pushed his hands into his pockets and tried to keep from shivering. He avoided looking at the woman, but he could feel her watching him.

'So what happened back there? I take it they didn't want their photos taken?'

Ben was uncomfortably aware that his teeth were starting to chatter from reaction. 'No, it, uh ... it was because I wouldn't take any.' He could feel himself starting to blush.

'Well, that's a new one. A photographer beaten up in a nightclub for not taking photographs.'

He couldn't help but respond to her amusement. 'Yeah, well, you've got to be selective about these things.'

Colin emerged from the club. Not even the neon light could disguise the flush on his cheeks as he strode over.

'Well, this is fucking great! Jesus, Ben, what the *fuck* were you thinking of?'

'What was *I* thinking of? They smashed my camera!'

'I don't give a shit about your camera! I've been working on this deal for the past six months and the day it's signed I get a singer who's going to need stitches and a bass player with a broken hand! And it's my fucking guest who does it! I mean, thanks Ben, this makes a *really* good impression, doesn't it?'

He had never seen Colin so angry, but a sense of injustice brought a spurt of his own anger. 'What do you expect me to do, smile and say thank you?'

'Would it have killed you to take a few fucking pictures just to keep things quiet, if only for my sake? But no, that's too much to ask, isn't it? You have to get into a fight with the singer and chuck the bloody camera in his face! Their manager's talking about *suing* you, for Christ's sake!'

Belatedly, it began to occur to Ben what an embarrassing position he'd put Colin in. 'I thought he'd catch it,' he said, lamely.

'Yeah, well, he didn't.' Colin ran a hand through his thinning hair. 'Look, I'd better get back in there. And you'd better make yourself scarce. They'll be coming out to go to the hospital soon. I don't want any more trouble if they see you.'

Ben nodded, chagrined. 'Sorry.'

Colin looked at him for a moment, as though considering whether to accept the apology or not, then sighed. 'Don't worry, I'll sort it out.' He gave a tired smile. 'It could be worse. At least it's only the bass player's hand that's broken. We're probably going to get rid of him anyway.'

Ben was about to laugh when he saw that he wasn't joking.

Colin turned to the young woman, who had been standing in the background during the exchange. 'Sarah, can you make sure he gets a taxi? And you might as well go home yourself then. There's no point you hanging about any longer.'

Without waiting for an answer he hurried back inside. There was a silence afterwards. Ben wanted to crawl under something. 'Come on,' Sarah said. 'We can get a taxi down here.'

They walked away from the club. 'I don't need a taxi,' he told her when they reached a side road. 'My car's parked down here.'

She stopped and looked at him. 'I don't think you should drive.'

'I'm okay. My eye isn't that bad.' He tentatively felt the swelling.

'I didn't mean your eye. How many drinks have you had?'

'I'm not drunk,' he retorted.

'Perhaps not, but don't you think tonight's been eventful enough already?'

The amused expression was still on her face. She had light brown, jaw-length hair tucked back behind her ears and a smattering of pale freckles running across her nose and cheeks. It was difficult to tell what colour her eyes were in the light from the streetlamps, but Ben thought they were probably hazel. She was quite attractive, he realised. He felt his scowl slipping away. 'Yeah, perhaps you're right.'

They flagged down a taxi. Ben offered it to her first, but she declined. 'Colin'll only quiz me about it tomorrow. I want to be able to tell him I saw you safely on your way.'

There was something vulnerable and yet aloof about her slim figure as she waited for him to get in. He felt strangely nervous. 'Where are you going?' he asked. 'We might as well share.'

She lived in Clapham. 'You've done me a favour, actually,'

she said, as the taxi pulled away. 'I'd have had to stay for another hour or so, and I don't like being late for the baby-sitter.'

'You've got children?' He was surprised at how disappointed he suddenly was.

'A little boy. Jacob. He's nearly two now.'

'Is your husband out tonight as well?'

'I'm not married.'

It was said without emotion, a flat statement. Ben realised he was pleased. *She's got a kid. Don't get carried away.*

'So are you a lawyer too?' he asked.

'No, just a lowly clerk. But I'm studying in my spare time. With a bit of luck I should take my articles in a few years. It's a roundabout way of doing things, but at least you get paid while you're doing it.' She shrugged, dismissing the problems of being a working single mother. 'How about you? Do you actually take photographs, or do you only use cameras as offensive weapons?'

He grinned, sheepishly. 'Only when provoked. When I'm not throwing cameras in people's faces, I do fashion shoots for magazines, bits and pieces for advertising agencies. Stuff like that.'

'Sounds glamorous.'

'About as glamorous as the music business.' He fingered his swollen eye and they both laughed. When the taxi stopped outside her flat he couldn't believe the journey had passed so quickly. As she climbed out of the cab he felt an urgency come over him he hadn't felt since he was a teenager.

'Look,' he said, hurriedly, 'if you aren't doing anything later this week, perhaps we could go for a drink some time?'

She smiled, bending to the open door. 'I can't really. It was difficult enough finding someone to baby-sit tonight. But thanks for asking.'

Leave it at that. Don't get involved, she's got a kid. She was straightening, beginning to close the door. 'How about lunch?' he asked.

She looked at him. Her smile had become quizzical, as though this wasn't what she'd expected either.

'Call me at work,' she said.

Two years later they were married. And two years after that a vein burst in her head and killed her.

Jacob sat on the settee in the crook of Ben's arm, watching *The Lion King* on video. It was one of his favourites, which for Jacob meant that he could watch it through to the end, then go back and watch the whole thing again straightaway. He'd learned how to work the video machine when he was four, but never bothered rewinding if a tape was halfway through. He just watched it from whatever point it started. The narrative never interested him, only the visuals.

He yawned now as he watched the cartoon. Ben knew that he should really put him to bed. They had a strict routine – Jacob would wash his hands when he arrived home from school, watch children's TV for half an hour, eat his tea, spend some time playing or watching more TV with them, then have a bath and go to bed. Routines for Jacob meant safety and security, and any departure could upset him. Ben had already helped him assemble a rudimentary car from Lego bricks, and now they were running into his bath-time. But he hadn't seemed to notice, and Ben was loath to put him to bed just yet. He needed the contact as much as Jacob did. More, perhaps, right then.

The phone had been ringing all night, various people wanting to see how he was. He was touched by their concern, but was glad when the calls had finally stopped. Most of 'their' friends were really Sarah's, parents of children who either went to Jacob's school or that she had met through autistic contact groups. Ben didn't feel he had much in common with them, and the conversations only made him more aware then ever that Sarah wasn't there. Only Jacob.

And he couldn't look at Jacob any more without thinking about the newspaper cuttings.

He'd been tempted to tell Colin about them when he'd phoned, but in the end he hadn't. He wanted to think it through first, satisfy himself that he wasn't being paranoid. One moment he would be convinced of the worst, the next certain that there was a mundane explanation. Sometimes a conviction that the entire thing was ludicrous would blow away his suspicions like a spring wind. He had seen photographs of Sarah when she was pregnant, for one thing, talked with her parents about the birth of their grandson. He knew that she had been seeing a bastard called Miles, who dropped her when she became pregnant (there was the usual surge of jealousy-tipped anger at the thought), and that she had moved in with her friend Jessica afterwards. Ben had dubbed her The Awful Jessica because in his opinion she was, although Sarah didn't like him poking fun. But, awful or not, she had been a trainee midwife, and when Jacob had been born prematurely and suddenly it had been Jessica who had delivered him in the middle of the night.

That was the truth as he had known it. He would remember it and feel relieved, but then, imperceptibly, his certainty would slip through his fingers and the whole process of argument and counter-argument would begin again.

Jacob gave another yawn and rubbed his eyes. Ben smiled despite himself as he watched him struggling to stay awake. 'Come on. Time for bed.' He gave him the expected piggyback upstairs and ran the bath. The boy was so tired he was yawning continuously, but he still followed the routine detailed in the little pictograms on the bathroom door. Sarah had drawn them herself, basing them on the Rebus symbols used at the school. They were simple drawings showing matchstick figures flushing the toilet, washing their hands and brushing their teeth. Some had a sun added to them to show they were for the daytime, others a crescent moon, and Jacob stuck to the sequences religiously. Ben had once made the mistake of trying to remove them, thinking they were no longer needed, but Jacob had made such a fuss he'd quickly put them back. Needed or not, the pictograms themselves had become part of the comforting order.

Ben kissed him goodnight and stood back as he pulled the quilt up to his chin, turned over and fell asleep instantly. He felt guilty for keeping him up so long. The boy had given no outward indication of being aware of his mother's death but it must have affected him. Ben was sure that, on some level, at least, he knew something was wrong. He didn't expect Jacob to understand what a funeral was — an ordinary day was full of confusion enough for him — but during the service he had stared at the coffin and rocked, which he only did when he was disturbed. Maggie, with her usual subtlety, had tried to persuade Ben not to take him, arguing that nothing would be gained by it and that he'd only cause a fuss. But Sarah would have wanted him there. She had always believed in treating Jacob as much like a normal child as possible, giving no more concessions to his autism than she had to.

'He's a bright boy,' she had said. 'I'm not going to patronise him because he's autistic. He isn't retarded.'

For a time they'd thought he might be. At least Ben had. He had never said as much to Sarah, even though he was sure it must have occurred to her. As a baby, Jacob had been slow first to crawl, then to walk. When he was three he still hadn't spoken so much as a word, and the excuse that he was a 'slow starter' no longer held any conviction. But it was his lack of *response* that convinced Ben there was something wrong. It seemed to make no difference to Jacob if he was being cuddled or left in a room by himself. He rarely smiled, and when he looked at anyone, even Sarah, it was with no more recognition than he would give a piece of furniture. For a long time Ben found his indifferent stare eerie, though that was something else he never mentioned.

Eventually, even Sarah couldn't deny that there was a problem. She had taken Jacob to have his hearing tested, and Ben got the impression that she hoped he actually was deaf, that the problem was a straightforward physical one. He didn't believe it himself. Jacob didn't seem to understand anything that was said to him or recognise his name, but there were some sounds he unmistakably reacted to. He would look towards the door of whatever room he was in when the doorbell sounded, and once when Sarah was out Ben had experimented by standing behind him and opening a packet of sweets. The little boy had twisted around immediately, a look of anticipation replacing his usual remote expression.

He had been nearly four when he had been diagnosed as autistic. Not long after that Ben went to Antigua on a shoot. The second night one of the models had come on to him after a group of them went to a bar together. She had a fabulous body, a golden tan, and he knew no word of it would ever get back to Sarah. He had seen the promise of suntanned and easy sex smiling in front of him and thought back over the strain of the previous few months. Taking Jacob to see specialists. Waiting for test results. Vainly trying to comfort Sarah as she cried, for the first time since he'd known her, when they were told. Did he really want to tie himself down to a woman with an autistic child that wasn't even his? The answer hadn't really surprised him.

He made his excuses to the girl and spent the night alone in his hotel room. The day he arrived back in London he asked Sarah to marry him.

Now he stood by Jacob's bed and looked down at her son, searching for some resemblance that would put the question of parentage beyond doubt. There was nothing. The boy's hair was a ruddy brown, not Sarah's paler colour. His eyes were a pale, tawny brown, and his features had none of the fineness of her bone structure. Ben had always taken for granted that the boy took after his father.

Perhaps he does.

He left the bedroom and went downstairs. The house was quiet. He took an old tobacco tin from the bag that held his camera equipment, collected a beer from the fridge and went into the lounge to roll himself a joint. Sarah never liked him smoking them at home, but Jacob was in bed, and if ever there was a time when he needed one this was it. He lit up and drew on it, holding his breath. When he finally let it go it was explosively, as if he could expel everything else along with the used smoke. Taking another drag from the joint, he crossed to the bookshelf and reached up for the strongbox. He carried it back to the settee and spread out the newspaper cuttings on the cushion next to him, where Jacob had been sitting earlier. He picked out the one that had a photograph of the baby's parents. It was impossible to make out what John Kale looked like but at least, if Jacob didn't take after Sarah, he didn't resemble the newspaper picture of Jeanette Kale either. Ben tossed the cutting on to the rest. He had already gone through them countless times without learning anything else. A newborn baby had gone missing, and it happened to coincide with Jacob's birth. So what? Hundreds of babies would have been born on the same day. It didn't mean anything.

So why had she saved the cuttings?

That was where all his reasoning, all his reassurances, fell apart. He could tell himself that it was ridiculous to be disturbed by a few pieces of old newsprint, that the dates were only a fluke. Reading about it on the same day she gave birth herself was probably what had prompted Sarah to save the reports in the first place. Then she'd put them to one side and typically forgotten to throw them away.

Simple.

Except it didn't work. Sarah might have kept an entire newspaper, or even several, but he'd never known her cut out individual stories. That sort of neatness wasn't part of her character. He couldn't even begin to think why they'd been in a locked box with the birth certificate.

Or rather he could.

Confusion gouged at the rawness of his grief. He pushed his hand through his hair. Even that brought a pang – she had liked it long, liked running her fingers through it. 'Jesus, Sarah,' he said. The need to talk to her, to see and hear her again, was so vast it terrified him. He couldn't believe he never would. It was as though someone had cut holes in the world where she should have been. He felt his throat begin to constrict and took a last steadying pull at the dying joint, welcoming the hotness of the smoke. He held his breath, but when he let it go it came out in a sob, and suddenly he was crying.

When it passed he felt drained but more himself. Sarah had been his wife and he had loved her. Jacob was her son, and that was all there was to it. He despised himself for doubting her. He stubbed out the roach and blew his nose. The cuttings were still spread out on the settee, but now they had lost their potency. They were just scraps of paper. He felt slightly foolish for overreacting. And ashamed.

He gathered them together, intending to throw them away. The phone rang as he was screwing them up. He sniffed and cleared his throat, banishing the last of the tears before answering. 'Hello?'

'Hello, Ben. It's Geoffrey.'

Ben felt a twinge of conscience at the sound of his father-in-law's voice. 'Sorry, Geoffrey, I was supposed to call, wasn't I?' It had been the last thing he'd said to Sarah's parents after the funeral the day before.

'Not to worry. You've got enough on your plate at the moment without worrying about us. I just thought I'd ring and see how you were getting on.'

'Oh ... okay.' He changed the subject. 'You got back to Leicester all right?'

'No trouble at all.'

'You could have stayed here overnight, you know.' He knew Geoffrey didn't like driving.

'I know we could, lad, but Alice wanted to get home. You know how she is.'

Ben did. She had never forgiven Sarah for moving to London twice, the first time to find work, the second after they had taken her back home when Jacob was born. 'How's she coping?'

'Not bad.' His tone said otherwise. 'She's in bed now. You've got to take these things a day at a time, haven't you?'

An awkwardness came between them. Ben sensed the older man's reluctance to end the conversation, even though there was nothing for either of them to say that hadn't already been said. He knew how keenly his father-in-law felt Sarah's death. Talking to her husband was a way of holding on to her, a cold comfort but all he had, and better than the lonely house with the mourning wife asleep upstairs. It was as much to prolong the contact between them as to appease any final doubts that Ben said, 'I've been thinking about when Sarah had Jacob.'

'Only seems like two minutes ago. I can't believe it's six years.'

'Was it a quick birth?' he asked, already knowing the answer.

'Two hours, that's all. We always said he was in a rush. Poor Alice was hopping mad. We'd only just been down to London a day or two before, and if she'd known the baby was going to be born six weeks early you couldn't have dragged her away in chains. Myself, I was just glad Jessica had been there.'

'There was no sign that Jacob was going to be premature, then?'

'None at all. No, that was why it was such a surprise. Sarah'd had cramps a few days before — that was why Alice insisted on going down to see her. But they'd stopped by the time we got there. Alice dragged her off to the doctor's, but he said everything seemed fine.'

A note of consternation entered his voice. 'There isn't a problem, is there? With Jacob, I mean?'

Ben felt the last trace of doubt slough away. 'No, he's fine. I was ... well, I was just curious.'

Her father abruptly sounded tired and old. Whatever brief comfort he'd drawn from the reminiscence had gone. 'I often wondered if Jacob being early had anything to do with ... you know. The autism.'

'I don't think so.' There were different ideas about what caused autism, but so far as Ben knew premature birth wasn't one of them.

'No, I expect you're right.' Geoffrey made an effort to sound cheerful. 'Wasn't as if he was a poor tiny thing, or anything.'

Later, Ben wished that he'd stopped the conversation there, with the question of Jacob's birth resolved in his mind. But he didn't.

'Wasn't he?' he said, no longer really listening.

Sarah's father chuckled. 'We always kidded that someone had got their dates wrong. He weighed over six pounds. If you didn't know better you'd have thought he was a full-term baby.'

Chapter Three

Jessica lived on the fourth floor of a block of squat council flats in Peckham. The lift was working, but when Ben saw the vomit drying on the floor and spattering the wall he took the steps instead. He was out of breath before he had reached the third level. He reminded himself that he ought to get back into playing football fairly soon. Or doing something. It was too easy to let it slide, and before he knew it he'd be forty and a fat bastard. There were still eight years to go, but already he'd found it only took a few weeks for the rot to set in, and it was becoming more of an effort to shake it off again.

Trying to pretend he wasn't winded, he hauled himself up to the fourth floor. The walkways ran along the front of the flats, open except for a chest-high concrete wall. He had never been there before. He and Jessica had never made any pretence of liking each other. He'd generally gone out whenever she called around to see Sarah, and on the few occasions when they couldn't avoid one another they barely managed a minimal degree of civility for her sake.

The antipathy between them had been immediate and instinctive, on Ben's part largely because he could tell that she disliked him, on Jessica's for reasons she kept to herself. But he thought he could guess. She resented him. Before he had come along and spoiled things, Sarah and Jacob had been part of her extended family. Sometimes he felt she thought they had *been* her family. Jessica had treated the small one-bedroom flat that Sarah had moved into after Jacob was born as a second home. She would drop in unannounced for meals, stay overnight, and answer the phone as if she lived there. Once, when he and Sarah had been seeing each other for only a few months, Jessica had let herself in and found him there alone, preparing dinner.

She had stopped dead. 'What are you doing here?'

He gave her a grin because he knew that would infuriate her. 'Cooking. What about you?'

She ignored his question. 'Where's Sarah?'

'Jacob's got a cough. She's taken him to the doctor's.'

She had stood in the doorway of the lounge, on the other side of the work surface that separated it from the tiny kitchenette. He saw her take in the makings of a dinner for two spread out next to the open bottle of wine. 'She didn't tell me.'

'It wasn't something she'd planned in advance.' Seeing her there, plain and heavy in her midwife's uniform, he'd relented. 'Do you want a glass of wine? She shouldn't be long.'

Her eyes flashed to him again. Her mouth tightened. 'No.' Without another word, she had turned and left.

'Poor old Jessica,' he had joked to Sarah one evening. 'I think she's jealous of me.'

'Of course she isn't. She's just shy with people, that's all.'

'With men, you mean. If the woman was any further in the closet she'd be in Narnia.'

Sarah pushed him. 'Don't be rotten. And you're thinking of wardrobe.'

'Okay, she's a wardrobe lesbian.'

She laughed, but he could see she was uneasy.

'Come on, you know she is,' he said, teasing but exasperated too. 'Admit it, it's no big deal.'

'Why go on about it, then?'

'I'm not going on about it. I just can't see why you won't admit it.' It genuinely puzzled him. They both had gay and lesbian friends, so Sarah's defensiveness towards Jessica's sexuality seemed odd. 'You two don't have any dark secrets, do you?'

His smile dropped as Sarah turned on him. 'No, of course we haven't! Don't be stupid!'

She had flushed angrily, her freckles standing out more than ever.

'It was a joke,' he said, surprised.

'I know, but you shouldn't laugh at her.'

'I wasn't laughing. Well, not much.'

The red was fading from her cheeks, but she still seemed unhappy.

'There wasn't anything between you, was there? I mean, it's none of my business,' he added, hurriedly. 'I just wouldn't want to upset you without knowing why, that's all.'

'She's a friend, that's all. I suppose I just feel a bit protective towards her.'

Ben couldn't think why. Jessica was more than capable of looking after herself. But after that he tried to keep his opinions of her to himself.

Even so, when they'd moved to the house in Camden he had made it clear that he didn't want Jessica to have a key. He needn't have bothered, because she'd hardly been there. There was too much of him in it. Sarah had only spoken to her once or twice in the past few months, and without really thinking about it Ben had been quietly pleased that the two of them were finally drifting apart. Friends or not, Sarah always seemed subdued when Jessica was around.

And now, he thought, reaching the right door number, they had both lost her.

He paused to catch his breath before knocking. When he realised the bumping of his heart wasn't just exertion he clenched his fist and rapped on the door. There was no answer.

A small spyhole was set in the centre of the door, and he had the sudden feeling that Jessica was watching him through it. He knocked again, harder. This time, after only a short wait, the door was opened.

Jessica regarded him without expression. Sometimes, when she was with Sarah and didn't know he was looking, she would smile and for a transient moment achieve an animation that was close to prettiness. That was rare, though, and she wasn't smiling now. She wore her starched midwife's uniform like armour. Her hair was parted in the centre and drawn severely back by a black plastic clip, while her moon face was free of make-up. Ben was faintly shocked to notice that her skin was clear and young-looking. He wondered if the absence of make-up was a denial of vanity, or because of it.

'I'm going to work in ten minutes,' she said without preamble, and stood back to let him in.

He went through the short hallway and into the lounge. It was uncluttered and almost clinically clean. There was a neat three-piece suite, only one chair of which looked used, and a laminated cabinet that contained a hi-fi unit and a few books. Other than that the room was bare. There wasn't a single plant.

He didn't sit down, and when Jessica followed him in she made no attempt to offer him a seat. She stood in front of the unlit gas fire, arms folded. 'Well? You said you wanted to talk to me.'

They had barely acknowledged each other at the funeral, and she had been openly unwelcoming when he had phoned. He'd had to insist that it was important, but now he was there he didn't know where to start. 'It's about Sarah.'

She looked at him, waiting.

'Look, I know we've never hit it off, but you were Sarah's best friend,' he went on. 'You knew her before I did.'

Jessica gave no sign of unbending. She stared at him, as hard and ungiving as stone. Ben couldn't imagine how someone so cold and unsympathetic could be a midwife, and not for the first time wondered about her motives for choosing it as her career.

But this wasn't the time to think about that.

'I wanted to ask about when the two of you shared a flat. When she was pregnant. Sarah told me some things, but not in any detail.'

'And?'

'It's a part of her life I don't know very much about.'

Jessica was almost smiling, although there was nothing pretty about it. 'So now you want to take that from me as well?'

Ben hadn't expected her animosity to be so naked. 'I don't want to take anything from you. I never did.'

Her expression said she didn't believe him. He felt more uncomfortable than ever. 'This is a bad time. Perhaps we ought to leave it for a while.'

'There isn't a good time as far as you're concerned,' she said, and there was no mistaking the hate now. 'I said I'd see you because of Sarah. But after this I don't want to set eyes on you again. Ask what you came for and then go.'

'All right. The real reason I came was to ask you about Jacob.' He was watching for some reaction, but couldn't see any.

'What about him?'

'You delivered him. I just want to know what happened.'

'What do you mean, "what happened"? She went into labour and I attended. That's it.'

'Why didn't she go to hospital?'

Jessica's mouth was a thin line. 'Didn't she tell you any of this herself?'

'Yes, but I wanted to ask you.'

She glared at him, then gave a terse shrug. 'It was the middle of the night. There wasn't time. She started suddenly, and by the time we realised what was happening the baby was on its way.' She lifted her chin fractionally, staring him down. 'Besides, there was no need for her to go to hospital. I was there.'

'You were only a student, though. What if there'd been any problems?'

'Then I'd have sent for help. But there weren't.'

'Didn't you send for a doctor?'

'I told you, there was no point. We called for one the next morning, he came and made sure they were both okay, and then went. I knew more about childbirth than any GP would have. Or her mother, though you wouldn't have thought it to hear her.' She gave an angry shake of her head. 'She insisted her little daughter had to go back home with them. As if I couldn't have given her everything she needed.'

She was no longer looking at him, lost in the anger of six years ago, and Ben felt sorry for her. And sorry he had come. He felt more and more that he was wasting his time. There was only one thing left he had to ask.

'Sarah's father told me Jacob was a big baby. Over six pounds.'

'Six pounds three ounces.'

The figure was thrown at him. He accepted its accuracy. 'He said he didn't look premature at all.'

'So?'

'Isn't that unusual?'

Jessica's look was full of contempt. 'Not particularly. He might not even have been very much premature anyway. Sarah's periods weren't regular, so it was difficult to know how far into her term she was. And some babies are bigger than others, you know. Like anything else.' There was derision in her voice. 'Is there anything else you want to ask?'

He didn't even feel relieved. Just stupid. 'No.'

'Good. In that case you might as well go.'

She went and stood by the lounge door. Shamefaced, Ben went past her into the hallway. Another doorway led off it into a kitchen that was as barren and clean as the rest of the flat. A solitary place mat was set out on the small table, with a stainless-steel salt-and-pepper cruet and glass vinegar bottle positioned at its top. They had the look of permanent fixtures. A newspaper lay neatly folded to one side of them, face up. Ben walked past, then stopped and went back.

The newspaper was the *Daily Mail*.

Jessica was standing behind him. 'Now what?'

'I didn't know you were a *Mail* reader.'

'I can't see that it's anything to do with you what I read.'

'I'd have thought you were more the *Guardian* type.'

'Well, I'm not. I've always read the *Mail*, and it's none of your business anyway.'

Ben turned to face her. 'Did you read it when you lived with Sarah?'

It seemed to him that her irritation wavered. 'Perhaps. I can't remember.'

'I thought you said you'd always read it?'

'What difference does it make? Look, I've got to go to work, even if you haven't.'

She brushed past him towards the front door. Ben stayed where he was. 'I found the cuttings.'

He thought she paused fractionally, her back to him. When she turned, her face was guarded.

'What cuttings?'

'The cuttings about the baby that someone took from a hospital when Jacob was born.'

'I don't know what you're talking about.'

'Sarah kept them in a box with Jacob's birth certificate.'

He watched Jessica for some reaction. She shrugged. 'So what?'

'So why would she do that?'

'I've no idea. Does it matter? She's dead. Or have you forgotten?'

'I haven't forgotten. I just can't see why she would have saved them.'

Jessica gave a derisive snort. 'Is that what all this is about? You think she took somebody else's baby? What's the matter, are you tired of looking after him already?'

'I just want to know the truth, that's all.'

'The truth? The truth is that Sarah gave birth to an autistic child, and now she's dead you've decided you don't want the responsibility. Well, you married her,' she spat. 'Now live with it!'

'So Jacob is hers?'

'Of course he's hers! I delivered him! Or are you going to call me a liar as well?'

Ben was never sure if he'd planned what he said next or not. But the fabrication came smoothly, as if rehearsed. 'So how come they've both got the same birthmark?'

Jessica frowned. 'What?'

'The newspaper said the baby had a birthmark on his right shoulder. Jacob's got one there as well.'

He expected scorn for the transparent fabrication. Jessica's gaze went blank for a moment. Then it snapped back into focus. 'That doesn't prove a thing. Lots of children have birthmarks,' she went on, but the hesitation had been too long. He felt a horror begin to uncurl in him.

'Oh Christ,' he said.

'I've told you, it's just a coincidence. It doesn't mean anything.'

'She did it, didn't she? She took the baby.'

'Don't be ridiculous! Just because two babies have similar birthmarks—'

'There *isn't* any fucking birthmark!'

She blinked. Her eyes broke away from his gaze. 'Look, you're going to have to leave now. I've got to ... I've got to go to work.'

The bluster lacked conviction. Her hands fluttered, then

fell limply to her side. Ben felt himself swaying. His legs barely supported him as he went unsteadily to the nearest kitchen chair and sank on to it. In spite of everything, he hadn't really believed it. He realised he hadn't come to be told this; he'd come to be reassured.

Jessica hadn't moved from the doorway. Her face was sullen and resigned, the colour leeched from it. The midwife's uniform seemed like a costume.

'Why?' he asked. 'What made her do it?'

'She lost the baby.' Her voice was lifeless and flat. 'I came home one night, and found her sitting in the dark. She'd spontaneously aborted that afternoon. In a public toilet.'

She came to the table and sat down herself. She looked shapeless, as if only the starched fabric was holding her together. 'I wanted to call for a doctor, but she got hysterical when I tried. So I didn't. I made sure she wasn't still bleeding or anything. It wasn't as if they could do any good anyway. They'd only want to know where the foetus was, and then the police would've had to be called in. She'd been through enough already after that . . . that *bastard* left her when she was pregnant.' She looked at him, viciously. 'Did you know she tried to kill herself?'

She gave a nod of triumph when she saw he hadn't. 'No, I didn't think so. Well, she did. She took an overdose not long after she came to live with me. I found her and made her sick before she was too far gone. I thought she might miscarry then, but she didn't. I wanted to spare her anything else. I thought . . . I thought if I could find the baby and bring it back I could say she'd lost it in the house, and that way there'd be no police, no fuss about it.'

Her fingers teased at her skirt, pinching a fold of it, then smoothing it down and repeating the process.

'She wouldn't talk at all, at first, but eventually she told me she'd left it in a bin near Piccadilly Tube station. I put her to bed, but it was late by then. I thought I'd have a couple of hours' sleep and go to Piccadilly first thing. She was still sleeping when I went. I wanted to be back before she woke up, but when I got to the station I couldn't find the right bin. I started looking in all of them, until the streets started getting busier and I had to stop. I never did find out where it was. There was no mention of it being found, so I suppose it just got taken away when the bins were emptied. I couldn't do anything except go back home, and when I got there Sarah had gone. I didn't know what to do. I couldn't call the police, so I just waited and hoped she'd come back. But when she did she'd got a baby with her.'

A corner of her mouth lifted in a smile. 'She looked so *happy*. Like the day before hadn't happened. Like Sarah *should* look. I tried to get her to tell me where she'd got it from, but she didn't seem to know what I was talking about. And when I asked whose baby it was, she just said, "Mine." I tried to make her realise what she'd done, but it only made her confused. I was frightened she'd sink back into the state she'd been in earlier. I couldn't think what to do. And then, all of a sudden, it came to me. I didn't have to do anything. Sarah had been pregnant, and now she'd got a baby. It was big for a premature one, but not so big that it'd cause problems.'

He couldn't keep quiet any longer. 'Problems? It wasn't hers! Jesus Christ, she *stole* it!'

Jessica gave him a look of contempt. 'What did you expect me to do? Go to the police?'

'Yes! Yes, you should have gone to the fucking police! They wouldn't have prosecuted, not for something like that! She'd have been given psychiatric help!'

'Put away somewhere, you mean? You think I'd have let them do that to her?'

'It would have been better than what you did!' He felt he had fallen through to another, less rational pocket of reality. 'Did she know? What she'd done, I mean? Did she know afterwards?'

Jessica raised her shoulders, listlessly. 'I don't know. She might have, at some level. I'd cut out the reports from the newspaper and saved them in a drawer, but when I looked after she'd gone back with her parents they'd gone. She never said she'd taken them, and I never asked her.'

'You never spoke to her about it?'

She shook her head, but for the first time there was something subtly defensive about her. Ben thought he understood why Jessica had kept the cuttings. And why Sarah had been uneasy discussing their relationship.

The woman had wanted to tie Sarah to her.

He didn't bother to keep the disgust from his voice. 'Didn't you worry that someone might have found out?'

'Who was going to find out? I was nearly a qualified midwife, no one would doubt what I said. The doctor hardly even examined her when we called him out the next day. If I'd been based at the hospital the baby had been taken from somebody might have wondered, but I wasn't. There wasn't any risk.'

'No risk? She'd taken somebody else's baby! All right, she was ill, she didn't know what she was doing. But you're supposed to be a ... a fucking *midwife*, for God's sake! How could you do it?'

'Because it was for Sarah.' Jessica stared back at him, defiant and serene. 'I'd have done anything if I thought it would help her.'

'Help her! That wasn't *helping* her! You were just letting her hide from what happened! And what about its real parents? Didn't you care about what they must have gone through?'

'Why should I?' she flashed. 'Some pathetic squaddie and his stupid breeding-cow? Why should I care more about them than Sarah? I see their kind every day, squeezing out one brat after another! They've probably got three or four by now. They'd get over it, but Sarah wouldn't have! Care about *them*? I'd have taken it myself if she'd asked!'

Her eyes were bright and moist. 'Have I shocked you?'

she sneered. 'Didn't you think plain old Jessica was capable of something like that? God, you make me sick. You married her, you fucked her, but you never loved her. You don't know what love is.'

Ben couldn't bear to stay there any longer. The small kitchen was suddenly airless, dense with the possibility of violence. He stood up, startling himself with the sound of the chair legs scraping across the lino-covered floor.

'I don't know what you'd call what you did,' he said, thickly, 'but it wasn't love.'

He got as far as the door, then stopped. 'I can't pretend I don't know about this. I can't just ignore it.'

Jessica didn't look up. 'Do what you like,' she said, dully. 'I don't care any more.'

She was still staring at nothing when he went out.

Chapter Four

━━━━◆◇◆━━━━

Jacob selected a piece of jigsaw puzzle, held it in his hand for a second, then exchanged it for another and pressed it neatly into place. The puzzle, a scene from *Star Wars*, was nearly half completed. The box for it lay open close by, but Jacob never so much as glanced at the picture of the finished jigsaw on the lid. It wouldn't have helped if he did, because he was assembling it face down. He would sit through the whole of the *Star Wars* trilogy time and time again, entranced by the fast-moving images and sounds coming from the TV screen, but a static photograph from it held no interest for him. Ben was pretty sure that he recognised what it was, could make the association between one and the other, although he wasn't entirely certain. It was more likely that he simply regarded the picture itself as incidental. It was fitting together the little cardboard shapes which engrossed him, not what was on them when he had finished. He could assemble them with the picture upside down or sideways on with equal dexterity. It seemed to be all the same to him.

Ben watched from the other side of the lounge as he broke off from the puzzle and gazed at something out of the window. Or perhaps at the window itself. Ben couldn't see what had caught his eye, but he could guess. Jacob would scrutinise a cracked windowpane, a broken piece of glass, the chipped rim of a milk bottle in the sun; anything that refracted light and split it into an unexpected jewel of colour. They had realised what he was doing only after they saw him squinting into the spray of a lawn sprinkler, moving his head about to catch sight of an indistinct rainbow in the haze. Sometimes, generally after a joint, Ben wondered if he saw something in the refractions invisible to a less fractured mind.

Whatever he'd seen now failed to hold his attention, though. Jacob went back to the jigsaw. He gave no sign of being aware of either Ben's scrutiny or his presence. Normally he would have tried to encourage the boy to talk, asked him about school, anything to steer him towards some sort of communication. Now he couldn't find it in himself to make the effort. Jacob didn't mind. Jacob was locked in his own world, as usual. Sometimes Ben wondered if he wasn't happier there than when he was forced to acknowledge an exterior one that made little sense to him.

What am I going to do?

Jacob's elbow brushed the pile of unassembled pieces and knocked several to the floor. His face creased up as they pattered to the carpet. He looked down at where they'd landed, his breathing growing faster as he became more agitated, but made no attempt to pick them up. Sometimes it was difficult to know what would upset him, or see why it should. Jacob was generally placid, but if he became frightened or disturbed it could take a long time to calm him down. Once, when Sarah had misguidedly taken him to another little boy's birthday party, he'd become hysterical when a balloon burst behind him, rocking and screeching so violently with his hands clasped to his ears that he had set all the other children crying as well. That had been the last party she'd insisted he go to.

He stopped himself from thinking about Sarah. Jacob had begun banging himself about in the chair in frustration. Ben went over and picked up the fallen pieces of jigsaw. Jacob subsided as he dropped them back on the table, gathering them back into the pile as if nothing had happened. Ben stared down at the back of his head as he bowed over the puzzle. Normally he would have ruffled his hair, made some sort of contact. This time he didn't touch him. He went back to where he'd been sitting without a word.

What the fuck *am I going to do?*

Jacob's head shot up as the doorbell rang. He looked in the direction of the hallway. 'Mummy?'

Oh, Christ. 'No, Jacob,' Ben said. He felt full of ashes. 'It isn't Mummy.'

'Mummy.'

It isn't bloody Mummy! 'No. It's someone else.'

Jacob remained in the same attitude for a second or two, then went back to his jigsaw. When the doorbell rang again he took no notice. He didn't so much as glance up as Ben left the room to answer it.

Colin stood on the steps. He had obviously come straight from work, although the slightly loosened tie indicated that he was now officially in his own time. 'Sorry I'm late. Last-minute crisis.'

He broke off, gawping at Ben. 'What's happened to your hair?'

Ben resisted the urge to touch the stubble on his scalp. He'd stopped off at the barber's on the way back from seeing Jessica. He'd remembered Sarah running her fingers through it as he told the man to take it off. 'I've had it cut.'

'I can see that.' Colin tore his eyes from it, looking at him with concern. 'Are you okay?'

'Yeah.' Ben closed the door. 'Did Maggie mind you coming?'

'Naw, she's used to me being late. So long as I get back before it's time for Scott and Andrew to go to bed there's no problem.' Both Colin's sons were older than Jacob. On the few occasions when they 'played' together it was obvious they were under instructions from Maggie to be nice. It usually ended with Jacob sitting by himself while the two brothers did whatever they wanted.

'Let's go in the kitchen,' Ben said, as Colin started towards the lounge. Colin looked surprised but made no comment.

'I'll just say hello to Jacob first.' He always made an effort to treat Jacob normally, and if he tried a little too hard it was still better than Maggie's forced good humour.

Stop being so hard on them. It isn't their fault.

'Hi, Jake,' Colin said, striding over to the table. Jacob didn't look up from his jigsaw, but Ben could see him stiffen and knew what was coming next.

'Hang on,' he began, but Colin had already bent down in front of the boy. Jacob tucked his head on to his chest and thrust his arms out at him in a pushing-away gesture.

'No! Nono!'

Startled, Colin slowly backed away. 'Okay, Jacob, sorry.' He raised his eyebrows at Ben.

'He's been a bit edgy the past few days,' Ben told him. Jacob sat rigidly, head down, arms still held out. 'It's all right, it's only Uncle Colin. You know him, don't be silly.'

The arms remained raised, warding off.

'Come on, stop it, Jacob!' he snapped.

'Easy, Ben,' Colin said, shocked.

Ben took a hold on himself. He tried to say something to reassure Jacob, but it was like digging in a dry well. He just stood there, unable to think of a single thing to do.

Colin was looking from one of them to the other, worried. He came forward again, reaching into his pocket for a tube of Smarties. 'I've brought you some sweets, Jacob,' he said, giving it a little shake as he set it down on the table. Jacob's eyes flickered to it. After a moment he tentatively brought his arms down and picked it up.

Ben felt some of the tension leave him as Jacob visibly relaxed. The boy turned the tube around in his hand, apparently soothed by the motion and the sliding rattle of the sweets.

'Are you going to say thank you?' Ben asked.

'It doesn't matter,' Colin said quickly, taking Ben's arm and leading him away. They went into the kitchen. Ben blocked open the door so he could see into the other room.

Colin still looked upset. 'What was all that about?'

'I told you, he's a bit touchy lately.'

'I didn't mean Jacob.'

Ben went to the fridge. 'Beer?'

'If you're having one.'

He handed Colin a can and a glass. He opened his own and drank straight from it.

'So are you going to tell me?' Colin asked.

Ben went to a kitchen drawer and took out the newspaper cuttings. He tossed them on the kitchen table. 'You don't have to read them all. The first one'll do.'

Colin quickly scanned it, then looked up, puzzled. 'Sorry, I don't understand.'

'It's Jacob.'

The words actually hurt, a real physical pain in his throat. Colin was frowning. 'I'm not with you.'

'The baby that was stolen. It was Jacob. Sarah did it.'

Colin stared at him, then looked at the cutting again. Ben could see him struggling not to show his disbelief. 'Ben—'

'I'm not fucking fantasising. I'm serious.'

He told him what had happened, from finding the cuttings to visiting Jessica. Telling it to someone else didn't help as much as he'd hoped. It just seemed to make it more real. When he had finished Colin glanced through the open doorway towards where Jacob was playing in the lounge.

'Christ.'

Ben gave a crooked smile. 'Yeah. That's what I thought.' He was shivering, although the house was warm. He drained the beer can and sat down.

'Have you told anyone else about this?' Colin asked.

'You're the first.'

'So no one else knows? You haven't mentioned it to your dad?'

'No.' Ben's mother had died while he was at university. His father had remarried, a woman ten years his junior who made it clear she regarded Ben as competition for her husband's affections. Her presence came between them whether she was actually there or not, an intangible barrier that became harder to overcome as time went by. She hadn't gone to Sarah's funeral, and even through the numbing grief of the day, he had heard his father's apologetic excuses and felt sorry for him. That had been the first time in a year they had seen each other, and the first time in six months they had spoken. His father was no longer someone in whom Ben confided.

'What about Sarah's parents?' Colin asked. 'Do they know?'

'I told you, I haven't told anybody.'

'I didn't mean that. I meant do you think they've known all along? Could Sarah have told them?'

'I doubt it. I don't think it was something she even acknowledged to herself. Not consciously. And if her parents ever suspected anything, I'm pretty sure I'd have picked something up from them before now.'

Colin pulled absently at his lower lip. Ben could see him beginning to sift and arrange the information, applying himself to it like any legal problem. 'Have you thought about what you're going to do?'

'I haven't thought about anything else. But I still don't have a fucking clue.'

Colin's hand unconsciously went to straighten his tie, entirely the solicitor now. Ben had always envied the way he could calmly tackle problems. 'I don't think you need to decide anything straightaway. At this stage the main thing is not to go off half cocked. You need to make sure that whatever you do is best for everyone concerned. For a start, have you considered that Jessica might be lying?'

'She wasn't.'

'I'm not saying she *was*, only that it's a possibility you shouldn't overlook. I mean, what have you actually got? Some old clippings, and the story of someone who, let's face it, isn't exactly out to do you any favours. Can you be one hundred per cent sure that she's not making this up just to cause trouble?'

There was nothing Ben would have liked to believe more. But, tempting as it was, he couldn't bring himself to accept it. 'She wouldn't do that. Not when it means incriminating Sarah.'

'Are you sure? She might not expect you to tell anybody. And you said yourself that Sarah had more or less lost touch with her. You might have handed her a way of getting back at you both.'

'I know what you're saying, but I can't—'

Colin held up his hand. 'Just think for a second. What actual confirmation have you got that what she said is true?'

'None, but—'

'That's right, none. Have you checked to see what else might have been in the papers about the story afterwards?'

Uncertain now, Ben shook his head.

'So for all you know, little Steven Kale could have turned up safe and well a week or two later. And Sarah might have just put the cuttings into a box and forgotten all about them. The point is, you don't *know*. If you go to the police or social services now you could be letting yourself in for a whole lot of trouble for no good reason. And Jacob as well, don't forget. All because of some vague suspicions and a story you were told by someone who hates your guts.'

Ben rubbed his eyes. He didn't feel any more hopeful, but he knew what Colin said made sense. 'I suppose you're right.'

'Okay, then. So what we've got to do now is find out if the Kales' baby ever turned up again. And also if its parents are still alive themselves.' The look he gave Ben was cautious. 'If they aren't, you might want to think again about what you're going to do. Regardless of whether their baby was found or not.'

He knew what Colin was hinting at. He didn't know how he felt about it, though. 'How do I go about finding out?'

'It'd mean a lot of digging around.' Colin sucked air through his teeth as he considered, making a tiny whistling noise. 'It'd probably be best to hire someone to do it for you. It'll cost, but it'd be faster and less trouble.'

'Do you know anyone?'

'Not personally, but I could ask around. We sometimes have to use private detectives at work.' He gave a dry smile. 'You'd be surprised the sort of messes musicians can get themselves into.'

Not only musicians, Ben thought. 'How soon can you let me know?'

'Tomorrow, probably.' Colin looked uncomfortable. 'Look, this might be jumping the gun a bit, but depending what the detective finds, perhaps you should start thinking about consulting a lawyer who specialises in family law. My field's entertainment. I haven't a clue what the custody situation would be if ... well, if the worst came to the worst.'

Ben nodded. Colin looked across at him. 'I'm assuming you'd *want* Jacob to stay with you.'

Ben studied his beer can. 'Let's wait and see what the detective turns up.'

The traffic seemed even heavier than usual, or himself less patient, as he drove Jacob to school the next morning. The car sat in the meandering lines of vehicles as they crept forward, snarling into knots at junctions. Early as it was, the June sun was already baking down, indistinct through the purpling haze of smog.

He made no attempt to talk to Jacob. He'd hardly spoken to him at all the night before, even when he'd bathed him and put him to bed. Whenever he looked at him he felt such a turmoil of emotions it was impossible to see past them. He knew he wasn't being fair, knew that whatever had happened wasn't the boy's fault. But telling himself that nothing had really changed didn't help.

Everything had changed.

The traffic thinned out as he neared the school. It was in Islington, and getting there and back twice a day, five times a week, was often a nightmare. There was a special-needs school closer to where they lived in Camden, but it catered for children with a variety of learning difficulties, not just autism. The Islington school was one of the few that was only for autistic children. He and Sarah had decided that the benefits of Jacob being given specialist education and treatment outweighed any inconvenience of transport. Sarah had even insisted on taking and collecting him themselves, an arrangement Jacob soon regarded as inviolable. He could stretch his acceptance to include Maggie, but not to the local authority's minibus, with its roundabout route as it collected other children.

They had been lucky to get him into the school at all. Jacob had been almost school age before he had finally been diagnosed, and it had taken letters, pleas and numerous phone calls to the educational services to enrol him in time for the next term. But if nothing else it had given Sarah — and Ben as well, he remembered — something to do to help ease the shock of the doctor's verdict.

The memory of the afternoon in the specialist's office had, until now, ranked along with his mother's death as being one of the worst moments of Ben's life. He had held Sarah's hand as the man had explained that, while Jacob wasn't mentally retarded, he had a disability which prevented him from communicating or relating to the people and world around him in the usual way. There were, he had said, wide-ranging degrees of severity, and, while Jacob didn't exhibit as extreme signs as some, he would still need special education and care. They had listened, numb, as he told them about the behavioural problems they could expect, from an obsession with apparently senseless, repetitive activity, to the fact that Jacob would find it difficult to understand normal human interactions, or even fully recognise how to use language to communicate. Ben had asked if there was a cure. No, the doctor had said. Autism could be helped, improved, yes, but not cured. Sarah had looked over at where Jacob was playing with a toy abacus on the floor, sliding the beads around on it as though he knew exactly what he was doing.

What causes it? she had asked. The doctor had spoken at length about brain development before, during and after birth, about genetic traits and childhood illnesses, and in the end shrugged his shoulders and confessed that no one really knew. And Sarah had stared at Jacob with a look in her eyes that Ben hadn't been able to fathom, but which now, he thought, he was beginning to understand. That night, as they lay sleepless in bed, she had stared up at the ceiling and said, 'It's a judgment.'

'Oh, come on!' Ben had been disturbed by the way she had withdrawn into herself since leaving the specialist's office.

She kept her gaze on the ceiling. 'It is. It's my fault.'

The matter-of-fact way she said it had frightened him. 'How is it your fault?' She didn't answer. 'Thinking like that it isn't going to help,' he persisted. 'I know it's hard, but it's just something we're going to have to come to terms with. It's no good blaming yourself.'

For a long moment she didn't reply. Then tears had run out of her eyes, trickling sideways towards her ears as she lay on her back, and she had turned to him and sobbed until, at some point, they had both drifted into an exhausted sleep. Next morning Sarah had begun determinedly telephoning around autistic schools. She had never mentioned judgment or responsibility again.

Ben thought about what she had said as he parked the dusty VW Golf outside the school gates. He turned to where Jacob was belted into the back seat. The little boy had one hand close to his face, moving it from side to side as he stared out of the window through his spread fingers.

'We're here, Jacob. Are you going to undo the seat belt, or shall I?'

There was a momentary hiatus in the swinging hand, then Jacob carried on as before. Suppressing his anger, Ben climbed out of the car and opened the back door. Jacob peered up at him through his fingers, and continued to do so as Ben unbuckled him from the seat belt. Holding his free hand, Ben led him towards the school gates, and it wasn't until Jacob gave a grunt and began tugging at him that he realised he had forgotten the routine.

'Okay, okay, I'm sorry.' Ben let the boy pull him towards an old postbox set low in the wall surrounding the school. He waited while Jacob stood on tiptoe and inserted both hands, first his right, then his left, into its slot. Jacob had seen someone posting a letter in the box not long after he started at the school, and since then insisted on performing the ceremony every morning before he went in. Not when he came out, though; when school had finished he had to walk down the length of the car, top to bottom, brushing his left hand against it. Ben had learned from experience that, no matter how much of a rush he was in, it was better to let Jacob complete his rituals than try to interrupt them.

The formalities completed, Jacob took Ben's hand again and they went through the gates.

The Renishaw School was set in the grounds of an old vicarage. The vicarage itself had been demolished long since, but most of its garden remained, except a small area that had been asphalted to serve as a carpark. Tucked behind the chest-high stone wall, it formed a small oasis of shrubs, trees and lawn in the surrounding desert of brick and concrete. Someone had cut the grass, and the rich scent of it masked the petrol fumes from the road and hit Ben like an essence of childhood. The nostalgia eased past his defences and deepened without warning into the poignancy of loss. Angrily refuting it, he took Jacob over to the prefabricated units that stood on the site of the old house and went into the second one.

At first glance it seemed like any classroom; childish paintings on the wall competing with colourful posters full of bold lettering. But it was a much smaller group than a normal class, only eight other children in it besides Jacob, and only two of them girls. The other thing that set it apart was that there was less chatter than usual. Unless they were encouraged, the children tended to play by themselves instead of with each other, and when Ben had first taken Jacob there the classroom's relative quiet had struck him as eerie.

Now he barely noticed. The teacher, Mrs Wilkinson, smiled at him over the head of a little boy who was standing in front of her. He was talking almost without pausing for breath, all the time looking down at the wheel of a toy car he was spinning instead of at her.

'Excuse me, Terence, Jacob's here with his daddy,' she said, easing past. The narrative continued without a break as the boy turned and followed her, still concentrating on the car wheel.

'Morning,' she said to Ben over the top of the monologue. She was a plump woman in her forties, with a saint-like patience that made Ben feel both envious and mildly guilty. 'Terence, why don't you and Jacob go and see what Melissa's doing?'

The teacher gently ushered the boys towards the other children, and Ben tensed as he saw what was coming next. 'I was so sorry to hear about your wife,' she said, and the sympathy in her voice almost choked him.

He nodded, retreating from it. 'Thanks. I, uh, I've arranged for someone to pick Jacob up this afternoon. Anyway. Got to dash.'

He gave her the best smile he could manage and headed for the door before she could say anything else. He couldn't bear to see the understanding look he knew she would be giving him. It was a look he was beginning to know well. He hated it.

Outside the sun was still shining, and the air was still thick with the smell of cut grass. Ben took deep breaths as he walked through the peaceful scene. He felt he had no right to be in it. He kept his head down as he went back to his car. When he reached the gates he looked up and saw Sarah coming towards him.

It wasn't her, of course. The impression lasted only an instant, the woman's hair and clothes giving a fleeting illusion, but Ben felt as though he had been kicked in the heart. The woman gave him an odd glance as she came through the gates, and he realised he had stopped and was staring at her. He went quickly to his car and got in. He gripped the steering wheel and banged his head softly up and down.

'Oh, fuck, Sarah, why did you do it?'

He sat with his head resting on the wheel for a while longer, then started the engine and drove away.

The studio was on the top floor of an old factory. He had taken a lease out on it when the lower three floors were almost derelict. Since then they had been split into units and let out to design companies, marketing agencies and recording studios, and Ben paid less for nearly twice as much floor space than any of the tenants in the cramped, post-renovation quarters.

He let himself in and turned off the alarm system. The sunlight was dazzling through the three large skylights he'd had fitted to replace the rotting originals, and through the floor-to-ceiling windows that ran the full white-painted length of the east-facing wall. In the afternoon it would be equally bright through the windows on the other side. One of the reasons he'd taken the place was because it was perfect for shooting in natural light; the only way he could have got more would have been either to go outside or have the roof taken off.

It also made it like a greenhouse. Ben turned on the big overhead fan, and as it cranked up like the idling blades of a helicopter, he went to the drawstrings that lowered the blinds over the skylights and windows. The sunlight was reduced to a soft, muted glow.

He slipped off his shoes and socks, enjoying the feel of the varnished floorboards on his skin. He preferred working barefoot in summer, although Sarah had grumbled about the state of his feet when he got home and made him wash them before he got into bed. It gave him a sense of freedom that he knew was slightly ridiculous, as he was as much dependent on the income from his photography – and on pleasing his clients – as any office worker. But he felt it put him in contact with the studio itself; feeling the bare boards beneath his feet, he could walk around without taking his eye from the viewfinder, relying on their touch alone to guide him.

He was arranging the big reflective screens for that day's shoot when the door opened and Zoe came in. She flung her canvas rucksack on to one of the two overstuffed couches.

'Fucking Tube strikes!'

'Morning, Zoe.'

She fanned herself with the tight black T-shirt that showed a band of skin above her white jeans. 'I'm *really* sorry I'm late, but I was stuck in traffic on the *fucking* bus for nearly an hour before I gave up and walked, and now I'm sweating like a *pig*! God, what's happened to your *hair*?'

'I felt like a change.'

Zoe tilted her head to one side, considering it. She was in her early twenties, slim but without the angular shapeliness of a model. Her own hair was cropped and currently dyed black, although the colour changed regularly. Not long ago it had been blond; before that red. Once it had been green, the accidental result of a cheap dye. She hadn't been fit to talk to for days.

'Looks okay,' she said. Judgment given, she resumed the heated account of her journey. Ben took no notice. Zoe was bad at mornings, and in the twelve months since he'd hired her as his assistant he'd grown to ignore her pre-eleven o'clock tirades. It was just her way of geeing herself up for the day.

He began sorting through a drawer for a screwdriver as she slammed around the studio. 'Oh, great! We're out of fucking milk!' The fridge door was banged shut. 'Have they phoned to say what time the clothes are going to arrive? What time is it? Half past ten? Shit, they should be *here* by now! Where's their fucking number?'

The waterfall of words and curses was actually quite soothing, a balm of normality after the solicitude he had been smothered in. The first day he had gone to the studio after Sarah had died, Zoe had awkwardly told him she was sorry, then crept around as though the slightest noise would make him shatter, shooting him anxious glances every few minutes until finally he had turned on her and told her to for God's sake stop it. She had looked hurt and shocked, and Ben had thought, *Jesus, please don't let her start crying,* because he didn't think he'd be able to stand it. Then her cheeks had flared red and she'd thrown down the armful of clothes she had been carrying.

'Pardon me for fucking breathing!'

It had put her in a bad enough mood to make her forget he was part of the alien species of bereaved and treat him like a normal person again, and pushed him back on to his precarious platform of self-control. Half listening to Zoe berating the people responsible for delivering the model's clothes for the shoot, Ben closed the drawer and began setting up the lights.

Thank God for this, he thought, fervently.

It was after seven when he pulled up outside Maggie and Colin's house. They lived in a curving row of villas not far from the Portobello Road, with half a dozen steps running up to the heavy, lustrously black-painted front door. They had been there three years, and Ben wondered how soon it would be before they took the next step up the housing ladder. Not long, he guessed, judging by Colin's success in the music law business, and Maggie's capacity for advertising it.

Ben pressed the stiff brass bell and yawned, though not exactly from tiredness. The shoot had gone well, but the sense of satisfaction he'd felt had been snuffed the moment he emerged from his universe of angles, light and shade to an awareness of the real world again.

The door was answered by Scott, who greeted Ben with a brief lift of his chin before turning away and leaving him to come in and close the door himself. At nine he was already showing signs of being an objectionable little shit, although Ben wouldn't have dreamed of telling Maggie or Colin that. He suspected that Colin already knew, but Maggie was overseeing to the point of blindness.

And of course I don't have any problems of my own.

There was a rich smell of beeswax from the antique furniture as he went down the long, thickly carpeted hallway. From somewhere deeper in the house he could hear the murmur of Colin on the telephone. A door opened at the far end of the hall and Maggie came out. In the brown knee-length dress with its white lace collar she looked, as always, like she was caught in a 1980s Laura Ashley time warp. She faltered when she saw his hair, then, obviously deciding not to mention it, fixed her eyes on his face and smiled her stuck-on smile.

'We thought you weren't coming,' she said, jovially, but Ben knew her well enough to detect irritation at his late arrival.

'Sorry. It ran on for longer than I expected.'

'Yes, so we gathered.'

The effusive offers of help that Maggie had made after Sarah had died were clearly wearing thin. He knew he would soon have to make other arrangements for the days when he was too busy to collect Jacob from school, and hope it didn't take him too long to adjust to the change in routine. Then the thought came to him that he might not have to worry about such things for much longer.

He couldn't say how that made him feel.

'He's in here,' Maggie said, going into what she called the 'TV room'. Jacob was sitting cross-legged on the floor watching Tom and Jerry do violence to each other on the big colour screen. Scott was sitting next to his younger brother. Both of them sat apart from Jacob.

'Hi, Jake, had a good day?' Ben asked, doing his best to sound cheerful. Jacob looked at him blankly for a moment, then gave him a rare smile before turning back to the TV. Ben felt pierced by it.

Colin came into the room. He had already changed into his 'at home' outfit of jeans and a T-shirt, but his solicitor's persona was so strong that the casual clothes looked unnatural on him. 'Hi, Ben, fancy a beer?'

Ben was about to decline when Colin gave him a look and jerked his head towards the door. 'Er, yeah, perhaps a quick one.'

Conscious of Maggie's disapproval, he followed Colin into the kitchen. Colin glanced back to make sure no one else had followed them, then closed the door.

'I've got you the name of a detective.'

Chapter Five

———◆◇◆———

Ben couldn't park near the address Colin had given him. The road, just off Kilburn High Street, was being dug up by workmen and was down to a single lane. The yammer of pneumatic drills vibrated through Ben's skull as he walked past, each decibel a punishment for the beer, joints and finally vodka he had worked his way through the night before. The street was a run-down line of shuttered shop windows and disappearing small businesses. He slowed as he reached the number he was looking for. A disreputable-looking second-hand jeweller's was on the ground floor, but the row of buzzers by the doorway at the top of the three cracked steps indicated the presence of other occupants in the building. The sun bore down on the top of Ben's head like a Klieg light, making him squint. He shuddered as a clammy wave of nausea left him prickling with sweat. The air was full of diesel and dust from the roadworks. He took deep breaths of it anyway and went up the steps.

There was a small, clear plastic strip containing a name next to each of the buzzers. The one that said 'IQ Investigations' was right above the jeweller's. Ben hoped that meant it was on the first floor. He didn't think he could make it any higher than that. He pressed the buzzer and waited. There was a crackle of static and then a woman's voice said simply, 'Hello?'

'I've an appointment with Mr Quilley.' He waited for a

response. After a second the door hummed as it was unlocked. Ben pushed it open and went inside.

The hallway was lit with a flickering fluorescent strip light, redundant with the sunshine coming from windows on the stairway and at the far end. It added another notch to his headache as he passed underneath. Little fluff balls of dust were gathered in the angle of each linoleum-covered stair, and the banister wobbled beneath his hand. The first-floor landing was small, with only a single door. 'I. Quilley Investigations' was stencilled on it in scratched white paint, apparently put there before the introduction of the snappier abbreviation. Ben tapped on the glass and heard a distant 'Come in'.

The office was long, dark and narrow. A girl and a desk were crammed into an alcove to one side, together with a battered computer monitor and a fax machine that looked as though its owners had beaten their money's worth out of it. The girl glanced up from the computer screen, unsmiling.

'Hi,' Ben said. His head thudded. 'I'm Ben Murray. I spoke to Mr Quilley yesterday—'

A door that Ben had assumed led into a cupboard opened and a man poked his head around it. 'Come in, Mr Murray.'

The head disappeared. The girl went back to her typing. Ben went through the door into the next room. The man was already sitting behind an old teacher's desk. He was in his fifties. His hair was brushed straight back, mostly dark but receding in two deep bays above his temples. It had the oily sheen of Brylcreem. He waved Ben to sit down in the chair opposite with a hand that held a half-smoked cigarette and continued to write on a notepad. Ben sat down, glancing around. It was smaller but brighter than where the receptionist sulked, with a large sash window overlooking the street. The window was closed, muting the rattle of the pneumatic drills from outside but doing little to air the cramped space. The room was sour with stale cigarette smoke. Ben watched a curl of it drifting up from the stub tucked between the man's brown-stained fingers and felt queasy again.

The detective finished writing with an emphatic full stop and gave Ben a smile. 'Sorry about that.' He had a southern Irish accent. His teeth were small and the same yellow as his fingers. Rising half out of his seat he reached across the desk and offered the hand not gripping the cigarette. He was taller than Ben would have thought, with a heavy frame folded with office flab. His palm was damp and hot when Ben shook it. 'Don't mind if I smoke, do you?' he asked, waving the cigarette with little inclination of putting it out.

'No, go ahead.'

Quilley was dragging on the filter before Ben finished speaking, the request clearly a formality. His cheeks hollowed as the tip of ash raced towards his fingers. He stubbed the cigarette out in a surprisingly elegant cut-glass ashtray that was already overflowing and let the smoke out through his nose and mouth.

'Now, Mr Murray,' he said. 'What can I do for you?'

Ben took his eyes from the twin plumes of smoke issuing from the man's nostrils. 'I, er, I want you to locate somebody for me.'

The detective took a blank form from a drawer. It looked like one he had typed up and photocopied himself. 'What's their name?'

'Kale. John and Jeanette Kale.'

'Man and wife or brother and sister?'

'They're married. At least, they were, the last I heard of them.'

'And when was that?'

'Six years ago.'

The detective wrote on the form without looking up. 'Can you give me any more details?'

Ben told him as much as he knew from the newspaper reports. Quilley didn't interrupt, and broke off writing only to light up another cigarette. He dropped the match into the ashtray and picked up the Biro again.

'Why do you want them locating?'

'Why . . . ?' Ben faltered. Quilley looked up. He had a habit of half smiling that made him seem to be recalling some private joke.

'You needn't tell me, of course, but sometimes it makes my job easier. I don't like to get involved in anything without knowing the reason.'

Ben had worked out his story beforehand in case he was asked. He'd hoped he wouldn't be. 'I'm researching a book about the Gulf War. John Kale served there, and I'd . . . well, I'd like to interview him.'

He'd decided against making any mention of the Kales' son. Lying wasn't one of his strong points, and he didn't want to give anyone any hints as to what he was really trying to find out. If the detective was any good he would learn about the abduction for himself. He might even tell Ben if the baby had been found without him having to ask.

Quilley's grey eyes seemed speculative as he gazed across at Ben. 'Have you been in touch with the MOD?'

'The what?'

'Ministry of Defence.'

'Uh, no, no I haven't. Not yet.'

He felt completely transparent, but the detective simply made another note. 'And when I've located the Kales, do you want me to approach them?'

'No, just . . . just find out where they are now, what they're doing. That sort of thing.' He hoped he sounded natural. 'I'll get in touch with them myself.'

Quilley took another deep pull on the cigarette, head bowed over the form. Smoke trailed up lazily through his hair. 'Who's publishing it?'

'Sorry?'

'The book.' The detective looked up at him again. 'Who's

publishing it? You did say that's why you wanted to find the Kales, didn't you?'

'Oh, right.' Ben's mind raced, conscious of the man calmly watching him. 'I'm not sure yet.'

Quilley nodded, smiling faintly.

'It's still in the early stages,' Ben went on. *Shut up.* The detective regarded him for a moment longer, his smile lingering, then asked for Ben's address and telephone number. He set his pen down on top of the form.

'Well, I think that's all I need to know for now. I can't say exactly how long it'll take, but I should have something for you by the end of next week. Is there anything you'd like to ask?'

'I don't think so.' Ben just wanted to get away from the hot, smoky office. He felt sure his lies were written on his face. The detective raised his eyebrows.

'Don't you even want to know how much this is going to cost you?'

Feeling somehow at a disadvantage, Ben said he did. The detective told him a daily rate that seemed surprisingly cheap. He agreed and pushed back his chair to leave.

'Oh, one last thing,' Quilley said, pen still in hand. 'What's your occupation?'

'Photographer.'

'Really?' The detective's half-smile was back. 'Rather unusual, a photographer writing a book, isn't it?'

You sneaky bastard. Ben stared at him coldly. 'It's mainly photographs.'

'Ah.'

'Do you need references?'

Quilley chuckled, unperturbed. 'Oh, nothing like that. I just like to know a little about who I'm working for.' He came from around the desk and opened the door for Ben. 'Leave it with me, Mr Murray. I'll be in touch.'

He shook Ben's hand again. Up close his breath was heavy

with coffee and cigarettes. His smile hid whatever he was thinking as Ben went out. 'And good luck with the book.'

It was a purer, more simple vision through the camera. Sifted through the membrane of lens and filter, aperture and viewfinder, the world was changed, reality reduced to bite-sized, manageable slivers, immeasurably small fragments of time plucked out by the click of a shutter. Ben found it comforting to be able to close out the world except for that one rectangle of light, framed by blackness. He could manipulate it, make it into what he wanted, before, during and even after the image had been captured.

It was reassuring to think he was still in control of something.

When he first became interested in photography, in the second year of his fine art degree, it had been its apparent objectivity that had attracted him. He had seen a camera as a medium connecting the eye to the subject, but without the filter of an artist's perception to distort it. He had believed that through it he could show truer, more valid images than he could achieve with paintbrush and canvas. Even when he had begun accepting, and actively seeking, commissions for commercial work, he told himself that was completely different, financially necessary but separate from what he was trying to achieve through his more personal efforts. Disillusionment came when he found himself employing the techniques learnt in one for the other, trying not to capture the moment but improve on it as he would the looks of any model. He had been rocked by his own infidelity and, looking at everything he had done up until that point, he had suddenly seen that it was every bit as subjective as any painting. What he'd thought was objectivity was only another form of manipulation. There was nothing intrinsically truthful or real about it; his photographs didn't reveal, as he had believed, only distort in a more subtle way.

Ben had come close to throwing out in disgust everything he had done. In the end, though, he hadn't. Nor did he have much time to dwell on his failure. Ironically, as if to compensate, the commercial side of his work had begun to pick up almost immediately. He accepted the commissions and the money gratefully, cynically rationalising that, if what he had been doing was worthless, then one type of photograph was as good as another.

Sometimes, though, he would still surprise himself.

There was one photograph of Jacob that even now could make him think he had almost caught something. The boy's lack of self-consciousness made him an ideal subject. Provided Ben didn't use a flash and the shutter mechanism wasn't too noisy, Jacob would continue with whatever he was doing as though he weren't there. On this occasion, only a few weeks before he had been diagnosed as autistic, he had been watching television through his fingers, waving them to give a strobe effect. It was a favourite trick of his, but when Ben had tried it himself he found it hurt his eyes. Jacob didn't seem to tire of it, though.

Ben had already taken most of a film, experimenting with different shutter speeds to vary the effect of the moving fingers. The nice thing about photographing Jacob was there was no rush. He adjusted the focus for a final close-up, and just as he pressed the shutter release Jacob suddenly looked straight at him. He had gone back to watching the television again a moment later, but for that instant it had been surprisingly disconcerting to have him unexpectedly staring *back*. Ben had lowered the camera feeling he'd somehow been found out.

It wasn't until he'd developed the film that he was sure he'd caught the moment. In thirty-five of the thirty-six frames Jacob was looking away from the camera, but in the last one he was looking directly at it. His gold-flecked eyes gazed out in perfect focus from behind the blurred bars of his fingers, and Ben felt an echo of the same shock as when he had taken the shot. He had experienced a similar feeling years before, when he had been working on a project for his degree. He had been given permission by a café owner to set up his camera in a darkened back room, from where he could look out at the customers without being seen. He had lost himself in the illicit fascination of photographing the unknowing diners with impunity when one man had turned and looked into the room at him. Ben had frozen like a thief. The man had simply looked away again and gave no sign of having seen anything, but Ben ended the session soon afterwards. He didn't go back. The security of his hiding place now seemed illusory. He'd felt exposed. Known.

The photograph of Jacob gave him the same feeling. It was uncomfortable, but that was what made it so effective. When he'd shown it to Sarah she had looked at it for a while, then quickly handed it back.

'It's horrible.'

He tried to make light of his disappointment. She had given him an apologetic smile, but there were shadows in her eyes.

'Sorry, I didn't mean to sound so blunt. I mean, it's very *good* as a photograph, but ...' She hugged herself. 'He just looks ... so *different*, that's all. Cold. And peering out through his fingers like that. It's like he's in a cage.'

Ben didn't say that those were the very reasons he was so pleased with it, that it worked because that single shot somehow communicated all of Jacob's isolation, his *differentness*. He had put the photograph away and later presented Sarah with a shot that caught Jacob smiling, which he knew she would like. But he had kept the other, and although he hadn't hung it even at the studio, not wanting Sarah to see it and be upset, he had given it pride of place in his portfolio. It was as near as he was going to get to what he had originally set out to do.

None of the photographs he produced now gave him anything resembling that sort of satisfaction. But he took pleasure in doing his job, and doing it well, just the same. He threw himself into his work as he waited to hear from the detective, trying to bury any other thoughts under the sheer weight of it. Quilley had said he would be in touch by the end of that week, and as it approached Ben's nerves became strung out like harp strings, twanging at the slightest provocation.

On the Friday morning he had to go out to check on a possible site for a location shoot for a jeans ad. He kept his mobile with him the whole time, but the detective didn't call. It was mid-afternoon before he got back to the studio. Music was blasting from the sound system and the red warning light outside the darkroom was on. There was rarely anything for Zoe to do in the studio when Ben wasn't there, but she often went in anyway to develop her own work. She was only two years out of art college, following a route similar to that Ben himself had taken. She seemed to regard the time spent as his assistant as a sort of apprenticeship, and he knew she looked up to him as a role model. It either flattered or depressed him, depending on what mood he was in.

She came out as he was opening the post. 'Didn't hear you come in,' she said, going to the coffee machine. A faint chemical smell clung to her. 'You should have knocked. I'd have come out sooner.' Zoe felt guilty about using the darkroom, although he had told her there was no need.

'I've only just got here.' He shook his head when she held up the coffee jug in invitation. She poured herself one and leaned against the back of the couch. She was wearing black jeans and a yellow vest top that clung to her small breasts. With her black hair it gave her a faintly bee-like appearance. She regarded him over the steaming rim of her mug.

'You okay? You look knackered.'

'Just tired.' Two of the envelopes contained cheques. He pocketed them, went on to the rest. 'Any messages?'

He had given the detective only his home and mobile

number, so he knew none of them would be from Quilley. 'The photo editor of *Esquire* wants you to phone him back, didn't say what for. You've got to call Helen about the shoot next week, as well. Oh, and some guy called and asked for you but didn't leave a name. Sounded Irish.'

Ben stopped in the act of opening another envelope. 'Did he say anything?'

'No, just wanted to know if this was where "Mr Murray" worked.' She looked worried, the brash shell crumbling at the thought she had done something wrong. 'Was it somebody important?'

'No, I don't think so.' It couldn't have been Quilley. Ben realised he was biting his lip. He threw the rest of the unopened post on to the battered pine table by the sink. 'I'd better go and pick Jacob up.'

He phoned the detective as soon as he was in the car. The line was engaged. He tried twice more, then tossed the handset on to the passenger seat. 'Fuck it.' He was being paranoid. If the man had any news he would have heard.

Unless he'd left a message on the answerphone at home.

Suddenly Ben was certain that was what had happened. He cursed himself for having an old-style machine that couldn't play itself back over the phone. He pulled out into the traffic, almost knocking over a motorcycle courier. The rider swerved and jabbed two fingers at him. 'Get fucked!' Ben shouted.

He fretted at every stop-start of the clogged roads as he drove to the school. Knowing he had a clear afternoon, he'd told Maggie he'd collect Jacob himself, but now he regretted it. By the time he parked outside the school gates he was in a foul mood. He said hello and goodbye to Mrs Wilkinson as quickly as he decently could and hurried back to the car with Jacob. He forgot to let him run his hand down the side of it before they got in, and had to close the door again until he had.

He barely looked at the little boy as he buckled him into the back seat.

For a change there was a space miraculously close to the house. He parked and hurried Jacob inside. He went straight to the answerphone on the old cherrywood cabinet in the hallway. Its light was flashing. He pressed play.

It was from Maggie, inviting them to lunch on Sunday.

He listened to the tape rewind and then snatched up the receiver. Fuck it. He dialled the detective's number, tasting his nervousness at the back of his throat, a metallic sourness like blood. The phone rang four times and then a recorded message cut in. Ben looked at his watch, incredulously. It was just after five o'clock. He waited, hoping someone would pick up the receiver at the other end, but no one did. He slammed down the phone.

'Fucking great!' He slapped the wall. 'Five past *fucking* five and they've gone home! Fucking brilliant!'

He hit the wall again, harder this time, and kicked the door nearest to him. It swung back with a bang. Ben turned, looking for something else to take his frustration out on, and saw Jacob standing where he had left him in the hallway.

The little boy was rocking himself, covering his ears. *Don't start.* 'It's all right, Jacob, it's just me being silly.'

'No noise! No noise!'

Ben ran his hand over the stubble of his hair. The rasp of it still surprised him. 'Okay, okay, no noise, I've stopped now.'

'No noise!'

'*I said OKAY!*'

The shout hurt his chest. He looked down at his clenched fists, forced them open. Jacob was quiet, but his rocking had grown even more pronounced. He had his head down, although not so far that Ben couldn't see the utter misery on his face.

The anger went out of him. 'Oh God, I'm sorry, Jacob.' He went and crouched in front of the boy. 'It's okay, it's all right, don't be frightened.'

Jacob shook his head, violently. 'Not you,' he moaned. 'Not you, not you, not you.'

He reached out, but Jacob thrust him away. 'Mummy. Mummy.'

Oh Christ. 'Mummy can't, Jacob. Mummy isn't here.'

'Mummy. *Mummy!*' The boy was crying now, and Ben knew that would make things worse because Jacob didn't understand what tears were, was frightened by them. And Ben could feel his own control starting to crack. He clutched the small body to him, holding it tight against its struggles, his own tears running to dampen the back of Jacob's shirt. He squeezed his eyes shut. 'It's all right, it's all right, it's all right,' he chanted, even though he knew that it wasn't, that nothing was all right, but he repeated the words until he felt the rigidity go from the boy's body.

He held him for a while longer, then wiped his eyes as best he could and sat back on his heels. Jacob's face was red and shiny with tears, his long lashes glistening. His chin was still on his chest, but Ben knew the worst was over. He ran his finger across the boy's cheeks, brushing away the runnels of water.

'There we go. That's better.'

Jacob glanced up. He reached out and tentatively touched Ben's cheek, then his own. He regarded his fingers. 'Wet.'

Ben gave a shaky laugh. 'Yeah, that's right. We're both wet.' He stood up and hoisted Jacob on one arm. 'Come on. Let's make some tea.'

After that, Ben felt he had stepped into a bubble of calm. It was as though he'd come through a high fever and been left drained but in a state of fragile peace. The fact that he hadn't heard from the detective no longer gnawed at him. It wasn't that he was holding out any false hopes, simply that there would be time enough to deal with that, and its consequences, later. The weekend seemed to exist by itself, and he accepted the respite gratefully, all the more so because he knew that it *was* only a respite.

The pain left by Sarah's absence was still there, but at least now it was uncluttered with resentment and anger. He hadn't even realised he had felt any of those things until they had gone, and if the keenness of the hurt was undiminished, he would rather have that than the maddened, confused rage which had mocked everything he and Sarah had been together. No matter what she had done he still loved her, and missed her. It was almost a relief to recognise that.

On the Saturday he took Jacob swimming. It was always difficult to know which activities he would enjoy, and which would either leave him indifferent or, worse, would bewilder and agitate him. Swimming had been a surprising success from the start. To begin with Sarah had been worried that he would not understand the concept of water, would try to breathe with his head submerged or drown himself in some other offbeat way, but her fears proved groundless. Jacob splashed about as enthusiastically as any other child his age, and although he didn't know how to swim he was safe enough in a pair of water wings. He looked all head and ribs in his swimming trunks, and Ben felt a surge of protectiveness towards him. *He's mine as much as Sarah's*, he thought; and then, *We're a family. We've only got each other now.*

But that was too sombre a mood, belonging to the week ahead, not the present. Turning away from it, Ben took Jacob down the easiest water slide, and was rewarded with a beaming grin. The problem then became convincing him to stop while they still had some skin left on their legs and behinds.

They went to a pub with a beer garden for lunch, and as Ben watched Jacob carefully shred his paper napkin into strips he reflected that at least the boy's condition made him indifferent to the charms of McDonald's. There was always a bright side, he thought, wryly.

Jacob was yawning before they reached home. Ben knew he would want to go to bed early, but there was a brief flurry of rebellion at bath-time, when he refused to get into the tub.

'Orange. *Orange,*' he repeated, brushing away the orange juice and fruit he was offered. Ben was at a loss, until he made the connection with the water. With his dayglo armbands on, Jacob got happily into the bath and let himself be washed.

Ben had been dreading the prospect of another Saturday night spent alone, with nothing to hold back the cold truth that Sarah wasn't there to share it with him. But the buffer of calm that had sustained him all day didn't desert him now. Tinged with sadness, it let him get through the hours easily enough, a bottle of wine and the occasional joint helping, until he began to doze on the couch during a late-night horror film and took himself off to bed.

Maggie had been tartly surprised when he had declined the offer of Sunday lunch. Instead the next day he took Jacob to the river near Henley. It had been a favourite picnic spot of Sarah's, and he'd wondered if going there now was a good idea. But somehow it seemed the right thing to do. They walked along the riverbank, Jacob's hand small and warm in his. Jacob was *la-la*-ing a tuneless song, a sign that he was enjoying himself. He fell silent as they approached the familiar nest of willow trees that hung over the water. His eyes were big and solemn as they flitted over the two other groups of picnickers already there, and Ben felt his throat tighten as Jacob turned to look behind them, as though expecting to see someone following.

We shouldn't have come.

But the boy's quietness didn't last long. By the time Ben had spread out the picnic blanket, Jacob was humming softly to himself again as he plucked the seeds from stalks of grass and arranged them in a line on his bare leg. Ben had packed hard-boiled eggs and ham-and-tomato sandwiches, cut into the thin strips that Jacob liked. After they had eaten he brought out a football, but Jacob wasn't interested. Sometimes he would play with it, sometimes he wouldn't. Now he was more interested in the ripples his trailing hand made in the slow-moving water.

Ben watched him tilting his head to catch the light sparkling from them and quietly took his Nikon from the bag.

Storing up your memories in advance. The thought came without warning. He lowered the camera, feeling the balance he'd held all weekend begin to disintegrate. But the movement attracted Jacob's attention. He rolled over on to his back and smiled upside down through splayed fingers. Ben grinned back, glad once more that they had come.

They stayed until the heat had gone out of the sun and all the other picnickers had left. Jacob had fallen asleep, and Ben had to wake him when it was time to go. When he was bathed and in bed, Ben took a chair and sat out in the small back garden, watching the sun set behind the sycamore tree at the bottom.

If I could hold on to things like this I'd manage, he thought. It wouldn't be as good, but I could cope.

But he knew that was only a weekend mood, and would disappear just as quickly. And when he woke up the next morning the heaviness was waiting for him, ready to be put on again like a pair of dirty jeans. He grabbed for the serenity he'd felt the day before but it had gone, already as faded and insubstantial as a childhood holiday.

He took Jacob to school and went to the studio. At eleven o'clock Quilley called to say he had found the Kales.

Chapter Six

The girl looked as tired as the last time Ben had seen her. She greeted him as unsmilingly as before. 'You can go straight in.'

He went to the door and tapped. Quilley's voice came from inside. 'Come in.'

The detective was sitting behind the desk. The small room was still thick with stale cigarette smoke, but at least the pneumatic drills outside were silent. Quilley motioned Ben towards the spare chair without looking up from what he was writing. 'Take a seat, Mr Murray. I won't be a moment.'

Ben sat down. He stared at the top of the detective's head and wondered if he went through the same rigmarole with every client. He felt an irrational burst of dislike for the man.

Quilley put down his pen. 'There we go.' He sat back. 'And how are you keeping?'

'Fine.' *Get on with it.*

'Locating the Kales was a bit more complicated than I thought it would be. It involved ... well, quite a lot more digging around, shall I say, than I expected.'

His smile was blandness itself.

He opened a cardboard folder. 'Right, here we go. John Kale. Currently lives with his wife in a place called Tunford, which is a small town halfway between Northampton and

Bedford. Kale's from the area originally — he was brought up in an orphanage, don't know if you knew that — and moved to Tunford when he left the army four years ago. He was discharged after he was wounded in a border incident over in Northern Ireland. Leg injury. That was after his first wife was killed, so perhaps—'

'His first wife was killed?'

'Sorry, didn't I mention that? That was Jeanette, who you already know about. She died in a road accident six years ago. Quite tragic, really.'

Six years. The significance of that wasn't lost on Ben. Quilley was watching him with that half-smile. 'Are you all right, Mr Murray? You look quite pale.'

'I'm fine. Go on.'

'Where was I? Yes, John Kale. Remarried about the same time he moved to Tunford. His second wife's called Sandra. Met her when he was stationed at Aldershot after he was wounded, not long before he was discharged.' The detective turned down his mouth. 'Doesn't look a very select article, Mr Murray, if you don't mind my saying. Works as a barmaid in the local pub. Kale's employed in a scrapyard in the next town. Quite well thought of, from what I can gather. Bit of a local hero. You know, local boy goes off to fight, wife dies, he comes back injured. All very tragic.'

He looked across at Ben, as though waiting for him to say something. Ben took it as his cue to ask what he had been dreading.

'Do they have any children?'

There was a subtle change in Quilley's attitude, as though the question pleased him. 'No, and that's another tragedy. Kale had a child by his first wife, a little boy, but it seems the baby was stolen from the hospital not long after it was born. Jeanette Kale was staying down in London with her parents at the time. They never did find out what happened to it.' He tut-tutted. 'Makes you wonder if that had anything to do with what happened afterwards. You know, her getting herself killed, him getting shot. Almost like everything went to pieces for them after that.' His smile remained, but his eyes were unmistakably watchful now. 'Still, they say things happen in threes, don't they?'

Ben told himself he was being over-sensitive about the man's manner. 'Did they have any idea you were checking up on them?'

'Oh, no need to worry about that. I wouldn't be very good at my job if I let people know when I was checking up on them, would I?'

The impulse to get out of the office and away from the man on the other side of the desk was growing stronger. 'So is that everything?' He found himself hoping it was.

'I think it more or less covers what you wanted to know, wouldn't you say?'

Ben found himself nodding. 'How much do I owe you?'

The detective's smile was no longer so bland. He settled back in his chair, folding his hands across the top of his stomach. 'Well, now we come to a bit of a problem, actually.'

Ben's hand slowed on the route to his cheque book. 'I'm not with you. We agreed on a rate.'

'Yes, yes we did. But that was before ... how shall I put it? Before I was fully aware of the nature of the research.' He nodded, as if appreciating the phrasing. 'You see, Mr Murray, the reason I'm so good at my job is that I believe in thoroughness. I don't like leaving things half done. And if I come across something that puzzles me ... Well, I can't rest until I've got to the bottom of it, if you take my meaning. How is the book going, by the way?'

The walls of the office seemed to be closing in. 'Okay.'

'Good, good. Because I got to thinking that it's rather unusual for a writer – or a photographer, such as yourself – to hire a private investigator to locate someone just to interview for a book. To say nothing of expensive. Anyone doing that must either want to interview them very badly indeed or ...' The smile broadened. 'Or have their own reasons for doing it. Now you might say that those reasons are none of my business, and perhaps you're right. But as I pointed out to you at our last meeting, I do like to know a little about who I'm working for. And so I took the liberty of carrying out a little "extracurricular" research, for want of a better term.'

Ben thought about the phone call to the studio. The detective had been checking up on him. *Oh, Jesus, what have I done?*

'I must offer my condolences on the death of your wife.' Quilley shook his head, slowly. 'A terrible thing to happen at that age. Terrible. And leaving you to look after a little boy as well. A handicapped one at that. It can't be easy. Particularly when, if you'll pardon me saying, he isn't actually yours.'

'What's that supposed to mean?'

'Only that he's your stepson. What else could I mean?'

The edge of the chair seat dug into Ben's palms where he gripped it. 'If there's a point to this why don't you get to it?'

'No need to be defensive, Mr Murray. I'm only commenting on the facts. And I'm sure that when you come to interview Mr Kale for your book you'll find it helpful that the two of you have so much in common. Quite a catalogue of coincidences, really. His first wife also having died young, and you both having sons – or in your case a stepson – born on virtually the same day. Except that Mr Kale doesn't know where his son is, of course.'

The urge to walk out and the desire to lunge at the face across the desk were equally strong. 'I don't see how any of that's relevant. Or anything to do with you.'

The detective grinned as if Ben had made a joke. 'I take your point, Mr Murray. Of course, it isn't anything to do with me. Nothing at all. And I do apologise if I've touched on a nerve. I'm sure you're very fond of the boy. Look on him as your own after all this time, I dare say.'

Ben felt uncoordinated as he took out his cheque book. 'I asked how much I owed you.'

'So you did, Mr Murray. And, as I said, it's a difficult question. You see, what we basically have here are two separate issues. On the one hand there's the fee for my time and expenses, which is fairly straightforward. But then there's the question of ... how shall I put it? The value of information, let's say. And I'm sure you can appreciate that's less easy to put a price on. What's worth one thing to one person may be worth much more to another. How do you judge these things?' The detective's smile was indulgent. 'I'm sure you appreciate the problem.'

The pen seemed cumbersome as Ben wrote out a cheque. 'It's six days by my reckoning. I'll give you the benefit of the doubt and include Saturday at the same rate. There's fifty pounds for expenses as well.' He tore out the cheque and dropped it on the desk. He stood up. 'I'll take the report with me.'

Quilley's smile had shrunk a little but it was still there. He handed Ben the cardboard folder. 'As you wish, Mr Murray. As you wish.'

There were signs that Maggie's charity was wearing thin. Her smile was glassy as she served the lasagne. Ben sat next to Jacob. On the other side of the table Scott and Andrew whispered and cast glances across at him, sniggering from time to time. Colin still wasn't home. He had called to say that he would be working late. Maggie ordered them all to the dinner table as she announced the news.

'He says it's unavoidable, so that's all right, isn't it? Still, never mind. I'm sure we can manage without him. And if his dinner's burnt when he decides to get back, that'll just be too bad, won't it? If he doesn't like it he's always welcome to find himself some other hotel.'

Ben said nothing. He wished he hadn't accepted Colin's invitation. He had called him at work as soon as he had left the detective's office. A secretary had said he was in a meeting, but Ben had insisted on talking to him.

Colin had listened to his ranting account and then said, 'Shit.' He'd told Ben he couldn't get away just then, couldn't even talk for long because he'd got a room full of record company suits and an angry band, and if he didn't get back soon they'd start breaking the furniture on each other. 'Come over for dinner tonight. We can talk then,' he'd said.

But when Ben and Jacob had arrived at the house he'd found that Maggie wasn't expecting them. Now she had the toothpaste smile of the self-martyred as she handed out the plates. 'I just hope there's enough to go around. Of course, it would have been nice if Colin had had the consideration to tell me he'd invited guests, but I suppose that would be asking too much. After all, that's what I'm here for, isn't it? I don't have anything better to do than stay at home all day while he goes off with his bands.'

Maggie seemed convinced that Colin's work was mainly socialising because most of his clients were musicians. Ben hadn't heard her complain about the money he earned, though. 'Don't bother about me,' he told her. 'I can eat later.'

'No, of course you won't. If there isn't enough Colin'll just have to go without. Perhaps then he'll make more of an effort to get home on time when I've gone to the trouble of cooking.' The serving spoon rattled against china. 'Scott, it's rude to whisper to your brother at the dinner table.'

Scott ignored her, whispering behind a cupped hand to Andrew. Although Ben couldn't hear what was being said he could guess its subject by the way they were looking at Jacob, who was busily picking out the pieces of onion from the sauce and arranging them end to end around the rim of his plate.

Andrew giggled as his elder brother finally lowered his hand. Scott glanced at Ben indifferently, still smirking. Ben stared back at him, fighting the desire to ram his fork up the little bastard's nose. *He's only a kid, for God's sake. Don't be so touchy.* He turned to Jacob.

'Come on, Jacob. Eat your tea.'

Jacob looked up, blankly, at the sound of his voice, then went back to sifting out the onion.

Maggie finished dishing out the lasagne and sat down. For a while there was no noise except the scrape of cutlery. 'This is really nice,' said Ben, dutifully. To give Maggie her due, she was a good cook.

'Thank you. Nice to know someone appreciates me.'

Oh God. Scott and Andrew were giggling and nudging each other. 'If you two boys don't hurry up, you won't get any dessert,' Maggie said with forced jocularity.

'That's all right, because I don't want any,' Scott told her.

'Well, perhaps we'll let you go without all week, then, shall we?' The bright smile was set on her face now, as convincing as a party mask on a mugger.

'Good.'

Maggie's mouth twitched, and Ben hoped for a moment that she would resort to violence against her first-born. Instead she tore her eyes away and noticed Jacob, still arranging the onions in a line.

'Eat up, Jacob. Don't play with your food when Auntie Maggie's gone to the trouble of cooking it, dear.'

Jacob didn't even look up. 'Did you hear Auntie Maggie, Jacob?' she persisted. 'Be a good boy and do as you're told.'

Because your brats certainly don't. Ben gripped his cutlery. He had seen Maggie in her picky moods before. They ran off Jacob, and usually Ben took no notice. Right then, though, he wasn't in a good mood himself.

'He'll get round to it,' he said, as casually as he could manage. 'No need to push him.'

Maggie's smile glittered. 'Was I pushing? I'm sorry, I'm sure I didn't mean to. It's just a little annoying when you see something you've cooked go to waste.'

Scott and Andrew had fallen silent and stopped eating, aware of the sudden tension between the adults. Only Jacob seemed unaware of it. Ben told himself to ease off. A scene wouldn't do anyone any good, and Maggie had been helpful since—

—*since Sarah died.* The thought snuffed the heat out of him.

'It won't be wasted. If the worst comes to the worst I'll finish it myself,' he said, doing his best to smile naturally. Maggie backed off a little herself. At least she seemed to.

There was an interval while she put green salad on the side of her plate. Then she asked, 'Have you any idea yet what you're going to do about Jacob?'

Ben felt the lasagne clog his mouth. He took a drink of water. 'I'm not with you.'

'About his school, I mean. Not that I mind running him backwards and forwards for you.' She smiled, saccharin again. 'He's such a treasure. But it isn't always convenient, and I expect you'll want to sort out something more ... well, more permanent, won't you?'

His relief was followed by irritation. Here it comes, he thought. First the favour, then the bill. 'Yes, I will.' He knew he wouldn't ask her to collect Jacob again, no matter how difficult it became.

'I don't want you to think there's any hurry as far as I'm concerned,' she went on, back-pedalling now she had made the point. 'I know it's not easy for you, though, and I just wondered if you'd had chance to think about any other options.'

'What sort of options?' He could guess.

'Well, I don't know, really. Perhaps some sort of ...' She

glanced at her two sons, who were no longer paying the slightest bit of attention, and lowered her voice conspiratorially. '. . . of residential school. Of course, it's only a thought. I don't know what you've got in mind, but with Jacob being a . . . a *special* little boy, and you being busy and all, well . . .' Her smile was failing against his silence. 'You don't mind my mentioning it, I hope?'

'Why should I?' He stood up. 'Excuse me.'

He left the table, knowing it was rude of him, but also knowing it was less rude than what he might have said if he'd stayed. The bathroom was at the top of the stairs. Ben locked himself in. He hadn't particularly wanted to urinate but now he was there he did anyway. It gave him something to do to take his mind off his anger. When he had finished he put down the pink marble-effect seat and pressed down the gold-plated flush handle. The washbasin taps were even more ornate, a pair of stylised and vaguely Japanese-style dolphins. As he dried his hands on one of the soft pink towels he remembered what Colin's room had been like when they had been students. The décor hadn't run beyond posters and empty bottles of Newcastle Brown. It didn't take much guessing whose hand had been behind decorating the house.

He went back downstairs, cooler-headed than when he went up. It wasn't worth falling out with Maggie, if only for Colin's sake. And, after helping out with Jacob for the past three weeks, he supposed she had a right to ask what his plans were.

It wasn't her fault that he didn't have any.

The thick oriental carpet silenced his footsteps as he returned to the dining room. He heard voices from it before he reached the doorway.

'. . . well, he *is*,' Scott was saying. 'I don't see why he's got to come here!'

'I don't care, I've told you not to call him that!' Maggie snapped, trying to whisper.

'Why not? He can't understand.'

'That's not the point! It isn't a nice thing to say.'

'So what? He *is* a mong. And you don't want him here either. I've heard you telling Dad.'

'You shouldn't have been listening! I won't tell you again—' She broke off as Ben came in. 'Oh.' She hastily tried to assemble a smile. 'We, er ... we were just—'

'Yes, I heard.' He went over to Jacob. The boy sat with his chin tucked on his chest, eyes downcast. Ben's jaw muscles hurt to think of him sitting there as they talked about him. 'Come on, Jacob, time to go home,' he said, taking his hand. He shot a glare at Scott, who was sullenly staring at the table. 'Thanks for dinner, Maggie. Tell Colin I'll talk to him later.'

'Ben, there's no need to ... I mean, I don't want you to think—'

'Don't bother to get up.'

She still followed them into the hallway, smiling anxiously. 'Are you sure you won't stay for dessert?'

'I don't think so, Maggie.'

He opened the door and went out before she could say anything else. His Golf was parked further up the street. He hoisted Jacob up and carried him, even though it wasn't far. He felt he wanted to cry. He thought about Maggie again and let himself feel angry instead.

He set Jacob down when he reached the car. As he unlocked it there was a shout. He turned to see Colin hurrying from his BMW. There was no sign of Maggie.

'Where're you going?' Colin asked, breathlessly.

'Jacob's tired, so we're going home.'

'Home? I thought you wanted to talk.' He took hold of Ben's arm. 'Come on, you can have a quick drink—'

'It's okay, I'll give you a ring.'

Colin let his hand fall. 'What's wrong?'

'Nothing. I just want to get Jacob home, that's all.'

They looked at each other. Colin glanced towards the

house. He seemed to sag slightly, then drew himself up. 'If you're in a rush let's talk in the car.'

Jacob played with a puzzle in the back while they talked. Ben described the meeting with Quilley. When he'd finished Colin kneaded the bridge of his nose. The flesh of his face was pale and puffy. His scalp showed through his thinning hair. *He looks middle-aged,* Ben thought, with a slight shock.

'I'm sorry, Ben. If I'd any idea he'd pull something like this I'd never have recommended him.'

'You weren't to know.' But he still felt resentment, unjustified or not.

'I know it doesn't help but I'll see to it he doesn't get any more work from our firm. I'll put the word out to other people as well. It's just a pity you didn't tell him you'd got his name from us. I don't think he'd have tried anything if he'd known.'

'I'm more worried about what I'm going to do now than what I should have done.'

'I can call him, if you like. Tell him we represent you. That might make him think twice before he does anything else.'

'Are you sure you want to get your firm involved?'

Colin didn't say anything, but Ben could see he wasn't.

'I don't have any choice, do I?' he went on. 'I've got to assume it's all going to come out.'

'You don't know for sure there's anything *to* come out.'

'Oh, come off it.'

Colin looked at Jacob playing on the back seat. He gave a sigh. 'Okay, then. The next thing to do is to get some advice. I can ask around, see if anyone knows a good family law solicitor. The number of divorces our clients go through I shouldn't think that'll be a problem.' He gave Ben a sheepish glance. 'I'll make sure it's someone reliable this time.'

The streetlights had come on, although it wasn't dark. Ben looked at the weak yellow glows. 'You don't think I should go straight to the police?'

'Christ, no. If you do they'll be all over you. You could wind up being held on a kidnapping or aiding-and-abetting charge and Jacob in care before you know what's happening. You need legal representation before anything else.' He paused. 'The question of custody's going to be tricky enough as it is.'

Ben was aware that Colin was watching him, trying to gauge his reaction. In the rear-view mirror he could see Jacob's face, unconcerned. He felt an urge to hug him.

'What I can't stop thinking about,' he said, in a voice that wasn't quite steady, 'is how the other poor bastard must feel. You know who I mean. It's been over six years. We're sitting here, calmly discussing what we should do, and he's sitting somewhere not knowing if his son's alive or dead. I keep thinking about what he must have gone through, and what happened to his wife, and ... fuck, I don't know.'

He broke off and turned to stare out of the side window. Colin was quiet for a while, giving him a chance to recover.

'You've got to think about yourself, Ben,' he said gently. 'And Jacob. I'm sorry for this guy too, but it doesn't alter the fact that you're in a vulnerable situation. If this does all come out you're going to have to prove you knew nothing about it until now. You're going to have to decide fairly soon what you're going to do, and to do that you need expert legal advice.'

'I know.' Ben cleared his throat and nodded. 'I know, you're right, and I will, but ...' He realised he'd already come to a decision. 'I'd like to see him first.'

'Oh, now look, Ben——!'

'I don't mean I want to meet him. I just want to see where he lives, what he looks like. Try and get some idea of what sort of a man he is. I can't decide anything until I know that.'

He expected an argument, but Colin was silent. 'When?' he asked.

'I don't know.' He hadn't thought that far. 'Tomorrow morning, perhaps.'

Colin passed a hand over his face and shook his head. But whatever objections he had he kept to himself. 'I'll come with you,' he said.

Chapter Seven

It took almost as long to get out of London as it did to get to the town itself. There was another Tube strike, and the roads were clotted with slow-moving snakes of traffic. The air was unbreathable. It was a close, muggy morning but they kept the window up, preferring the heat to the atmosphere of exhaust fumes.

They had taken Ben's Golf. Colin had objected to travelling in what he called 'a biscuit tin', but couldn't deny that his black BMW would look conspicuous in a scrapyard. Ben guessed it was the thought of what might happen to it there that finally convinced him.

Once on the M1 Ben made good time to the turn-off. The main suburban sprawl was quickly left behind, but the countryside was still marred with blotches of industry, man-made cankers of brick and metal amongst the green. Some of the fields they passed still had yellow snatches of rape clinging to them, and then suddenly there was a brown patch of houses and they were in Tunford.

It was a new town, or at least had been in the 1950s. The brave new face of postwar housing development now looked ramshackle and depressed. They went along the high street, a short stretch of squat, dun-coloured shops, until they left the town again on the other side. Ben turned the car round in a lay-by littered with plastic bottles and tin cans and headed back for the town centre.

'What's the address?'

Colin opened the folder the detective had given Ben. 'Forty-one Primrose Lane.'

The shops came into view again. Prefabricated semi-detached houses ran off to either side. 'Do you think there'll still be primroses there?' Ben asked, trying to conceal his nervousness.

'If there are they'll be under the tarmac. Shall we try the next turning?'

Since they didn't know where Primrose Lane was, one street was as good as another. They had no map of the town, and didn't want to draw attention to themselves by asking for directions. Not that there were many people about to ask. Neither of them spoke as they drove through the empty streets at random. On one they passed a mongrel dog shitting on the pavement.

'Welcome to Tunford,' Colin said.

Primrose Lane was at the edge of the town, running parallel with the fields beyond. They drove down it slowly, counting house numbers. Colin pointed. 'There.'

The house was set behind a four-foot-high wire mesh and concrete post fence. The neighbouring properties were run down, with shaggy lawns and unkempt flower-beds, and the garden in front of 41 was heaped with rusting piles of metal. Car wings, doors and bumpers, engine parts and motors were stacked haphazardly, grown through with uncut grass and weeds.

'Obviously a man who takes his work home with him.'

Ben didn't respond to the joke. He drove past slowly, taking in the peeling paint on the doors and window frames. A woman appeared in an upstairs window. He had a glimpse of yellow hair and plucked eyebrows, and then the house was behind them.

Colin craned his head to see. 'Was that the wife?'

'I suppose so.'

They were quiet as they went back to the main street. 'It might not be as bad as it looks,' Colin said, after a while. 'Just because they won't get in *House and Home* doesn't mean they might not be nice people.'

'No.'

'You can never tell from appearances.'

'Just leave it, Colin, will you?'

He headed out the way they had originally gone, before they had turned back. According to the detective's report the scrap metal yard where Kale worked was on the outskirts of the next town along, about three miles away. For a while they were back in open countryside, but the taint of civilisation was in the litter-strewn hedgerows. They passed an untidy farm, then a garage. The scrapyard was the next building after that.

Ben pulled into the edge of the road before he reached it. The yard was surrounded by a high brick wall, topped with barbed wire and shards of broken glass. Mounds of decaying cars were visible above it, stacked one on top of another. A battered sign saying 'Robertshaw's Reclamation Yard' arched across the top of the entrance. Below it, the spiked double gate was open.

Colin stirred. 'You sure you want to do this?'

Not really. Ben didn't answer. He could see some sort of heavy vehicle moving about inside the yard. A crane. 'What is it we're supposed to be looking for?'

'Spares for an MG. But I'll ask about that. You just keep your eyes open.'

Quilley's report had given a basic description, but other than that Ben didn't know what the man looked like. The car spares story had been Colin's idea, a pretext for wandering around the yard until they identified him.

'Shall we go in, then?' Colin said.

Ben started the car and drove through the gates. Once

through them the yard opened up, bigger than it appeared from outside. The long drive ran between stacks of wrecked cars. It led to a two-storey brick building with a steeply pitched corrugated roof. In front of this was a clearing where two obviously still-roadworthy cars were parked. Ben pulled in behind them. They got out.

There was an earthy smell of rust and oil. From somewhere behind the building a dog barked twice, then abruptly stopped. There was the sound of heavy machinery, but they couldn't see where it was coming from. No one came to meet them. A dirty window on the ground floor looked into an office.

'Let's try in there.'

The door was down a short passageway. At the far end was a flight of concrete steps that presumably ran up to the next floor. A tinny radio played inside the office. Colin knocked and pushed the door open when there was no answer. The room was empty. A tatty Formica desk was covered with stained mugs and folders. The radio served as a paperweight on a pile of grubby papers. Nude calendars were tacked on the walls. Big-breasted girls leaned across gleaming cars and straddled shining motorbikes, offering various body parts to the camera.

'Anybody here?' Colin shouted.

They heard someone coming down the steps. Ben tensed, but the man who appeared in the doorway was too old to be Kale. He was in his fifties, heavy with muscle and fat. Strands of greasy hair poked out from under a trilby, a darker grey than the silvery stubble on his chin. He wiped his hands on an oily rag as he came into the office.

'Mornin', gents. What can I do for you?'

He had a wheezy, phlegm-filled voice. Ben looked quickly at Colin, all thought of their story vanished. But Colin was unperturbed.

'We're looking for spares for a 1985 MG.'

Ben saw the dealer take in the lightweight woollen suit and

silk tie and wished that Colin hadn't come dressed for work. But he had to be back for a meeting at twelve. The man rubbed his chin. 'MG?' He sounded doubtful. 'What parts are you after?'

'Depends what you've got. I'm renovating one virtually from the bottom up, so I need just about everything. Provided it's in reasonable condition.'

'Don't think we've got anything from an MG,' the man muttered, partly to himself. His fingers rasped on his stubble again.

'Can we have a browse around anyway?'

The man wasn't listening. He cast another glance at Colin's suit. 'I might be able to sort you out with something,' he said, obviously loath to let such a wealthy customer go empty-handed. 'Come with me.'

'It's okay, really——' Colin began, but the man was already on his way out.

There was nothing to do but follow him. He led them around the back of the building. The machine noises grew louder. A small crane on caterpillar tracks was behind the office. A man was in the cab, working control levers to manipulate the flat magnet that swung from hawsers and chains from the jib, suspending a burnt-out Ford by the roof. He wore a rimless leather skullcap and also looked too old to be Kale, Ben saw after an anxious second. The scrap dealer shouted up to him.

'You seen Johnny?'

The man in the cab cupped an ear, and the dealer repeated the question more loudly. The crane driver nodded towards the far end of the yard. 'He's with somebody by the crusher.'

The dealer set off again. 'I'll ask one of my blokes,' he said as they trailed after him. 'He knows what we've got inside and out. If we've anything, he'll be able to put his hands on it.'

Ben glanced worriedly at Colin, who shrugged helplessly. Neither of them had missed the significance of who 'Johnny' might be. Seeing Kale from a distance was one thing, but Ben was feeling less and less prepared to meet him face to face.

The scrap dealer took them past a towering stack of flattened cars, compressed to no more than thin stripes of colour, layers of red and blue, yellow and white. The angular bulk of a crushing machine was tucked behind them.

'Johnny!' the dealer bellowed. 'Got a customer!'

There was a movement from the end of the machine. A man appeared, and Ben found himself looking at Jacob's father. There was no doubt who he was. John Kale had written his features on his son's face almost verbatim, discernible even under the blurring of childhood. There was the same colouring, the same cheekbones and straight nose, firm chin and mouth. He had Jacob's deep-set eyes, and as they settled on Ben the sense of recognition was so great that for an irrational second he felt sure it must be two-way. Then Kale looked away again, uninterested.

The dealer motioned with his thumb towards Colin. 'Fella here looking for MG parts, John. We got anything?'

'No.' There was no doubt or hesitation.

The older man scratched at the open neck of his soiled shirt. 'You sure? I thought there might be something—'

'That was a Midget. It went.' The voice was medium-pitched and inflectionless. Kale no longer so much as glanced towards either Ben or Colin. For all the attention he paid them they might not have been there. He wasn't particularly tall, two or three inches shorter than Ben's six foot, but there was a sense of restrained physicality about him. The muscles in his bare arms were clearly defined, and he looked compact and fit in the oil-stained T-shirt and jeans.

The dealer's regret was palpable, but he didn't question the information. 'Sorry, gents. If Johnny says we don't, then we don't. Wish I could help you.'

Ben couldn't stop staring at Kale, who was standing motionless by his boss. He must have felt the scrutiny because his eyes suddenly flicked to Ben with a gaze as direct and unblinking as an animal's. *Christ, he even stares at you like Jacob.*

Ben made himself look away as Colin gave a convincing shrug of resignation. 'That's okay. Thanks anyway.'

They turned to go. Ben was desperate to get out of the scrapyard now, to give himself time to think. He wondered if Colin would mind him smoking a joint in the car. Then another voice spoke from behind them.

'Well, fancy seeing you here, Mr Murray.'

He looked around, and felt himself deaden into shock as Quilley emerged from behind the heavy crushing machine.

The detective's smile was more mocking than ever. 'Talk of the devil. We were just discussing you, weren't we, Mr Kale? Oh, sorry, you haven't been introduced, have you?' he said in response to Kale's puzzled frown. 'Mr Kale, this is Ben Murray. He's the photographer I was just telling you about. The one who might have got your son.'

Oh, Jesus. Oh fuck, no.

'Now, hang on a second,' Colin began. Kale ignored him. The Jacob-stare was fixed on Ben.

'That true?' His face was still expressionless, only now there was a terrible intensity about it. 'You've got my boy?'

'It isn't how it seems—' Ben stammered.

'Okay, that's it. We're leaving now,' Colin said, taking hold of his arm.

But Kale had already started towards them. One leg was stiff and unbending, and Ben remembered Quilley saying how he had been wounded in Northern Ireland.

Colin stepped forward. 'Okay, let's all calm down a little—'

Kale didn't so much as glance at him as he rammed the heel of his hand into his face. There was a solid meat-and-bone impact. Colin rebounded from the out-thrust hand and staggered backwards. Ben moved to help him and suddenly found himself lying on the rough concrete floor. He had no memory of getting there. He became aware of a commotion near by and turned his head to look. The movement caused a shaft of pain that served as a vanguard to a much bigger one throughout his entire body. A few yards from his head he saw two pairs of boots scuffling, and followed them upwards to see the scrap dealer struggling to restrain Kale. Kale was staring fixedly at Ben, and although the dealer was straining with his full weight he was being pushed inexorably backwards.

'Go on, fuck off out of it!' he snapped. Ben felt a hand under his arm as Colin helped him up. His mouth and chin were shiny with blood.

'Come on, let's go.' Colin's voice was clogged and nasal. Ben tried to get his feet under him and the world tilted to one side. He nearly vomited.

'Where's my boy?' Kale didn't shout, but the demand was no less imperative for that. Ben was still searching for some way of taking them back to a better start as Colin began pulling him away. Behind them Quilley watched, no longer smiling but making no attempt to intervene.

'Let 'em go, John!' the dealer gasped, feet scrabbling for purchase in his effort to hold Kale.

'Get out of the way. Now,' Kale told him.

There was a final warning in his voice. The dealer said, 'Leave it, John, for Christ's sake!' but dropped his arms. Kale thrust him aside. Ben knew the man was beyond reasoning and hobbled into a shambling run as Colin urged him to go faster. He couldn't remember what Kale had done to him but he felt he had been transposed into an unfamiliar, pain-racked body. As they stumbled past the stacks of flattened cars he glanced back and saw the ex-soldier limping after them with grim determination. But he was falling steadily behind, slowed by his unbending left leg. They reached the crane, ignoring the bewildered looks from its operator as they ran by. The office building was just ahead of them, the car around the other side of it.

'Get the keys ready,' Colin panted. Ben was pulling them from his pocket when there was a piercing whistle.

He looked round. Kale had two fingers hooked into his mouth, and without breaking stride he gave another short, sharp blast. A low brown shape streaked out from amongst the wrecked cars. Kale didn't speak, simply snapped his fingers in their direction. The dog tore towards them

Ben said, 'Oh fuck,' and they began to run in earnest. The Golf was in sight now. He sprinted for it, Colin beside him. The sound of the dog's claws on concrete grew swiftly louder. It was closing fast. 'Get on the bonnet!'

They leapt on to the car at the same time. The dog overshot, its claws scrabbling as it braked in a tight circle. It was a Staffordshire bull terrier, all wedged-shaped head and slabbed muscle. Ben slid off the bonnet and thrust the key into the lock. He threw himself inside and slammed the door as the dog came tearing back. There was a bang and the car rocked as the animal hit it. He reached across and unlocked the passenger door. Colin had climbed on to the car roof. He scrambled inside while Ben fumbled with the ignition and the dog jumped up at the window on the driver's side. Ben heard him say 'Shit!' and looked up to see Kale heading for them from around the building. The dog snarled and slavered at the glass inches from his head as he crashed the gears into reverse and accelerated for the gates. The car shot through them backwards into the road. He stamped on the brake, crunched into first, and put his foot down hard. The scrapyard disappeared behind them.

He took turnings at random until he felt sure that Kale had no chance of following, then pulled into an overgrown lay-by and switched off the ignition. The car subsided into silence. Ben kept his hands on the steering wheel. Beside him Colin held a carmine-splashed handkerchief to his nose. His shirt was dappled with blood.

'You all right?' Ben asked.

'I don't think it's broken.' His voice still sounded honky and strange. 'How about you?'

Ben looked down at himself. He didn't even seem to be bleeding. But it wasn't the physical hurt that stopped him answering. What had happened was too calamitous for him to take in. It was as though he'd been gored, knowing it was serious but too numbed by shock to gauge how bad the damage was. He couldn't begin to think what the consequences would be.

He turned on the ignition. 'I think now's the time to find a good solicitor.'

Chapter Eight

The sun had almost disappeared behind the rooftops. The small garden was dappled by shade. Jet contrails criss-crossed the orange-to-indigo vignette of evening sky, slowly dispersing into petrochemical imitations of cirrus clouds. Ben blew his own contribution up at them and stubbed out the joint on the heel of his sandal. He dropped it in his empty beer bottle and leaned back against the garden wall. The bricks still retained some of the sun's heat, but that was the only comfort to be had from their ungiving roughness. There were perfectly good wooden sun chairs a matter of feet away, and Ben had no reason not to sit in them instead of on the hard-baked ground. But he wasn't uncomfortable enough for it to merit the effort of moving.

The creak of the swing provided a metronomic counterpoint to the sweeter but unstructured birdsong from the trees. Whenever it began to slow, Ben reached out with his foot and set it going again. The empty seat arced lazily backwards and forwards. Jacob could sit on it for hours without growing bored, just watching the grass zip by under his feet. Ben had taken photographs of him, using a high-speed film to capture the movement without blurring. A camera lay beside him now. He'd focused it once on the untenanted swing, but had put it down again without pressing the shutter release. It would have made too bald a statement.

Another plane crossed the sky, invisible except for the white chalk mark that trailed behind it. Ben raised the camera and took a couple of shots of the geometric tracery above him. He knew it was the wrong sort of camera, wrong sort of film, and that he was in the wrong sort of mood to get anything decent, but, just as there was no reason to go and sit in a chair, neither was there a reason why he shouldn't waste some film if he wanted to. Nothing seemed any more or less worthwhile than anything else.

It was amazing how quickly things could turn to shit.

Objectively, it was only three months since the disastrous visit to the scrapyard, but so much had happened that to his subjective timescale it seemed much longer. When he had gone to see the solicitor the day after the encounter with Kale he still hadn't any real idea what was in store for him. Ann Usherwood was in her late forties, tall and sparely built with greying hair and a severe business suit. Her office was smart but unpretentious, functional almost to the point of being spartan. She had been professionally blunt as she told him he was in a legally vulnerable position. 'A step-parent doesn't have any automatic rights to their spouse's children. You ought to have made an application to the court for something called a "residence order" as soon as your wife died, so Jacob could continue living with you.'

'Won't Kale be able to just take Jacob back anyway?' he'd asked.

'It doesn't work like that. Although, from what you say, there's no doubt that John Kale is the natural father, the child's welfare is always the first consideration. No one's going to simply tear Jacob from his home and hand him over to a total stranger, natural father or not. Mr Kale will still have to apply for a residence order himself, unless you voluntarily agree to return Jacob to him. The fact that Jacob was, er . . .'

'Stolen,' supplied Ben, brutally.

'I was going to say unlawfully taken by your wife, but however you put it a child isn't a piece of property to be returned to the original owner, regardless. Taking him was a criminal act, however, and I imagine the midwife will be investigated and quite possibly charged.' She paused. 'You'll have to satisfy the police that you didn't know anything about what your wife had done until you found the cuttings. Taking steps to find Jacob's father will weigh in your favour, although it might be argued that you should have gone to the police straightaway instead of going to the scrapyard.'

'I only wanted to see Kale for myself.'

'Hopefully the police will accept that. In any event, you've got to make a decision on how you want to proceed. Given that John Kale will probably make an application for residence, are you going to contest it?'

Ben rubbed his temples. 'What'll happen if I do?'

'A court welfare officer — or in this case perhaps a social worker — will be appointed to consider Mr Kale's application and make recommendations. Then the court will decide where Jacob's going to live. They'll take into account his own wishes and feelings, which is obviously more difficult when there are communication difficulties. But under normal circumstances you'd probably have a reasonable prospect of keeping him.'

He felt too tired to think. 'And if I don't contest it?'

'Then, after a period of assessment, Jacob will probably go to live with his natural father.'

'Will I still be able to see him?'

'You might be allowed some contact, but I can't say how much. That'll depend on what's felt to be in his best interests.'

Best interests? Ben thought about the shabby little town, the house with its junk piled in the garden. He hated the idea of Jacob living somewhere like that. He didn't want to give him up, couldn't imagine how he'd feel if he did. The thought of what Sarah would say, what she would think, was a dry anguish in his gut. The rights and wrongs of how she came by him apart, Jacob was her son. She had loved him, looked after him. And so had he. How could he just let him go now?

But against that was the memory of Kale limping forward with six years' pent-up grief. *Where's my boy?*

He realised the solicitor was waiting. He gave her his answer.

John Kale saw his son for the first time in a dirty concrete-and-glass social services building. Ben held Jacob's hand as they went with Ann Usherwood to the room where the meeting was to take place. The social worker appointed to carry out the assessment was a man called Carlisle. He was a few years older than Ben, with a stubble cut, chinos and a habit of looking down his nose. John Kale and his wife were there already, Kale in a dark green suit that was too heavy for the weather, his wife in a short, sleeveless pink dress. Ben braced himself as Kale stood up, but the other man didn't so much as glance at him. He was staring at Jacob.

Everyone in the room seemed to hang on the moment. Kale limped over and stood in front of his son, never taking his eyes from him. His face was as unrevealing as it had been in the scrapyard, but now Ben fancied there was a tentativeness about him. He squatted down, looking intently into the boy's face without speaking. Ben expected Jacob to make his pushing-away gesture, but he didn't.

'Hello, Steven,' Kale said. 'I'm your dad.'

Jacob kept his gaze averted, then cautiously shifted it to the man crouching in front of him. They looked at each other, and Ben felt a little slip of unreality at the resemblance between them. Then Kale turned and fixed him with an unblinking stare.

'What have you done to him?'

The social worker stepped forward. 'I think perhaps we should all just take a seat. This is going to be very difficult for everyone, and it's important to keep calm and remember that we're here to discuss what's best for Jacob.'

'Steven,' Kale said. His head swivelled from Ben to the social worker. 'His name's Steven.'

Carlisle faltered, then rallied. 'I'm sorry, Mr Kale, but unless you want to confuse and upset him, you'll have to start thinking of your son as Jacob now. That's the name he knows and has been brought up with, and trying to change it now could prove very difficult for him.'

Ben saw Kale's jaw muscles bunch as he looked down again at Jacob. The social worker turned in silent appeal to the overweight man with a thick moustache and glasses sitting with Sandra Kale. By his dandruff-flecked suit and briefcase, Ben guessed he was their solicitor. The man reluctantly rose to his feet. 'Why don't you sit down, Mr Kale?'

Kale ignored him. He fished in his pocket and brought out a small parcel. 'Here.' He offered it to Jacob. Jacob just looked at it. Kale unwrapped it for him. Ben saw that his hands were square and broad, the fingers stubbed and callused. The object was a puzzle, a clear plastic case in which two or three tiny silver balls rolled freely. It was similar to the ones Jacob had at home. Kale gave it a little shake, rattling the balls, and offered it to him again. This time the boy accepted it. He shook it himself, copying Kale, then began trying to manoeuvre the balls into holes in the puzzle's base.

Kale passed his hand softly over the boy's head before going back to his seat. As if that were their cue, the rest of them also went to the collection of low chairs set around a squat rectangular table. The informal setting did nothing to relieve the atmosphere in the room.

'Before we go any further, I think one thing I have to stress is the need for us all to co-operate,' the social worker said. He was careful to address all of them, not just Kale.

'This is a very emotional time for everyone concerned, but we mustn't lose sight that our priority is Jacob's welfare, not, ah, not venting personal differences.'

'I want my boy,' Kale said. He was hunched forward on the edge of his seat, still watching Jacob. In the next seat his wife was chewing on one corner of her red-painted mouth as her eyes darted from her husband to her stepson. Her eyebrows were plucked into thin dark lines. Her face was sharp-featured and the roots of her straw-coloured hair were dark brown, but there was a vulpine, shopworn attractiveness to her. An edge of white bra strap was showing on one shoulder. She looked up and caught Ben watching her. He turned away.

Carlisle nodded placatingly. 'I know you do, Mr Kale, that's why we're here. But you must understand it isn't a simple matter of you taking Jacob home with you. There are still procedures we have to go through.'

'Like checking up on us, you mean.' It was the first time Kale's wife had spoken. She had a cracked cigarette voice.

'We're not "checking up" on you as such, Mrs Kale. But we can't simply turn a child over to someone without assessing what's best for him.'

'I'm his father,' Kale said. Ben could see him rhythmically squeezing his fists, pumping the veins on his forearms until they stood out. 'He's got no right to him.' His chin jerked in Ben's direction. 'He's kept him from me all this time. He's not keeping him any more.'

Ann Usherwood shifted forward slightly in her seat. 'Mr Murray won't contest your residence application if the local authority and social services are satisfied that it's in Jacob's best interests to live with you and your wife, Mr Kale. And for the record I must remind you that no blame for what happened is attached to my client whatsoever. The police have accepted that he believed the boy was his wife's natural son until after her death, and if not for him acting on that information none of us would be here now.'

There was a snort from Sandra Kale. 'Give him a medal.'

She had a cigarette in her hand. As she raised it to her mouth the social worker said, 'I'm sorry, it's no smoking in here.'

She looked across at him, the cigarette gripped between her lips. 'You're trying to tell me that I can't have a fag?'

Carlisle looked flustered and strained. 'No, I'm sorry.'

'Put it away,' Kale said without looking at his wife. She glared at him, then angrily snatched the cigarette from her mouth. Ben noticed the red smudge of lipstick on the filter as she threw it in her handbag.

The social worker looked at her, then away. 'As Ms Usherwood said, Mr Kale, there's no question of anyone contesting your application for a residence order. But these things do take time, and meanwhile, although you'll be allowed frequent contact, it's best if Jacob remains with Mr Murray—'

'No.'

'I appreciate how you must feel, but—'

He broke off as Kale abruptly rose to his feet. Ben stiffened as he came around the table.

'Ah, Mr Kale . . . ?'

Kale ignored the social worker as he went over to where Jacob was standing. He crouched down in front of him as he had earlier. 'Steven?'

'Mr Kale, I really must ask you not to—'

'Look at me, Steven.'

Jacob continued playing with the puzzle as though he were unaware of Kale's presence. Kale reached out and slowly pushed it down. Jacob gave a little grunt of annoyance and jerked away.

'You'll upset him,' Ben said. Kale took no notice.

'Steven.'

He took hold of Jacob's chin and gently lifted it. 'Don't,' Ben began, but stopped when he saw that Jacob was paying attention.

'I'm your dad. Tell them you want to come home with me. Tell them.'

No one moved. Father and son regarded each other, and for an incredulous second Ben thought that Jacob was going to respond. Then the boy turned back to the puzzle.

The tinny rattle of the silver balls had broken the quiet. 'He can't help it,' Ben had said, feeling obscurely sorry for Kale. Yet at the same time he couldn't deny he was pleased. Both emotions had chilled as the man turned to him with his wide-eyed stare. It was unsettling in its blankness. *You can't tell what he's thinking, what he's going to do. He's like a fucking Rottweiler.*

Kale went back to his seat and didn't speak again for the rest of the meeting.

After that the days had sunk into a montage of dour offices and stern, official faces. The police interviewed Ben several times and took the newspaper cuttings. He didn't care if he never saw them again. Besides, if it was newsprint he wanted, there was plenty of fresh material. The media had latched on to the story of 'Baby Steven's Return' with glee. Seeing the number of 'exclusive' interviews that Quilley gave, Ben guessed that the detective had finally found a market for his information.

He hoped he choked on it.

He had called Sarah's parents before the news broke, wanting to spare them hearing about it first on the TV or radio. He spoke to her father, the words tripping him up so that he had to backtrack constantly to untangle himself.

'I don't understand,' Geoffrey said when he'd finished. His voice was an old man's.

'I didn't want to tell you like this, but the press have found out. It's ... well, it's going to get pretty bad.'

'Oh no. Oh no.'

'I'm sorry.'

But his father-in-law wasn't listening. 'What am I going to

tell Alice?' he asked. Ben was trying to think of something to say when the receiver was fumbled down at the other end.

His mother-in-law called him that same night, after it had been on the evening news. 'Are you satisfied now?' she hissed. 'You couldn't leave well alone, could you? Isn't it enough that Sarah's dead? Did you have to destroy what we've got left?'

'Alice—'

'He's our grandson! He doesn't belong to you! He's all we've got left, and you're giving him away! God, I despise you! I *despise* you!'

Ben couldn't blame her. He didn't feel too good about himself.

The garden was completely in shade now. The swing creaked, almost at a standstill. Ben gave it a final push with his foot and stood up. His flesh under the thin white shirt felt brittle with goose-pimples. He went inside. The front of the house was west-facing, and the lounge was still bright. A rhomboid of yellow light was shafting obliquely on to the carpet through the window. Ben sat in it, closing his eyes and turning his face up to the day's last dregs of sun.

His vision became a red field. Red on red, backed by red, lit by a red glow. He gave himself up to it. It was a Friday night. He didn't want to have to think about what he was going to do with himself for the rest of the weekend. Or the ones after that. Weekends spent with Sarah and Jacob had developed a rose-tinted distortion in his memory that he knew wasn't real but didn't question. He didn't want to think about that either. It was easier to tilt his head to the dying sun and think of nothing.

The red universe darkened to black. He opened his eyes. The sun had shifted so that a horizontal shadow of window frame fell across his face. The patch of sunlight had shrunk to a stripe, too narrow to sit in. Ben put his hand down to push himself up and felt something hard. A single piece of jigsaw puzzle was lying face down on the carpet, concealed by the tassels of a rug. He picked it up. The shiny side was bright blue. A thick orange line cut across it. Ben couldn't imagine what it could be a part of, or which of Jacob's jigsaws it was from. He turned the irregular piece of cardboard in his hand, then looked at his watch.

It was time for the news.

It was one of the last items, a feel-good wind-down to the programme. The newsreader had a smile as she announced that Steven Kale was now back with his real father. *It's Jacob. Not Steven.* There was no mention that he'd been seeing the Kales more and more frequently as part of a supervised 'rehabilitation' process. The coverage showed John and Sandra Kale outside the social services building that afternoon, with Jacob between them. Journalists and photographers scurried alongside and in front. Kale acted as if they didn't exist, but his wife was loving every second of it. She played up to the attention, cheaply sexual as she posed and postured, the only one of the reunited family who was smiling. She beamed at the cameras, holding on to Jacob's hand, and Ben could see that her knuckles were white with the effort of keeping it there. Jacob's head was down, refuting the activity around him. Ben felt his own chest tighten.

He almost didn't recognise the brief shot of himself, hurrying away like a criminal.

Kale's residence application had been approved, and that afternoon Ben had taken Jacob for the final handover to his new parents. He'd told himself all the way through that it was the best thing to do. Best for Jacob. To have contested Kale's right to his son would have been selfish. No matter what he felt personally, no matter what Sarah's parents thought, John Kale was Jacob's father. All the other arguments failed in the face of that. If the social services had found anything, any reason why Jacob shouldn't be returned to his natural father, then that would have been different. But they hadn't, and Ben had agreed to abide by their decision. And he had. Right up till the end.

I'm sorry, Sarah.

He remembered how Jessica had accused him of not wanting the responsibility of looking after Jacob, and wondered if his motives for giving him up without a fight had been completely pure after all. His reasoning now seemed blurred and muddied. He watched as the television report cut to an elderly couple in a tiny flocked-wallpaper living room. Jeanette Kale's parents. The woman was in a wheelchair, obviously uncomfortable in front of the TV cameras. Her husband sat holding her hand, a composed-looking man being slowly dragged down by age. Yes, they were very happy, they said. Yes, they wished their daughter were alive to see her son's return. When they were asked if they had seen their grandson yet, Ben saw the woman glance at her husband. He hesitated. 'No, not yet.'

When would they be seeing him? the interviewer pressed. Again there was an awkwardness.

'Soon, we hope,' the man answered. He didn't look at the interviewer as he said it.

The item ended with a shot of the Kales taking Jacob into their house. The cameras had obviously stayed at the top of the path and were filming over the gate. The overgrown garden with its piles of junk wasn't shown. Its squalor would presumably have struck the wrong chord for the 'up' tone of the rest of the piece. Ben watched as Jacob was absorbed into the black rectangle of the hallway and a smiling Sandra Kale reluctantly closed the door.

He turned the set off. He went into the kitchen, got himself another beer from the fridge and sat down at the table to roll himself a joint. He was smoking too many and drinking too much lately. *Fuck it.* He drew down a lungful of the bitter-sweet smoke, held it, then blew it out and took a gulp of beer to cool his mouth.

Once a month.

That was his reward for doing the right thing. That was how often he'd been granted access to Jacob. Not that it was called 'access' any more. The new word was contact, as if the name made any difference. It still meant he would only be allowed to see him one day out of every twenty-eight.

Once a fucking month.

Even Ann Usherwood had been confident that it would be weekly, or fortnightly at most. But although the police had absolved Ben of any guilt, any complicity in what had happened, the social services had still decided that it wouldn't be in Jacob's 'best interests' to see him too often. They appeared as taken with the romantic story of little boy lost, little boy found as the lowest of the tabloids. Not that they admitted it. It was all couched in the most respectable, reasonable terms. Jacob was already settling into his new home surprisingly well, Carlisle, the social worker, had told Ben. In view of the circumstances, and his condition, far from helping that process, frequent contact with his former stepfather might actually disrupt it. He said they were sorry.

Which made everything all right, of course.

Ben drained the bottle of beer and went upstairs to Jacob's room. What *used* to be Jacob's room, he corrected himself, drawing on the joint. He looked at the toys and clothes that Kale hadn't wanted, the Rebus symbols and brightly coloured posters on the wall. He didn't know which was worst, seeing what was left behind or noticing what was missing. He'd taken the previous day off work so they could spend it together. They'd gone to the zoo. He'd carried the boy on his shoulders around the caged and penned animals, trying to make him laugh, wanting it to be a day they'd both remember. Jacob seemed to have had a good time but it had been too emotionally loaded for Ben to enjoy it. A part of him was forever standing back, self-consciously observing everything they did in the awareness that it was their last day. Telling himself that he'd be able to see Jacob again in a month's time didn't help. He knew it would be different then. His mood had continued even when they were back home. That morning he'd helped Jacob dress, made his breakfast, all with the knowledge that he wouldn't be doing any of it again.

It was harder than ever to convince himself that he had made the right decision.

He closed the door on the room that Jacob wouldn't be spending any more nights in and went back downstairs. He killed the joint and took another beer from the fridge. A photograph of Sarah stared down at him from the kitchen wall. He had always liked it because she seemed to be smiling even though, taking each of her features in isolation, she wasn't. It had only been recently that he could bring himself to put it up. Sarah thought it was vain to have photographs of herself on display unless either Ben or Jacob were in them too, and after she had died he'd found it too painful to see it every day. He looked at it now, but even after several joints and beers he couldn't fancy that he saw any reproach or criticism in it. It hadn't changed. It was just a photograph.

The doorbell rang. Ben stayed where he was. He didn't want to see anyone. He had switched off his mobile, and as soon as he had arrived home he had taken the phone off the hook to pre-empt the sympathy calls he knew would be coming. He felt a little guilty for avoiding Colin, but he could always phone him later. It was even possible that his father might feel obliged to ring again, and Ben felt bad enough already without having to go through that. There had been a call when the story first broke, a short conversation that left Ben more depressed than ever. Most of the conversation had been taken up with his excuses for staying away, an apologetic ramble that boiled down to his wife feeling under the weather. Ben had noticed that she always came down with something whenever anyone put any demands on her husband's attentions. 'You know how it is,' his father had finished, and Ben had agreed that yes, he knew how it was. Thanks, Dad.

The doorbell shrilled again. Ben resolutely sat at the table, but this time it didn't stop. He pushed back the chair and went to see who it was.

Zoe was leaning with her thumb on the bell. She jerked it away when he opened the door. A taxi was double-parked on the road behind her, its engine still running. She gave a grin that didn't manage to conceal her nervousness. 'Hi. I tried to ring, but the phone's been engaged.'

Ben was still trying to adjust to seeing her. 'I took it off the hook.'

'Oh.' She put her hands in the back pockets of her tight black jeans. They rode low on her hips. The movement hunched up her shoulders. 'I heard about what had happened on the news. I thought I'd see if you were okay.'

'Yeah, I'm fine.' He remembered his manners. 'Are you coming in?'

'No, it's all right. The taxi's waiting.' Zoe watched herself stub her toe up and down on the step. Her hair was red this week. 'So what are you doing now?'

Ben recalled the solicitor's talk of an appeal over his contact with Jacob, but it had been half-hearted. And just then it seemed too abstract, too effortful for him to concentrate on now. 'I don't know.'

She looked down the street as if something there had caught her attention. 'There's a party in a new club in Soho. I've got an invite. Fancy going?'

It occurred to him that perhaps she hadn't been asking about his long-term plans after all. He took in the lipstick and make-up. The orange top she had on was even briefer than the ones she wore to work, little more than a bra that clung to her small breasts. 'No, I don't think so. Thanks for asking, though.'

'You got something else on?' She squinted up at him.

'I don't really feel like going out.'

She nodded. 'So you're just going to stay in and get shit-faced by yourself.'

'Zoe, it's nice of you to come round, but ...'

'But you're going to stay in and mope, yeah?'

He felt too enervated to be angry. 'I'm not feeling very sociable.'

'Who said anything about being sociable? You can get shit-faced in company.' She looked more serious. 'I just don't think you should stay in by yourself tonight.'

That was exactly what he wanted, to stay in and surround himself with memories of Sarah and Jacob, to wallow in his lost family. It was easier than making the effort to drag himself out of the hole he was sliding into. All he wanted to do now was give up and enjoy the ride down.

Except that Zoe was looking at him, waiting for an answer. He tried to produce one, but somehow couldn't get beyond shaking his head.

'Come on,' she said, sensing blood. 'You'll feel better.'

I don't want to feel better. But it was too much of an effort to argue. 'I can't go like this,' he said, feebly, glancing down at the creased trousers and the shirt smudged with dirt from the garden wall. He realised when he saw the grin spread across Zoe's face that she'd won.

'I'll tell the taxi to wait while you get changed.'

The club was a sweat-box. It was small and dark and cramped, humid with the breath and perspiration of too many bodies. Anonymous buttocks, hips and crotches pressed up to their table, leaning on the edge, the sharp corners digging into denim and leather and satin and flesh.

'They don't know what causes it,' Ben said. 'They say it's some kind of brain disorder, like epilepsy, but when it boils down to it they haven't a clue why some kids are autistic and some aren't. It might be hereditary, it might be linked with childhood illnesses or vaccinations, lack of oxygen at birth. You name it.'

Zoe sat with her elbows propped on the table, chin resting on cupped hands as she listened, sitting close to him to hear above the thump of music. She took another drink from the neck of the beer bottle. Ben nursed his own, peeling off the corner of the label. Paper scraps were scattered around it.

'It's not something like Down's syndrome, where it's obvious if a kid has it or not. It isn't always easy to diagnose. Sometimes it's so mild kids can go to a normal school, and sometimes it's so bad they have to wear nappies all their lives. And it changes all the time, you get different symptoms as the kid grows up.' He took a drink from the bottle. The beer tasted warm and stale, although it was a new bottle. Or was it? His head was fuzzy. It was difficult to tell. He set it back down and carried on peeling the label.

'Jacob's pretty mild compared to some of the poor little sods. With him it's more of a communication difficulty. He couldn't cope at an ordinary school yet, but there's always the chance he'll improve. Sometimes, he looks at you and you feel he's just on the edge, that one little nudge and he'd be a normal kid. And then he'll go away again, and it can be like he's from a different planet. It's really frustrating, you feel he's sort of stuck inside his own head, but if you could only get him to come out ...'

He broke off. 'Sorry, I'm talking bollocks.'

'No, you're not.' Zoe shrugged. 'It's interesting bollocks, anyway. You don't normally talk much about him.'

'There's nothing more boring than listening to people going on about their kids.' *Especially when they're not really theirs.* He raised his bottle to his mouth again but it was empty.

'Did you ever think about adopting him?' She immediately grimaced. 'Sorry, that was tactless.'

'It's okay, I don't mind. Sarah and I talked about it,

and agreed that I should at some point. We'd talked about having kids of our own as well. But there didn't seem to be any rush.'

That sank the conversation like the *Titanic*. Ben felt his mood going down with it. He knew he was on the way to being drunk and maudlin, that he should stop talking and stop drinking and go home, but the thought was whisked away from him almost as soon as it occurred. 'It wouldn't have made any difference,' he said. 'I'd probably still have let Kale have custody — sorry, I mean "residence" — anyway.' *Would I?* He moved on to safer ground. 'I just can't believe they'll only let me see Jacob once a month. Once a fucking *month*.'

'Can't you talk to his father? Explain, I mean. He might let you see him more often.'

Ben thought about the way Kale looked at him. He shook his head slowly and deliberately from side to side. 'Not a chance.'

'But that's so unreasonable!'

'I don't think he's a reasonable man.' It struck him that he had put his finger on a simple truth. Whatever reasoning processes went on behind Kale's tan-coloured eyes were unfathomable. Perhaps he was like Jacob in more than just looks. Ben tried to pin the idea down so he could scrutinise it further, but it got away from him. Another thought replaced it. 'I hope Jacob's okay with him.'

Zoe put her hand on his arm. 'I'm sure he will be. They wouldn't have let him have him if there was any doubt.'

'God, I hope so.' But he remembered the house, and the junk piled up outside, and Sandra Kale's feral face that had only smiled for the cameras. Jacob seemed small and vulnerable amongst all that hardness and sharp edges.

Someone nudged him. He looked up. Zoe was holding out a glass. He hadn't even noticed that she'd been to the bar.

'Beer time's over,' she said. 'Time to get serious.'

He sniffed at the drink. Vodka. Zoe anticipated the refusal before he could make it.

'I thought you wanted to get shit-faced,' she said.

There were windows of sobriety, when he would emerge from the alcohol like a drowning man coming up for air, just long enough to look around and see where the current had carried him before he sank under its pull again. The club became hotter and more crowded. The air was thick with body odours, perfume, cigarette smoke and spilt beer. The angry lights and screaming music pounded with migraine intensity. The only way they could hear themselves speak was to lean close and shout. He found himself at one point aware of the sensation of Zoe's mouth brushing his ear as she shouted into it. Her breath was hot on his skin. She smelled of sweat and a spicy perfume, and ever so faintly of garlic. She had her hand on his shoulder as she spoke. It was warm and damp through his shirt. He could feel the heat coming off her bare flesh. The halter top clung to her, exposing her midriff, arms, shoulders and chest. He closed his eyes. Everything was physical sensation, noise and touch without sense. He could hear her words but no longer understood them. He went away for a while and when he came back he was in the same place and nothing had changed. There was a pressure in his ear, small pushes of air that he finally associated with someone talking to him. He opened his eyes. Zoe's head filled his vision, too big to focus on. He drew back and watched her lips forming shapes. He made an effort not to drift off again.

'What?' he asked. His voice sounded far away.

'I said are you going to dance?'

Ben shook his head. It felt heavy, unattached. 'You go.'

She said something else, but he couldn't hear what. She stood up. Ben found himself looking at her stomach, pinkly suntanned and sweetly curved. When she turned and began to push through the crowd jammed up to the table, the waistband of her jeans moved away from her back, exposing a further inch of knuckled spine below the imprint it had left of itself.

She vanished into the wall of bodies. Ben felt he had strands of tar pulling at him. Every movement had to fight their resistance, but every now and again they would snap and his limbs would move in uncoordinated lunges. He knocked over an empty beer bottle as he raised his arm, and two more as he tried to grab it. They chinked but the noise was lost in the larger cacophony. He was suddenly thirsty. There was beer left in some of the bottles on the table but the thought of it nauseated him. He picked up a glass that had liquefying ice cubes in the bottom and tipped them into his mouth. Then he drank the dregs of lukewarm ice-melt from the other glasses on the table. It made him more thirsty than ever.

He looked above the people bunched in front of him. The ceiling over the dance-floor was mirrored. He could see heads and shoulders suspended upside down, rhythmically bobbing and heaving, outflung hands waving like seaweed in the erratic blue and red lights. He felt sick.

Zoe came back. He had no idea how long she'd been gone. Her hair was plastered to her forehead and her arms and torso were flushed and shiny with sweat. Her breasts rose and fell after the exertion. The halter top was dark in patches, sticking to her. She carried two glasses. She grinned as she gave one to Ben. He was aware that he had already had too much to drink but the glass was cold and had ice cubes in it. He emptied it while he was still wondering if it was a good idea.

Then they were somehow outside and it was quiet and cool. Ben had a buzzing in his ears. His arm was around Zoe's shoulders and he felt hers around him. They were in a taxi and she was leaning against him. Her skin was burning hot and slick. The thought circled that he was going to fuck her. Somewhere miles away in his head was a protest but it was too distant to bother with. His hand stroked her bare back under the flimsy top. Her mouth was covering his. Her tongue and teeth seemed huge, covering him. The hard pebble of her nipple pressed into his palm through a thin layer of fabric.

Cold air hit him as he climbed out of the cab. He looked up at the sky. There was a faint lightening towards the horizon. The stars wheeled above him. He stepped backwards to keep his balance, swaying as she unlocked a door. For a moment of clarity he saw Zoe again, the girl he worked with. Then he was going into an unlit hallway. A door creaked open and he was in a bedroom. She was pressed against him, cooling skin and hot, wet mouth. His hands were down the back of her jeans, inside her pants. His shirt was open. Her hands were on his chest, his stomach. The buzzing in his ears grew louder. It went away and he was looking down from a dizzying height at the top of a dark head. He felt a chill on his naked skin, but no sensation other than that. He didn't know where he was. The head wasn't Sarah's. He felt panic, and then it came back to him in a rush that she was dead, that he was at Zoe's, and he stumbled away from her.

'I've got to go.' His voice sounded thick and unfamiliar. He began pulling on his clothes.

'What's wrong?'

He didn't answer, not knowing, not able to speak anyway. He began to dress, and the buzzing returned with the motion. He overbalanced and almost fell. His trousers were on now, and his shirt, and he was searching for his shoes. Zoe was a shadow kneeling on the floor, watching him. She didn't say a word as he went out but he knew without looking that she was crying.

On the street he began walking without any idea of where he was or where he was going. He wanted only to get away, to put distance between him and the memory of what had happened. The sky was lighter now, the stars beginning to pale out. A police car slowed. Two white faces watched him. He shivered without feeling the cold and walked past them.

Unfamiliar streets stretched out ahead and behind. He took them at random until he came to a main road. The sodium lamps on the pavement had winked out before he flagged down a taxi.

Chapter Nine

Jessica's trial was held three weeks after Jacob's final handover to the Kales. It fanned fresh interest in the case, and as Ben walked into the court building on the day he had been called as a prosecution witness he was treated to a media phalanx barring his way.

'Mr Murray, are you relieved not to be standing trial yourself?' one woman demanded, walking backwards to keep pace with him. She held out a microphone like a baton, as if she expected Ben to take it and run with the question. He brushed past without even giving her the benefit of a 'no comment'. When he was inside the court and safely out of camera shot he stopped and leaned against a corridor wall until he felt less like punching it, and the spasm that had gripped his stomach had passed.

He had tried not to think about what the trial would be like. But even reminding himself that his first contact day with Jacob was soon afterwards didn't make the prospect any more palatable. He had done his best to move his life back to some sort of normal footing, or at least as normal as it could be now that two-thirds of it had been cut away. The only way he could think of to do that was to throw himself into his work. Ironically, he had never been so busy. The same events that had wrecked his private life had brought a boom to his professional one. When the phone calls first started coming in he had thought it was a sign of support from editors and designers he'd known for years. That had been before he saw how his name had suddenly acquired a cachet that had nothing to do with his photography. One magazine editor had run a series of fashion shots that Ben had done months earlier completely out of context, hanging the piece entirely on his new notoriety. He had phoned her in the blazing heat of discovery and told her graphically what he thought, the result being one source of work he could cross off his Christmas card list.

There were plenty of others to replace it. Once his initial indignation had died down, he stifled the self-destructive voice that urged him to tell them all to fuck off and accepted everything he could. It was all work, and anything that kept him occupied at the studio and away from the hollow bricks and mortar he'd once thought of as home was welcome.

He contented himself instead with raising his fees.

It meant he could pay Zoe more, which helped ease the guilt he felt after their night out together. He'd woken on the Saturday with a sense of curdling shame and a full-body hangover. He'd folded himself over the toilet and vomited until only dry heaves were left and the sweet stink of it blocked his nose. Even then he'd had to wait until the throbbing in his head had eased enough for him to pull himself feebly to his feet. Rinsing his mouth and splashing cold water on his face and neck made him feel cleaner but no better. He'd braced his arms on the washbasin and studied the palsied wreck of his reflection in the mirror. His face was pouchy and colourless, except for his lips, which were an unnatural red. There were lines under his eyes he'd never noticed before. He felt racked with self-hate as he'd looked at himself. His thirty-third birthday had been the month before. Christ had changed the world and been crucified by that age. Ben didn't give much for his chances of founding a religion, but the way things were going he felt that crucifixion wasn't out of the question.

He'd taken a pint glass of water and a bottle of paracetamol and gone back to bed.

The prospect of trying to apologise to Zoe over the phone was too daunting, so he'd waited until Monday morning. He hadn't been sure if she'd turn up at the studio, but she had, no later than usual but uncharacteristically subdued. They'd skirted around each other, quietly polite, until Ben had finally blurted, 'Look, I'm sorry for running out like that.'

She stopped with her back to him. 'It's okay.'

'It was just too soon.' He winced at the cliché. Zoe had turned but didn't look up. She ducked her head in agreement.

'Yeah. Bad idea all around, really.'

There was a pause when they both found other things to look at. 'Do you still think we can work together?' Ben asked.

She was very still. 'Do you want me to leave?'

'No, course not. I just didn't know if you wanted to.'

'No. Unless you want me to.'

'I don't.'

Zoe nodded. She put her hands in her pockets, then took them out again. Ben picked up the camera and examined it.

'So how did you feel on Saturday morning?' he asked.

She pulled a face. 'Like death.'

They had grinned at each other, and although there was still some embarrassment, at least it had been faced. When he heard her swearing down the phone at someone later he knew things were back to normal.

Yet not quite. Once, as Zoe crouched to adjust the hem of the model's dress, an image of her kneeling in front of him had flashed into Ben's mind. He'd looked away, quickly, but the memory had triggered something else that had been tugging at his subconscious. Reluctantly, he'd let himself acknowledge it.

He couldn't remember having an erection.

Specifically, he could remember *not* having one. He'd been drunk, anaesthetised with alcohol, and he was glad nothing more *had* happened, but he couldn't deny that he'd been up for it until the point when he'd pulled away.

Except that part of him obviously hadn't been.

What was even more unsettling was the realisation that he hadn't had an erection since Sarah had died. Which might or might not be a natural reaction, but the fact remained that it had been over four months now. Not a long time in itself, and it wasn't as if he was ready to sleep with anyone else yet. But even the guilt he felt at thinking of such a thing couldn't stop him worrying about it.

As he sat outside the courtroom in the roped-off waiting area, though, his lack of a hard-on wasn't foremost in his thoughts. There were other people waiting to be called as witnesses but he didn't recognise them. No one spoke to anyone else. There was a heavy-set, middle-aged woman whose bust filled her dress like a roll of carpet. She had red hair piled up into a bun and squinted with concentration at the paperback novel she held with the cover bent back against the spine. The hand that gripped it had thick sausage fingers, scrubbed pink as if they were used to being in water.

Ben decided she was a nurse from the hospital Jacob had been taken from. The Asian man a few seats away he tagged as the doctor who'd attended Sarah after the 'birth'. There were two policemen, one in uniform, one in plainclothes but with a jacket, trousers and short haircut that identified him just as clearly. He kept scratching in one ear with a finger, giving it a surreptitious wipe afterwards on his trousers. There was another man, and two other women, but by then Ben had tired of the game.

He'd probably guessed them all wrong anyway.

His turn came in the afternoon. He felt something like stage fright as he went into the courtroom and took the stand.

His voice sounded unnaturally loud when he read the oath. He couldn't see Jessica at first; there were too many faces all staring at him. And when he saw the woman in the dock it wasn't the Jessica he remembered.

She'd lost weight. Her brown frock hung on her like a sack. She was still pudding-faced but now the line of her jaw and cheeks was visible, and a wattle of loose skin hung below her chin. Her skin was pallid, her hair lank and lifeless. Even across the court, Ben could see the streaks of grey in it. She only once looked at him, an apathetic glance without recognition or interest, before staring off again at some point on the floor. With a peculiar mingling of revulsion and pity, Ben realised that the trial was irrelevant. Nothing anyone did would make any difference to her now.

The prosecuting counsel questioned him, then he was passed over to the defence. It was as bad as he'd expected. When he was told to stand down his legs shook. He kept his eyes set straight ahead as he left the court.

The verdict was reached two days later. Ben heard it on the radio as he was driving. Jessica had been found guilty of aiding and abetting, and sentenced to three years.

He turned the radio off.

Once the trial was over there was nothing to get in the way of his anticipation of seeing Jacob. He expected to feel excited, but as the Sunday he was due for his first contact approached, the anxiety he'd felt over the court case seemed simply to be transferred to the new target.

Colin had offered to go with him but he'd declined. There was still a bump on the bridge of Colin's nose from the last time he had provided moral support, and Ben's relationship with Maggie was strained enough as it was. He didn't want to risk anything making it worse, if only for Colin's sake.

But the real reason was that he wanted to see Jacob by himself.

The journey seemed quicker now that he knew the route. It was a close, cloudy day. The fields were stripped bare, bleached to a golden stubble instead of the lush green they'd been the last time. Some of them were blackened from fires that in places were still burning, trailing curtains of smoke like mist across the road. Ben had thought that stubble-burning was illegal now. If it was no one around Tunford seemed to care.

He had phoned the Kales the night before to arrange what time he should arrive, but there had been no answer. He hadn't been in touch with them since the handover — not that they'd spoken much then, either. He'd been tempted to call several times to see how Jacob was, rehearsed what to say, assured himself it could be kept casual. But he hadn't. No matter how much he worried about Jacob, he wanted to be seen to be keeping his side of the bargain. He didn't want to give John Kale an excuse not to keep his.

The possibility that Kale might not need an excuse was something he tried not to dwell on.

As he drove through Tunford he wondered if they could have forgotten it was his day for contact and gone away for the weekend. Or remembered but gone away anyway. That stirred up all the other fears, and he was wondering if Jacob could have forgotten him in a month when he turned on to their road and saw Kale's car outside the house.

It was an old Ford Escort, a 1980s model, dappled with rust but with a serviceable air about it. A coating of dried mud and dirt dulled the original red paint. He had seen the Kales getting into it once outside the local authority building, but he would have known who it belonged to anyway. It seemed to fit Kale, somehow.

At least they're home. He parked behind the Escort and looked inside as he walked past. The seats were covered with a black nylon stretch fabric, holed and gritty with crumbs. A puzzle like the one Kale had given Jacob at their first meeting lay on the back seat. The sight was strangely painful. Ben turned away and went down the path.

There was even more junk in the front garden than he remembered. It was all car parts; chrome bumpers spotted with corrosive acne, doors with gaps where the handles used to be, decaying bonnets, wings and headlamps. The colours were gradually oxidising into a universal shade of brown. Grass and weeds sprouted through glassless windows, tangling dead metal with splashes of living green. Where pieces had been moved there were telltale imprints of flattened yellow stalks and slimy soil. Wondering why anyone would want to litter his own outlook with scrap metal, and what the hell Kale did with it all anyway, Ben skirted the radiator grille of a Mini and went to the front door.

It had been white once, but what paint was left was peeling away like fragments of eggshell. The wood underneath was grey and weathered. The entire house and garden were a working model of entropy, a physical reminder of the natural trend towards dissolution and decay. Ben felt fresh outrage that this was the environment to which Jacob had been entrusted, and immediately ashamed for thinking it. *Don't be a snob.* But the objection he felt was both more intrinsic and less definable than that. Using the mottled flap of the galvanised letterbox, he knocked and stepped back.

The sound was loud in the Sunday stillness. It died away. There was a noise from the next garden. He turned. A woman had emerged from the house, holding a long-handled sweeping brush. Ben gave her a smile.

'Morning.'

The greeting went unacknowledged. She regarded him coldly, making a few half-hearted sweeps at the path with her brush. Across the street a man in a vest was leaning on his gate, openly watching. Ben turned his back on both of them. *It's the Village of the fucking Damned.* He knocked on the door again.

He was conscious of their scrutiny as he waited. The scrape of the woman's brush punctuated the quiet. He wished someone would hurry up and answer the door. He counted to ten then knocked again, harder.

The door opened. Sandra Kale regarded him sullenly. Her eyes were puffy and her bleached hair rumpled and uncombed. She had on a pale pink bathrobe that ended mid-thigh. It needed washing. A sour, warm smell of bed came from her.

Ben waited for her to say something. When she didn't he said, 'I've come for Jacob.'

She folded her arms under her breasts. The movement pushed them up against the terry-towelling bathrobe. 'He's not here.'

There wasn't as much anger as he would have thought. It was as though he'd been expecting it. 'But I'm supposed to be picking him up today. It's my day to see him.'

She hitched one shoulder indifferently. It caused the bathrobe to gape, showing cleavage where her arms pressed her breasts together. Without make-up her face was younger and less hard, but no more friendly. 'Tough. I've told you, he isn't here.'

She began to close the door. Ben put his hand flat on it to stop her. He caught a waft of the odour of the house from behind her, a staleness of fried food and unemptied ashtrays. 'So where is he?'

'Gone out with his dad.'

'When will he be back?'

'Don't know.'

'Can I wait?'

'Do what you fucking like,' she said, and pushed the door shut.

A shard of loose paint shot off and stung his face like miniature shrapnel. He heard the woman with the brush chuckling in the next garden. Feeling his face burning, he banged on the door with the side of his fist. The sharp-edged paint crunched underneath it, digging into his flesh before flaking off. He carried on hammering.

The door was yanked open. Sandra Kale's face was pinched and angry. 'He's not fucking here! Now fuck off!'

'Not until I've seen him.'

'Are you fucking deaf? I've told you—'

The door was pulled from her hand. Ben instinctively stepped back as Kale appeared in the doorway. He was naked except for a pair of brief black shorts. His wife looked startled, then moved meekly aside.

He had been exercising. His entire body was beaded with sweat and flushed pink, as though he had been scalded. The thin shorts moulded his hips and genital bulge, but tight as they were there was no overhang of fat. Each muscle was clearly defined, not with the sculptured physique of a body-builder but with a cleanness that was entirely functional. Ben automatically pulled his own stomach in.

'I've come to collect Jacob,' he said. Kale was breathing deeply and rhythmically. He didn't answer. Ben went on. 'It's my day to see him. We agreed on every fourth Sunday. That's today.'

Moisture dripped from Kale's brow. He made no attempt to wipe it. Ben looked past him into the hallway. There was no sign of Jacob.

'There's nothing here for you.'

Kale spoke flatly. Ben turned to him.

'Where's Jacob?'

'I said there's nothing here for you.'

'I'm not going without seeing him at least.' He held his ground against Kale's stare. It was like leaning into the wind.

Kale moved his head fractionally towards his wife. 'Fetch him.'

'John—'

'Fetch him.'

Her face reflected her unease for a second longer, then settled into the hard lines of irritation. She disappeared inside the house.

Kale remained where he was. Ben watched the empty hallway, glad of the excuse to look away. He'd always thought that Kale's eyes were expressionless, but that wasn't true. Their gaze was unsettling because it gave a view of a personality that, like his body, had been rendered down and stripped of inessentials. It was like looking into the sun.

Sandra Kale came back into the hallway. She had Jacob by the hand. Ben could see that he didn't want to go with her. He squatted in front of him.

'Jacob? It's me. Ben.'

Jacob kept his head down, but Ben thought there was a glimmer of recognition. He seemed healthy enough. He wore a T-shirt and a pair of shorts that, if not completely clean, were not exactly dirty either. His hair was longer than the last time Ben had seen him.

'I've come to take you out, Jacob. Would you like that?'

'His name's Steven.' Kale bent and effortlessly lifted the boy. He held him easily in the crook of one arm as Ben straightened. 'You wanted to see him. You have done.'

'I'm supposed to be taking him out.'

Sandra Kale came forward, her face pinched with spite. Her bathrobe was flapping loose, revealing more of her breasts. 'Why don't you just get lost? Just leave us alone!'

'Cover yourself up,' Kale said. She glared at him, then flounced into the house. A door banged.

Ben tried again. 'I'm entitled to contact once a month. That was part of the agreement.'

Kale stared at him, then raised his free hand. Ben tensed but there was no blow. Kale rotated it, studying it as he slowly flexed his fingers as if its workings were new to him.

'It killed her,' he said, still watching his hand, almost absently. 'Losing him. It killed her. They said it was an accident, but it wasn't. I knew her. I'd seen it coming, but I couldn't do anything. Jeanette carried him for nine months, bled and screamed to get him out, and then some bitch came along and took him before she'd even had a chance to hold him properly.'

The hand clenched into a fist. The curled edge of the forefinger was thickly callused and cross-hatched with ingrained oil. Kale rubbed his thumb over it. It made a faint rasping noise. He lowered the hand as though he'd grown bored with it and looked at Ben again. His eyes were unbearable.

'He never knew her. His own mother, and he never knew her. Now he doesn't know me. He doesn't talk. Your whore did that to him. She took my wife and kid away from me. Six years. That's how long she had him. That's how long I thought he was dead. Six years. Now you come here wanting to take him away again.'

Ben wanted to tell him he was wrong, that he was being unfair. But he knew it wouldn't make any difference. The man's viewpoint was as rigid as his body. 'It isn't like that. I'm only—'

'He doesn't want you. He doesn't need you. You're not part of the pattern any more.'

Ben didn't know if he'd heard right, didn't know what the fuck the man was talking about. 'Look, it was agreed. Jacob won't understand why he doesn't see me—'

'His name's Steven.'

Ben bit back the objection. One thing at a time. 'You can't just cut us off from each other.'

'I can do what I want.'

It was said without petulance or bravado. Looking at him, Ben saw that nothing he could say, no talk of rights or court action, was going to alter anything. Jacob sat on his arm, apparently content. He was wriggling his fingers. After a moment Ben realised that he was copying Kale's earlier movements with his hand.

'Can we at least talk about this? You know, perhaps sit down—'

'I don't want you in my house.'

'Oh, come on, this is getting stupid!'

Kale's whistle made him jump even as he was regretting the choice of words. There was a scrabble of claws from within the house. *Oh fuck*, Ben thought as he saw the bull terrier from the scrapyard materialise in the hallway. It trotted towards them, bow-legged with muscle. He felt childishly betrayed when he saw Jacob trying to whistle himself.

The dog stopped at the doorstep and glared up at him. A threatening rumble came from its throat. He quickly checked to see how far away the fence was. Kale held his hand over the animal's head, restraining it without touching it.

'Go on.'

Ben thought that Kale was speaking to the dog before realising it was to him. He flinched back as it gave a single, yapping bark, its front legs bouncing clear of the ground. Then Kale pushed it back into the hall with his foot and shut the door in his face. He angrily raised his hand to bang on the peeling grey wood, then lowered it. He knew it wouldn't do any good. All he'd achieve would be an assault by Kale, or the dog. Or both. He didn't want that to happen in front of Jacob.

He didn't want that to happen full stop.

He turned to leave. The woman with the brush hadn't moved. Other people had also come out of the nearby houses to watch. Ben tried to ignore their collective hostility as he went down the path. When he reached the Mini radiator grille he gave it a savage kick that sent it spinning into the overgrown garden. It hurt his foot, but he refused to limp as he walked back to his car.

Across the street, the man in the vest leaned over his gate and spat on the pavement.

Chapter Ten

The floodlights caught the fine drizzle as it fell and turned it into beads of silver. The harsh glare bathed the football pitch in unnatural brightness, shifting once-familiar colours into an unreliable spectrum and giving objects a hard-edged focus that was both more vivid and unreal. Beyond the light there was only blackness, so that the floodlit pitch seemed to exist by itself in an ocean of shadow.

Ben's head hung between his knees. Next to him Colin squatted with a football between his legs. His hands were bulky in the goalkeeping gloves, and his track suit was smeared with mud. He nudged Ben and offered him a plastic bottle of water.

'You okay?'

Ben nodded without lifting his head. He was still too winded to speak. His throat hurt as he drank. He lowered the bottle after a couple of swallows, swilling the last of it in his mouth before spitting it out. He was thirsty but he knew if he had any more it would only give him a stitch in the second half.

He handed the bottle back. Colin's Adam's apple jerked as he drank deeply, eyes shut. Ben felt the burning in his thighs and calves and wished he played in goal himself. His breath was beginning to come back, but his chest still ached.

Colin's chin shone wetly when he lowered the bottle. He wiped it with one gloved hand. 'How's the leg?'

Ben examined the scrape on his shin. Dried blood and dirt obscured it. 'I'll live.'

Colin looked over to where the opposing team were sprawled around the goalmouth in a mirror image of their own. 'He's a dirty bastard. He has somebody down every game.'

The match was a 'friendly' between Colin's firm and a rival practice. The teams were supposedly made up of lawyers from each, but a blind eye was turned to ringers such as Ben, provided they weren't too good. Which, right then, he certainly wasn't. He kneaded his calf muscle and looked over at the player Colin had indicated. He was in his twenties, with curly black hair and an arrogant strut. He had brought Ben down with a late tackle, unnoticed by the referee, and run on without a backward glance. Ben hadn't seen him before, but then he hadn't played for weeks. He felt every one of them now in every part of his body.

Since seeing Kale's ripped torso and corrugated belly he'd been making an effort to get fit. He'd been drinking less and cutting down on joints, even doing sit-ups and push-ups at home. It didn't seem to help. Having a bruised and scraped leg helped even less. During the game he had been too busy to dwell on it, but now, with time to catch his breath and thoughts of Kale and Jacob still in his mind, he looked over at the laughing player with a gathering of animus.

The second half was easier than the first. Either he had caught his second wind or was pacing himself, and he no longer envied Colin his stationary spot in the net quite so much as he huffed around in midfield.

There was still no score when the ball came to him on the break. He ran with it, seeing the greyhound-thin shape of one of the forwards sprinting towards the goal. He swung his leg into the pass, and suddenly he was sprawling face down in the wet grass. He looked up to see the curly-haired player running off down the pitch.

Ben was barely aware of the whistle blowing as he scrambled to his feet. The other player turned around just as he reached him. Ben threw a punch and felt the jar shoot along the length of his arm. He was hit himself, and then they both slipped in the mud and fell over.

They scrabbled about on the ground for a few seconds before they were dragged apart. As Ben was pulled to his feet the curly-haired player caught him on the cheek. Ben kicked him on the thigh, then other players were between them. Colin had both his hands on Ben's chest, pushing him back.

'All right, Ben, all right, cool it!'

'The bastard hacked me!'

'I know, I know, but—'

'The cunt!'

'Look, calm down, will you? I've got to fucking work with these people!'

The intensity in Colin's voice penetrated even Ben's anger. He looked at his friend, took in the thinning hair stuck darkly over his scalp with the rain, the face that was beginning to show incipient jowls where a jaw line used to be, and felt as though he were looking at someone he didn't know. The heat went out of him.

'Sorry.'

Colin took his hands from his chest, giving him a warning look. 'What's the matter with you?'

'I'm sorry. I lost it a bit.'

'A *bit*! Jesus, Ben!'

Ben mutely accepted the reproof. The referee, an older solicitor from Colin's firm, beckoned him over. He hung his head as he stood next to the player who had fouled him, saying nothing as they were first told off, then sent off. His boots squelched desolately through the mud as he made his way from the pitch to the sports hall's changing room. Good move, he thought, hitting a lawyer with twenty other lawyers as witnesses. His opponent walked parallel with him, a few yards away. The heavy slap of the ball being kicked resumed behind them.

'Fucking bastard.'

Ben looked around. 'What?'

The other player's lip was swollen. He gave Ben a look of contempt. Their studs made clacking noises as they reached the path. 'You heard, wanker.'

The hot anger that Ben thought had gone suddenly boiled up in him again. 'If you've got something to fucking say, fucking say it!'

'Fuck off.'

'Are you going to make me?'

He felt disbelief as he heard himself, but the desire to lash out was a thick pumping of blood behind his eyes. He could barely contain it. The other man looked away with a snort of derision.

'You're not fucking worth it,' he said, but Ben was attuned enough now to see his uncertainty. It fuelled him.

'Come on, you curly-haired twat!' He had his fists balled. 'Come on!'

The other man kept his head averted. 'Just leave me alone.'

There was a moment of savage joy when Ben almost hit him anyway. It burst as swiftly as an overfilled balloon. He stopped and let the other man go into the sports hall ahead of him as the shame rose up. He wanted to chase after him and say he was sorry, that he wasn't really like that.

Aren't I? He could exorcise his frustration on a football pitch, with someone he didn't feel threatened by, but not when it mattered. He would never have dared do it with Kale. So what did that make him?

Lavish with self-disgust, he went into his team's changing room to get showered.

* * *

Both teams went for a drink afterwards, filling one side of the pub with the smell of wet hair, deodorant and talc. Some of the players ignored him, especially on the opposing side, but others grinned and made boxing jokes. He'd only gone to the pub because he'd hoped to restore some of his self-esteem by apologising to the curly-haired player. He'd visualised shaking his hand, buying him a drink, laughing about how stupid they'd been in the heat of the moment, until he'd begun to feel as though it had actually happened. But in the pub there was no sign of the other man. Ben heard someone say that he'd gone straight home.

He stood with Colin at one end of the bar. He could tell by Colin's stiffness that he had something to say. Knowing he had deserved it, Ben waited.

'It's no good taking it out on everybody else,' Colin said finally, when no one else was in earshot. He occupied himself by unwrapping the cellophane from a cigar. It was a habit he had only recently acquired, and Ben still wasn't used to seeing him smoking them.

'Taking what out?' he asked, even though he knew.

'This business with Jacob. I know it's frustrating but you're going to have to get hold of yourself.'

'I lost my temper, that's all.'

Colin just looked at him. Ben sighed.

'All right, I'm sorry. But it's just ... shit, it's just so *frustrating!*'

'Kale's only stopped you seeing him once. He might change his mind once things settle down.'

'He might let me sleep with his wife as well.' Ben wondered why he'd made that particular comparison.

Colin lit the cigar and puffed on it self-consciously. 'I admit it isn't very likely, but you're just going to have to be patient and hope he comes round. You can't do anything on the basis of one visit.'

'It isn't going to make any difference whether it's one visit or twenty. Kale isn't going to budge. He doesn't have to, he's got Jacob now. Everything's on his side.'

Colin tapped his cigar into an ashtray, frowning. 'He can't stop you from seeing him indefinitely.'

Ben swirled the beer around in his glass. 'Can't he?'

He'd already told Jacob's social worker what had happened. Carlisle had listened with the weary expression of someone who'd heard it all before. He'd grudgingly agreed to contact the Kales, but his manner grew downright frosty after Sandra told him that Ben had arrived late and drunk. Ben's protests that she was lying were met with a stony insistence that the local authority couldn't intervene in 'personal squabbles'.

Incensed, he'd gone to see Ann Usherwood. He'd expected reassurances and promises of action. Instead she warned him that the social services were notoriously reluctant to become involved in arguments over contact. If Kale continued to prevent him from seeing Jacob, Ben could eventually take him to court, she conceded. But such disputes were always expensive and messy, and any rulings difficult to enforce.

Thinking about Kale, Ben knew it might be impossible.

As a last-ditch attempt he had phoned Sandra Kale, calling when her husband would be at work in the hope of persuading her to appeal to him. 'I know we got off to a bad start,' he'd said, before she could hang up. 'But I'm not trying to take Jacob away again. I only want him to let me see him occasionally.'

'It's nothing to do with me,' she'd said, indifferently. 'He's John's kid, not mine.'

'But you're his wife. Can't you——?'

'No, I can't,' she'd cut in. 'So why don't you just fuck off?'

It took an effort not to shout at her. 'I'm not going to just give up.'

He could hear her breathing. 'You would if you'd any sense,' she'd said, ending the conversation.

But he couldn't. The alternative was to let each month put more distance between himself and Jacob. The boy was only six, and autistic. He didn't make the normal associations, might not remember a relationship with someone from a half-forgotten life. And then Ben's last memories of his marriage to Sarah, the family he'd thought he'd had, would be proved ultimately worthless, would turn to dust and blow away.

He stopped playing with his beer and took a drink of it instead. 'I just don't know what else I can do,' he said, setting down the glass. 'Kale's already made up his mind, and I can't see him having a spontaneous change of heart.'

The cigar sent aromatic smoke around Colin's head. 'Is there anyone else you could speak to? Somebody like a neighbour or friend, who could act as an intermediary. Talk some sense into them.'

'I don't think so,' Ben said. But even as he spoke he'd already thought of someone.

It was the first Saturday he had taken off in weeks, since the hangover hell after the night with Zoe. He woke early and cooked himself scrambled eggs and grilled tomatoes. He ate them at the kitchen table, which seemed too big now he was the only person who sat at it. Afterwards he was still hungry, so he had a dish of cereal. He'd noticed he was tasting his food more since he had cut down on the joints.

He would have set off straightaway, except for the feeling that he ought to visit the cemetery. He'd only been once since the funeral, but that didn't bother him. He didn't feel the need to stand over a patch of ground when he carried thoughts of Sarah around with him every day. That morning, though, he felt an impulse to go.

The wind held a hint of rain as he made his way to the

grave. Sarah had told him that she wanted to be buried during a drunken 'when I die' conversation one night. Ben had said he wanted to be cremated except for his penis, which she could save as a keepsake. The memory of her laughter was carried away on the wind before he had a chance to smile.

The grave was part of a row of other new ones. There was no stone yet because the ground had to be left to settle. The grass was growing over it nicely, though, which pleased him. He put the flowers he'd brought in one of the two earthenware vases at the grave's head. Someone, her parents probably, had recently left another bunch. They were nearly dead, but he left them where they were because he didn't want to risk upsetting her mother by throwing them away. He felt a twinge of conscience that he hadn't been in touch since the whole mess with Jacob had come out. He hadn't wanted to make things worse, but enough time had passed now to soften what had happened. Wiping his hands dry, he told Sarah that he would make the effort, but reminded her that her mother was a difficult cow, so he couldn't promise anything.

He stood remembering while the wind plucked at him, then went back to his car.

Irthlington was ten miles north of Tunford. Ben came off the motorway at the same junction and followed the same route for a while before turning off. The road signs led him past an industrial estate and then back out into a brief splash of green countryside before the town began.

The house was on a short terraced row with a corner shop at one end, and a rubble-filled space bordered by a tall wire fence at the other. Inside it were yellow JCBs and workmen's huts, quiet and deserted for the weekend. A lot of the houses were boarded up, waiting their turn at demolition. Others were obviously still tenanted. The number Ben was looking for had neat flowered curtains and a colourful window box on the downstairs sill. He parked outside and climbed from his car before he had chance to have second thoughts about what he was doing.

He didn't know what he hoped to gain by visiting Jeanette Kale's parents. He had no reason to think they would have any more time for him than Kale. Kale had lost a wife, they'd lost a daughter, and Ben was the nearest thing to a scapegoat they had. When he'd seen them interviewed on TV, though, Ron and Mary Paterson hadn't seemed bitter. He thought they might be prepared to listen to him, if nothing else.

It wasn't much to hang a Saturday morning on, but it was all he had.

The Patersons had moved out of London after their grandson went missing. Ben had traced them by going through the recent newspaper reports in the library until he found a reference to the town where 'baby Steven's' grandparents now lived. Then he had gone through the telephone directory until he found their address. He'd considered phoning before making the journey, but in the end he'd decided not to.

Over the phone it would have been too easy for them to say no.

He knocked on the door. It was grimy from the dust thrown up by the destruction of its neighbours, but the underlying blue paint was sound. They're not going to be in, he thought, but was proved wrong by a muffled 'It's not locked'.

He went inside. The door opened straight into the kitchen. The walls were covered with a yellow floral paper. In the doorway a small rubber mat covered the brown-and-cream swirl-patterned carpet. A sturdy drop-leaf table stood against the wall facing him, a potted geranium in its centre. There was a smell of old cooking, not rancid like the Kales', but one that spoke of Yorkshire puddings and roast meats. It reminded Ben of his childhood visits to his grandparents.

An elderly man was standing by the sink. He wore brown pleated trousers and a white vest. A peeled hard-boiled egg was in one hand, while the other was cupped underneath it to catch the crumbs. He looked at Ben without saying anything, flecks of yolk around his mouth. Ben recognised him from the TV as Jeanette Kale's father. He felt suddenly embarrassed at seeing him like that, knowing he wasn't whoever the man had been expecting.

He hovered in the doorway, uncertainly. 'I'm sorry, I heard you say it wasn't locked. I'm Ben Murray—'

'I know who you are.'

Paterson turned back to the sink and went on eating the egg. He pushed it into his mouth and delicately brushed his lips with his fingers.

'I'm sorry if I caught you by surprise.' Ben somehow felt he was the one at a disadvantage.

Small dewlaps of flesh swung under Paterson's arms as he wiped his hands on a towel. He had the fleshy build of a once-powerful man overtaken by time. He hung the towel on a hook by the sink. 'What do you want?'

Ben was already sure it was a wasted journey. 'I'd like to talk to you and your wife. About Jacob.' *If he says 'Steven' I'll turn around and go.*

'What about him?'

The man's look was neither hostile nor encouraging. It compelled Ben to be direct. 'John Kale won't let me see him. I wondered if you could help.'

Paterson turned back to the sink. 'There's nothing we can do to help you.'

'I thought you could perhaps talk to him. Explain that I'm not trying to take Jacob from him. I just ... I just want to see him every now and again.'

Jacob's grandfather shook his head without looking around. Ben remained by the open front door, unable to bring himself to leave but not knowing what else there was to say. A mechanical whine came from a doorway on the other side of the kitchen. Paterson glanced at him, then went out. The noise grew louder, an electric motor of some kind. It stopped and he heard voices. There were other sounds he couldn't identify, and then the door at the far end was pushed back. A woman in a wheelchair came through with Paterson pushing it, and Ben realised the whine had been from a chairlift.

Mary Paterson was stick thin, with hair that must once have been red but was now turning orange from the grey in it. Her eyes were beady and dark, like a bird's as she regarded Ben.

'Shut the door,' she said.

They sat around the drop-leaf table, drinking tea. A plate of digestive biscuits had been put out next to the geranium. Ben had taken one out of politeness and then found his hand straying back of its own accord until the plate was half empty.

He didn't even like digestives.

'She left him, you see,' Mary said. She was still in her wheelchair, lower than either Ben or her husband, who sat in the hard-backed dining chairs. She looked like a wrinkled child. 'She came back to live with us a few months after Steven — after *Jacob*,' she corrected herself, annoyed at the slip, '... after Jacob went missing. We'd moved back up here by then. We'd only gone down to London to be near my sister, when Ron took his early redundancy. But after what happened at the hospital ... Well, you tell yourself it isn't your fault, but if Jeanette hadn't come down to stay with us ...'

She left the sentence unfinished. 'John never said as much, but we always felt he blamed us. Partly, anyway. And then when she left him and came home that was the final straw. I don't think he ever forgave us for that.'

'But Jacob's your grandson. Surely you're entitled to see him.'

She looked across at her husband. A wordless message

seemed to pass between them. 'So are you. But with John Kale that doesn't make a lot of difference, does it?'

Ben didn't know whether he was pleased to have found someone else against whom Kale was exercising his unreasonableness, or frustrated that another avenue had come to a dead end. Sympathy for the Patersons overruled either. 'What has Kale said?'

'Not a thing.' Ron Paterson broke a biscuit in half over his plate, then in half again. He had put on a shirt, explaining that he had thought Ben was a friend of his when he'd knocked on the door, a widower he went shopping with every Saturday. He noticed what he was doing to the biscuit and put it down. 'We haven't spoken to him. Only that woman. She told me not to bother phoning again.' His lips set in a stern line. 'Foul-mouthed little tart.'

'Ron,' his wife warned. His nodded acknowledgment was also an apology. She turned to Ben. 'We've written, but we haven't had any reply. Not that we expected one. But you still hope, don't you?'

Not any more, Ben thought. If Kale wouldn't even let Jacob's grandparents see him, there was no chance for him. 'It isn't any of my business, but why did Jeanette leave him?'

Again they shared a silent look of communication. 'He'd changed,' she said. 'He'd always been a quiet type. Deep. But after Stev ... after Jacob disappeared he wasn't the same. No disrespect intended, but it shattered him. Shattered them both, but in a different way. He got harder.' She frowned, shaking her head. 'No, not harder exactly, that's not right. But like he didn't care. And Jeanette ... well, she never really got over it. You'd have thought they'd have helped each other, but it went the opposite way. Perhaps Jeanette was as much to blame as John, I couldn't say. But she needed someone to support her, to help her through it. And he didn't do that. I suppose it was his way of coping with what had happened, but he just got more wrapped up in himself. More intense. They'd come around to see us, and he'd sit for hours, staring at nothing, not saying a word. And most of the time he was away anyway, you know, serving overseas. Jeanette was left by herself down in Aldershot. So in the end she came back home.'

Ben dreaded the next question, but it had to be asked. 'Kale said ... he told me that it was my wife's fault that Jeanette died. What did he mean?'

She didn't answer. Her husband folded his hands together on the table. His knuckles were white. She reached out and patted them. Her own hands were swollen and deformed.

'He meant she killed herself.' She drew in a deep breath that had only a hint of tremor in it. It seemed to inflate her bony frame. 'But I don't know.' She gave her husband's hands a squeeze before removing hers from them. 'I don't know. They say she walked out into the traffic without looking, but whether she meant to, or just didn't think ...' She shook her head. 'John had been around the day before. He was on leave. Compassionate leave.' She gave a humourless laugh at the thought. 'He turned up and said she was going home with him. Like that. No asking, no talking. Just straight out with it. Ron told him she wasn't doing anything she didn't want to, and ... and John knocked him down.'

She glanced at her husband. His hands were clenched tighter than ever. He spoke without looking at either of them. 'If I'd been ten years younger he wouldn't have done it. Soldier or not.' His voice was gravelly with emotion. His wife's hands twitched on her lap, as if she were about to touch him again. This time she didn't.

'John walked out after that without another word,' she went on. 'The following morning Jeanette went for a walk, and the next we heard she was dead.'

Oh Sarah, what did you do?

'We haven't seen John since then, except at the funeral,' Mary said. 'And he didn't speak to us there. So I don't think there's much we can do to help you. I'm sorry.'

Ben couldn't look at either of them. 'He blames me,' he said. 'Me and my wife. He blames us for Jacob being autistic.' He felt as though the words had been cut out of him. He had to go on to fill the silence that followed. 'The doctors say it isn't caused by anything like that, being taken from his mother, but he still thinks it's our fault.'

He heard Mary Paterson's chair creak as she stirred. 'I think sometimes things just happen. It doesn't do any good trying to guess why.'

'I'm sorry,' Ben said, and it was only after he'd said it that he realised it was the first time he had apologised for what Sarah had done.

'You've got nothing to apologise for.' She sounded weary. 'You weren't to know. And your wife ... Losing a child does strange things to you. Your wife did what she did because of it, and our Jeanette did what she did. One way or another you never get over it.'

That was as much absolution as Ben could hope for. He wanted to thank her, but when he looked across he saw her face was drawn and pale.

'You'll have to excuse me now,' she said. Her voice was slurred with fatigue. 'Ron ...' In response her husband stood up and silently pushed her out of the room. Ben heard the chairlift start up, then her husband returned. His face was stoic.

'Is she all right?' asked Ben.

'Just tired. It's arthritis. Some days are better than others.'

'I'm sorry, I shouldn't have stayed so long.'

'She's glad you did.'

He didn't sit back down, though, or invite Ben to stay any longer. Ben stood up to leave, but there was one more thing he had to ask. 'Do you think Jacob'll be all right with him? With Kale, I mean?'

'He's his son. He's been missing him for the last six years.'

That wasn't what Ben asked. He rephrased the question.

'He's your grandson, as well. How do you feel about Kale bringing him up?'

Paterson seemed to deliberate before he spoke. 'I don't know John Kale any more. I can't say what he's like now. The last time I saw him I thought he was a man on the edge. And that was before he got shot up in Northern Ireland. But it isn't for me to say.'

'What about his wife?'

Paterson's expression darkened. 'That one. I've heard—'
He broke off.

'What?' Ben asked.

'Nothing.'

Ben would have liked to have pushed, but he could see the old man had said all he was going to. He went to the door.

'Can I ask a favour of you?' Paterson asked, abruptly. 'Photographs ... We haven't got any. Of Jacob, I mean. I wondered if you could let us borrow some. It'd mean a lot to Mary.' There was a minute trembling in his lip. 'Just so we can see what he's like.'

He tried listening to the radio as he drove back to take away the silence in the car, but soon switched it off again. The quiet oppressed him, but the noise and chatter ran against his mood. He reached a junction where he had turned off earlier. A road sign pointed to Tunford. The indicator arrow on his dashboard clicked softly as it winked on and off, pointing in the opposite direction. Ben flipped it the other way and followed the sign.

He didn't know why he was doing it. But he couldn't come this close to where Jacob was and just go home again. He tried to keep his mind clear as he approached the town, as though if he didn't think about what he was going to do something would occur to him. There was an acid tightening in his gut as he came to the shops, but no inkling of a plan.

If Kale's car isn't there I'll stop and knock at the door. He took the first of the turnings that would lead him to the house. *If it is I'll keep going.*

A group of small boys were playing football in the middle of the road. They grudgingly moved to the pavement as he drove past. There was a sudden bang that made his foot leap for the brake before he saw them sprinting away, and understood that they had kicked the football at the car. *Little bastards.* His grin of nervous relief faded as he turned on to Kale's street.

The rust-coloured Ford Escort was parked outside the house.

Ben gripped the steering wheel, agonising over whether or not to stop anyway. He slowly cruised past. He saw the piles of junk in the garden, gathered now into two big piles instead of several smaller ones; he saw the guttering hanging loose from the eaves, but he didn't see either of the Kales or Jacob. He stayed rigid with indecision until the house disappeared from the rear-view mirror, and the moment when he might have stopped was gone.

He continued to the end of the street, deflated, as if he had failed some kind of test. The road curled away around the last of the houses before climbing a hill behind them. Ben hadn't followed it this far before, but he didn't want to turn around and go past the Kales' again. The hill was covered with scrubby woodland, so that he soon lost sight of the town. Towards the top there was an overgrown lay-by leading to a wooden five-barred gate, thick with nettles. Impulsively, he pulled into it and switched off the engine. It ticked like a time bomb as it cooled. He sat in the car for a while, then got out.

The wind had picked up. It slapped his coat around him, watering his eyes and tugging at his hair. The field beyond the gate dropped steeply to a flooded gravel pit. Each gust sent a shiver racing across its surface like goose bumps. He turned away and went across to the other side of the road. An old and uneven stone wall bordered the woods. Through the trees he could see snatches of the houses below. The branches thrashed in the wind, their remaining leaves showing dark green, pale green as they whipped about. Others were wrenched off, spinning through the fast air, abandoned to the death of another season. Ben thrust his hands in his pockets and faced the wind. He felt as though he had been torn loose from everything that had anchored him, that he was on the verge of being ripped up and blown away himself.

A section of the wall had tumbled to a low heap of individual stones. It was topped with rusted barbed wire, but the posts that had held it up had also slumped and given up. Ben stepped over it into the woods. The trees were mostly scrubby and stunted oaks. He picked his way through them, no longer able to see the town as he descended. He came to a path, little more than a worn track. He followed it without really caring where it led, wanting only to lose himself for a while in an unfamiliar landscape. The path meandered gradually down the hillside, snaking around the trees, broken every now and then by exposed roots. It was uneven enough to make him watch his footing, and when it suddenly emerged from the trees on to an open slope he was surprised to see how close to the houses he'd come.

Their back gardens butted up to the field at the bottom of the hill like an uneven strip of patchwork quilt. He could see the tarmac ribbon of road he'd driven on continue from where they ended and curve away up the hill to his right. He couldn't make out which was Kale's house, but he knew it couldn't be far away.

He went back into the woods and began to head in its direction. He wasn't sure why he didn't just walk out in the open, but something in him didn't want to be seen, not just by Kale but by anyone. The grass was longer off the path, still wet from the last rain, and the bottoms of his trousers were soon soaked through. He slipped and skidded across the hillside, trying to gauge whereabouts on the street the Kales lived. He needn't have bothered. He could hardly have missed it.

When he next paused to get his bearings he saw it immediately. The rear of the house was a scrapyard in miniature, a Pyrenees of metal crammed into the confines of a semi-detached garden. Ben carried on through the woods until he was looking directly down on the sprawl of junk. He could see now that it wasn't a solid pile, as he'd first imagined. There was a clear area at its centre.

In it were Kale and Jacob.

The tree line was about a hundred and fifty yards from the garden, too far away to make out any details, but Ben could tell it was them. Jacob was sitting on something low to the ground. He was occupied with an object in his hands, and although Ben couldn't see what it was he guessed it would be some sort of puzzle. He felt a lump form in his throat at the familiar sight.

Kale was a few feet behind his son. He was standing with his legs braced apart, and had something gripped in both hands behind his neck. It looked heavy. As Ben watched he slowly hefted it above his head, then lowered it in front of him until he was holding it outstretched directly over Jacob's head.

Ben stiffened, but Kale was already raising the weight again. Keeping his arms straight, he reversed his motion until it was again grasped behind his neck. He held it there for a second, then repeated the entire procedure.

Jacob continued to play, unconcerned with what was going on above him. The scene had the appearance of being a routine they were both used to, and Ben felt his anxiety give way to fury. It increased with each repetition until he was quivering with a hatred for the man he had never felt before. Whether Kale was doing it as a test of strength and endurance or just showing off, there was no excuse for it. It was fucking irresponsible, dangerous, *stupid* ... The epithets trailed off as he saw Kale's movements begin to slow. The arms were taking an age to thrust the weight above his head. Once there they hesitated. Even at that distance there was an unmistakable wobble in them.

Oh, please, God, don't do it ...

They began inexorably to descend. The weight came to a halt over Jacob's head. It stayed there longer than before, hovering unsteadily. Ben could almost feel the strain on muscle and tendon. Jacob played on beneath it all, oblivious. *Please ... Lift it. Fucking lift it.*

Slowly, the arms began to rise. They got so far and then stopped. The weight began to pull them back down. It halted above Jacob and slowly came up again. Now it looked as though Kale was deliberately rocking it from side to side as he struggled to raise it over his head. There was a long moment of impasse. Then he managed it, and in the same movement he pivoted and let it drop.

The weight landed next to Jacob. Ben saw him turn to look at it, then go back to his puzzle as Kale collapsed to his knees.

'Oh, you fucking mad bastard,' Ben said out loud. 'You fucking mad bastard!' He wanted to run down the hill and fling himself at the fence, climb over and club Kale with some of the metal he was so fond of. He wanted to hug Jacob and carry him away, back to safety, back to his fucking *home*, where he belonged.

Except he knew if he tried Kale would beat him to a pulp.

Kale had come to his feet but was still bent over, in the attitude of a man fighting for breath. Behind him, there was a movement as a figure appeared in an upstairs window. The yellow hair identified Sandra Kale. She seemed to be looking down at her husband.

At that distance Ben couldn't be sure, but it looked like she was naked.

The tableau held for a while. Then Kale limped over to a shed that was half obscured with junk. He went inside, closing the door behind him. When Ben looked back at the bedroom window it was empty.

But he had seen enough. He felt as weak as if he had been the one lifting the weight. The memory brought a fresh resurgence of anger. Tamping it down into a hard core of resolve, he took a last look at Jacob and began to make his way back to the car.

Chapter Eleven

———◆◆◆———

Ben could tell the social worker didn't believe him. 'Look, he could have been killed! If Kale had dropped that thing it would've stove his head in!'

Carlisle's face was studiedly neutral. 'But you didn't try to stop him.'

'I've told you, I was too far away.'

'So you just left without doing anything or letting him know you were there.'

'I knew it wouldn't have done any good! He's already made it clear what's going to happen if I go there again. Christ, what more do you want?'

He tried to calm himself down, knowing that losing his temper wasn't going to help. But the thought that those macho repetitions — and God knew what else — could be going on regularly made him break into a sweat. The more he thought about it, the more convinced he was that the testosterone-driven bastard wasn't just an unreasonable man.

He was insane.

Carlisle pulled on the lobe of one ear. 'What made you go around the back of the house in the first place?'

'I don't know. Curiosity I suppose.' Ben could feel his face growing red. The fact that he felt guilty made him angrier than ever. 'I'm not making this up. If you don't believe me go and see for yourself! The place is like a . . . a scrapyard! God knows how you could let Jacob go somewhere like that!'

The last remark came out before he could stop it. A flush darkened the social worker's neck. 'Contrary to popular belief, we aren't complete idiots. We visited the house and satisfied ourselves that it was a safe environment.'

'It might have been then, but it isn't any more! Did anyone actually look in the back garden?'

Ben knew he was moving the meeting towards a confrontation but was unable to stop himself. Carlisle's cheeks had now reddened.

'We know our job, Mr Murray.'

'Well, then, do it! Jacob isn't safe there! That madman's going to end up killing him!'

'I don't think histrionics are going to get us anywhere.'

'It isn't histrionics! I saw what he was doing!'

'So you say.'

Ben clenched his fists, fighting for restraint. 'What's that supposed to mean?'

The social worker too seemed to be trying to bring things back to a more controlled level. 'Mr Murray, I explained last time that this sort of situation, when a child has been taken from one parent, or step-parent, and placed in the care of another, is always difficult. Okay, I appreciate that it can't be easy to accept that Jacob no longer lives with you, but I've got to remind you that, you know, you didn't contest Mr Kale's residence application. Now I know that there was a misunderstanding over your first contact day – no, please, hear me out.' He held up a hand as Ben tried to interrupt. 'But there quite often are disputes to begin with, until both sets of parents have come to terms with the new situation. I have stressed to Mrs Kale that you are entitled to your contact days, and she had no objection to that—'

I bet.

'—so what I suggest is that you wait until your next

contact is due, and I'm sure that all these ... these problems will be resolved amicably.'

The man genuinely believed there was nothing to worry about, Ben saw. As far as the social worker was concerned, the happy ending had already happened. 'And what if Kale drops a lump of metal on Jacob's head before then?'

Carlisle looked as though he had made a tasteless joke. 'We will look into your complaint, obviously. We take everything like this seriously, but you have to understand that we can't act on an uncorroborated allegation.'

'In other words you think I'm making it up.'

'It isn't that I think you're making it up.' The implication in his voice was that he didn't think Ben was telling the whole truth, either. 'We just can't do anything without evidence.'

'So that's it, then?'

The social worker spread his hands. 'I'm sorry, Mr Murray. I can assure you that—'

Ben walked out. His head seemed to hum with the force of his frustration.

I'll get you fucking evidence, he thought.

He bought the lens from his usual supplier. He already had zoom lenses for detailed and portrait work, but nothing that was up to the kind of specifications he had in mind now. It was a 600mm telephoto, a more-than-half-metre-long beast that still wasn't as powerful as some of the long lenses press photographers used, but with muscle enough for his needs.

When he fitted it to his Nikon and looked through it he felt as though he had an artillery gun strapped to his head.

On the afternoon he collected it he told Zoe not to expect him back and set off for Tunford. A thin and insincere afternoon sun broke through the clouds as he left the motorway. Bypassing the town altogether, he headed directly for the hill. He parked by the same overgrown gate as before, shouldered his camera bag and set off through the wood. This time when he hit the track he knew exactly where to go. He caught glimpses of the houses through the trees. When he thought he had gone far enough, he left the track and cut straight downhill.

He was a little too high, but he backtracked until he was directly above the house. There was no sign of anyone, but he'd expected that. Jacob would be at school, Kale at the scrapyard and Sandra at the pub where she worked as a barmaid. He looked around. Not far from where he had stood the previous Sunday was a cluster of bushy young oaks, their lowest branches almost sweeping the ground in places. Ben cautiously pushed his way through them. They clutched and scratched at him but once he was inside there was a relatively clear area where he would be hidden. He set his camera bag and lens case down and snapped off one or two small branches that were in the way. After he had broken off the overhanging twigs in front of him, he had an uninterrupted view down into Kale's back garden.

He took out the telephoto lens and fitted it on to his Nikon. The weight made the familiar camera feel unbalanced. It would have been unmanageable without a tripod. When it was fully supported he put his eye to the viewfinder, and suddenly the back garden was in his face. He drew back, startled, then looked through the camera again. 'Wow,' he murmured, adjusting the focus.

Compared to this the zoom lenses he was used to were like bifocals. The rear of the house leaped into close-up; the grainy texture of the bricks, the flaking paintwork, even the brand-name of a box of matches on the windowsill above the sink, all were as clear as if he were only a few feet from them. He panned around the garden, which he now saw was contained by a high wire fence. In the centre of the bare, compressed earth was the car seat where Jacob had sat while Kale performed his lunatic exercises. Embedded in the ground next to it was the weight he had used, a finned metal cylinder which looked like part of an engine. He couldn't tell if it had been moved again or not.

The scene had a flat, slightly unreal quality as the compression of distance made the perspective lose its depth. In the foreground the mounds of scrap became individual metal shapes, precariously stacked and pockmarked with corrosion. Ben felt his anger mount at this further proof of Kale's irresponsibility. Ragged and razor-sharp edges protruded like traps, waiting to stab, crush and slash. He couldn't believe anyone could entrust a child to such a lethal playground, and wondered again how Kale had got away with it. Surely *somebody* for Christ's sake, should have made him clear the garden before Jacob was allowed to live with him.

Unless it hadn't been there then.

Ben began taking photographs of the junk, making sure that at least part of the house was also clearly in view in each frame. He shot three rolls of film before he felt he'd done enough for a dry run. He took his eye from the viewfinder. It was odd returning to an unmagnified perspective, like coming out of a cinema into a mundane world. The Kales' house looked shrunken and insignificant. There was still no sign of life. Ben felt disappointed, but only mildly. As he looked down the hill, it was another feeling altogether that gripped him. It was a moment or two before he recognised it as anticipation.

Not sure why that made him uncomfortable, he packed his gear away and went home.

He planned to finish work early and go the woods again the next afternoon, but by lunchtime the rain had started coming down with the steady determination of a long-distance runner. It continued over the next few days, a sullen downpour from a dour sky that didn't permit a glimmer of sun. If it left him frustrated, he could at least console himself that Kale and Jacob were unlikely to be out in it either.

The bad weather was doubly annoying because he had a location shoot scheduled for the end of the week. It should have been carried out during the summer, but penny-pinching by the fashion designer meant that now they had to try and juggle it into what sunny days the autumn grudgingly provided. The designer, spurning the idea of going abroad, had booked Ben for two days on the basis of the long-range weather forecast. Ben, Zoe, the make-up woman and two models had huddled around the cars on a deserted and windswept beach since first light, waiting for the low cloud to lift while the designer fretted and snapped at his assistant, chain-smoked black cigarettes and got on everybody's nerves. After lunch the sun had begun to break through. They had hurriedly set up and Ben had gone as far as taking final light readings when the first fat spots of rain splattered down.

They waited it out for another hour before Ben announced that he'd had enough. To the accompaniment of the designer's tantrum, they packed everything away, helped by the male model, who had obviously taken a shine to Zoe. As Ben was sitting with his feet out of the car, kicking the sand off his boots, she came over to him.

'Do you need me for anything else?' she asked, overly casual. 'Daniel's asked me out for a drink, so I'll go back with him if that's okay.'

'No problem.' He winked at her. 'See you tomorrow.'

She smiled, blushing, and went over to the model's black 1960s BMW. Ben watched her slim hips push from side to side as she waded across a patch of soft sand, self-consciously aware of being observed. But not by him, he realised. The studied insouciance was for the hunk waiting in the car, and Ben was wryly amused to find that his ego was pricking him. It was one thing to turn someone down. It was another to see how quickly they'd recovered from it.

The other model, a girl, had travelled down with the designer, and Ben felt obliged to offer her a lift rather than abandon her to the man's spleen. She was young, twenty or twenty-one, with short, curly auburn hair and a long upper lip that could look either sulky or sensuous. 'Thank God for that,' she said, as they set off. 'I thought I'd have to listen to that wanker whining all the way home. Mind if I smoke?'

Ben did, not liking even the smell of stale joints in his car, but he always felt picky saying so. He told her to go ahead. She lit up a St Moritz, offering him one which he declined. She put her head back on the seat as she inhaled, gratefully. 'He doesn't like models smoking when they're in his "creations",' she told him, making a parody of the last word. 'Says he won't have them smelling of ashtrays. I mean, I know he's the designer, but come on! God, what a tosser.'

Ben smiled non-committally. He had learned never to engage in slanging sessions with people he worked with. Particularly not when the subject was the one paying his fees. The girl took another languorous drag of her cigarette, turning her head to look at him.

'A friend of mine worked with you last year,' she said. 'You shot a piece on young British designers for *Vogue*. She was one of the models. Black. Tall, looks sort of Egyptian.'

Ben blanked, then recalled the shoot she was talking about. It had run over several pages in the magazine, and involved several models. It disturbed him that he couldn't remember one of them. A year ago, that was all. It seemed an age. Back in prehistory, when Sarah had been alive, and Jacob had been their son. A year ago he'd had a family. He felt his stomach drop. 'Oh, yeah. Right.'

'She said you were pretty good.'

The girl took a final drag of the cigarette, wound the window down an inch and slid it out. It was whipped away in a flare of sparks by their slipstream. She closed the window and moved around in her seat, so that she was half leaning against the door, facing him.

'I saw about you in the news,' she said. Ben felt his stomach drop some more. 'They warned us at the agency not to say anything. They didn't want anybody putting their foot in it and annoying you, but it seems like a lie, sort of, to pretend I don't know, doesn't it?'

Ben didn't want any part in this conversation. He gave a shrug, hoping she would take the hint. She interpreted it as agreement. She nestled down in the seat, settling herself into the topic.

'You must have been really upset. Some of the things they said. I mean, I thought they were really horrible.'

'That's the press for you.'

'I know but, you know, it seemed so un*fair*. I don't know how you could stand it.'

I didn't have any fucking choice. And when he had he'd made the wrong one. 'It's past now.'

Her hand shot to her mouth. 'Oh, I'm sorry, I didn't mean to—' She put her other hand up with her first, so it looked as if she were praying with clenched fists. 'Shit, I shouldn't have said anything, should I?'

'It's okay.'

'I just thought ... well, I don't know what I thought. I just wanted to let you know that I knew about it, and ... shit, I'm doing it again, aren't I? Look, I'm really, really sorry. Just ignore me, okay?'

'Don't worry about it.'

'No, but you must think I'm really callous, or stupid, or something.'

The assured pose had left her now. She looked so contrite and young that Ben felt old and shopworn, which didn't help. He sighed. 'It's all right. Forget about it.'

She subsided for a while. 'What made you want to be a photographer?'

Christ. He stifled his impatience, knowing she was only trying to be sociable. 'I was studying fine art, and started experimenting with film. It went on from there.'

'I didn't want to be a model. I wanted to be a dancer. But I was too tall and couldn't dance.'

Ben smiled dutifully. She took it as encouragement, and for the rest of the journey chatted about herself, telling him about her background, her childhood and her favourite foods. Practising for all the interviews when she was rich and famous, he thought. But at least it didn't require much input from him. He switched off, nodding occasionally to give the impression he was listening while his mind went off on its own track.

He dropped her outside the house she shared with two other girls, parts of whose life histories he had also been treated to *en route*. 'Do you want to come in for a drink?' she asked, stooping slightly to talk to him through the open passenger door. 'Or there's a good pub on the corner. Irish. Serves great Guinness.'

'No, thanks, I've got a lot to do.'

She said that was fine, she would see him tomorrow. It was only when he was almost back at his own house that it suddenly struck him that the girl wasn't just being friendly, that there had been, if not a come-on, then a shy offer behind the invitation. His first reaction was surprise, not so much that it had been made, but that he should have missed it.

His second was dismay that he wasn't interested anyway.

For a time he'd been able to convince himself that the utter lack of arousal he'd felt since Sarah had died was only normal. Or, if not normal, then at least understandable. It had only been five months, and it wasn't as if he *wanted* to go to bed with anyone else. He still missed her too keenly.

By the same token, he didn't like to think that he might be permanently dead from the waist down.

He could excuse the episode with Zoe as a drunken fiasco. The guilt and disloyalty he felt for even thinking about such things no doubt added their own contribution. Even so, he knew his own body, and if five months was short in terms of grief, it was still a hell of a long time to go without a hard-on. On a couple of occasions he'd deliberately tried to provoke a response, but they'd seemed seedy and furtive. The faces and bodies of models and past partners he'd pictured all blurred and became Sarah, and he would feel that he was somehow desecrating her. When he tried remembering the two of them making love, the sense of loss would overwhelm him. Even the purely physiological reflex, the morning glories, the hangover erections that would pulse in time to the painful throb in his head, seemed to have deserted him. It was as though the sexual side of his nature had been cauterised.

If he didn't even notice any more when an attractive girl more than ten years younger came on to him, he thought, sourly, as he unlocked the studio, it must have been burnt out altogether.

He was planning to make an early start the next morning, but one look at the way the rain was sheeting down told him there was little point. The fashion designer shouted and swore when he called and suggested delaying the shoot until the afternoon, but finally agreed after convincing himself it was his own idea.

Ben phoned Zoe to tell her the new arrangements, then made a flask of coffee and some sandwiches. He couldn't say if the idea of going to Tunford had presented itself to him before or after he'd decided to postpone the session. He wasn't even sure why he wanted to go, since it was a weekday and they would probably all be out.

But it was better than sitting in the house by himself.

The rain cleared before he reached the town, although it was still overcast. Ben parked in the usual place and headed for the oaks where he'd hidden the previous time. As he neared them he saw two men walking a dog up ahead. He cut deeper into the woods, letting them get well past before dropping down to his hiding place. The wind and rain had stripped some of the leaves from it, but enough remained to conceal him. He looked down towards the Kales' house as he gave the branches a shake, dislodging the rain in a silver shower. The garden was empty, but someone was apparently home because the back door was open. He pushed into the trees and sat on the low, collapsible fisherman's chair he'd brought with him this time. He was setting up the tripod when Sandra Kale came out.

She wore what looked like a long white T-shirt. Even at that distance, unmagnified, he could see that her legs were bare. She went to the bottom corner of the garden, where the junk was lowest. She stepped over it, and Ben noticed for the first time that there was a gate made from the same wire mesh as the fence. She opened it and glanced quickly up and down the track that ran along the backs of the houses, then turned to the house and beckoned. A man appeared and ran down the garden in a low crouch. He reached the fence and said something to her. She nodded, hurriedly pushing him through the gate, and it was only then that Ben realised he was gaping like an idiot.

'Shit!'

He grabbed for his camera, fumbling to attach the telephoto lens. A film was already loaded, but there wasn't time to waste with the tripod. The man was already moving down the track as Ben hefted the Nikon, struggling to support the huge lens while he focused. He only managed to fire off a couple of shots before the man cut up a path between two of the houses. Swearing, he shifted his attention back to the Kales' garden.

Sandra had shut the gate and was almost at the door. Before she went in she took a last look around. Under the magnification she seemed to be standing right in front of him. Her face was without make-up, the bleached hair uncombed and ruffled. Its dark roots contrasted with the artificial yellow of the rest. One cheek was marked by an angry-looking red spot, and her lips were puffy and bare of lipstick except for a smudge at one corner. Her nipples pushed at the T-shirt, and the bounce of her breasts as she moved suggested that she wore nothing under it. As she stepped into the house the T-shirt rode up fractionally, giving him a glimpse of a bare buttock. The door closed behind her.

There was a shadowy glimpse of her walking past the kitchen window, heading into the house. Ben automatically raised the camera. One of the upstairs windows was frosted, obviously the bathroom or toilet. He shifted his attention to the other. It was the one where he'd seen Sandra the first time he was there. The telephoto lens didn't have a zoom capacity, but by sharpening the focus he could make out some of the details of the dark interior through the glare on the glass. There was the pale square of a double bed, the bright sliver of a dressing-table mirror. Then a door opened and Sandra Kale appeared. Only her white T-shirt and yellow hair stood out in the room's shadows, but she became more visible as she moved nearer the window. Ben took several shots as she changed the sheets on the bed, then bundled the dirty linen in her arms and left the room.

The ache in his arms made him lower the camera. The house was again reduced to an innocent part of the row. He stared down at it with a hollow feeling of excitement.

'You randy bitch,' he said, wonderingly.

He began setting up the tripod.

Chapter Twelve

———◆◆◆———

'Of course, that's only my opinion,' the woman said. 'But the courts are far too lenient. It's so obvious I can't believe there's any argument about it. Sentences have dropped, and crime's increased. Even a blind man could see the correlation. And yet – and this is what really amazes me – yet you *still* get these people crying on against sending criminals to prison!'

The woman looked around the table, hands spread, her incredulous smile inviting everyone to share her amazement. The other guests looked back at her with uniformly bland expressions. Ben felt pins and needles starting in his legs and recrossed them. He took another drink of wine and silently congratulated Maggie on another rip-roaring success. She was sitting opposite him at the far end of the table, her russet-coloured dress clashing in an unhappy combination with her dark red lipstick. Neither of them suited her. The party was to celebrate her and Colin's tenth wedding anniversary, but her inverted Midas touch applied to social events as it did to everything else. By some perverse gift of planning she had managed to invite exactly the wrong number of guests; too many for a dinner party and too few for anything else. Even so, the food had been good, the wine even better, and it might not have been so bad if the chemistry between the guests hadn't been non-existent. Sometimes a mix of different types could make an evening, but in this case they had simply cancelled each other out.

Except for the woman.

She had started before the cheese course, and as the other conversations had dried up, hers had expanded to fill the gap. Attractive in an overfed way, she had the loud, monied confidence that came from never having her opinions challenged, and not listening when they were.

'It's like the whole question of capital punishment,' she explained, smiling reasonably. 'Everyone knows its a deterrent, so why in God's name we don't use it heaven only knows! These people wouldn't be so ready to murder and rape at the drop of a hat if they thought they'd be strung up for it. Instead, what do they get? Something ridiculous like a suspended sentence or community service half the time. I know that certainly wouldn't deter *me!*'

Ben didn't doubt it. It would take beheading just to shut her up. He looked across at Colin, surprised that he hadn't stepped in to steer the party back on course. But Colin was staring with absorption into his glass, either unaware of or indifferent to the woman's monologue. He had seemed subdued all night, which Ben thought was understandable after ten years with Maggie. She was shooting her husband meaningful glances, a fixed, desperate smile on her face. Colin didn't seem aware of that either. He drained his glass and silently refilled it. Ben thought that was a good idea and did the same. The woman droned on.

'Our entire society's too soft, that's the trouble. And it isn't just the prison system. There's no discipline in schools any more, so it's hardly surprising we're turning out generation after generation of uneducated louts. And as for this new vogue for parents not smacking their own children, well, I ask you!' She laughed at the absurdity of it. 'I'm sorry, but children need to be taught right from wrong. That's why we're getting so much crime amongst youngsters, because there's no discipline and no respect for authority. It needs to be drummed into them.'

Ben had been drinking steadily since he had arrived. He'd had a couple of beers before he went out, partly because it was Saturday night and partly because he'd been to Maggie and Colin's parties before and knew what to expect. But it wasn't until his muttered 'Hang 'em all' came out louder than he'd intended that it occurred to him that he was drunk.

Oh shit, he thought as everyone turned to look at him. The woman regarded him as if she'd only just realised he was there. She wore a faintly condescending smile, but her eyes were bright as spikes.

'I know common sense isn't very popular these days. It's much easier to mock than actually do anything about it. Perhaps you'd like to tell us what you think should be done.'

Ben didn't want an argument. He wasn't even sure how much he disagreed anyway. It was just the woman herself he didn't like. He felt every glass of wine conspire to make his tongue lie thick and heavy in his mouth. 'Not really.'

'No?' The woman looked around at the other guests, clearly considering herself to be their spokesperson. Ben felt his anger rise and tried to ignore it, knowing he'd had too much to drink. 'Do you have any children yourself?' she asked.

'Only by marriage.'

'Er, shall we—' Maggie began, but the woman wasn't going to be diverted.

'And do you smack them when they misbehave, or let them run riot?'

'Since he's autistic he wouldn't understand why you were hitting him, so there wouldn't be much point,' Ben said. 'Unless you think I should beat him anyway as a matter of principle.'

The woman's cheeks flooded with colour. She turned her head away sharply. The room was dreadfully silent. *Well, that's one way to kill a party*, he thought, and then Maggie was lurching to her feet.

'Coffee, anyone?' she asked with a cheerfulness that was almost hysterical. Ben saw the quiver in her smile and felt ashamed of himself. As relieved conversation began to spread once more, he left the dinner table and went upstairs to the bathroom.

He urinated, avoiding looking at himself in the mirror as he washed his hands. Time to go home. He hadn't been in a party mood before, and he was even less so now. Apart from his guilt at making a scene, the mention of Jacob had stirred up all sorts of emotional silt. Which was his own fault, but that didn't make it any better. He would quietly make his excuses and leave, he decided.

He didn't think he'd be missed.

He opened the bathroom door and found Colin waiting outside. 'I hoped it was you in there,' he said, straightening.

'Look, I'm sorry about what happened, I know I should have kept my mouth shut,' Ben began, but Colin wasn't listening.

'I need to talk.' His voice was low and urgent. He took hold of Ben's arm and led him away from the stairs. He opened the door to his study and turned on the light. Maggie's heavy hand was apparent even in here, unless Colin's taste in colours ran to mauve. The new computer monitor on the leather-topped desk seemed both anachronistically modern and honest in comparison to the expensive but chintzy reproduction furniture

Colin closed the door. His eyes had a glazed look, and with surprise Ben saw that his friend was drunk. 'What's the matter?'

Beneath the alcohol blush his friend's face was drawn. He glanced nervously at the door. 'I'm having an affair.'

The attempt at sounding casual failed. He gave a weak smile at Ben's expression. 'I know. I can't believe it either.'

Ben had the feeling that there must be a sort of etiquette for this kind of conversation, but he had no idea what it was. 'Who is she?'

Colin ran his hand along the edge of his computer keyboard, checking for non-existent dust. 'She works for a management company. They represent one of our bands.'

There was a peculiar relief that at least it wasn't anyone more glamorous. 'How long has it being going on for?'

'Nearly a month. I've known her for longer than that, but not ... it's always been in a professional context before. Then a few weeks ago there was a party to celebrate the band's new album release, and we got talking, and ... it sort of happened.'

'Have you seen her since?'

'About half a dozen times. She doesn't live far from the office, so we go to her flat at lunch-time. And once or twice I've told Maggie I've been working late.' He gave a humourless laugh. 'That old chestnut.' He sat down. 'I just can't believe it's happened. I never thought I was the affair type.'

Neither had Ben, but he didn't say that. 'Does Maggie know?'

'Oh, Christ, no!' Colin looked horrified. 'She's no idea. No, no one knows. I wasn't even going to tell you, but ...' He ran a hand through his hair, leaving one thin strand sticking up. 'I just feel such a fucking shit. She wanted me to make a *speech* tonight.'

'So are you going to finish it? With the girl, I mean?'

Colin took a moment to answer. 'I don't think I can.' He sounded miserable.

'What about her? The girl. What does she think?'

'We haven't really talked about it.' He gave Ben a peculiar look. 'She's only twenty-two.'

It was almost a boast, and Ben found himself on the verge of a grin, an automatic slide into male collusion. But both of them seemed to draw away from it at the same time. Ben thought of Maggie and her frumpy dresses, in competition without realising it with a girl ten years younger, and felt an unexpected pity for her.

'What are you going to do?' he asked.

'I haven't a fucking clue.'

There was a silence in which Ben wished he could think of something constructive to say. Colin stood up.

'Well, I suppose we'd better go back to the party.'

Ben stayed till the end. Not just for Colin's sake, but also for Maggie's. He felt that leaving early would be a slap in the face for her. One she might not actually notice, he admitted, but he still couldn't bring himself to do it. As the two of them came to the door to say goodnight he wished Colin hadn't told him about the affair. He didn't want to feel sorry for Maggie but he couldn't help it.

'Thanks, it's been great,' he lied, leaning into the aura of her flowery, unerotic perfume to kiss an over-powdered cheek.

'Glad you've enjoyed it. Thank you for coming,' she said, and for a second, as they looked at each other, social smiles firmly in place, he felt that the insincerity was openly exposed between them. His smile became stiff as he broke the contact and said goodnight to Colin, trying to make it seem as natural as he could. Feeling shoddy and two-faced, he hurried down the steps to the waiting taxi before he gave anything else away.

He shared the cab with a couple from the party who lived on the same side of town. The polite conversation petered out before the first mile, and they rode in the silence of people who have nothing in common, masking the awkwardness by staring through the windows. After they had been dropped off, Ben spread himself out on the taxi seat and realised that he didn't feel remotely tired. Or drunk. Since his brief clash with the woman and Colin's revelation, he had stuck to coffee.

The cab trolled through the dark streets, the meter clicking softly in the background. He couldn't make up his mind whether the affair showed that Colin wasn't as staid as he was beginning to look, or if it was part of a premature mid-life crisis, a last kick against the social and family shackles that were tightening around him. Ben felt relieved that he wasn't in that situation, until the barrenness of his own came back to him. What the fuck did he have to feel smug about? He tried telling himself that at least he and Sarah had had a good relationship, that they'd been faithful to each other, but the irony was too obvious for him to draw any comfort. Looked at in another way, their entire marriage had been a sham, built around the illusion that Jacob was Sarah's real son.

He knew that wasn't true, but the guilt he felt for thinking it fed his growing mood of self-disgust. And self-pity, if he was going to be honest. He stared morosely through the window. The taxi was coming to a commercial area, darkened shops with neon signs, and pubs with the last of the night's customers still spilling from them. He looked at his watch. It wasn't even midnight. It just felt as if the evening had gone on for ever.

The cab turned down a side street. It was quieter than the main road and badly lit. Two girls were standing under one of the few working streetlamps. They were heavily made up, with short, tight dresses showing fleshy thighs. One of them gave Ben a smile as they watched the taxi go past. It was a professional invitation, but in his loneliness even that seemed to offer comfort. There was a hot constriction in the pit of his stomach. He leaned forward to tell the driver to stop, then sank back in his seat without speaking.

He hadn't sunk that low. Not yet. *Besides, I'd only be wasting my money.* He wondered who he was to have felt even briefly smug about Colin's infidelity.

At least Colin could still get it up.

Further along another girl was walking slowly up and down in the dim blue glare from a closed newsagent's window. She had dark hair and her face was in shade, but for some reason Ben thought of Sandra Kale. His gut tightened again, and for an instant there was a tug of something so dark and illicit he didn't recognise it. Then it was gone, leaving an unspecified sense of depression. He tried to lift himself out of it by thinking about going to Tunford the next day, but that only made him feel worse. It seemed to him now that there was something not quite wholesome about his eagerness to return. The justification that it was for Jacob rang false. He was struck with the sordidness of what he was doing, skulking around with his long lens like some sweaty voyeur.

And enjoying it.

His self-loathing was so thick he could taste it as he paid off the taxi driver and went inside. He stood in the dark hallway, listening to the sound of the untenanted rooms. The house pressed in on him, claustrophobic in its vastness. No Jacob. No Sarah. He realised he was crying. He lashed out and punched the wall and felt the jolt sear from his knuckles to his shoulder. Goaded by the pain, he seized the cherrywood cabinet and tore it down. It toppled against the wall on the other side and lodged at an angle. There was a crack of breaking wood, a chime of the telephone falling off. He thought of how he and Sarah had bought the cabinet when they were first married, and the stab of remorse incensed him. He kicked wildly at it, punishing himself with each splintering blow, stamping on it until it crashed over sideways and its mirror shattered in a cascade of silver fragments.

Ben stood over it, panting. The rage dwindled and vanished. He looked at the shattered cabinet and felt a sadness so great he thought he would never climb out of it. He stepped over the wreckage and went into the lounge. There was enough light coming through the window to guide him to the sideboard. He groped inside until he found the bottle of vodka and took it with a glass to the settee.

Then he sat down and set about getting drunk.

The light was shining directly into his face. It seemed to have a physical weight, pressing on his temples and eyelids like a vice. He turned away from it, trying to retreat from the pain back into sleep. The movement made it worse. His head throbbed and there was a stiffness in his neck that stabbed from his shoulder to his skull. Dimly he became aware that something was wrong. His posture was cramped and uncomfortable, the surface under his head too firm to be a pillow.

Reluctantly, he opened his eyes.

A textured pattern, like seaweed, swam into focus. Ben blinked at it, but the distant panic at not recognising what it was paled in the face of the way his head was hurting. The pain seemed to increase with consciousness, until finally the discomfort of his position outweighed his reluctance to move.

He rolled over. The banging pulse behind his eyes made him shut them. When he tentatively opened them again he found himself looking up at the living-room ceiling. He was on the settee. The seaweed pattern had been the tasselled edge of a cushion he'd had screwed up beneath his neck. He lay there as memories of the previous night returned to him.

He sat up and sucked in his breath at the sudden pain. Holding his hands to his temples, he slowly swung his feet to the floor. They struck something hard and cold. He looked down and saw an overturned tumbler lying in a stained patch of carpet. The memory of vodka nauseated him. He took a few deep breaths through his mouth until the feeling had passed, and then stood up.

He'd been expecting the clamour in his head, but it was still almost enough to make him sit back down again. He swayed on his feet, waiting until the worst of it subsided, and then gingerly made his way into the hall. It was the first real hangover he'd had since he'd been out with Zoe. His body felt as though it had been taken apart during the night and badly reassembled, so that none of the parts fitted together properly.

He paused when he saw the wrecked cabinet. It was ruined beyond any hope of repair, but just then he felt too ill for the regret to make any impression. One self-punishment at a time. He took two paracetamol, followed them with a glass of liver salts, and splashed cold water on his face and the back of his neck. Then he sat at the kitchen table with his head in his hands and waited for it to stop hurting.

The self-disgust he'd felt the night before had been pushed aside by the more immediate misery of his hangover. It seemed inconsequential now, and he was already forgetting it as he looked at the clock and estimated how soon he could pull himself together and go to Tunford.

When the worst of the shivers had passed, he poured himself a glass of orange juice and went to load his camera.

By lunch-time his hangover had subsided to a general malaise. It lingered as a dull throb behind his eyes as he peered through the viewfinder at the Kales' back garden. Kale and Jacob were in the central clearing surrounded by scrap. Jacob sat in the car seat while his father moved pieces of scrap around. Sandra was at the kitchen sink, still wearing her bathrobe. During the half-hour that Ben had been watching, none of them had spoken.

He'd hoped he might see them all together, since it was a Sunday, and he'd been so eager to reach his vantage point that he'd almost blundered into a group of children playing in the woods. They were too close to the huddle of oaks for him to risk going to it, so he'd had to wait until their game took them out of sight before he could go down to his den.

He'd urinated against a nearby tree before he'd settled himself inside, knowing that if the children returned he might be stuck in there indefinitely. He'd heard them – or another gang – playing in the distance, but so far they hadn't come back. He hoped the dying leaves still clinging to the branches would be enough to screen him if they did. As he set up the camera and lens, he entertained notions of camouflage netting before deciding that would be going too far. He wasn't doing anything wrong, he told himself.

Not really.

He massaged his temples as he watched Kale place a last piece of scrap and stand back to regard his handiwork. Ben couldn't see what difference any of it made, but he presumed there must have been some reason. Even Kale wouldn't shift heavy lumps of metal around for the fun of it.

He yawned as Kale went inside the house. Jacob played on, regardless. He had a puzzle game in his hands, a complicated arrangement of steel hoops, and every now and again he would stop and hold one close to his eyes. Trying to catch a glimpse of the spectrum in the reflected sunlight, Ben thought, smiling. He seemed well enough. There were patches of what looked like oil on his shorts and T-shirt, but that wasn't exactly surprising considering his father's choice of garden furniture.

There was a movement in the doorway. The bull terrier hobbled down the steps like a muscle-bound golem. Ben had forgotten about the dog. He willed Kale or Sandra to reappear as it sniffed around the garden. There was no sign of either of them. He drew in his breath as it approached Jacob and lunged up at him, but the animal only licked the boy's face. Jacob irritably pushed it away. The dog wagged its tail and flopped down at his feet, tongue hanging from its grinning mouth.

Ben had risen half out of his seat. He sat back down, the thud of his heart echoing painfully in his head. Now Kale came out of the house again, carrying something. He stepped in front of Jacob, blocking him from Ben's view, and let the object fall to the ground.

It was a crumpled car wing. The chrome rim of the headlight was still set in it, spiked with jagged shards of glass. Kale disappeared inside again and returned a few moments later with a dented car bonnet. It rocked unevenly on the floor when he dropped it next to the wing. Ben focused on them as Kale went back inside. They were the same colour and appeared to be from the same car. It had obviously been involved in a bad crash. The damage was too comprehensive to be from anything other than a collision.

Something about that pricked his consciousness. He shifted the camera to look at the scrap pile itself, adjusting the focus until the individual pieces became clear. Mangled car roofs, radiators, doors, bumpers. There wasn't a smooth or undamaged surface anywhere. Not one. He hadn't really considered it before, except for the danger it posed to Jacob, but now he saw that, like the bonnet and wing, everything there showed the scars of some horrendous impact. He panned around the tortured shapes, and for the first time it came to him that Kale wasn't just collecting junked car parts.

It was accident wreckage.

Ben sat back and rubbed his eyes. His head was throbbing badly. He wondered if he wasn't reading too much into things. And what did it matter anyway? Perhaps Kale was simply a morbid, as well as mad, bastard. But the feeling remained that this was significant in a way he couldn't yet grasp.

He bent back to the camera. Kale was back in the garden. Ben watched as he continued to move the scrap around, painstakingly shifting and realigning pieces of it as if their precise position actually mattered. Every now and then he would pause to consider the effect, but Ben was at a loss to see any sense to it all. The changes seemed pointless, yet too deliberate to be wholly random, as though there were a purpose to it only the ex-soldier could fathom.

But what the fuck was it?

The door opened and Sandra Kale appeared. She had dressed. Her face was made up, her hair combed. Ben guessed she would be going to the pub for the afternoon shift. She looked from her husband to Jacob and said something. It was like watching a film without sound. Kale didn't appear to hear her either. Sandra stared at him, thin-lipped, then jabbed two angry fingers up at his back and flounced back into the house. The door slammed behind her. A heartbeat later the sound of it carried from the bottom of the hill.

Ben grinned. Sunday harmony *chez* Kale.

After she'd gone, Kale brought out two plates of sandwiches and gave the smaller to Jacob. He hunkered down on the floor beside him and they both ate, in silence as far as Ben could tell. At one point they were sitting in almost identical positions, the boy in the car seat, his father on the ground, chewing in unison. When he'd finished, Kale threw some scraps to the dog, which had been sitting hopefully at their feet. Jacob copied him and went back to his puzzle as Kale took the plates inside.

Ben ate his own sandwiches while he waited for him to reappear. Jacob remained in the garden, moving only once to urinate against the wooden wall of the garden shed. Ben shook his head, angry at this evidence of his new parents' laxness.

It was more than an hour later before Kale came into the garden again. Ben had begun to wonder if he'd gone out somewhere as well, leaving Jacob at home by himself. He had changed into a creased T-shirt and shorts, and now he began a series of stretching exercises. The section of engine he'd hefted over Jacob's head lay near by. Ben felt a rush of adrenalin. He waited, both hoping for and dreading what was going to happen.

But Kale ignored the blunt metal weight. Instead he picked up two house bricks, one in each hand, and began slowly raising and lowering them, rotating his arms and varying the movements so that all of his upper-body muscles were included in the workout. It reminded Ben of t'ai chi, an almost graceful exhibition of control. Only Kale's injured leg spoiled the effect, nailing him to the same spot like a wooden post. By the time he dropped the bricks, dark patches of sweat were staining his T-shirt. He was breathing deeply but steadily as he went and stood behind the car seat where Jacob was sitting. He looked down at the puzzle his son was playing with. Then, without warning, he bent and lifted both the seat and Jacob straight above his head.

The boy's eyes widened in surprise, but instead of the panic Ben expected his face split into a delighted grin. Kale began raising and lowering the seat while Jacob smiled above him. Ben began taking pictures, but then stopped. Jacob was laughing now, and Kale was actually smiling himself as he effortlessly bench-pressed his son. Ben felt a sense of exclusion and loss crystallise inside him as he watched. Those two smiles seemed to undermine any reason he had for being there.

But he made no attempt to leave.

'Fucking action man,' he muttered as Kale smoothly set the seat down and went back to his exercises.

The afternoon passed without further event. Kale continued to workout while Jacob played with his puzzle. He didn't so much as glance at the engine embedded in the ground, but Ben continued to watch, all the same. When Sandra Kale returned from the pub, he switched his attention to her. She seemed no happier now than when she'd left, peeling potatoes at the sink as if she bore them a personal grudge. She didn't tell her husband she was back, and if Kale was aware of it he gave no sign. It was like a dull soap opera, Ben thought, one in which the characters didn't do anything or talk to each other. Yet there was something hypnotic about it. He found himself drawn into the viewfinder's reality, fascinated by the Kales' lack of communication, the absorbing minutiae of their lives.

It stopped him thinking about his own.

It was becoming harder to see. He looked up from the camera and found with surprise that the light was fading. He hadn't realised it was so late. Or that he'd been there so long.

Rubbing his stiff neck he decided to pack up. He didn't relish the prospect of walking through the woods in the dark.

He reached down to remove the lens and saw the tiny figure of Kale disappear inside the garden shed.

He had gone in there after lifting the engine over Jacob's head, Ben remembered, looking through the viewfinder again. The small wooden shack expanded to fill the world. There was a window in it, but from that angle it was impossible to see inside. He decided to wait for Kale to re-emerge and try to catch a glimpse then.

Twenty minutes later his curiosity had given way to impatience. The dusk was settling into a dim twilight, but Kale showed no inclination to come out. Ben wondered what the fuck the man could be doing in there. He was beginning to think there must be another exit when the shed door opened.

Kale staggered out. His T-shirt was stuck to him, dark and wet as if he'd been swimming in it. There were livid red marks around his wrists, legs and neck. One ran across his forehead like a bandana. His face was congested and shiny with sweat as he held on to the shed door and gulped air.

'Jesus Christ,' said Ben, awed.

His imagination balked at what he could have been doing to get into that state. The shed wasn't that big. He focused quickly on the dark gap through the doorway. There was an impression of something vaguely mechanical inside, then Kale had closed the door. His limp was even more pronounced than usual when he went over to Jacob.

Still breathing heavily, though slightly less so now, Kale pointed to the car wing and bonnet that he'd brought into the garden earlier and said something to his son. When Jacob didn't look up from his puzzle, Kale bent and took it from him. Ben's finger pressed on the shutter release as he recorded Jacob's angry protest. Kale said something else, but he was wasting his time. Ben knew from experience that Jacob was winding up to a tantrum. He could hear his frustrated cries drifting up the hillside as he tried to grab the puzzle back. Kale withheld it for a few seconds longer, then let go.

Jacob went into a protective huddle, clutching the puzzle to his chest. Kale looked down at him, but whatever he felt didn't show on his face. He picked up the bonnet, seemed to consider for a moment, then laid it on the pile. He shifted it several times before he seemed satisfied, then did the same with the car wing.

He stood in the centre of the garden and regarded his handiwork.

He didn't move when the kitchen door opened and Sandra came out again. Her expression was pinched and mean as she stared at her husband's back. Ben wondered if he knew what else went on behind it while he was at work. He didn't think so. Kale was the possessive type.

He'd kill her if he found out.

Sandra was speaking. The heat in her words was evident even though Ben couldn't hear them. Kale didn't answer. His wife gesticulated angrily towards the kitchen, then said something else when Kale still didn't respond. *Your tea's on the table.* No, Ben amended, seeing the forms her lips made. *Your fucking tea's on the table.* Without turning around, Kale abruptly snapped something at her. The effect was immediate. She subsided, and in her face was something that could equally have been either hate or fear. It didn't stop her from mouthing 'Fuck off' at her husband's back as she seized Jacob's arm and pulled him into the house, but something made Ben think she hadn't spoken the words out loud.

The light had almost gone. He straightened with a groan, kneading his back, and began to pack everything away. When he made his way through the darkening woods, Kale's shadowy figure was still standing in the garden.

Chapter Thirteen

———⟤◆◆◆⟣———

Gradually, with each visit, he began to discern the patterns that the Kales lived by, the rhythm and routines which ruled them. He was literally seeing just one side, only what went on at the rear of the house, but from that he was able to draw conclusions about the rest. He picked it up piecemeal, making the hour-and-a-half journey to the woods whenever he could steal the time from work, until he was able to fit the pieces of their lives together like Jacob would a jigsaw puzzle. Slowly, a picture of the whole began to emerge from the separate parts.

On weekdays Kale and Jacob would have left before he arrived. He presumed that Jacob would be taken to school by the local authority's minibus while his father went to work. But that was part of the front life of the house, the part that Ben never saw. All he observed was their absence. And the time they spent in the garden.

As far as he could tell Kale hadn't endangered Jacob again. The lump of metal he'd hoisted over his son remained where it had landed that first time, and Ben was finding it harder to convince himself that it had been anything other than an isolated incident. Yet the rest of Kale's activities there followed a strict order. While Jacob lost himself in one of his puzzles, he would exercise and busy himself with his scrap. He would switch pieces around, arranging them with such precision that Ben began to wonder if he was missing something obvious. Perhaps it depended on the angle. Perhaps, if he could see through Kale's eyes, he would be able to understand what the point of it all was. He even considered the possibility that the entire scrap pile was some sort of free-form sculpture, tried to imagine Kale as an aspiring artist. But no matter how he tried to rationalise it, he always came back to his earlier theory.

The man was a fucking nutter.

His exercise regime always ended with him going into the shed. Even on Sundays, when he would be at home all day, he didn't go into it in the morning or afternoon. Only in the evening, at final light, and Ben would wonder what part of the picture that he was piecing together was concealed by the flimsy wooden walls. He toyed with the idea of slipping down to look inside when the Kales were at work, but the prospect of having to climb over the high fence in full view of the neighbours was too daunting.

Often when Kale came out, drenched in sweat and streaked with red weals as though he had been whipped, he would set a piece of scrap on the ground in front of Jacob like an offering. He would sit close to the boy and begin to talk to him, making Ben wish that he could hear as well as see them. Kale would eventually stop, looking expectantly at his son as if he were waiting for a response. When he didn't get it he would calmly move away and contemplate the mountain of wreckage surrounding him, his own little kingdom of rust. Ben would always be driven out of the woods by darkness before he tired of it.

That was the pattern that Kale and Jacob's back-of-the-house lives took. But, except for weekends, they weren't played out until the evening.

During the day the house belonged to Sandra Kale.

No friends or neighbours called round, and if the man he'd seen sneaking out of the garden went to visit her again it was when Ben wasn't there. She rarely did any housework except washing dishes and making the bed. Most of the time she stayed in the kitchen, drinking coffee (instant, with milk and sugar) or just sitting at the table, smoking and staring into space. The main event of her day came at about half past eleven, when she would leave for work.

Sometimes she dressed in the bedroom.

The first time it happened Ben had guessed she was going to get ready when she stubbed out her cigarette and left the kitchen. On the previous occasions he'd been there that had been the signal for the bathroom light to come on, and for her to reappear fully clothed twenty minutes later, with wet hair that she would dry with a blower next to the sink. That morning, though, she had gone straight into the bedroom. He waited for her to gather her clothes together and go out. Instead she unbelted the bathrobe she was wearing and tossed it on the bed.

The glare on the window restricted his view, but he could still see her clearly enough to tell that she was naked underneath.

She crossed to the dressing table and picked something up. Deodorant. Her breasts lifted as she rolled it under her arms, jiggling with the brisk motion. They were low, heavy but not sagging, with small, very dark nipples. Her stomach was flat and, he saw when she came nearer the window, had lines across it, as though the folds of her bathrobe had dug into her flesh. Below them the trimmed black stripe of her crotch made a lie of her bleached yellow hair.

Ben had watched as she pulled on bra and pants, short skirt and blouse. She had gone out, and as he'd waited to see if she would return a bird clattered in the branches above him.

He jerked away from the camera, then gave a nervous, silent laugh. *Shit.* He began to lean forward to look through the viewfinder again, but stopped.

What the fuck am I doing?

There was no excuse for spying on her when she was getting dressed. That wasn't why he was there, but even as he told himself this he felt a tight band of excitement in his chest. And not just his chest, he realised.

He had an erection.

He didn't know whether to be relieved or disgusted. Although the unexpected resurrection delighted him, he felt uncomfortable over its cause. And confused. It wasn't as if Sandra Kale was anything special, and nudity was hardly unusual in his line of work. Models changed in front of him as a matter of course, with neither he nor they thinking anything of it.

But they knew he was there.

You closet voyeur, Murray, he thought, but the attempt to laugh it off was a thin one. He didn't stop going to the woods behind the house, though. And he didn't stop watching Sandra Kale.

She puzzled him. Boredom and dissatisfaction were shouted from everything she did. She and Kale hardly seemed to speak, while Jacob she treated with either indifference or barely suppressed irritation. Unless Ben had completely misinterpreted what he'd seen when the man left the house, she was unfaithful as well. Yet she had helped Kale get his son back, had lied to protect him.

Was still lying for him.

The week before his next contact day was due, a shoot was cancelled at the last minute. Ben had gone out the evening before with some people from an ad agency, and as he went into the studio the next morning, he was regretting it. What had started out as a quick beer after work had developed into a full-blown whose-round-is-it-next session. At some point they'd stumbled off to a Lebanese restaurant where one of them insisted that the *mezzes* were to die for. Ben wasn't wild about Middle Eastern food, but he let himself be carried along in their slipstream. It was either that or go back to the empty house.

They'd been led to their table by a waitress who was coldly unimpressed by their noisy arrival. The restaurant wasn't busy, but she took them into a back room, as far away from the main part of it as possible. Only two tables here were occupied, a family group at one and a man and woman at the other. The man was Colin.

Ben hadn't seen him since the anniversary party. What with work and travelling to Tunford whenever he could, he'd been too busy. And Colin had a new draw on his time himself. The shared knowledge of his affair – and Colin's clear shame over it – had made them both uncomfortable. Which, Ben admitted to himself, was probably the real reason they hadn't seen each other.

But that night the drinks had diluted any awkwardness he might have felt. And also any subtlety. 'Colin!' he'd exclaimed, delightedly, and it was only when he saw the guilty shock on Colin's face that he realised that the dark-haired woman with him was young, slim and obviously not Maggie.

The girl from the record company, Ben thought. Oh fuck.

But it was too late to do anything other than keep on smiling and go over. 'I wasn't expecting to see you here,' he said, belatedly aware of how tactless that sounded.

Colin's face was crimson. 'Er, Ben, this is Jo.'

Ben had said hello. The girl seemed pleasant enough, but with a cool look about her he didn't entirely like. He had excused himself and gone back to his own table, and for the rest of the evening he had avoided so much as glancing across. Colin had said a quick goodnight when he and the girl left, but Ben could see from his face that he was still flustered.

He regretted meeting them, not only because he knew it had spoilt their evening, but because it complicated things. Before, he had only known about Colin's affair in abstract terms. But having seen him and the girl together, he felt implicated in it. Not that he could say he actually *blamed*

Colin. Christ knows, he had spent long enough trying to dissuade him from Maggie before they were married. He just couldn't bring himself to approve either.

He was thinking more about that than the day's shoot the following morning when he arrived at the studio, until Zoe told him that it had been cancelled. The designer had fallen out with the modelling agency over unpaid bills, and been blacklisted as a result.

'You don't seem very upset,' Zoe said, when she broke the news.

He was already wondering how quickly he'd be able to get to Tunford. 'It can't be helped.'

'I know, but that's the third this month. It pisses me off.' The others had been postponements rather than cancellations, but Zoe took them all personally. At one time so would Ben, but not any more. He had seized those opportunities as well. 'I wondered about phoning that guy who wants some portrait stuff doing,' Zoe suggested. 'The writer. He said he wanted it as soon as we could fit him in.'

Ben struggled to remember who she meant. 'Oh ... no, it's too short notice.'

'It's worth a try.'

'No, let's leave it.' He could feel her disapproval. 'I tell you what, why don't you do it?'

'Me?'

'Yeah, why not? You're good enough.'

'But he wants you.'

'Tell him I can't do it. Say we're fully booked, but you can squeeze him in yourself.'

She was looking doubtful. 'Do you think he'll go for it?'

'Like you said, it's worth a try.' He went to put on his coat as she mulled it over.

'So what will you do instead?' she asked.

'I've got some things to sort out.'

'Anything I can help with?'

'No, it's okay.' He was at the door. 'Give that writer a ring and see what he says. I'll see you tomorrow, okay?'

She nodded, but she still didn't seem happy as he went out. He stopped off at an electronics shop and then headed straight for Tunford. It was late morning when he arrived at the woods. He parked in his usual place by the overgrown gate and took his bag and case with the lens in it out of the boot. An elderly couple walking a Yorkshire terrier gave him an odd look as he climbed over the fallen wall, clumsy with all the equipment. He gave them a confident smile and hoped they didn't recognise him, or realise what he was carrying.

A light drizzle had started by the time he reached his den, so he set up the camera and lens in their weatherproof jackets. It was cold and wet in the trees, a prelude to the final closedown of winter. Ben was shivering, but he still felt a buzz of anticipation as he focused on the house. Sandra was in her bathrobe in the kitchen, partially screened by the reflection of the garden on the window. Ben fitted a polarising filter on to the lens and the glass turned transparent. It was a new acquisition, expensive, but worth it for how much glare it cut out. With that attached to the lens he could see into the house much more clearly.

He delved in his bag again and took out the compact cassette recorder and tie-clip microphone he'd bought from the electronics shop on the way. He connected them and placed the microphone against the earpiece of his mobile phone. He'd tested the set-up earlier to check that it picked up both his voice and that of whoever he was calling. The sound quality wasn't wonderful, but he didn't need high fidelity. Just proof.

He glanced around to make sure that the woods were empty. The last thing he wanted was some local with a dog overhearing him. Satisfied, he looked through the viewfinder again. Sandra Kale was still in the kitchen, smoking a cigarette. Mounted on the wall a few feet from her was a telephone. Ben had seen her answer it occasionally, although she never seemed to call anyone herself. It was at the far end of the room, but with the new filter on the lens he could see it clearly. Still looking through the camera, he set the tape recorder running and dialled the Kales' number.

The ringing tone in his mobile coincided with an irritated glance towards the telephone from Sandra. She pushed back her chair and went to answer it.

'Hello?'

The thin reproduction of her voice was synchronised with the mime of her lips. In the background he could hear the tinny jangle of a radio. It surprised him. He'd taken for granted that the kitchen would be as silent for her as it appeared to him. He glanced at the tape recorder to make sure it was running.

'It's Ben Murray,' he said. 'I thought I'd remind you that it's my contact day this weekend.'

The microphone pressed against his ear like a cold button. It was a compromise solution he'd reached a few days earlier. He had at least to try to claim his contact rights, but he knew there was nothing to be gained by another *mano à mano* confrontation with Kale. This way he could prove he had made the attempt, and perhaps record Sandra saying something incriminating. The cancelled shoot was a bonus that gave him the opportunity to see her reaction as well as hear it.

He tried to disregard the accusing voice that sneered he was only avoiding Kale because he was afraid of him.

'So is it okay for me to come and collect Jacob on Sunday morning?' he prompted.

An exasperated sigh came down the phone. In the view-finder he saw her chest rise and fall in time to it. 'Are you thick, or what?'

'I'm entitled to contact every fourth Sunday. That's this weekend.'

Ben watched her draw on the cigarette and shoot out an angry line of smoke. The bathrobe gaped loosely. 'Big deal.'

'You wouldn't let me take him last time. Are you telling me I can't again?'

He'd wanted to spell it out for the tape recorder, but either she was naturally wary or something in his tone alerted her. Her voice became more cautious. 'Like I told the social worker, you were drunk and late. You weren't fit to have him.'

'I was on time, stone cold sober, and your husband threatened me. You were there, you know that.' He took a hold of his temper. 'Will you let me see Jacob on Sunday or not?'

There was a minute pause. He could see her chewing her lip. 'He's got a cold.'

'Cold?'

'Yeah, that's right, cold. Might even be flu. You know what flu is, don't you?'

'So you're saying I can't see him?'

'I've told you, he's not well. He's in bed.'

He'd watched Jacob in the garden the evening before. There had been no sign of a cold then. 'Have you sent for a doctor?'

She took a last draw on the cigarette and turned around to stub it out in something behind her. 'Not yet. We'll have to see how he goes on.'

She leaned against the wall, her back still to the window. *Turn round.*

'What?' she said.

Ben realised he'd muttered out loud. But she'd moved to face the window again. He could see her frowning, one hand cupping the elbow of the arm that held the phone. 'Nothing. So when can I see him?'

'How do I know? I'm not psychic. You never know how long kids are going to have something for, do you?'

Ben swallowed his anger. 'Perhaps I should speak to your husband.'

She glanced out of the window. At the scrap pile. 'He's at work.'

I know. 'I'll call when he gets back.'

'He works late,' she said, and Ben knew that he'd just lost any chance of getting Kale on the phone. She would make sure she answered it first in future.

Oddly, though, he didn't get any real sense of antagonism from her. He looked at her, bare-legged in the short robe. She was twirling the telephone wire as she waited for him to speak, unaware that he was watching her.

What colour underwear are you wearing?

The question popped into his head without warning, and he had to bite back a bubble of laughter. But at the same time it disturbed him.

'You still there?' she asked.

'Yes.'

There was a pause. She seemed to be almost smiling as she bit on her thumbnail. He wondered why she didn't put the phone down. Come to that, he wondered why he didn't either.

'Got anything else you'd like to ask?' she said, and although there was no mistaking the mockery there seemed something flirtatious about it. The high he'd felt a moment earlier was replaced by uncertainty.

'I don't think so.'

There could have been a laugh. 'Fuck off, then,' she said, and hung up.

He stopped the tape recorder. He rewound for a couple of seconds, then played it back. Her final 'Fuck off, then' sounded more contemptuous than ever. It was a strange kind of loyalty that let her sleep with someone else, yet still cover for Kale. But even though there was nothing on the tape that Ben could use, he was unable to feel disappointed. He packed away the recorder and microphone and switched off his mobile, not wanting it to ring while he was in the woods. When he looked at the house again the kitchen was empty and the bathroom light was on.

He blew on his fingers. It was bitterly cold. He took the Thermos flask out of his bag and poured himself a cup of coffee. He'd made it on the off-chance that he'd be able to go to Tunford before it got dark if the shoot finished early. He was glad of it now. Through the steam rising from the plastic cup he saw the tiny figure of Sandra Kale go into the garden. He dug into his bag for a Mars bar. The next time he looked she was walking away from the fence at the bottom.

The steam flattened and dispersed as he blew on the coffee. He took a sip and winced when it burned his mouth. The liquid scalded all the way down his throat. He hissed, sucking in cold air to soothe it. He took another sip, more careful this time, and when he lowered the cup a man was in the Kales' garden.

'Shit,' he said, spilling coffee down his front. He threw the cup to one side and dropped the Mars bar. By the time he was at the camera the man was already going into the house. Ben fired off half a film on motor drive but he knew he hadn't caught him. With the polarising filter still on, Christ knew what the shots would turn out like anyway. 'Fuck! Fuck, fuck, *fuck!*' Sandra Kale was already leading the man out of the kitchen. Ben raised the camera to the bedroom, focused and waited. 'Come on. Come *on!*'

The bedroom door opened and she appeared. The man followed her. Ben switched off the camera motor and took two shots as they entered the bedroom. He watched as they spoke. With the window glare reduced by the filter, he could make out quite a lot of detail. The man seemed tall in comparison to Sandra – dark hair, medium build. Ben put him in his late thirties. He was grinning as he moved towards her. She stepped back and said something, unsmiling. The man's grin faded. He spoke and went towards her again, but she shook her head. He shrugged, reluctantly nodded.

Now Sandra smiled and went to him. He was still frowning, but only until she reached out and put her hand on his crotch.

Click.

She steered him towards the bed. He was smiling again as she sat on the edge and unbuckled his belt. She pulled down his trousers. *Click.* He stood in front of her in his underpants. She peeled them off. His erection sprang up in front of her face. She said something and they both laughed. *Click.* She stroked it with her hand, looking up at him all the while, and then bent and took it in her mouth.

Click. Clickclickclick.

Ben came to the end of the film. He cursed as it automatically rewound, begrudging the few missed seconds. He took it out, dropped it into his bag and swiftly installed a new one.

The man had stripped off the rest of his clothes. He had a paunch, Ben was obscurely glad to see. Sandra was also naked. The striations he'd noticed before were livid on her white belly. They looked like stretch marks. She lay back on the bed. The man climbed on to it and knee-walked towards her. She opened her legs as he settled on top. There was some manoeuvring, and then he began pumping his hips up and down. Sandra lifted her legs higher and wrapped them around him.

Ben changed film again.

He ran off most of another before the man stopped thrusting. He flopped on to the bed beside her. Sandra propped herself on one elbow, her back to the window. It formed a clean curve to her buttocks. The man sat up and reached for his trousers. He took out a packet of cigarettes, offered her one, and then lit them both.

'You clichéd bastard,' Ben grinned. Cigarettes finished, they dressed on separate sides of the bed. The man tucked in his shirt and picked up his jacket. Sandra put on a T-shirt. She watched, still smoking, as the man took out his wallet and placed a couple of notes on the dressing table. She snapped something and the man laughed and added another to them.

Ben closed his mouth and finished the rest of the film.

By the time they came downstairs he had changed it. Like the last time, Sandra came out first before signalling for the man to follow. She locked the gate behind him but didn't go back into the house. She looked up at the hill that Ben was on, and for a moment he was convinced she was going to stare straight at him, acknowledge his presence. But her gaze came nowhere near.

Her cheeks hollowed as she sucked cigarette smoke deep into her lungs. Her expression was tight and unforgiving as she stared at the car wreckage. Abruptly, she seized the nearest piece of scrap and tugged at it. A distant clatter carried to Ben on the wind as it came free. She flung it aside and began tearing at the rest of it, but soon stopped with a grimace of pain. She examined her palm, then began sucking it. The fit seemed to have exhausted itself. She looked listlessly at what she had done and passed her injured hand tiredly across her eyes, leaving a smear of blood. She took a last, defeated drag of the cigarette which she'd held throughout.

Flicking it away in a trail of sparks, she turned and went back into the house.

The darkroom was full of wet eight-by-ten prints. In the dim red light they hung from the drying line like surrealist washing. His darkroom at home wasn't as well air-conditioned as the one at the studio, and he could taste the pungency of the developing chemicals at the back of his throat. Ben clipped the last print up and turned the fan higher as he studied the results. He was pleased with how well the new lens was working with the Nikon. Although the photographs of the bedroom were grainy, that was only to be expected. Even with the filter he could hardly expect good definition shooting from light to dark through glass.

It was good enough, though.

He examined one of the dryer prints. In it Sandra Kale

sat on the bed, the man's penis disappearing into her mouth. His lips were pursed in concentration, her face distorted as if she were mid-yawn. Both she and the bedroom were easily recognisable. Ben moved to another print. It showed the man putting the money on the dressing table, his wallet frozen on its way back to his pocket. Next to it was one of him leaving the house. His features were much clearer on that. Ben considered it for a moment, then unclipped it and went over to a filing cabinet. He opened a drawer and flicked through the index tabs until he came to the photographs he had taken weeks earlier, as Sandra's visitor hurried away from the garden. Ben compared them with the still-wet print he had just developed and gave an incredulous laugh. He hadn't been sure before, but there wasn't any doubt.

It was two different men.

Chapter Fourteen

———⊰●⊱———

'You can answer me any time today if you feel like it.'

Ben looked up from the reflector and stand he was dismantling. Zoe was waiting in front of him, a heavy tripod clutched in her arms, her face patiently exasperated. 'What?'

She sighed and rolled her eyes. 'I said shall I put this in the car?'

'Oh, right. Yeah, please.'

Zoe continued to look expectantly at him. 'And do I get the car keys as well?' she said in answer to his obvious incomprehension. 'Or am I supposed to smash a window?'

He fished in his pocket and gave them to her. 'Sorry. I wasn't thinking.'

'Tell me about it,' she grumbled, walking away.

Ben rubbed the bridge of his nose. He felt gritty and tired. The shoot had been for an advertising campaign for a new range of jeans 'to wear anywhere', as the ad would claim. They had been trying to find the right location for it since shortly after Sarah had died, and only recently settled on a sixteenth-century chapel in Sussex with beautiful stained-glass windows behind the altar. A mock wedding had been set up, with everyone in formal dress except the bride, who wore white jeans and T-shirt with her veil. It should have been straightforward enough, except that he'd left a box of filters he needed back at the house. It wouldn't have been so bad if he could have sent Zoe, but the box was in the darkroom, and the darkroom was full of prints of Sandra Kale. So he'd had to make the trip himself, leaving behind a chapel full of waiting models, make-up people and an apoplectic art director. By the time he got back the man – who Ben usually got on well with – was almost cross-eyed with frustration and Zoe was seething because she'd had to stay and bear the brunt of it.

The shoot had run on till late at night. Ben had silently blessed the fact that they were using artificial lights to simulate the sun shining through the stained-glass windows, and so could continue when it was dark. Afterwards he and Zoe had stayed to clear up, but when Zoe had only just managed to catch the tripod and camera he'd knocked over, he decided enough was enough and called it a day. Only the rector had another set of keys, so Ben had broken his usual rule of not leaving equipment untended, locked the big wooden doors on the mess and driven back to the hotel.

Now he regretted not finishing the previous night. The hire firm had taken away the big Kliegs they'd used to illuminate the chapel, and without them the air inside was cold and damp. The two of them worked with their coats on, breath steaming like ectoplasm within the dark stone walls. He knew he'd been unprofessional, and would have to come up with spectacular results if he wanted to work for the ad agency again.

More than anything, though, he resented the lost time.

He took the reflector out to the car. Zoe had the boot open and was moving the overnight bags to make room. Her latest hair colour was a blond that made her dark eyebrows stand out to startling effect. As he approached, she straightened.

'What's this?'

She was holding the telephoto lens. It was in its carrying case, but there was no escaping what it was.

'It's a lens,' Ben said.

Zoe snorted. 'Yeah, I think I guessed that. Bit big, though, isn't it? Can I have a look?'

She was unzipping the case as she spoke, used to handling all his cameras and equipment without thinking. 'God, what is it, four hundred millimetre?'

He felt caught. 'Six hundred.'

'*Six!* Fucking hell, you taking up astronomy, or what?' She looked up from the lens, grinning. 'What do you need a long lens for? Not turned into a paparazzo, have you?'

Ben's face was burning. 'I just felt like getting it.' He knew it sounded feeble, that it would have been better to have laughed with her. Instead he took the lens from her and put it back in its case. 'Come on, stop wasting time. We've got a lot to do.'

She stared at him. 'Well, excuse me! It wasn't *me* who forgot the fucking filters yesterday, was it?' She stomped off into the chapel.

Well, you handled that beautifully, he thought, closing the car boot.

The drive back to London passed in a constrained silence. He knew he should apologise but couldn't bring himself to mention it. He told himself he had nothing to be embarrassed about, that it was only a lens, for fuck's sake, and that in any case he was using it in a good cause. But his rationalisations had the feel of sophistry. He pulled up outside Zoe's flat. She got out of the car without a word. Her expression was stony as she jerked her bag from the back seat.

'See you tomorrow,' he said. She slammed the car door without answering.

Shit. He was on the verge of going after her, but something was tugging at his mind, distracting him as he watched her go into the house. He looked at her bleached hair, the eyebrows that appeared almost black in contrast, and an image of Sandra Kale naked in the bedroom came to him. The sound of the front door banging shut registered, but only peripherally.

As he pulled out into the traffic, he'd already forgotten about Zoe.

It was after lunch when he arrived in Tunford. He'd made no conscious decision to go, but neither did he ever really question where he was heading. He just avoided thinking about the reason. When he reached the turn-off that brought him to the woods, he slowed, then drove past. The house would be empty, so there was no point in watching it. Jacob would be at school, Kale at the scrapyard and Sandra at the pub. His mouth dried at that last thought, and finally he had to admit to himself where he knew he'd been going all along.

He pulled into the pub carpark.

He turned off the car engine but made no move to get out. The Cannon stood on the street corner, a few hundred yards from where the Kales lived. It was a squat block of dun brick, newer than the rest of the estate but still the worst sort of sixties architecture. A badly painted sign hung above the door. Ben looked at it and wondered what the fuck he was doing. His heart was thudding. He knew the sensible thing would be to drive off before anyone noticed him. But now he was there that would have seemed like cowardice. Not giving himself time to think about it, he climbed out, locked the car and went inside.

The carpet in the entrance was threadbare and sticky. There were two doors facing each other inside, one to the taproom, the other to the lounge. Ben went into the lounge first. The room was long, with a brown carpet, upholstery and curtains, and a pervading smell of stale beer. No one was about and steel shutters were drawn over the bar. He let the door swing shut and went into the taproom.

A blue haze of smoke hung in the air. A handful of men nursed pints at the Formica-topped tables. The solid crack of ricochet came from the pool table where two middle-aged skinheads played with stubby cues. The bar was lit but he couldn't see anyone serving.

One or two men glanced incuriously at him as he hesitated in the doorway. No one seemed to recognise him. He tried to appear relaxed as he walked in. There were only scuffed, non-coloured lino tiles on this side instead of carpet. An upbeat Elvis song was blaring from the wall-mounted juke-box, giving the room a semblance of liveliness.

'Bar, Sandra!' a man playing dominoes on a nearby table shouted as Ben reached the varnished wood counter. Suddenly what he was doing seemed like a very bad idea. In fact he couldn't even recall how he could have thought there was anything good about it. He made up his mind to leave, but before he could a door behind the bar opened and Sandra Kale came through.

She stopped when she saw him. Her mouth compressed into a thin line that matched her plucked eyebrows.

'What do you want?'

No reasonable answer presented itself, except the obvious one. 'A pint of bitter, please.'

She stared as if she wasn't going to serve him, then took a glass from below the counter, put it under an electric beer pump and pressed a button. She didn't speak as the glass began to fill, and Ben guessed she was trying to come to terms with the situation as much as he was.

Or perhaps she just had nothing to say.

She set the full glass on the counter. 'One eighty.'

Ben reached into his wallet and gave her a note. On impulse he said, 'Would you like one?'

Her eyes flitted to the room behind him. 'No.' She handed him his change then folded her arms below her breasts like a barrier. She wasn't wearing lipstick and her lips were pink and chapped. A wayward regret that he hadn't seen her getting dressed that morning blew across his mind. He brushed it away.

She regarded him, unsmilingly. 'Why've you come here?'

It was odd hearing her speak after the dumb-shows he was

used to. He took a drink of beer to hide his confusion. It was chilled to tastelessness. He put it back down. 'I was passing. I thought I'd see how Jacob was.'

'Steven's fine.'

'How's his cold?'

'Comes and goes.'

'I suppose it'll probably come when I'm due to see him again and go straight afterwards, won't it?'

Something that might have been a smile touched a corner of her mouth. She shrugged. Her breasts lifted, then settled again on her folded arms. Ben took another drink of beer and wondered what she would do if he told her he knew she had sex with men for money. The thought strengthened him. Whore, he thought. *Slag. Slut. Tart.* He realised he was growing hard inside his jeans and felt a rush of pure lust that left him light-headed and faintly shocked.

Jesus, what do they put in the beer in this place?

As if she had caught the drift of his thoughts, he sensed an imperceptible shift in the currents between them. The casual antagonism he'd felt from her was replaced by a sort of awareness. She tilted her head slightly to one side and moved her arms, pushing her breasts closer together and so out towards him. 'Have you any idea what he'd do if he knew you were here?'

There was no need to say who 'he' was. Ben drank some more of the tasteless beer. 'He doesn't, though, does he?'

'Supposing I tell him?'

He put the glass down. 'You don't tell him everything, do you?'

'What's that supposed to mean?'

It was his turn to shrug. He saw uncertainty touch her face and felt a corresponding throb in his groin. There was a movement next to him at the bar.

'Any problem, San?'

It was one of the pool players. He glared at Ben as he

asked the question. 'No. It's all right, Willie,' Sandra said, but the man stayed where he was. He was short and thick-set. He grasped the cue around its middle in an overhand grip as he looked Ben up and down.

'You're that cunt who had John's kid, aren't you?' he said, loudly.

The music didn't stop, but Ben could sense everything else in the room grinding to a halt; the desultory conversations, the domino games, all breaking off at this new entertainment. *Suddenly, it's fucking Deadwood.*

'I don't want any trouble, Willie,' Sandra snapped.

The man ignored her. His head wasn't completely shaved, Ben saw. It had a fine fuzz of pale stubble on it. His partner, also with a cue, came and stood behind and to one side of him. 'What the fuck are you doing here?'

'Having a beer, what's it look like?' Ben heard his own tone of voice and marvelled at it. On the juke-box Matt Monro began singing 'Born Free'. He felt giddy with an unexpected recklessness.

The one called Willie stared at him. 'We don't fucking want you.'

Ben stared back, gripping the pint glass like a weapon. 'I don't give a fuck.'

Part of him stood aside from himself, watching this stranger with amazement, but the rest of him was borne up in the thick, hot gorge of aggression. His limbs and head felt pumped full of blood. Only a thin membrane of sanity restrained him. He pressed against it, feeling it give, wanting an excuse to break through.

'You're already on one warning, Willie. Any more and you're fucking barred,' he heard Sandra say, and later he would wonder at her apparently taking his side, but right then her words didn't mean anything. He and the man faced each other, on the lip of violence. The man spat on the floor.

'Fucking London ponce,' he said, turning away.

The tension in the room was released. The other customers went back to their beer and dominoes. Ben watched the two skinheads go back to the pool table, laughing at some muttered insult, and felt as if he'd woken up on top of a precipice. He put his beer glass down on the bar with a hand that was suddenly shaking.

Sandra Kale shook her head. 'If you really want to kill yourself you should come here on a Saturday night.'

He didn't say anything. He would have asked for a brandy, but that would have made his weakness obvious. The thought of the pool players coming over again terrified him. He drank half of the beer left in the glass. It had warmed up but didn't taste any better.

Sandra was still watching him. 'So what did you come here for?'

I don't know. Reaction from the near-fight was setting in. He wanted to get out of the pub very badly. 'I'm not going to give up,' he said.

He immediately regretted the pointless bravado. Sandra Kale's face closed down again, but not before he saw the tiredness that stole across it.

'Please yourself,' she said, and walked out through the door behind the bar.

Ben finished his beer. He didn't want it, but he didn't want to be seen to be rushing out either. Putting the empty glass down on the counter, he walked out past the pool players without looking at them.

No one followed him out, but by the time he had unlocked his car and driven away he was clammy with sweat. He went past the Kales' house, noticing that the scrap in the front garden had also been added to and moved around since the last time he'd seen it, and followed the road up to the wood that overlooked the town. He pulled into the gateway where he usually parked and turned off the ignition.

'You fucking idiot.'

He shut his eyes and rested his head on the steering wheel. Jesus Christ, what had he been thinking of? The thought of how close he'd come to being worked over by two pairs of boots and pool cues made him feel sick. A pub fight was a different proposition to a scrap on a football pitch. Yet he hadn't just been ready, he'd *wanted* it to happen. That wasn't courage, it was fucking madness. But he hadn't cared. Even more incredible was that he had got away with it.

Perhaps that's the trick, he thought, you just have to not care.

A sudden spatter of rain against the windscreen made him lift his head. Fat drops the size of pennies were flattening themselves against the glass. The blue-black clouds bellied overhead like a water-filled awning. The rain came down more heavily, obliterating his view of the world outside. He looked out at the transient, spun-glass strands it formed as it bounced from the bonnet and told himself how stupid he'd been. This time, though, the self-flagellation lacked conviction. He was more relieved than surprised when he realised he didn't regret what he'd done. Not even the confrontation with the pool players.

You're getting as bad as Kale, he jeered, but he couldn't deny he was glad he hadn't lost face in front of Kale's wife. She's a fucking whore, he thought, angrily.

Then: *I want to fuck her.*

It was like lancing an abscess. He felt he couldn't breathe with the sheer pressure of lust, the need for rut. The rain beat against the car. Condensation had steamed the glass, making a dry, private cave of the interior. His fingers trembled with haste as he unzipped his fly and pulled his erection free. He gripped it and closed his eyes. He pictured Sandra Kale undressing in the bedroom, the man's penis in her mouth. With his eyes still shut Ben looked down and saw her sitting on the bed in front of him. She stared back, her plucked eyebrows mocking and callous as he thrust himself between her lips. He threw her on to the bed, ramming himself into her, and with a choked cry he came, arching his hips as the scalding white stream spurted over him, splashing the steering wheel, dashboard and the door panel until he felt he was pumping out his entire self and it would never stop.

Then it did. He slumped in the car seat. Gradually, his heart slowed to something like normal. The rain drummed on the car roof as he looked down at the sticky mess he'd made. He felt disgusted with himself, but not as disgusted as he probably should. Or guilty, since it was the first orgasm he'd had since Sarah died. He thought about the last time they'd made love, but it seemed unreal and long ago. A solitary ejaculation in a steamed-up car with the vision of a cheap prostitute for company seemed infinitely more real now. Far from bringing any sort of release, though, it had left him only with a dull and heavy sense of depression. With a sigh he began searching through his pockets.

He hoped he had some tissues.

Chapter Fifteen

It was only because of a sleepless night that Ben found out that Kale was keeping Jacob from school.

Insomnia had never been something that had troubled him before Sarah's death. Since then, though, and especially in the last few weeks, he was beginning to become familiar with its company. He'd fallen asleep when he went to bed but woken just after three, suddenly wide awake, a feat he wished he could achieve as painlessly at a more humane hour. There had been no reason for it, no noises or disturbance he could blame, but sleep was suddenly as far away as if he'd been up for ages. He'd lain watching the luminous digits of the clock radio beside the bed count off the night's passage with silent, infinitesimally slow beats. Sleeplessness, he'd found, distorted time more than the acid he'd tried at university. He would wait for one minute to flick into another. The numerals were an electronic cage that time seemed wantonly to wind in and out of, cramming more and more of itself into each sixty seconds until Ben became convinced that the clock had stopped. Then the numbers would change, and he would watch and wait again.

His mind began to run like an automated cinema projector, throwing up images that the dark had kitted out with spikes and poison. He reviewed his bravado in the pub and saw it as juvenile. It had been a ridiculous posture, a bluster to hide the fact that he daren't do anything where it mattered, with Kale. He replayed their encounters and felt shamed. He had backed down at every one. In the daylight he could tell himself that Kale was a trained soldier, used to violence, that he was unbalanced and provoking him would be suicidal. But the darkness stripped those rationalisations away.

The uncushioned truth was that he was scared of him.

He remembered a street fight he had seen when he was a student. A group of men had been arguing outside a pub, and as Ben had crossed to the other side of the road to avoid them the argument had suddenly exploded. He saw one man drop to his knees and have his head kicked like a football. The dull crack of his skull hitting the pavement had been audible even across the street, and as the fight spilled into the road Ben had hurried away from the sight of someone jumping with both feet on the fallen man's head.

He never heard anything about the fight afterwards, but he'd felt sick, sure he'd watched a man being killed. He'd hated himself for not doing anything, just as he hated himself now. *You're a fucking coward.* He visualised the scene again, only this time with Kale as the attacker, and himself the figure on the floor. As he stared at the bedroom ceiling he felt a four-o'-clock-in-the-morning certainty that there wasn't going to be any amicable ending between them. The soldier had slipped whatever restraints checked most people. If Ben kept on trying to see Jacob, sooner or later something would snap when there wasn't anyone around to intervene.

If that happened, Ben knew Kale wouldn't stop until he was dead.

At six o'clock he threw back the quilt and got up. It was still dark outside. He turned on the lights and tried to shrug off the disjointed feeling that still hung over him. He showered, treating himself to longer than usual, and under the hot needles he immediately began to feel tired. He was tempted to go back to bed, but he knew if he did he'd feel worse than ever when it came to getting up again in an hour or two's time.

He went downstairs, switched on the radio and set some coffee percolating. Jacob used to like morning TV, but Ben couldn't bear to listen to it now. He ate a bowl of cereal standing by the kitchen window while he waited for the toast. There was a faint paleness in the sky, but not enough to suggest that daylight was on its way. He put his dish in the bowl and spread sunflower margarine on the toast. Sarah had weaned him off butter and he still felt guilty if he spread anything remotely cholesterol-friendly on his bread.

By the time he'd finished breakfast it was almost seven. He had to be at the studio later that morning for the day's shoot, a fashion piece for a magazine. But he still had time to kill. He poured himself another cup of coffee and sat at the kitchen table. The salt and pepper mill lay exactly where he'd left them the night before. At the far end of the table was a ring from the coffee mug he'd almost knocked over the previous morning. He'd meant to wipe it up but forgotten. The stain would stay there until he did something about it. He looked around the kitchen. Everything in it would remain exactly as it was now, unless he made it otherwise. There was no one to scold him for not washing the dishes, no one to move a chair out of place, to disturb a single spoon except him.

It struck him with a painful clarity how alone he was.

He wondered why he didn't move to somewhere smaller. The house was far too big for him, and the empty rooms only reminded him of what he'd lost. He felt no sentimental attachment to it. It was part of the life he'd had with Sarah, but that life had ended. It made more sense to sell it and buy a flat, big enough to have a darkroom, not so big that he felt lost in it. Time to move on, cut his losses and get on with building a new life instead of living in the shadows of the old.

So why don't you? He couldn't answer that. Any more than

he could explain why he had held on to the old toys and clothes of Jacob's that the Kales hadn't wanted instead of getting rid of them as he had Sarah's belongings. He knew that the two issues were connected, but he wasn't ready yet to face up to them.

Not at seven o'clock in the morning.

Make that five past, he thought, glancing at the clock. Hours yet before he had to be at the studio. Fuck it.

He went upstairs to get dressed.

It had grudgingly lightened when he set off for Tunford, as though the day felt as unenthusiastic about starting as he did. He turned on the car heater full to drive away the chill as he set off. With luck he'd miss the heaviest of the rush-hour traffic and shave something off the one-and-a-half-hour run. He would have three-quarters of an hour there at best, and might just catch the Kales at breakfast. He knew there was no real point to the journey, but the town had become his magnetic north. He swung to it automatically when there was no other draw on his attention.

The sleepless night had made him gritty-eyed and irritable. He yawned as he moved into the motorway's inside lane for the Tunford exit. There were flashing red lights up ahead. The slip road was walled off by a line of orange cones, clustered with workmen and earth-shifting machinery.

'Fucking great.' He could still get to Tunford from the next junction but it would take longer, cutting into the time he could spend there. His mood deteriorated with each mile, and dropped still lower after he took the next turn-off and found there were no road signs. He consulted the map. He would have to come in from the opposite direction to usual, joining the road that linked Tunford and the next town at the halfway point. Tossing the map on to the seat in disgust, he set off again, sure now that Kale and Jacob would have left by the time he arrived. Although Sandra would still be there, perhaps still in bed.

Ben had never seen her getting up.

It took him ten minutes to reach the connecting road. He pulled up at a give-way sign, waiting for a gap in the traffic. One of the cars approaching was a rusting Ford Escort. That's like Kale's, he thought, a moment before he recognised Kale himself behind the wheel.

Jacob was next to him.

The car shot by in a blat of exhaust. He briefly considered the possibility that Kale might be taking his son to school, but somehow he knew he wasn't. There was a fleeting regret that he wouldn't see Sandra getting up after all, then he flicked the indicator the other way and went after them.

He hung back, keeping other cars in between himself and the Escort as he followed. He was already certain where they were going even before the scrapyard's barbed-wire-topped wall came into sight. He drove past after Kale's car had disappeared inside, then made a tight U-turn and parked a little further down the road.

From there he could see anything that came in or out of the tall gates. He felt a tight anger at himself for not realising sooner what Kale was doing. All this time he'd never given a thought to the fact that when Kale was at work, Jacob wasn't around either. He remembered the smudges and oil stains he'd noticed on Jacob's clothes and wondered how he could have been so stupid. He should have known that Kale didn't want anything coming between him and his son.

Including school.

Still watching the gates, Ben took out his mobile and found the number of Jacob's social worker from his address book. A woman told him that Carlisle hadn't arrived yet. He rang off and tried ten minutes later, then ten minutes after that, ignoring the woman's growing irritation until finally Carlisle himself answered. The social worker sounded wary. *So you fucking should.* The question boiled out of him. 'Jacob's been missing school, hasn't he?'

There was a hesitation. 'Who's told you that?'

'Never mind who's told me. It's true, isn't it?'

Ben counted to three before the social worker answered. 'There has been some problem about attendance, but—'

'Some "*problem*"? He isn't going, is he?'

'Mr Murray, I don't—'

'*Is* he?'

Again there was a pause. 'The situation is being monitored.'

'What the fuck is that supposed to mean?'

'It means exactly that. And I don't think there's any call for being abusive.'

Ben took a deep breath. 'I apologise.' He waited until the desire to scream at the man faded. 'How long's this been going on?'

'That's something I really can't discuss.'

'Look, if you don't tell me I'll ask the school myself!'

'I'm afraid I'm not—'

'Has he been at *all* since he's been living with Kale? He hasn't, has he?'

He could hear Carlisle's reluctance. 'Er ... well, actually no, I don't believe he has.'

Ben didn't trust himself to speak.

'There's been some confusion over whether or not Jacob's been well enough to attend,' Carlisle said, defensive now. 'Mr and Mrs Kale — well, Mrs Kale, really — claims that he has a virus. We've warned them that we need to see a doctor's certificate, and that it's illegal to keep Jacob off school without one.'

And I bet that made a lot of difference. Ben stared across the road at the scrapyard. 'Kale's been taking him to work with him. That's why he isn't at school, not because he's got a "virus".'

'How do you know?' The officiousness had crept back into the social worker's voice. He sounded more annoyed than anything.

'Because I'm outside the yard now. They're still in there, if you want to check yourself.'

'You've actually seen them?'

'That's right.'

He could sense Carlisle trying to juggle this information into an acceptable package. 'Perhaps there's no one to look after him at home.'

Ben's patience ran out. 'Oh, for God's sake. If he's well enough to go to a scrapyard, he's well enough to go to school! There's nothing wrong with him! Kale just doesn't want him to go!'

'I'm sorry, Mr Murray, but I can't see how you can be such an expert on Mr Kale's motives. And even if he has taken Jacob to work today—'

'He has.'

'—even if he has we can't jump to conclusions on the basis of an isolated occurrence.'

'Of course it isn't isolated! His wife's been feeding you this "virus" crap to keep you off his back, and you're letting him get away with it!'

'We're not letting him get away with anything, Mr Murray—'

'Then why don't you do something?'

'If it's felt there's a need then we will, but a heavy-handed approach isn't going to help, and we don't feel it's currently called for. It's an extremely sensitive case, and we don't want to be seen to be—'

'Don't want to be seen? That's the bottom line, isn't it? You're frightened of getting bad press!'

Carlisle's voice had a quaver of suppressed anger. 'I don't need telling how to do my job, thank you, Mr Murray. And if you don't mind I'd like to get on with it now.'

'Are you going to do anything about Kale?'

'We'll look into it. Goodbye.'

'Hang on—!' Ben began, but Carlisle had already hung up. 'Bastard!' There was a crack of plastic as Ben struck the phone against the dashboard. He subsided, then smashed it down twice more, each time harder, and flung it on to the passenger seat.

He stared through the windscreen, incensed. He visualised walking into Carlisle's office, kicking his desk over, banging the man's head against the wall until it was bloodied and crushed. Then he thought about Kale, and considered walking into the scrapyard to face him. He imagined knocking him down, incapacitating him with a kick to his crippled knee, towering victoriously over his beaten figure, but even his anger wasn't enough to make that seem credible. With a cold breath of realism his temper was snuffed out and left him back in the car, impotent and bleak.

Brooding, he glared at the gates.

It was the rumble of his stomach that roused him. He stirred, stiff and uncomfortable. The rumble came again. It occurred to him that he was hungry, and with that realisation he suddenly remembered what he should be doing.

Oh Christ, he thought, the shoot.

He looked at his watch, swore, and reached for his mobile. The sight of it lying smashed on the seat next to him was like a smug chastisement. He tried it anyway. Dead. He threw it down and scrambled to start the ignition. 'Fuck, fuck, *fuck!*'

There was an irate blare of horn as he shot out into the road. He ignored it and tore back the way he'd come, praying for a phone box. But there was nothing except fields and fences. He reached the junction where he'd seen Kale's car, decided to go into Tunford to find a phone and changed his mind at the last moment, raking the corner in a squeal of rubber. The car vibrated as he hammered down the outside lane. He was making good time until he neared London, where the traffic thickened to the consistency of sludge. When he reached the studio there were no parking spaces, and he had to meander further and further away before he found one.

He ran back to the building and pounded up the stairs.

He was breathless and sweating as he burst through the door, the apology ready on his lips. Zoe looked up from where she was sitting reading a magazine.

There was no one else in the room.

He stood in the doorway, panting. 'Where are they?'

Zoe went back to the magazine, idly flicking over the page. 'Gone.'

'Gone? Gone where?'

'They didn't say. Somewhere there's a photographer, I expect.'

'Fuck.' He sagged against the door. 'Couldn't you have told them to wait?'

She flung the magazine down and jumped up. 'What the fuck do you think I did? It's half past fucking two, Ben! Where the hell have you *been*?'

He closed the door. 'I got delayed.'

'Delayed? Well, that's just fucking great! You get delayed, so I have to make excuses, get yelled at over the phone by the fucking photo editor – who, by the way, says he's going to bill you for the models' time – and look like a fucking idiot because I don't have a clue where you are! You weren't at your flat, I couldn't get you on your mobile! I mean, what the fuck was I supposed to do?'

His throat ached. He wiped the sweat from his mouth. 'I know, I'm sorry.'

'Yeah, so am I, Ben.' She raised her hand, let it fall as though abandoning whatever else she had been going to say. 'I mean, what the fuck's the *matter* with you lately? It isn't just today. All I seem to be doing is apologising and making excuses for you. You're turning up late, you're forgetting things. You don't even concentrate when you're *on* a shoot! You just don't seem to give a shit any more!'

'Look I know I fucked up, I've apologised, let's forget about it.'

'No, let's not!' she flared. 'I've been ignoring it for weeks! I'm getting sick of it!'

'Well, fuck off, then, nobody's making you stay!'

Her face went white. She stared at him, then went to where her coat was hanging.

'I'm sorry,' Ben said. She ignored him, picked up her bag from the sofa. 'I didn't mean it, all right?'

She went around him to the door.

'Zoe ...' He put his hand on her arm. She shrugged it off, not looking at him. 'Look, come on ...' He reached for her again.

'Don't touch me, you bastard!'

Her mouth was set and trembling. He could see that her eyes were wet. 'I'm sorry,' he repeated. 'I shouldn't have said that.'

'No, you fucking shouldn't.'

'Can I move away from the door now, or are you still going to walk out?'

She moved back into the room. She dropped her bag on the sofa and stood in front of him, waiting sullenly. Ben ran his fingers through his hair, pushing it from where it was stuck to his forehead. It had taken it weeks to grow back after he'd had it cropped. 'I know I've been a bit unreliable lately ...'

Zoe gave a snort.

'... and I know it's given you a hard time. It's just that I've had a lot on my mind, and there's a few things I need to sort out. But I promise I'll try and get my shit together in future, okay?'

She looked at him, unimpressed. 'I'm not stupid, you know.'

'What's that supposed to mean?'

'Oh, come on! You suddenly start carrying a big bastard of a telephoto lens around with you, you're never at home, you're always turning up late and rushing off somewhere. It doesn't take a fucking genius to guess what you're doing.'

And you thought you were being so subtle. To give himself time he took off his coat and hung it up. Underneath, his shirt was plastered to his back. He pulled it away from his skin. 'They don't deserve to have him.'

Zoe didn't bother to ask who he was talking about. 'It's a bit late to decide that, isn't it? I'm sorry, and everything, but they've got him. You're just going to have to live with it.'

Ben shook his head.

'So what good is spying on them with a telephoto lens going to do?'

He didn't answer.

'Fucking hell, Ben, can't you see you're getting obsessed? And while you're playing at peeping Tom your career's going down the fucking tubes!'

'It's not that bad,' he said, stung, but he wasn't sure which part he was denying. He could feel the blood rushing to his cheeks.

'Isn't it? And what's it going to achieve?'

'I want him back.'

It was the first time he had admitted it, even to himself. He felt a superstitious unease at having finally voiced the hope, as though now the gods, providence and pure shitty luck would conspire against it.

Zoe seemed about to argue further, but then abruptly gave up. She flopped down on to the sofa. 'I just hope you know what you're fucking doing.'

So do I. Ben went to the fridge and poured himself a glass of water. Zoe watched him, worriedly chewing a nail. 'Is there anything I can do?'

The offer touched him. 'Thanks, but you've put up with enough already.'

She nodded, but still seemed abstracted. 'Can I ask a favour, then?'

'Yeah, sure. What?'

'The shoot tomorrow. Do you mind if I don't stick around after I've helped you set it up?'

'Not if you don't want to,' he said, eager to appease. He refilled the glass. 'Have you got something else on?'

She studied her bitten fingernail. 'Not really. It's just that Daniel's one of the models, and I'd rather not see him.' She gave a shrug that was meant to be unconcerned. 'We had a big row last week.'

It took a few seconds for him to realise what she was talking about. The model who had given Zoe a lift home from the shoot on the beach had been called Daniel. Ben hadn't known he was involved in the next day's shoot – or if he had he'd forgotten. He'd even less idea that Zoe had continued seeing him.

I really have been losing touch, he thought.

'Oh,' he said. 'I'm sorry.'

'Yeah, well, that's how it goes.' She stood up and stretched, affecting indifference. 'Things don't always turn out how we'd like, do they?'

Ben drank the water and pretended he hadn't heard.

Kale propped the car door on top of the wrecked bonnet, manoeuvred it until it balanced, studied it, then shifted it slightly. He picked up another, unrecognisable car part and placed that with it, going through the same careful process before he was apparently satisfied. They were part of a selection of new parts he must have gathered over the previous week. It had become too dark in the evening for him to do much when he arrived home at night, but each weekend he would still be out in the garden, arranging his recent additions with all the care of a stamp collector gumming in a Penny Black.

A few feet away, Jacob sat in his usual place on the car seat, a thick duffel coat buttoned up to his chin as he tilted and spun a puzzle block. His father's sole concession to the weather was that he now wore track-suit bottoms instead of shorts. The breath from the two of them misted in the cold air, exhaust from biological engines.

Ben cupped his hands and blew into them without taking his eye from the images in the viewfinder. It was, without a doubt, fucking freezing. The chill cut through the woollen hat that he wore pulled down over his ears and the fleece-lined Gore-Tex coat. His fingers were numb from handling the camera, but gloves would have been too cumbersome to work in. He rubbed the tip of his nose and considered having another coffee. He was eking out his flask, knowing that once it was gone there would be nothing to warm him until he was back in the car.

The long-term view won. He thrust his hands into his coat pockets instead. 'Come on, do something,' he said to the magnified figure of Kale. But Kale typically showed no inclination of obliging. He continued his rearranging with the same painstaking deliberation as ever, moving the tortured pieces of metal around as if seeing how they would fit. Ben felt something almost work its way from his subconscious. He grabbed for it, but it was gone. He sighed impatiently as Kale moved the battered car door from the position he'd seemed happy with five minutes before, and carried it to another part of the garden.

'It's just scrap,' he muttered. 'As if it matters.'

He shifted his attention to the house. Kale and Jacob had already been in the garden when he arrived, but there was no sign of Sandra. Judging by the drawn bedroom curtains she still hadn't got up. Ben hoped the idle bitch was enjoying her lie-in. He'd spoken to her the night before, taping the conversation as a matter of course as he reminded her that it was his weekend for contact with Jacob again. She'd replied that Jacob's cold had flared up, but neither of them made any pretence that the lie was anything other than a formality. Their tone had been quite bantering. Flirting, almost. When Ben had put the phone down he'd had a hard-on.

He stared at the closed curtains, willing her to open them. They remained drawn. Fuck it, he thought. He sat back from the camera and reached for the Thermos flask. The hot steam from the coffee condensed on his cheeks as he cupped his hands around the plastic cup, huddling himself around it. The air was damp and smoky. A crow caw-cawed from somewhere near by, but other than that the woods seemed to have shut down. In the last week the autumn colours had given way to the dripping blacks and browns of winter, a time of year and colour scheme that Ben found depressing at the best of times, let alone when he had to sit out in it. The small oaks that formed his den were stripped bare except for a few dead leaves that still clung to them like early Christmas ornaments. He no longer felt invisible in them, although the branches themselves overlapped so densely that he doubted that anyone could see him from more than a few feet away. But it gave an added insecurity to the time he spent in the woods, and on those occasions when he heard other people in them he wouldn't dare move until he was sure they'd gone.

He took a king-sized Snickers bar from his pocket and tore it open. The chocolate was hard and brittle with cold. He took another drink of coffee to wash it down and found that it had already turned tepid.

'Piss,' he said. He drank it anyway and ate half the Snickers. The rest he put back in his pocket before looking through the viewfinder again. The curtains remained resolutely shut. He tilted the camera so he could see Jacob and Kale in the garden again.

Kale had started the balletic movements of his warm-up routine. Ben watched him stretch and twist without interest. He had seen it all countless times, but still not caught him doing anything else that threatened Jacob. He no longer really believed that he would. The single incident he'd witnessed seemed like something even Kale wouldn't be reckless enough to try more than once.

He didn't let himself consider why, in that case, he continued watching them.

Since he'd discovered that Kale and Jacob spent their days together at the scrapyard, surrounded by the crushed and wrecked remains of cars, Ben's entire perspective had somehow altered. Some of it he could put down to jealousy and anger that Kale was selfishly spending so much time with his son. But the apparent obliviousness they displayed towards each other in the garden now seemed to him more like an acute familiarity, each so conscious of the other's presence that it was taken for granted. There were times when he could almost believe that Jacob's tireless absorption with his puzzles and Kale's behaviour were somehow linked, their apparently separate tasks both working towards the same obscure end.

Then he'd remind himself that Jacob was autistic and Kale had one foot in the funhouse, and wonder if his own sanity wasn't flapping in the wind.

He sat back and blew on his hands again, bored. A flutter of movement showed on the first floor of the house. He looked through the camera and felt animation return as the bedroom curtains were jerked back. Sandra Kale squinted against the daylight and quickly turned away. Ben expected her to leave the room, but she went to the bed and sat on its edge, rubbing her temples. He grinned.

Heavy night, was it?

He quickly slipped the polarising filter on to the lens and refocused. The inside of the bedroom opened up to him. Sandra's hair was dishevelled, the dark roots forming a ragged dark line down the centre of her scalp. The grubby bathrobe was belted loosely around her waist. It fell open as she pushed her hands back through her hair, revealing a breast and nipple. When she lowered her arms the breast remained carelessly exposed. His finger pressed reflexively on the shutter release as she stood up wearily and the robe hung open, affording him a quick glimpse of her navel and the tuft of black hair at her crotch before she turned and went out.

The small frosted panel of the bathroom window became yellow as the light was switched on. Ben waited, only dimly aware of the touch of the camera's icy case on his fingers. *The bedroom. Go back to the bedroom.*

The bathroom light winked out. The bedroom door opened and Sandra reappeared. Her hair was wet, slicked straight back on her head like an otter pelt, the chemical blond now darkened to a metallic sheen. Her face looked both younger and less formed without its covering of make-up.

She hadn't bothered to fasten the bathrobe, and now she slipped it off. Her nipples were erect. He wondered if she'd had a shower, and his guess was confirmed a moment later when she used the bathrobe to dry her back. Dropping it on the bed she opened a drawer in the dressing table and rummaged around. Without taking anything from it she impatiently pushed it shut and picked up a white scrap of cloth from the floor. It was a pair of pants. She gave them a quick shake before stepping into them. The stretch marks stood out like scars on her pale stomach.

She put on a bra, also from the floor, then pulled on a pair of tight jeans. With a wiggle of her hips she hitched up the waistband and fastened the zip with a swift tug. She took a cream-coloured sweater from the back of a chair, pulling it over her head as she walked out.

He continued to watch the bedroom until it became obvious she wasn't coming back. He straightened, becoming conscious of the erection trapped painfully in his jeans. Trying to dismiss the now familiar, vaguely soiled feeling that watching her gave him, he manoeuvred until he was more comfortable and took the Snickers bar from his pocket. Biting into it, he idly looked down the hill towards the house. The diminutive figures of Kale and Jacob were still in the garden.

Kale was holding the engine over Jacob's head.

Ben took in the strained stance, the way the weight was seesawing in Kale's hands, and the chocolate turned to clay in his mouth. He dived for the camera, fumbling at it with cold and clumsy fingers. 'Oh, please, please, please,' he breathed, not sure if he was pleading for Jacob's safety or enough time to photograph what was happening.

The garden swung dizzyingly across the viewfinder, then Kale and Jacob came into sight. He hastily adjusted the focus and changed the exposure as the engine slowly wobbled higher in what had to be the final lift. The filter was still on the lens but there was nothing he could do about that. As the tendons stood out in Kale's neck and his mouth opened in a silent grimace, Ben switched on the motor and pressed the shutter release, praying there would be enough film left.

The camera began to whirr a second before Kale twisted to one side and dropped the weight. It thumped down beside Jacob, and in the same instant the film came to an end and started to rewind.

How much did I get? Enough? He didn't know. He quickly snatched the filter from the lens and changed the film, then ran off half of it while Kale was still doubled over. He made sure the lump of metal embedded next to Jacob was included in each frame.

Kale straightened and began to limp away. Ben slumped back. He realised he still had a mouthful of semi-masticated chocolate. He spat it out. The rest of the Snickers bar lay at his feet where it had fallen out of the wrapper. He looked at the plastic film container in his hand and gave it a little shake to reassure himself.

Jesus.

He'd nearly missed it. All this time, all those weeks, and when it finally happened he almost hadn't noticed. He'd been too busy watching a woman take her clothes off.

You pathetic bastard. Over the top of the camera he saw the once again reduced figure of Kale going into the shed. Ben knew that when he came out he would go over to Jacob and deliver another of his monologues. There was a hint of movement in the kitchen window that would be Sandra Kale, doing whatever. Even through the bitter taste of self-contempt, Ben felt his curiosity piqued, felt himself drawn to bend forward and peer through the viewfinder again, to involve himself vicariously in their lives. Deliberately, he removed the lens from the camera.

He packed everything away, then stood up and folded the stool. He looked around to make sure he hadn't forgotten anything. The nest of flattened grass he had made for himself looked as familiar as home.

He wouldn't be going back.

The coffee and adrenalin had worked on his bladder. Leaving his bag and the lens by the oaks, he moved a few feet away to urinate. His piss steamed like yellow acid on the dead grass. He shook off the last drops and was zipping up his fly when a barking shape exploded from the undergrowth behind him.

For an instant he thought it was Kale's bull terrier, but the dog was smaller and white, a Jack Russell cross. It set up a hysterical yapping and snarling, prancing just out of kicking range as he sank back against a tree with relief.

'Bess! Get here!'

Two men were walking through the trees towards him. *I never looked*, he thought, his relief turning cold. *The first time I didn't check to see if the woods were clear* ... The dog's barks subsided to low grumbles as it trotted away. 'Sorry about that, pal,' said the man who had shouted. He gave the still-growling dog a nudge with his foot. 'Quiet!'

Ben fought the urge to look over at where his camera equipment was half hidden by the oaks. The film of Kale and Jacob was amongst it. He managed a smile. 'It's okay. Just frightened me to death.'

'She's a noisy little bugger,' the man agreed, and Ben felt a lightening of hope as he began to turn away. But his companion didn't move. He was staring at Ben.

'This is the bloke who told Willie Jackson to fuck off in the pub,' he said. 'The one who had John's kid.'

The wood's silence pressed in on them. Ben could feel the smile stiffen on his face, but couldn't seem to let go of it. The man who'd recognised him was short and sallow-skinned, with pinched, rattish features. Ben couldn't remember seeing him in the pub, but then he hadn't taken much notice. Off to one side, the Jack Russell was bouncing and snuffling through the wet grass.

Its owner had stopped. He was older than the other man, in his fifties but with the burly look of a manual worker about him. He glanced towards the Kales' house, visible at the bottom of the hill. His face was stony as he looked back at Ben. 'What you doing here?'

'It's a public wood, isn't it?' Out of the corner of his eye Ben saw the dog heading towards his den.

'He asked what you're fucking doing here,' the small man said, enunciating the words slowly, as if he were talking to an idiot.

Ben could hear the dog nosing around by the oaks. He tried to summon the reckless anger that had possessed him in the pub, but it wouldn't come. 'I'm going for a walk, okay?'

'Not round here it fucking isn't.' The small man's fists were clenched. They were as undersized as he was, like knotted lumps of bone. He took an eager step forward, but the other's voice checked him.

'All right, Mick.'

The small man turned, angrily. 'Is it fuck all right! What's he doing in our fucking woods?'

'He isn't doing anything. He's going.' Without taking his eyes from Ben, he jerked his head in the direction of the road. 'Go on. Fuck off.'

Ben hesitated. The dog yapped from within the oaks, then the branches thrashed and it reappeared, shedding drops of water as it sprang through the tall grass. 'Okay, I'm going.'

Rotting acorns crunched like marbles under his boots as he began to walk away, planning to wait near by and come back for his gear later. He'd only gone a few paces when the small man stepped in front of him.

'You're not fucking going anywhere.'

'Mick,' the older man warned.

'He's taking the fucking piss coming round here!'

'It's not your problem, Mick. It's John's business, not ours.'

'So let's take the cunt down and let John sort him!'

Ben's mouth had gone dry. 'Look, I'll just go, okay? I'm not going to come back.'

The small man's grin was almost a snarl. 'Dead fucking right you're not.'

An impulse to run crossed Ben's mind, but that seemed too abject even for him. The older man considered, then gave a short nod. The one called Mick reached out to give Ben a shove. Ben knocked his hand away.

'Keep your fucking hands to yourself.'

The man's grin disappeared, but before he could respond the older one moved between them. 'All right, come on.'

Ben thought about the film waiting in the bag. Without a word he turned and set off down the hill, leading them away from the vulnerable roll of celluloid.

The hillside was slippery with mud, dotted with scrubby patches of brier and bramble. They had to skirt around them, cutting diagonally across the slope, and when they reached the track at the bottom Kale's house was out of sight. Ben walked ahead of his escort. His mind seemed to have slipped out of gear, so that he coasted along in neutral without taking in what was happening. Once he looked back up towards the woods. They seemed a long way away, and completely unfamiliar. He couldn't pick out the spot where he'd spent so many days watching.

He was at the other end of the lens now.

Ahead, he could make out the tall wire fence at the bottom of Kale's garden. From this angle the scrap metal formed a screen that blocked out any view of what lay on the other side. As he drew closer he could hear Kale's voice. Ben wondered at what point he'd come out of the shed.

'... in everything, everything locks in,' Kale was saying, invisible beyond the wall of wreckage. Ben pictured him squatting next to Jacob, looking earnestly at him. He slowed, listening. 'We can't see it, but it's only a matter of looking, looking in the right place, looking hard enough. And once you've seen it, seen the pattern—'

'John!' The small man slapped his hand against the wire fence, rattling it. 'John! Got somebody to see you!'

Kale's voice broke off. They waited by the gate, still unable to see much of the garden. Ben felt the slipping gears inside him spin loosely, felt an almost out-of-body detachment. There was a noise and then the bull terrier bounded over the lowest point of the scrap pile. The fence shook as the dog hit it. It stood on its hind legs against the mesh, growling. Then Kale appeared, and Ben suddenly spiralled back into the here and now of himself.

They looked at each other over the metal wreckage.

'Found him sneaking about in the woods, John,' the small man said, barely containing his excitement. 'Thought you'd want to see him.'

Kale didn't say anything. His bad knee made him ungainly as he stepped through a gap in the scrap pile, taking a bunch of keys from the pocket of his track-suit bottoms. He was red-faced, the fleecy cotton of his sweat shirt dark with perspiration. He unlocked the gate and swung it open. The bull terrier shot through. Ben tensed but it was more interested in the Jack Russell. The smaller dog had its ears flattened and its tail curled between its legs as the other sniffed at it. As if at some signal they bolted off together into the long grass.

'Bess!' the older man shouted after them.

'She'll be all right,' Kale said, looking at Ben. But Ben had moved to see through the gap to where Jacob was sitting in the car seat. A mangled car radiator and hub-cap lay on the floor in front of him like a sacrifice.

'Jacob!' The boy looked up, blankly, and something inside Ben's chest felt like it was being crushed. *Oh, God, he doesn't even remember me.*

Then Jacob's face split into a smile.

He pushed himself off the car seat and began running down the garden. Ben made to go through the gate but the breath was suddenly jolted from him as Kale hit his breastbone with the heel of his hand. He staggered back. Jacob stopped dead, his smile vanishing.

'I told you not to come here again,' Kale said.

Ben tried not to show how winded he was. 'I've got a right to see him.'

'You've got no rights.'

'What about him? Doesn't he have any?'

'I'll decide what's right for him.'

'Like keeping him away from school, you mean?'

Kale stared back without blinking. 'He's my boy. Nobody's going to tell me what to do with him.'

Before Ben could say anything else there was another sound from the garden. He turned and saw Sandra Kale picking her way across the scrap. She was wearing the clothes he'd seen her put on earlier. It seemed like weeks ago.

She stopped at the gate. 'All right, Sandra?' the small man said, leering. She ignored him, looked briefly at Ben, then fixed her attention on her husband.

'What's going on?'

'Take Steven inside,' Kale told her.

'Why?'

'Take him inside.'

'For Christ's sake, John——'

'Now.'

Her cheeks flushed, then she turned and roughly grabbed hold of Jacob's hand. Jacob grunted and pulled against her. 'Nonononono!' She took no notice, dragging him squealing towards the house. She lifted him up the steps by his wrist before slamming the door.

Ben faced Kale. He shook, but from anger now rather than fear. 'You don't give a shit about what's best for him, do you? You're only bothered about yourself!'

Kale started towards him. 'Look, John, don't do anything stupid,' the older man said, half-heartedly, but Kale took no notice. Ben automatically stepped back and hated himself for it.

Fuck this, he thought, and swung at Kale's head.

Kale deflected the punch effortlessly. He clamped a hand just above Ben's elbow, thrust his other under his outstretched arm, and Ben felt himself swung weightlessly against the fence. The wire gouged his face as he smashed into it, then his arm was jerked between his shoulders and pain exploded in his lower back as something rammed into his kidneys.

It pistoned into him twice more, and if he hadn't emptied his bladder in the woods it would have emptied itself then. It hurt so much his cry strangled in his throat, but there was no respite before he was yanked round. He had a glimpse of Kale, impassive even now, and then a fist drove into him just below his ribcage.

It felt as if his heart had stopped. He doubled up, saw Kale's knee fill his vision, and there was a burst of light and pain.

Images of sky and ground wheeled about him. From far away there was an impact of landing. He felt soil beneath his fingers, then a sensation of being lifted. Dark shapes came between him and the grey light above. A heavy shock seemed to shatter his face, then he was falling back. He heard the crack of his skull breaking as the man outside the pub landed on it with both feet. He lay on the pavement, brain, membrane and blood seeping through the splits in his head. He could feel them with his fingers, wide and deep and cold, full of pebbles and dirt, rutted with the patterns of bicycle wheels.

People were shouting near by. His lungs surged against the pain in his chest, sucked in air, and as though that had cleared a blockage he rolled over and vomited. There was blood in it. He put his hand to his nose. It felt odd. His mouth was swollen and bloody. The voices were still shouting. He looked and saw that Sandra Kale had both arms around Kale's chest and was straining to push him back. The older of the two men who'd brought Ben down was hovering beside them, one hand on Kale's shoulder in a token restraint. The small man's face was lit with excitement as he watched.

'Leave him, John, do you want to fucking kill him?' Sandra was yelling. 'Just let him go, you've done enough!'

'Move.' Kale's eyes were fixed on Ben.

'What, so you can show everybody how fucking hard you are? Do you think anybody fucking *cares*?'

With a sudden twist he pushed her aside. She fell against one of the support posts, shaking the entire fence.

'Come on, John, enough's enough,' the older man said, but he made no attempt to stop him. Ben tried to get up but everything swung around. There was no strength in any of his limbs. Kale gripped the front of his coat in both hands and lifted him half off the ground.

'Next time I'll kill you.'

He let him drop. Ben fought the wave of nausea the movement caused. Kale turned towards his wife. She was clinging to the fence post, bleeding from a graze on her cheek. He levelled a finger at her.

'Don't ever get in my way again.'

He limped back into the garden. Sandra Kale wiped her cheek and stared at the blood smeared on her hand.

'You all right, Sandra?' asked the older man.

She didn't look at him. 'What do you think?' Unsteadily, she pushed herself off the fence and followed her husband.

There was a whoop from the small man. 'Fucking hell! Eh? Fucking *hell*!' His eyes were feverish as they fixed on Ben. 'Bet you won't fucking come round here again, cunt, will you?'

He came forwards, fists balled. Ben tried to push himself to his feet.

'Leave him, Mick.'

The small man turned in surprise. 'Why? Come on, Bri—'

'I said fucking leave him!' He walked over to Ben and took a large handkerchief from his pocket. He held it out. 'I didn't know this was going to happen.'

Ben knocked his hand away. He felt like crying. 'What the fuck did you think he was going to do?'

The man stood there for a moment, then put the handkerchief away and went to the edge of the track. He gave a sharp whistle. 'Bess!'

There was a rustling in the bushes further up the track. The Jack Russell emerged and ran towards him, tongue flapping in a dog grin. It trotted at his heels as he began walking back down the track. The small man followed sullenly a few steps behind.

For the first time Ben noticed the faces peering over fences and walls along the line of houses. One by one they disappeared, absolving themselves of any involvement. He climbed to his feet. He felt sick and weak. He leaned against the fence. His mouth and nose were swollen. Several teeth were loose. He probed them, testing them with his tongue, rubbing his bruised stomach. He turned to spit blood, and saw he wasn't alone after all.

The bull terrier was watching from the other side of the track.

Ben looked around for something to defend himself with — a stick, anything. There was nothing. He risked a glance at the dog again. A low rumbling came from its throat. Slowly, he pushed himself off the fence, not making eye contact with it. He took a hesitant step.

It came for him.

He fell back against the fence, lashing out with his feet in an attempt to keep it away from his groin and body. The bull terrier made a noise like an unoiled buzz-saw as it caught his foot in its mouth and shook it. Ben gripped the wire mesh to keep from falling, arms spread out across it in a posture of crucifixion. His foot felt as if it were in a vice. The dog's teeth pierced the thick leather of his boot. It let go of his foot when he stamped at its head, but slashed its teeth across his calf, tearing cloth and muscle. He heard shouts and saw the two men running back towards him. The Jack Russell bitch raced ahead of them. It ran up to the fence, barking excitedly, and the bull terrier rounded on it. The smaller dog yelped as it was bowled on to its back.

'Get off, you bastard!' the older man yelled as he pounded up. He tried to kick the dog away as the Jack Russell's screams grew more hysterical. Then Kale was there. He pushed the other man to one side and grabbed hold of the bull terrier's studded collar. It gave a hacking cough as he yanked it back, holding it so only its hind feet were on the floor. It made another lunge for the smaller dog but he cuffed it across its head and gave it a single, violent shake. Gasping, it subsided, its muzzle shiny and wet.

'Oh, Christ, oh, Christ,' the older man moaned, going down on his knees. The little dog was spasming on the floor, its white coat matted from the blood that pumped from its throat and stomach. 'Oh, look at her, look at her!' He slid his hands under it and held it to his chest. It twitched spastically, smearing his coat as he tried to staunch the wounds with the same handkerchief he'd offered

Ben. 'Your fucking dog, John! I'll kill it! I'll fucking kill it!'

Kale still held the bull terrier by its collar. It wheezed for breath, but the frenzy had gone out of it. He looked without expression at the Jack Russell, then turned and thrust his dog towards the gate.

'In.'

The dog ran into the garden, stubby tail wagging. Kale followed it.

The Jack Russell's spasms were dying down. Its owner was crying. 'Did you hear what I said?' he shouted into the garden. 'I'll have it! I'll fucking—!'

The explosion sent a cloud of birds clattering into the air. Ben and the two men froze, stunned, as its echoes died away. The small man, no longer smiling, ran to the fence and stared inside.

'Oh fuck! Oh fucking hell!'

Ben hobbled over, desperately trying to see over the scrap. The bull terrier lay in the centre of the garden. Most of its head was blown away. One of its legs twitched, then was still.

Kale stood over it with a shotgun.

'Fucking hell, John, you shouldn't have just shot him!' The small man sounded appalled.

Kale cracked open the shotgun and let a shell fall from one of its chambers. 'It's my dog. I'll do what I like.'

He looked at Ben as he spoke. Then he snapped the gun closed and limped back towards the house.

'Bastard,' the older man said, weeping over the motionless dog in his arms. He was covered in blood and shit. 'Bastard.'

The smaller man took his arm. 'Come on, Brian.'

They set off down the track. Ben waited until they were well ahead before he followed them.

Chapter Sixteen

—————◆◆◆—————

The solicitor took her time going through the photographs. Her eyebrows dipped into a frown when she saw the ones showing Kale lifting the engine above Jacob's head, rose for those of Sandra Kale and the man in the bedroom. She gave Ben a quick glance before moving on.

He waited silently until she had finished, resisting the urge to try to make himself more comfortable. The chair was well upholstered, but even after a week his lower back was still painful. The swelling around his nose and mouth had mostly gone, and he hadn't lost any teeth, but the flesh under his eyes remained discoloured. His calf itched unbearably as the chunk the dog had taken out of it slowly mended.

Usherwood came to the end of the photographs. She lay them on the desk in front of her, absently straightening the edges. 'Well ...' She drew a deep breath, cleared her throat. 'I can see why you're concerned.'

He waited for her to say something else. She looked down at the photographs again, chewing one corner of her mouth in thought. 'How long have you been watching the house?' she asked without looking at him.

Ben felt himself colouring. 'Quite a while.' He didn't let himself elaborate or make excuses.

She gave a small smile. 'Perhaps it's as well there aren't stricter privacy laws.'

'I wouldn't have cared if there were.'

It came out more emphatically than he intended. The solicitor looked again at the photograph on top of the pile, as though it could tell her something it hadn't already. Her fingers lightly touched the images of torn metal, as though they still possessed the power to cut her. 'So what exactly are you asking me?'

'I want to know how to get Jacob back.'

She pushed the photographs to one side with a sigh. 'I'm afraid it isn't that simple. Courts are very loath to take a child away from his or her parents — or parent in this case. And in Jacob's case it's compounded because he's already had the trauma of being moved from one home environment. It's extremely unlikely that anyone would want to submit him to another upheaval unless it was felt there was absolutely no other alternative.'

'What alternative is there? Leaving him in a dump full of scrap metal, with a stepmother who whores around and a father who's a f—' He stopped himself. '—a maniac?'

'I'm not saying nothing would be done, but taking a child from its parents is seen as a last resort. It would have to be felt that there was a real risk to Jacob in remaining where he is.'

'Kale dangles half a hundredweight of metal over his head. Isn't that risk enough?'

'But you admit yourself that he hasn't been physically harmed. I'm only pointing out what the situation is, Mr Murray.'

'I know, I know. I'm sorry.' He made an effort to calm down. 'What will they do?'

Usherwood sat back. 'Once you've voiced your concerns to the local authority they'll hold a case conference to decide what, if anything, needs to be done. If it was thought there was enough of a risk of harm to Jacob — either physical or emotional

– they might put him on the Child Protection Register. If the risk is considered significant, then an application for a care order can be made through the courts, and the child placed with a foster family. But that's only in very extreme cases. Which this isn't.'

'So there's no chance of them letting me have him,' he said, flatly.

A rare look of sympathy crossed her face. 'I'm sorry. You could make a residence application anyway. But for Jacob to be permanently taken from his father it would have to be felt that the situation was so bad there was absolutely no way he could ever safely live with him. And, to be blunt, that isn't likely to happen.'

'What about the photos? Don't they count for anything?'

She picked them up again, but she was shaking her head as she fanned them out. 'The fact that his wife's having an affair – or affairs,' she added, with a quirk of her mouth, 'isn't going to be seen as significant one way or another, whether she's accepting payment for it or not. Even prostitutes are allowed to have children. As for Kale himself . . .' She leafed through the photographs until she found one of him holding the block of metal above Jacob. The polarising filter had thrown out the exposure, but Ben had been happy to come out with anything at all. 'Yes, these show he's put his son at risk. On one occasion. There's no proof that he'll continue to do so.'

She held her hand up to forestall Ben's protest. 'He has a garden full of scrap metal – he'll be told to get rid of it. He's been reckless when he's weight-training – he'll be told to be more careful in future. The most serious charge against him is that he's been deliberately keeping Jacob away from school, but provided he starts toeing the line there, then even that won't weigh too heavily against him. I know you say he's unbalanced and dangerous, but there's nothing at present to actually prove it. Or to justify insisting he has a psychological assessment.'

Ben tasted a bitterness in his throat. 'How about beating me to a pulp and blowing his dog's brains out?'

'Didn't you say you tried to hit him first? And in front of witnesses?'

He looked down at his hands. 'What about the dog?'

'I'm afraid if the police aren't going to take action there's nothing we can do.'

Ben tiredly rubbed his face, accepting the truth of what she said. After he had retrieved his equipment from the woods he had driven – slowly – to the local police station in Tunford. The desk sergeant had perked up when he'd limped in, battered and bloodstained, but that had changed when he'd realised who he was talking to.

Ben wondered if there was anyone in the town who didn't regard him as lower than something they'd scrape off the bottom of their shoe.

'What exactly were you doing in the woods behind the house, sir?' the sergeant had asked.

Walking, Ben had told him, and held his stare while the policeman waited in silence for him to elaborate. He had tried to hold his anger in check as the questions became almost taunting in their bias. 'Sounds to me like he was defending himself, sir,' the policeman commented at one stage, with insulting courtesy. 'If I were you I'd think myself lucky to have got off so lightly.'

Ben knew then he was wasting his time, but he still tried. 'He shot his dog, for Christ's sake!'

'Perhaps he was just being public-spirited, sir. If it had attacked you, like you claim, it'd have to be destroyed anyway.'

'So it's okay for him to go around firing off a shotgun when he's got a child in the house?'

'Provided he's got a certificate for it, and I expect he has. He's a responsible man, sir. Not like some. He knows how to handle firearms.' The sergeant gave a supercilious smile. 'Besides, you get a lot of vermin in those woods.'

Ben had given up. He hurt all over, and reaction had left him weak and exhausted. He needed to have the bite dressed and his smashed nose looked at.

More than anything, he needed to get away from that town.

'Drive carefully, sir,' the sergeant had said as he left. 'You look a bit worse for wear. You don't want to get arrested.'

Usherwood was looking at Ben with concern. 'I know none of this is what you want to hear, but I can only tell you what would probably happen. There are very definite rules laid down in situations like this.'

Ben managed a smile. 'I didn't think there were any other situations like this.'

The solicitor looked down at the photographs. 'Can I keep these?'

He nodded. He'd printed several sets of the best ones. All the others, including those of Sandra Kale, naked and clothed, he'd burned.

'I'm not saying the local authority will ignore the evidence. If nothing else it should make them apply pressure to ensure Kale allows you your contact to Jacob,' Usherwood said, with the air of offering an unconvincing consolation prize.

'And what happens if he still refuses?' *When.* 'Will they take Jacob off him then?'

'No, but you've a legal entitlement. He's got to let you see him eventually.'

Ben gently kneaded the bridge of his nose. It was still tender. 'You've met him. Did he strike you as the sort of man who's got to do anything?'

He stood up while she was still considering that.

'I'll be in touch.'

There were too many hours in the day now that he wasn't travelling up to the woods behind Kale's house. He didn't know what to do with the free time, and so he filled it by working. Zoe was clearly relieved that he was reliable again, seeing it as a sign that things were returning to normal. But Ben couldn't even remember what 'normal' was any more. It was something that had stopped, perhaps for good, when Sarah had died. If anything he felt more out of synch with himself than ever. He seemed to be functioning on a purely surface level, going through the motions of talking, eating, going out, but without any of it making any impression on him. He couldn't even say he felt depressed, because he wasn't really feeling anything. It was as though he were using only a single room of a large house. Sometimes he was aware of the rest of the rooms waiting for him to retenant them, but he felt no urge to leave his emotional bed-sit. That would involve asking himself what his next step was going to be.

And facing up to the fact that there wasn't one.

He had come to the end, without accomplishing a thing. Kale wasn't going to change. He might appear to if he was forced, but only until he was left alone again, and then Ben would be in the same position as he was now. The closest he would be able to get to Jacob would be through a telephoto lens.

He'd already been down that route.

Two weeks after he had visited Ann Usherwood he was no nearer a decision. He hadn't been in touch with her again. There was no point. He was still only going through the motions of his life when the phone call came through to the studio. Zoe answered it, then cupped her hand over the receiver.

'Guy for you. Won't say who he is, but says it's important.'

Ben was on a pair of stepladders, replacing a light. 'Tell him I'm busy.'

He heard her repeat it. The model finished checking herself in the mirror. 'Do you think this top needs pinning at the back?' she asked, pulling it between her shoulder blades so it was tighter across her breasts.

He didn't really care but tried to apply himself to the question.

'He says to tell you his name's Quilley,' Zoe said from behind him.

Ben's mind emptied.

'Come on, Ben, do you want to talk to him or not?'

He climbed down from the stepladders. When she held out the phone for him he realised he still had the light bulb in his hand. For a moment he couldn't think what to do with it. He put it on the window ledge and took the receiver.

'So am I pinning this, or what?' asked the model.

He motioned vaguely for Zoe to sort it out. She gave him an odd look before she moved away. He put the phone to his ear.

'Hello?'

'Hello, Mr Murray. Long time no see, as they say.'

The anger seared through him without warning. Its strength was debilitating, like a fever. 'What do you want?'

'Just a chat, that's all. Are you still there, Mr Murray?'

There were so many insults and accusations clamouring to be shrieked they closed his throat. If the detective had been in the same room as him Ben would have gone for him. 'I've got nothing to say to you.' His voice was thick.

'You're still a little worked up, I can tell. You shouldn't have taken what happened personally. It was a simple business matter, that's all. Like I told you, I'm in the information business. If one person doesn't want to buy, then you take your wares somewhere else.'

'I don't give a fuck. You're scum. You're a piece of shit.'

He was dimly aware of Zoe and the model staring over at him. He turned his back.

'You're entitled to your opinion, of course,' Quilley said. 'But before you get too carried away I'll come to the point. While we're on the subject of information, I've come by some that I think will interest you. In fact, it's fair to say that I know it will.'

Curiosity won over the desire to slam down the receiver. 'About Jacob?'

'Indirectly, I suppose. Or perhaps directly, depending on how you look at it. Let's say it has a bearing on the current situation.'

'What is it?'

He heard Quilley chuckle. 'Ah, now that's the question, isn't it? And of course the next one is how badly do you want to find out?'

'Why should I believe you know anything?'

'I'd have thought you of all people wouldn't need to ask that, Mr Murray. You should know from personal experience that I'm rather good at digging around. Particularly when I think there's something there to be dug up, as it were.'

'So why have you waited all this time?'

'Let's say I found myself in something of a quiet patch, professionally speaking, so I decided to tidy up some loose ends.'

'You mean your work's dried up.' Ben couldn't keep the satisfaction from his voice. 'Stopped getting recommendations, have you?'

'I wouldn't worry yourself about that, Mr Murray. The fact is that I've got something to sell. What we need to establish now is whether you want to buy.'

'I don't know until I've got some idea what it is.'

'If I told you I'd be putting myself at a disadvantage, wouldn't I? I'm afraid you'll just have to take it on faith.' The detective's regret was cheerfully insincere.

Ben chewed his lip. 'How much do you want?'

'Well, now, that's open to negotiation, isn't it?'

'I've not said I'm interested yet. I know what Kale's been doing, if that's all you're offering.'

There was a momentary pause, then another chuckle. 'Who

said it was anything to do with him? But I tell you what,' Quilley went on as Ben was absorbing this, 'you have a think about it for a day or two. Ask yourself how much your stepson is worth to you. And then when you've decided give me a ring.'

The detective let this sink in. 'A word of advice, though,' he added. 'I wouldn't leave it too long. Nice talking to you, Mr Murray.'

He met Colin in a pub that evening. It was crammed with after-work City drinkers. There were no seats left but he found a corner to stand in by the cigarette machine and the bar. He ordered a pint while he waited. Colin was late. When he pushed through the pub doors his hair and overcoat shoulders were dappled with melting snow. 'First fall of the year and it isn't even Christmas yet,' he complained, brushing it off. Ben didn't say anything. The prospect of a Christmas without either Sarah or Jacob made him feel as if he had stepped out into a black void. It had been something else he had avoided thinking about.

It seemed to be a day for having things thrust on him.

'I can't stay long,' Colin said, shucking off his overcoat. 'I'm, uh, meeting somebody in an hour.'

'You mean Jo?'

'Er, yeah. Do you want a drink?'

'I'm okay. I'll get you one.' Ben turned to the bar, giving Colin a chance to get over his discomfort. The affair showed no signs of dying out, but he still seemed to find it embarrassing to talk about.

'So what did Quilley actually say?' Colin asked, taking the lemon from the tonic he'd requested and nibbling at it. He'd told Ben it was an appetite suppressant. If nothing else infidelity had made him cut down on drinking and lose weight. The cigar habit had been quickly snuffed as well. Ben wondered if Maggie was as unsuspicious of the sudden change as Colin appeared to believe.

He outlined the conversation with the detective. Colin sipped his tonic as he listened attentively, every inch the solicitor. 'Well, you've got two choices,' he said when Ben had finished. 'You either tell him to fuck off, or pay up and hope he really does know something useful. If you do that you've got to decide how much you're prepared to fork out, and how to make sure Quilley doesn't stiff you completely.'

'You think it might be worth taking a chance, then?'

'Can you just ignore it?'

Ben reluctantly shook his head.

'So there's your answer. But make him give you some idea what it is he's selling before you pay him, otherwise he might just take the money and tell you that Kale has All-Bran for breakfast. If he really does know something, and he's as strapped for cash as he sounds, he'll give you some sort of clue. If he won't then he's probably just trying to rip you off.'

'If he is I'll fucking kill him.'

Colin dropped his lemon rind into an ashtray. 'That'll certainly help you get Jacob back, won't it?'

The anger died as quickly as it had appeared. After the vacuum of the past two weeks the sudden onslaught of emotions was like eating over-rich food after a fast. 'There's no guarantee that what he tells me'll help anyway,' he said, despondent again.

'No, but there's only one way you can find out.'

Ben stared into his beer but found no inspiration.

'If you decide to risk it you still shouldn't let him think you're too eager. He'll only try to screw you for as much as he can if you do.'

'He warned me not to leave it too long.'

'He's hardly going to tell you there's no rush, is he? I'd make the bastard sweat for a day or two. Play it cool.' Colin looked at his watch. 'Sorry, I'm, er, going to have to go.'

'Where are you meeting her?'

Colin tried to hide his awkwardness with activity, putting his glass on the cigarette machine, slipping on his overcoat. 'Just some restaurant in Soho. Not Lebanese,' he added, wryly.

'What have you told Maggie?'

He regretted the question immediately. Colin looked momentarily stricken. 'She thinks I'm working late. What a cliché, eh?' He smiled wanly. 'Let me know what happens.'

Ben said he would. He watched him walk out of the pub, the expensive coat still wet on the shoulders, the thinning hair now becoming an actual bald patch, and hoped he hadn't spoiled his mood. Then he thought about Maggie, at home with the two boys, and felt sorry for her too. He hoped for Colin's sake the girl was worth it. He began feeling sorry for her as well before he caught himself.

Fuck it, he thought, resisting the drift towards self-pity. Who am I to feel sorry for anyone?

He finished his beer. Then, because it was still snowing outside and he had nothing better to do, he bought himself another.

He followed Colin's advice for a whole day before he gave in and phoned Quilley. The resurgence of hope had unsettled him, and when he heard the mechanical tones of an answerphone the anticlimax was killing. He waited ten minutes and tried again, with no more success. He continued trying throughout the afternoon, but each time was greeted by the secretary's recorded voice telling him to leave his name and number. He hung up without speaking. When there was no answer by the early evening he accepted that he would have to wait until the next morning.

He got the answerphone then as well.

This time he left a message, brusquely telling Quilley to call. After that he felt better for a while, knowing he had committed himself. It was up to the detective now.

But Quilley didn't get in touch.

Ben waited another day before he rang again. He phoned from home, and then from the studio, where he and Zoe were preparing for a shoot. He was so accustomed to hearing the recording that it took him by surprise when someone answered.

The secretary sounded even more truculent than he remembered. 'He's not here,' she snapped when he asked for the detective. She didn't enlarge.

'When will he be back?'

'No idea.'

'Will it be later today or tomorrow?'

'I've told you, I don't know.'

He tried not to lose his temper. 'Is there another number where I can get hold of him?'

There was a bitter laugh. 'Not unless you want to ring the hospital.'

'He's in hospital?' Some of his paranoia receded at hearing there were no darker motives behind the detective's absence. 'What's the matter with him?'

'He got beaten up.'

The paranoia returned. 'Who did it?'

'How should I know?'

'When did it happen?'

'I don't know, a couple of days ago,' she snapped. 'Look, it's no good asking me anything. I don't work for him any more. He owes me two months' wages, and I bet I'm *really* going to see that now he's stuck in there. I've only come in to collect some things. I don't even know why I bothered to pick up the phone.'

He sensed she was about to hang up. 'Just tell me which hospital he's in.'

She gave an irritable sigh, but told him before she broke the connection. Ben slowly set down the receiver. There were probably dozens of people who would like to give Quilley a kicking, he told himself. It didn't necessarily mean anything. He could have been mugged, even.

But he didn't believe that.

The shoot wasn't scheduled for a couple of hours. He promised Zoe that he'd be back in plenty of time and drove to the hospital. It took him a while to locate Quilley's ward. He'd been prepared to make up some story so he'd be allowed to see him, but it was all-day visiting. No one stopped him as he walked in.

The detective's bed was half screened by striped curtains. He didn't appear to notice Ben. He was lying flat on his back and wore a creased blue hospital gown. A drip fed into his arm from the chrome stand beside him. His face was so blackened with bruising it looked as though he'd been burnt. A dressing was taped across his nose, and another covered one ear. The hair around it had been shaved. An old man's silver stubble frosted his hollowed cheeks and the loose wattles of his throat.

He was staring at the ceiling. He glanced briefly at Ben when he reached the bedside, then away again. He showed neither recognition nor interest.

'Your secretary told me where you were,' Ben said.

Quilley didn't respond.

'It's Ben Murray,' Ben added, not sure how aware the man was.

'I know who you are.'

The voice was a weak croak. Quilley's gaze remained fixed above him.

'She told me you'd been beaten up.' Ben paused. 'Who did it?'

Nothing.

'Was it Kale?'

The detective's eyes might have flickered, but that was all.

'It was, wasn't it?'

'Leave me alone.'

Some of his front teeth were missing, Ben noticed. He sat on the armrest of the vinyl chair. 'Have you told the police?' There was no response. 'You told him you'd found something out, didn't you? What did you do, say you'd tell me if he didn't pay you? Then what? Were you going to go with whoever offered the most, or take money from both of us? Except Kale beat the shit out of you instead.'

Quilley didn't look at him, but his chin was quivering.

Ben leaned nearer. A smell of antiseptic and unwashed body came from the bed. 'What did you find out?'

The detective stared resolutely at the ceiling. The tremor in his mouth grew more pronounced. His Adam's apple looked as though it would break through the skin as he swallowed.

'I'll pay you,' Ben said.

Quilley closed his eyes. A tear ran out from the corner of one and ran sideways towards his ear.

'Please. It's important. Was it something about Kale?'

It seemed that Quilley was going to ignore this also. Then he moved his head fractionally from side to side.

'What, then? His wife? I know she has men round while Kale's at work. Is that it? Or is it something else?' There was no further movement. Ben took a deep breath, trying to control his frustration. 'Why won't you tell me? Because you're frightened of him?'

The detective turned his head away.

Ben stood up. He'd thought he'd feel some satisfaction in seeing the man broken. He didn't, but he didn't feel any pity either. He walked away from the bed without another word. On the way out he stopped at the nurses' station. A plump young nurse was writing behind it. She looked up as Ben approached.

'I'm a friend of Mr Quilley's. Does anyone know what happened to him?'

It took her a moment to place who he was talking about. 'Oh, the man who was beaten up? No, I don't think so. He says he can't remember. We think it must have been more than one person, though, from the extent of his injuries. There's a lot of internal bruising. He's lucky he wasn't killed.'

Ben thought he was very lucky.

Chapter Seventeen

He felt the pull of Tunford even after he had driven past the turn-off that led to it. For several miles afterwards he was conscious of where it lay behind him, as though part of his brain were looking backwards, watching it recede.

The snow had lingered here, piles of dirty white melting slowly by the roadside, staining the bare trees and dead grass like mould. Ben had turned the car heater up high, but the frigid damp still seemed to cling to his clothes.

Or perhaps it was him it was clinging to.

The industrial estate had an abandoned Sunday air about it. The town itself looked similarly deserted. One or two windows of the terraced houses were decorated with tinsel and coloured baubles, but they seemed unconvincing in the grey daylight. When he reached the street where the Patersons lived he saw that more of the boarded-up houses had gone. The strip of semi-levelled rubble now extended halfway along the row of terraces. The JCBs and earth-shifting machinery stood patiently amongst the bricks, waiting to be loosed on the rest.

Ben parked outside the house and knocked on the door. The window box held only soil. The glass above it was misted over. He stamped his feet, feeling the dank atmosphere penetrate his lungs.

The door was opened. Ron Paterson nodded a greeting

and stood back to let him in. The kitchen smelled of roasting meat. A coal fire burned in the small grate set into the tiled fireplace. Ben felt the warmth close around him, snuffing the chill in an instant.

Paterson closed the door. 'Give me your coat.'

Ben took it off and handed it to him. He went out to hang it at the bottom of the stairs. 'You sure you don't mind me coming?' Ben asked when he came back.

'I'd have said if I did.' He nodded at the table. 'You might as well sit down.'

Ben had phoned the day before to ask if he could call around. Paterson had told him to come before lunch — he'd called it 'dinner' — the next day. He hadn't asked why. It didn't need to be said that it would be something to do with Jacob.

'How's Mary?'

Paterson was filling the kettle. 'In hospital.'

'Is she all right?' Ben had thought she must be upstairs.

'They're doing tests.' He said it matter-of-factly, keeping whatever he felt out of sight. He plugged in the kettle. 'Want a cuppa?'

He set out the teapot and mugs, then came and sat at the table. 'So what can I do for you?'

'You said something last time I was here. About Sandra Kale.'

'I said a lot of things.'

'But you started to say that you'd heard something about her, and then you stopped. I wondered what it was you'd heard.'

Ben had remembered the conversation after he'd visited Quilley. He knew he might have made the journey just to hear a piece of useless gossip. But it wasn't as if his Sundays were so fun-filled any more that he couldn't spare the time.

Paterson sucked on a tooth. He didn't look at Ben, but

he didn't give the impression of looking away from him either. 'Just rumours.'

'What rumours?'

'I don't spread gossip.'

'It might be important.'

Paterson considered that. 'Why?'

Ben told him.

Jacob's grandfather listened without making any comment. Once he got up to unplug the kettle, although he didn't bother making any tea. Other than that he didn't move as Ben described Kale's activities in the garden, and Sandra's in the bedroom. Ben told him how Jacob was being kept off school, and what had happened when the two men had found him in the woods. He left nothing out, except the fact that he'd almost allowed himself to be sidetracked by Sandra Kale's ruttish sexuality. He wanted to emphasise how Kale was unbalanced, not only unfit to bring up Jacob but an actual danger to him.

But he saw the grimness in Paterson's face and knew there was no need.

There was a silence when he had finished. The coals of the fire tumbled in on themselves in a swarm of sparks. The gas oven hissed softly. Paterson went over and turned it down.

'We don't keep drink in the house,' he said, fetching Ben's coat.

He took Ben to the workingmen's club. It was non-political, an old and ugly brick building with an even uglier 1960s extension tacked on to its front. An elderly fat man in a three-piece brown suit sat behind a table in the entrance. He greeted Paterson with a wheezed 'Afternoon, Ron' as he pushed across a book for him to sign. Ben wrote his own name in the 'guest' column and followed him inside.

It was a big room with a high stage at one end. Brightly

coloured paper streamers ran from the edge of the ceiling to its centre, and already deflated balloons hung limply on the walls. The stage itself was fringed with gold plastic tassels that could have been a part of the Christmas decorations except for a tired look of permanence about them. Round, dark wood tables and matching stools filled the floor space with no clear aisles in between. A few were occupied, mainly by men, but most were empty.

Ben tried to buy the drinks but Paterson would have none of it. 'You're my guest,' he said, in a tone that spoke of protocols and tradition. They carried their pints to a table by the window. Paterson exchanged nods with one or two of the other customers but didn't stop to talk. They sat down, taking the top off their beer in the ritual that had to precede any conversation. The beer was cold and gassy. Ben stifled a belch as they set down their glasses.

The lull wasn't so much awkwardness as not knowing where to start.

'Gets busy in here at nights. Specially weekends.' Paterson lifted his chin towards the stage. 'Get some good acts on, as well.'

'Right.'

'Used to come in here a lot, Mary and me. Before we moved to London, and then for a bit when we first moved back. Till Mary got really bad. It's difficult now, though.' He looked around the room as if noticing it for the first time.

They took another drink.

'I can't vouch for anything,' Paterson said, abruptly coming to the point. 'It's only what people have said. Nothing specific.'

Ben nodded.

Paterson studied his pint. 'She's supposed to have a bit of a history, that's all.'

'History?'

'Been a bit of a bad 'un. Taking money for it.' He looked across at Ben to make sure he understood.

'You mean she was a prostitute?'

'That's what I've heard. One of the club members' sons had a mate who was based at Aldershot with Kale. Reckoned she'd sold it to half the regiment before she married him.' He pursed his lips disapprovingly. 'Sounds like she's still at it, from what you've said.'

Ben felt let down. Even if it were true it wasn't the revelation he'd hoped for. 'Was there anything else?'

He could see Paterson struggling with some decision. 'There were stories about some trouble she'd been in,' he said at last. 'Other trouble. But I couldn't tell you what. I don't listen to that sort of thing.'

'Do you know anybody who might know?'

The other man considered, then shook his head.

'How about the member's son you were talking about?'

'The family moved away last year. Couldn't tell you where they are now.' He must have read the frustration in Ben's face. 'You thought I could tell you something to help get him back.'

It wasn't a question. Ben hadn't mentioned anything about why he wanted to know, only that he was worried about Jacob. 'I've been told there's no chance.'

Paterson took a pull from the pint. 'John Kale's not going to let him go. It won't matter what anybody tells him.'

Ben didn't answer.

'He was always possessive. Didn't like our Jeanette going out or doing anything without asking him. He was bad enough that way then. Now he's got his son back he won't let nobody take him again.' He tapped his finger on the table for emphasis. 'I mean nobody. And I wouldn't like to say what'll happen if anyone tries.'

'You think I should just give him up.'

A weariness seemed to come over the older man, then it was

gone. 'I don't like to think of my grandson in that house any more than you do. But John's not going to deliberately hurt him. He's all he's got. Forget her, that tart.' He made a dismissive brushing-away gesture. 'She's just a bit of nothing. It's the boy he'd lay down his life for. If he thinks he's going to be taken away again, it'll be like losing everything twice. I don't think he'll care what he does then.'

'I'll be careful,' Ben said.

Paterson reached for his glass. 'It's not you I'm thinking about.'

They had another drink at the club — which Ben bought, so obviously the protocol of guests not buying applied only to the first round — and then went back to the house. Paterson invited him to stay for lunch. 'I've done enough for two,' he said. 'Force of habit.'

Afterwards they watched the football match on the small TV in the lounge. Ben felt drowsy and comfortable. The beer, the roast lunch and the coal fire popping in the grate combined to make him feel more relaxed than he had in ages. Whole swathes of the afternoon passed without them talking, but there was no awkwardness in the silences. When Paterson announced that he would have to get ready to visit his wife, Ben offered to go with him to the hospital. The decline came without fuss or self-consciousness.

'She's not at her best just now. You can call round again when she's back at home.'

Ben understood, without feeling offended, that it was time for him to go. Paterson saw him to the door, but they didn't shake hands. It wouldn't have felt right.

'Don't push him too far,' the older man told him as he left.

Ben almost said okay.

But he didn't.

*　　*　　*

He spent Christmas in the Caribbean. It was one of the plum jobs that came along every now and again, a scramble from an advertising agency who had decided to switch photographers at the last minute and needed something to show their clients early in the New Year. They sounded relieved when Ben accepted the job.

Almost as relieved as he felt.

He sent Jacob a big parcel of Christmas presents, but he had no idea if he'd understand who they were from. Or if Kale would let him have them. Before he went away he spoke to Ann Usherwood about investigating Sandra's background. The solicitor had been doubtful. She'd warned it would be expensive, and probably not tell them anything they didn't already know. 'If there was something incriminating the social services would have it on record,' she pointed out. But Ben insisted.

If it had got Quilley nearly killed, it had to be worth knowing.

He left for the shoot without having heard anything. At the last minute a heavy weight of reluctance descended and almost made him back out. He felt certain that he was letting down his guard, struck by a superstitious conviction that something disastrous would happen if he wasn't at hand to prevent it. Only the fact that he wouldn't hear anything from Usherwood over Christmas anyway, and the knowledge that his professional reputation might not stand another dent, made him go.

When he came off the plane and felt the sun bake down on him he was glad he had. It was so far removed from anything he associated with Christmas – and any stinging reminders of Sarah and Jacob – that the period he'd been dreading slipped by almost without him noticing. Even Christmas Day passed relatively painlessly. They worked in the morning then spent the rest of the day getting slowly pissed at a beach bar. By the evening Ben had even forgotten what time of the year it was.

There was no escaping New Year's Eve, though. He was back in London by then. He had been invited to several parties, more even than usual, but while he knew the reason for it and was grateful, he had no intention of going to any. He planned to lock the door, turn the clocks to the wall, then watch videos and drink until January had safely started.

But memories of other years came at him like a juggernaut. Only four of them; that was all they had spent together. It seemed incredible that it had been so few. The best had been their second, when he and Sarah had left Jacob with her parents and gone to a New Year's Eve party in Knightsbridge. The house had been ridiculously opulent but they hadn't known many people there and had left not long after midnight. Slightly drunk, they had returned home, gigglingly stripped off and made love on the lounge floor. Sarah had gone down on him, teasing him with hands and tongue, and when he came in a spine-arching spurt she had grinned up at him and mock-roared, 'Hap-py New Year!'

The previous year's hadn't been so memorable – Jacob had come down with flu, so they'd stayed in – but looking back on it now as the last they would spend together, the last Sarah had been alive for, made it if anything more poignant. It seemed at once close enough to touch, yet much further removed than a mere twelve months.

He put the vodka bottle on the floor within easy reach and chain-watched one mindless video after another.

When the phone rang it startled him out of a doze. He jumped, spilling vodka from the glass loosely balanced on his chest. The room spun as he stood up. On the TV a mass of images refused to congeal into any coherent picture. The phone continued to ring. He wished he'd thought to disconnect it. He didn't want to hear anyone wishing him a Happy New Year.

He didn't think there was any such thing.

Resenting the intrusion, he answered it. 'Yeah?' he said, deliberately surly.

Sounds of a party came down the line; cheers, hooters, the cracks of party poppers. 'Ben? Is that you?'

The unexpected voice cut through the vodka. 'Dad?'

'Can you hear me?'

'Yeah! Where are you?'

'We're at some friends' house.'

Ben couldn't stop the drop of disappointment that he wasn't near by, even while he recognised its absurdity.

'I thought I'd call and see how you were.'

'Oh ... not bad. You?'

'Fine!' There was a pause. 'I just wanted to say ...'

Don't. Not 'Happy New Year'. Please don't.

'... Well, you know. I'm thinking of you.'

Ben felt a lump rise in his throat.

'You there, Ben?'

'Yeah.'

Somebody whooped in the background. There was a burst of laughter. He could hear someone calling his father's name. It sounded like his stepmother.

'I'd better go,' his father said, but didn't break the connection. Whoever was calling his name grew louder. 'Look after yourself.'

Ben tried to say something, but the background noise of the party had been replaced by the dialling tone.

He put down the receiver. Fireworks were being let off outside. It couldn't be long after midnight. He wiped his eyes.

'Fuck it,' he said, for no particular reason, and went over to where he'd left the vodka.

The New Year carried on from where the old had left off. There was work, and there was going out after work, and there was going home to an empty house. January had always been his least favourite month. He told himself it was just a matter of getting through it. One rainy Sunday afternoon he realised as he watched a video that it should have been his contact day. He'd forgotten about it. It upset him not because he'd held out any hope of Kale letting him see Jacob, but because he was already starting to let things slide. It seemed to foreshadow the way things would be in future.

He wondered if he shouldn't stop clutching at straws, aim for something more attainable like his contact rights, as Usherwood advised. But the same arguments still applied. Kale wasn't going to share his son, no matter what anyone said. As long as he had Jacob he would continue to do what he liked, until he ultimately did something that even the authorities couldn't ignore.

Ben hoped Jacob could survive his father's free will for that long.

He expected to hear from Ann Usherwood soon after the New Year, but February arrived without any word from her. He had begun to regard Sandra Kale's past as another dead end when the solicitor called him one morning.

'How soon can you get in to see me?' she asked.

He was at the studio, just about to start a shoot. His first impulse was to cancel it, then he thought about Zoe and decided against. 'Not till tomorrow. Have you found something?'

'Enough to know that the social services didn't check up as well as they should,' she told him. 'Sandra Kale's got a twelve-year-old criminal record for prostitution and drug offences. She's been married before, to a pimp and drug pusher called Wayne Carter. It was in Portsmouth, under a different local authority, and when she divorced him she reverted back to her maiden name. Unless the social services here ran a pretty thorough check on her background – which they obviously didn't – they could easily have missed it.'

Excitement and disbelief blew away Ben's depression. But Usherwood hadn't finished.

'That's not all they missed,' she went on. 'Sandra and Wayne Carter had a child, a little girl. She died from parental abuse when she was eighteen months old.'

Chapter Eighteen

◆◆◆

The rain had stopped for a while, but by the time the figures began straggling out of the pub it had started to come down again. Most were men. They turned up their coat collars and bunched their shoulders against the wind-lashed downpour, apparently preferring pasted-down hair and soaked shoulders to the effeminacy of an umbrella.

Ben watched the last of the afternoon drinkers hurry away. The street became deserted again. He cracked open one of the car windows a little to clear some of the condensation. A fine spray of rain gusted in, making him shiver. He'd turned the engine off when he'd parked twenty minutes earlier, and the warmth the heaters had built up had largely gone now.

He tucked his hands under his arms and waited. After another half-hour the pub door opened again and a woman came out. She was half hidden behind a telescopic umbrella which she struggled to keep from blowing inside out. Ben wiped the misted glass, not sure if it was her. Then a gust of wind plucked open her coat and revealed the shortness of the skirt underneath, and he knew it was.

Her umbrella blew inside out just as she reached the car. She stopped as she wrestled with it. The wind tried to tear the passenger door from Ben's fingers as he reached across and opened it.

'Want a lift?'

Sandra Kale squinted through the rain, trying to see him. He could tell when she realised who he was by the way her face suddenly became set. With a jerk she inverted the umbrella right side out again. Her high heels tapped on the wet pavement as she strode on as if he weren't there.

'I can always come round to the back of the house instead,' he said.

She stopped and looked at him, trying to gauge his meaning. He was getting a twinge in his back from leaning over to hold open the door. 'There's no point walking in this,' he said.

She stood, indecisive. Then, with a quick glance up and down the street, she folded the umbrella and got in.

She sat next to him, breathing slightly heavily as he pulled away. The inside of the car smelled of her perfume and wet cloth. Damp and cold had entered with her, but he thought he could detect her heat underneath it. Her hair, darkened to something like its natural colour by the rain, stuck to her forehead and the back of her neck. Water beaded the skin of her face like sweat.

He noticed a large bruise on one cheek, unsuccessfully disguised with make-up.

'What do you want?' she asked.

'We need to talk.'

'Do we?'

'I think so.'

'I don't. I've got nothing to say to you.'

'You might have when you know what I want to talk about.'

He wasn't as confident as he tried to sound. His excitement over Ann Usherwood's news had faded when she'd told him that an undisclosed criminal record — particularly one twelve years old — didn't have any bearing on the current situation. It would embarrass the social services, but that was all. And while the death of Sandra's own child was more serious, only her husband had been prosecuted. He'd been found guilty of manslaughter; the worst charge against her was neglect.

'Kale can't be held responsible for what his wife did before she met him, in any event,' the solicitor had said. 'And even if she was deemed unfit to live in the same house as another child, which frankly I can't see, who do you think he'd pick if he was forced to make a choice between them?'

The answer to that didn't need thinking about. What did it take? he'd wondered, wearily. What the fuck did it take? Usherwood had gone on to tell him how it put them in a much better position to insist on his contact rights, and asked if he wanted her to present his case to the local authority now. No, he'd said. Not yet.

There was someone he wanted to talk to first.

He was aware of Sandra Kale's scrutiny in the close confines of the car, but kept his own gaze on the road. They drove in silence until they reached the house. He parked and switched off the ignition.

'Say what you've got to say, then,' she said.

'I'd rather tell you inside.'

'You can't come in.' Beneath the aggression she sounded almost frightened.

'If we stay here the whole street can see us. He won't like that if he hears about it, will he?'

Her mouth tightened, then she got out of the car. Ben picked up his bag from the back seat and followed her. The rain was bouncing up off the pavement, and he was soaked even in the few seconds it took him to reach the house. He half expected her to slam the front door behind her, but she left it open.

He went inside and wiped the water from his face. The hallway was dark and chill. There was a sour smell he couldn't identify. From further inside he could hear Sandra moving about. He headed towards the noise.

The hallway went past the lounge. The door was ajar. He paused, taking in the clothing strewn on sofa and chairs, the toys and magazines on the floor. One of Jacob's T-shirts was hanging over the back of a chair. He could remember Sarah buying it. He turned away, skirting a car wheel propped up against the wall as he went into the kitchen.

The kitchen seemed at once familiar and strange, like somewhere visited in a dream. He was used to seeing it from the outside, framed first by the window, then the viewfinder, as two-dimensional as an image on a TV screen. The reality was both more vivid and yet somehow less real. He couldn't quite believe he was there. *I'm inside the looking-glass.* He glanced through the window, but the hillside was obscured by the rain and mist, reduced to a vague shape.

In the foreground, the mound of wreckage formed a darker one below it.

Sandra finished plugging in a convector heater that stood against one wall and turned to face him. She leaned back against a work surface with her fists on her hips.

'Well?'

Now he was here Ben didn't know how to start. He put his bag on the floor.

'I want Jacob back.'

Sandra stared at him, then put her head back and gave a laugh. 'Oh, is that all?' Her expression became heavy with disdain, but there might have been an element of relief there, too. 'If that's all you wanted to say you might as well fuck off back to London. Thanks for the lift.'

The hot air from the convector heater hadn't yet warmed the room, but he was already feeling stifled in his bulky coat. 'What are you frightened of?'

'I'm not frightened of anything. I just wish you'd piss off and leave us alone.'

'Leave *you* alone?' he said, incredulous. 'All this started because you wouldn't let me see Jacob.'

'If you're so bothered about the little bastard you shouldn't have given him away.'

'I didn't know what Kale was like then.'

She dropped her arms, stepped towards him. 'He's not a fucking dog! He's got a first name!'

Ben refused to back down. 'You know what he's doing isn't right.'

'Do I?'

'I think so. And you don't want Jacob here any more than I do.'

'What makes you such an expert on what I want?'

Because I've watched you. 'Tell me I'm wrong.'

She looked away. 'It doesn't make any difference anyway. What I want doesn't matter,' she said, and the bitterness was so close to the surface he could have touched it. Abruptly, she turned back to him. 'You think it's going to do any good, coming here? You think I'd really help you? Even if I fucking could?'

'I hoped you might.'

'Well, you hoped wrong! Sorry to disappoint you.' She went to her handbag and took out a packet of cigarettes.

'Even if I can't get Jacob back I want to make sure he's properly looked after,' Ben said. 'He needs special schooling, he needs to mix with other kids. He's not getting any of that.'

Sandra had a cigarette clamped tightly in her mouth. She struck a match and held it to the tip. 'Life's hard, isn't it?'

'What about all that macho shit with the weight, lifting it over Jacob's head in the garden? What happens if he drops it?'

She looked at him sharply, but didn't ask how he knew. The fear he'd thought he'd detected earlier flared in her eyes again for a moment. She blew smoke towards the ceiling. 'John won't drop it.'

'That's it, is it? One slip and Jacob's dead, but you just pretend it can't happen?'

She shrugged.

'Wasn't it enough letting your own daughter be killed without letting it happen again?'

Her face went white. The bruise on her cheek was like a strawberry birthmark against it. 'Who told you that?'

Ben hadn't wanted to bring it up quite so brutally, but now he had there was nothing to do but carry on. 'I know you've been married before. And about your criminal record.' He tried to convince himself he'd nothing to feel bad about.

Sandra swayed slightly, as if she were about to faint. She closed her eyes. 'This is that fucking detective, isn't it? I wish John had killed him.'

He nearly did, Ben thought. 'Did he ask for money?'

Her face was drawn as she nodded. 'He told John he'd tell the social services if he didn't pay him. Stupid bastard.'

'So Kale beat him up.'

He thought she would shout at him again for using Kale's surname, but she didn't. They'd already gone beyond that. She just looked at him, as if the question didn't deserve an answer.

He felt himself reddening. 'Didn't he know about your past until Quilley told him?'

'He knew. It didn't matter to him, though. It never seemed to occur to him that anything could stop him getting Jacob back. He was his son, and that was it.'

'Didn't it occur to you?'

'Of course it fucking occurred to me! But what do you think I was going to do? Tell him? I'd have been out on my ear if he'd thought I might stop him getting his precious little son back. I didn't have one night's sleep for months, worrying about them finding out.'

The colour had come back to her cheeks, but she still looked tired. 'When they didn't I was so fucking *relieved*.'

'Weren't you worried someone might recognise you on TV?'

'You think I still look anything like I did twelve years ago?' she said, scornfully. 'Christ, I wish. Anyway, by then I thought it was all over. The social services hadn't traced me back to that stupid, doped-up little tart who let her husband beat her kid to death. I thought I'd finally put it all behind me. I'd earned a bit of limelight.' The brief animation went out of her. 'Then that fucking detective turned up again.'

'How did Kale take it?' Ben asked.

She glared at him. The bruise stood out lividly on her cheek. 'How do you think?'

He looked away, embarrassed.

'That was the first time he's ever hit me.' Ben thought about how Kale had thrown her against the fence. His disbelief must have shown. Her face hardened. 'I'd married one man who knocked me about. Do you think I was going to marry another?'

But she seemed to lack the energy to sustain any anger. She sank back against the work surface again, pulling on the cigarette as if it were a lifeline. 'God, I wish I'd never heard of you or your son. Why couldn't you just have left well alone?'

It was something Ben had asked himself often enough. He didn't have an answer. 'I didn't ask for this. If your husband had been' – he was about to say 'reasonable', but that word no longer seemed to apply even remotely to Kale – 'had been different, I'd have settled for seeing Jacob once a month.'

He wasn't sure if that was true, though. He couldn't think of any one point where things between him and Kale could have been otherwise. There seemed an inevitability about it, as though they were both chained by personality and events to tracks that had led to him being there, now, talking to Kale's wife in that room. And from there – where? He had a dizzying sense of standing outside himself, looking back on something that had already happened. He felt that the conclusion had already occurred, and was simply waiting for him to catch up with it.

Then the feeling passed.

'How did you meet him?' he asked.

'Oh, please.'

'No, I'd like to know. Really.' He meant it. He wanted to make her lower her guard, but there was also a genuine curiosity.

She looked disgusted for a moment longer, then shrugged. 'After I left Portsmouth I lived near Aldershot, not far from where he was based. I used to knock around with a lot of the soldiers. You know.'

Ben thought he probably did.

'I was working in this pub one night and two of the locals started giving me a hard time because I wouldn't go with them. I told them to fuck off, but they'd had a bit to drink and they started getting rough. So then John comes up and tells them to pack it in. I didn't know him, but you could tell he was a soldier. I don't mean just the haircut. There was something about him. He just stood there and didn't say a word while they mouthed off. It was after he'd been shot, not long before he got discharged, and his limp was pretty bad. Even so, they should have known not to mess with him. But they were pissed and he was by himself, so one of them took a swing.'

She fell quiet, remembering. It brought a smile. 'They wouldn't have tried it on with anyone else for a while after that.' The smile died as she returned to the present. 'They'd got more sense than you.'

Ben went to the window. It brought him closer to her. He could feel her watching him suspiciously as he looked out at the garden. 'What's he doing out there?'

'He's not out there, he's at work.'

'You know what I mean.'

'No I don't.'

The denial lacked conviction. He saw her shoot a glance through the window at the garden. Her mouth was puckered to one side as she chewed the inside of her cheek. Ben felt oddly comfortable with her.

'Is he building something?' he asked.

'Why don't you ask him?'

'Because I'd like to see my next birthday.'

The smile came back, but it was short-lived. He waited. She stabbed out the cigarette.

'He's looking for the Pattern.'

'The what?'

'The fucking Pattern. With a capital fucking P.' She made it a mock proclamation, but there was no humour in it. 'He thinks that there's a pattern to everything. A reason for whatever happens, except we just can't see it. He says it's everywhere, it's just a matter of knowing what to look for.'

She waved her hand at the window. 'That's why we've got all that junk out there. Because if he looks at it hard enough it might show him this Pattern. He thinks it's easier to see in anything that's been smashed up. Nearer the surface, or something. He's got one of those radio scanner things, so he can listen to the police wavelength for road accidents. Whenever there's a car crash he's always the one who goes out to bring it in. The bigger the better. There was a pile up on the motorway a while back, and he ended up having to borrow a lorry from the yard to carry all his bloody souvenirs home.'

Ben thought about Kale moving the pieces of metal around, studying each new arrangement. Something nudged his memory, and he remembered the first time he had gone to the house to collect Jacob. Kale had said something then about him not being part of 'the pattern'.

He didn't like to think what that could have meant.

'What does he expect it to show him?' he asked.

'God knows. Something that'll explain why everything's happened. His son getting stolen, his wife stepping in front of a bus, him being wounded and his mates killed in Northern Ireland. Even being brought up in an orphanage. He thinks there's got to be some reason for it all. And he thinks if he can see the Pattern it'll tell him.'

She stared through the rain-smeared window at the distorted metal, as if hoping to see an explanation there herself.

'Was he like this when you first met him?'

Sandra shook her head without looking round. 'He seemed different to most of the other squaddies I'd met, but that was all.' Her mouth twitched. 'He didn't try and drag my knickers off in the first five minutes, for a start. That was one of the things I liked about him. And he was quiet. Not shy, just quiet. Most of them tell you their life stories at the drop of a hat, but he was more interested in listening to me talk about mine. I didn't tell him everything, not straightaway, and it wasn't until I told him what had happened with Kirstie – my little girl – that he said anything about what had happened to him.'

She sniffed. Ben wasn't sure if she was close to crying, or whether it was the dry heat of the kitchen. His own nose was tickling from it.

'When he found out about Kirstie he went quiet for ages. I thought I'd put him off, that he was blaming me the same as everybody else did. Then he started telling me about his son being taken from the hospital, and his wife killing herself. He said people like us, who'd had their lives messed up, were damaged for a reason. That was how he put it, "damaged". He was as excited as I've ever seen him. He said we must have been meant to meet, after we'd both lost our kids and everything. He said something then about it being part of a pattern, but I can't remember what. I just thought he was being romantic. A bit soft, but romantic.'

She gave a short, bitter laugh. 'I was just another fucked-up piece of scrap.'

He felt a desire to put his arms around her. He kept his hands in his pockets. 'Was he as obsessed about it then?'

'I don't know. I don't think so. Hang on a second, I'll show you something.'

She went out of the kitchen. He heard her go down the corridor to the lounge. There was the sound of a drawer being opened. A few seconds later she came back, carrying a large, vinyl-covered photograph album. She set it down on the work surface next to him. He could smell her perfume, the tobacco odour on her clothes, a faint musk of underarm sweat.

He took his hands back out of his pockets.

'This is John's,' she said, opening it. She quickly flicked past the first few pages. Ben caught glimpses of a younger Kale, sitting on a motorbike, standing in a green army uniform, smiling with his arm around a pregnant young woman.

He recognised Jeanette Kale, Jacob's mother, but Sandra had already moved on.

'Here,' she said. 'He took these when he was in the Gulf. During the war.'

She moved slightly to one side so he could see. He felt the heat from her hip, almost touching his, as he came nearer. There were four photographs, two on each page. One of them was a long-distance shot of a blazing oil well. The rest showed blasted areas of desert littered with debris. In one of them was a tank, its nearside track torn off. A charred body was folded over the blackened turret. In another was the wreckage of a helicopter, the limp rotor blades hanging like the veins of a dead leaf.

'He took these before his wife was even pregnant,' Sandra said. 'Before everything went wrong for him. I don't think he'd got a thing about wrecks back then, these were just like souvenirs, you know? It wasn't until after we were married that he dug them out and stuck them in here.'

They weren't the sort of souvenirs Ben would have chosen. If Kale's obsession wasn't yet formed, the seeds of it were still evident. The pictures on the next page displayed the same morbid fascination. Most had been taken on a road instead of open desert. Military and civilian vehicles were scattered along it, burned, lying on their sides, tyres flat or melted, the bodywork crumpled like paper. In some shots the road stretched to the horizon – no sign of life on it, only the numberless wrecks. The bodies that lay among them looked insignificant.

Ben went through the rest of the album. To begin with there were ordinary snapshots included; a Middle Eastern shop with grinning British soldiers outside, what looked like the same group outside a tent pitched on sand. But these soon petered out until the photographs were solely of wreckage.

The desert was abruptly replaced by a colder, more familiar landscape. A troop carrier lay on its side in the road. Behind it were grey clouds, green hills and bushes. A shattered car, half in, half out of a bomb crater.

'That's Northern Ireland,' Sandra said. He could feel her breath on his ear. He turned the page. More of the same. Now, though, the photographs seemed to have been taken with more care paid to angles and light. Whereas the earlier ones had been little more than snaps, dramatic only because of their content, there was a self-consciousness about these that suggested a new intent. In one the wreckage of some vehicle was partially silhouetted against either a sunrise or a sunset. The sun reflected off some parts while turning the rest black. It was corny and badly executed, but not ineffective.

'Was this his last term over there?' Ben asked. 'After Jacob had gone missing and his wife had died?'

'Yeah, I think so.' Sandra sounded more suspicious than surprised. 'Why?'

'I just wondered.' He told himself he was reading too much into a few photographs. But he couldn't shake the conviction that, whereas the early ones had been coloured by a morbid curiosity, in the last few Kale had already started looking for something.

He turned over again. There was only one photograph left.

It was black-and-white and had been cut from a newspaper. It showed two army Land Rovers. The first was on its roof. The second, behind it, had its doors open and its windscreen smashed. There were dark marks on its bodywork that looked like bullet holes.

'That was the ambush where John got shot,' Sandra told him. 'He should have been in the first car, the one on its roof, because he was the corporal. But its radio wasn't working, so he went in the other. About a mile after he'd changed the first car went over a land-mine and everybody in it was killed. Then the bastards started on them with a machinegun.'

Ben closed the album.

'Don't see many of me in there, do you?' she said.

The bitterness had given way to hurt.

'When did he start bringing the scrap metal home?' he said, to get away from it.

'Almost as soon as we came here.' She moved away. He wasn't sure if he was relieved or not. 'He started looking for a job. I thought he'd get something in a garage, or somewhere. You know he's a qualified mechanic? He can fix anything mechanical, he's got a knack for it. That's why he joined the Engineers. But he came home one day and said he'd got this job in the scrapyard. I didn't mind, I thought it'd only be temporary. I didn't even take any notice when he started bringing bits and pieces back with him. I supposed he wanted to mess around with them. Hammer them out for spares, or something, I don't know. Then he started talking about this Pattern.'

She glared at Ben as if it were his fault. 'It was bad enough before, but when he found out Steven' – *Jacob*, he thought – 'was still alive he started bringing back twice as much. I told him the social services would have a fit if they saw it, but he didn't take any notice. And they never went out back anyway. They had a look round the house, but that was all. I just drew the curtains when they came in the kitchen so they wouldn't see it. Pricks.'

There was no heat in the insult. Her skirt tightened around her thighs as she leaned against the edge of the table. 'Now John's not got time for anything else. He could get a job in any garage and earn decent money, but he won't. And he has to pay for everything he brings home. That fat bastard he works for takes it out of his wages, as if there's enough of them to start with. He won't listen to me any more. He hardly even talks to me. All he cares about now is his bloody wreckage. And the kid. Won't let his precious little son out of his sight. He's got this idea that he can help him see what the pattern is, because of how he is with jigsaws and things.'

'That's stupid! A lot of autistic children are good at puzzles. It isn't anything unusual!'

'Try telling that to John,' she said, dryly. 'He thinks it all ties in. Steven's going to help him first, and once he has he'll be able to make Steven better. Or something like that. It's all part of the *Pattern*, isn't it?'

Her tone was loaded with sarcasm. Ben remembered how Kale set pieces of metal in front of Jacob, as if waiting for his reaction. Waiting for him to help decipher whatever he thought they held. 'Oh, Christ.'

'Oh, you don't know the half of it,' Sandra said. She was smiling again, but it wasn't a pleasant one. 'He exercises until he's sick. He tries to work himself into a state where he can "see" this fucking pattern of his. I mean, he hasn't managed it yet, obviously, so that just means he has to go at it harder. He says he's "purifying" himself. Well, that's what he said once. He doesn't talk about it at all now. Not to me, anyway, but you can hear him telling the boy sometimes. As if he can bloody understand him.'

'Is that why he lifts the engine over Jacob's head? To push himself harder?'

An expression of suspicion smoothed her face, then was gone. 'I suppose so,' she said, examining her nails. 'I haven't asked.'

She still hadn't asked how he knew what Kale did in the garden, either. Ben wondered if she didn't want to find out what else he might have seen.

'What does he do in the shed?' he asked.

The look she gave him was a mixture of fear and dislike. It was quickly replaced by resignation. 'You can see for yourself.'

She brushed past him and went to the back door. He began to follow and walked into her as she stopped suddenly. He stepped back, blushing.

'Sorry,' he mumbled.

'I forgot the key.' There was a satisfied air about her as she took a key-ring from a drawer in one of the kitchen units, as though she had somehow proved something to herself. Ben felt the advantage had been subtly taken from him. A gust of rain and icy air swept into the kitchen as she opened the door. He clutched his coat around him as he went out, conscious that Sandra hadn't even bothered to put hers on. The garden was muddy. Broken paving slabs had been embedded in the grassless soil like stepping stones. Through the rain Ben saw the encircling wall of metal.

There was more of it than he remembered.

He skirted a jagged piece of bodywork that protruded from one side of the pile. The seat where Jacob had played while Kale suspended the engine over him looked wet and abandoned. In front of it sections of broken cars had been left like parts of a dismembered animal.

Sandra unlocked the padlock and opened the shed door. It tore out of her hand and banged against the wooden side. Ben went in after her.

There was a pungency of bitumen, pine resin and stale sweat. It was dark and cramped, forcing him to stand close to Sandra. Her hair was flattened against her head by the rain. He could feel water from his own trickling over his face and neck. He blinked it out of his eyes, trying to work out what the object that filled most of the interior was.

At first he thought it was simply an exercise machine, a multigym of some sort. There was an impression of a steel frame, pulleys and ponderous weights. Then he took in the straps attached to the long wooden bench and dangling from cables, the oil-covered cogs of what appeared to be gear wheels.

It looked like something designed to tear apart rather than exercise.

'This is why he comes in here,' Sandra said. She was shivering. 'He built it himself.'

Ben was still trying to work out what it was. He thought he knew, but couldn't quite believe it. 'What is it?'

'It's a rack, what's it look like?'

There were small straps for wrists and ankles, and a larger harness that had a forehead band and a chinstrap. Each was joined by cables to the weights, which hung like steel fruit at the head and foot of the bench, and were connected in turn to the heavy gear wheels. Sandra ran her fingers lightly over the frame. Her nails were bitten and ragged.

'He fastens himself into it and takes the brake off the weights. The gears stop them just smashing straight to the floor, but once they've gone past a notch you can't pull them back. He's worked it so the further they go the heavier they get. The only way you can stop them's by that.' She pointed to a mechanism at the top end of the bench. It had a smaller set of weights, and was attached to the head harness. 'It's a clutch, or something. But you have to use your neck to lift those weights off the floor far enough for it to trip in.'

'Jesus.'

'John lets it go as far as he can, and then just holds it there. Tries to keep himself at breaking point for as long as he can. When he first built it and I came and saw what he was doing I panicked and made him lose concentration. It nearly killed him. When he managed to get out he threw up and told me never to come in here again. I thought he was going to hit me, but he didn't. Not then.' There was a deadness in the way she said it. 'I've never watched him since, but I can tell by how long he stays in here and what he looks like when he comes out that he's taking it further and further. One of these days ...' She didn't finish.

Ben tried to imagine what it would feel like to be strapped into the machine. 'Why does he do it?'

'To help him see the Pattern. Why else?' She hugged herself and rubbed her arms. 'He thinks the pain focuses his mind. All part of being "pure". Can't be impure if we want to see the Pattern, can we?'

He stared at the sweat-stained straps. In places the edges of them were marked with what looked like dried blood. 'Are you sure he isn't just trying to punish himself?'

Sandra looked at the rack as though she were frightened of it. 'I'm not sure about anything.' She turned away suddenly. 'Let's go in. I'm freezing.'

As they went out he noticed the shotgun lying on a shelf to one side of the door. He remembered what it had done to the dog's head. *At least he keeps the place locked*, he thought as he watched Sandra snap the heavy padlock shut. He followed her back to the house. The kitchen began misting up as soon as they closed the door. They were both soaked, but at least he'd had a coat on. Her clothes were stuck to her. The outline of her bra was etched under her sweater. Her nipples stood out through both layers of fabric.

'You're dripping all over the carpet,' she told him. 'If you're going to stay you might as well take your coat off.'

He did, draping it over his bag. She handed him a towel. 'Here.' It was already damp and didn't look too clean, but he took it anyway. Sandra rubbed her hair vigorously with another.

'I'm wet through.' Without coyness she pulled off her

sweater and dropped it on a chair. The skin of her arms, chest and stomach was pale and covered with goose bumps. Her white bra was semi-transparent.

'Don't mind, do you?' she asked, pushing her wet hair back with her fingers so that it hung behind her ears. Her heavy breasts lifted with the movement.

'No.' He tried to remember what he'd been going to say next. 'Look—'

'Coffee?'

'Uh, please.'

There was a small roll of flesh above the waistband of her skirt. She went to the sink and filled the kettle. To the left of her spine below her bra strap was a mole the size of a small fingernail. He hadn't noticed it when he'd watched her through the long lens.

He made himself look through the window at the scrap metal.

'Why only wrecked cars?'

'What?' She pushed the kettle plug into the socket with a firm jab from the palm of her hand. A muscle jumped down the side of her ribs.

'All the scrap. Why is it just cars? Why not bits of fridges and washing machines as well?'

'Because a car wreck's violent. One minute it was driving around, the next it's junk. And somebody with it. He thinks each piece he brings home is some sort of memento of that. Somebody's life being smashed.' She had turned to face him, but for a moment she seemed to forget he was there. Then she came back from wherever she'd been and smiled.

'I can't see the point in looking for reasons,' she said. 'Things happen, don't they? You just have to make the most of what you've got.'

Ben didn't say anything because she had started walking towards him. She didn't take her eyes from his. The smile was still on her mouth. She came close and stood in front of him. He was surprised at how small she was. He could feel the fabric of her bra brushing his shirt. The weight of her breasts was an implied threat. She rested her hands flat on his chest. They felt cold, then the heat of them came through.

'What have you got?' she asked, looking up at him. She began to slide one hand lower. It burned a slow path down his stomach. There was a thrumming in his head, twinning the one in his crotch. Her hand reached it, pressed against it, and a vibration went through him as though she had struck a tuning fork. He stepped back slightly for balance and something crunched under his shoe.

He looked down. One of Jacob's puzzles was crushed under his heel. Tiny silver balls had spilled from the broken plastic. He lifted his foot and more of them escaped, running like beads of mercury across the dirty carpet.

'Don't worry about it,' Sandra told him. 'John's bought him loads of them. They're all over the place.'

But Ben felt something shifting inside him, something that had nothing to do with the pressure of her hand. He took another step backwards. She looked surprised, then her expression grew closed at whatever she saw in his face. Her hand fell to her side.

'Well,' she said, looking away. She self-consciously folded her arms across her breasts. 'Sorry if I'm not good enough for you. I expect you're too used to models.'

Ben couldn't think of anything he could say that would make things any better. The kettle clicked off, its steam adding to the fog on the window. He moved further away, careful not to step on any of the silver balls. He tried to reassemble his reason for being there.

'I'm going to tell the social services that I don't think your husband's mentally fit to look after Jacob,' he said.

Sandra went to where her sweater was discarded on the chair. 'Do what you like.'

'All that stuff in the shed. He's self-destructive. I'm not

going to let anything happen to Jacob because he's got some fixation.'

'Bully for you.' She felt the wet sweater and dropped it back down with a grimace of annoyance. She picked up a sweat-shirt from another chair.

'Will you back me up?'

She paused in the act of pulling on the sweat-shirt and stared at him. 'Back you up? Don't be fucking stupid!'

'You've just told me what he's like.'

'That doesn't mean I'm going to say he's some sort of nutter so you can get his son taken off him.'

'He needs help.'

She laughed, harshly. 'Don't we all!' She jerked the sweat-shirt over her head. 'And don't pretend you're bothered about John. You don't give a shit about him. You're only worried about the kid.'

'Wouldn't you be?'

She raised a shoulder, indifferently. 'He'll just have to take his chances with the rest of us. And since that's all you came for you can fuck off. I've got to get tea ready.'

Ben went to his bag and took out the photographs of her and the men in the bedroom. Her expression became hunted as he held them out. 'What are they?'

When he didn't answer she came forward and took them. She stared at the first one, then quickly at the next few.

She flung them at him.

'You bastard! You fucking—!'

He thought she was going to hit him, but she let her arms fall. She hung her head. 'I hope you enjoyed watching. You fucking shit.'

His cheek was stinging from the edge of one of the photographs. He put his fingers to it. They came away coloured with blood. He groped in his pocket for a tissue. His arms seemed sluggish. He felt he was moving through a mire of shame.

'So what are you going to do with them?' she asked. 'Do a Quilley? Blackmail me into saying John wants locking up?'

He held the tissue to the cut. 'I only want you to tell the social services what you've told me.'

'So you can get Jacob taken away? What do you think he'd do to me if I did that?'

'What will he do if he finds out you've been sleeping with other men while he's at work? And taking money for it?'

She covered her eyes. Something inside Ben was curling up and withering. He did his best to ignore it. 'They probably won't take Jacob off him, anyway.' *You fucking hypocrite.* 'But if somebody doesn't do something, sooner or later he's going to kill one of them. Either Jacob or himself. You'll lose him then either way.'

Her throat was jumping in little spasms. She wiped her hand across her cheeks, dragging the skin like a rubber mask. Streaks of mascara followed her fingers.

'You think you can leave things behind,' she said. 'You think you've got away from them, but you never do. You take it all with you. When I met John I thought ...'

She didn't finish. The smeared mascara made her face look like something left out too long in the rain.

'We haven't had sex in a year.'

I don't want to hear this, Ben thought, but he didn't move. He owed her that much.

She stared at the photographs scattered on the floor. 'Not since before all this started. He isn't interested any more. He's like one of these bloody monks. Sex is "impure", it'll stop him seeing his Pattern. Specially with someone like me. He doesn't say as much, but I can tell by the way he looks at me. I'm a cheap tart. More pricks than a pin-cushion, that's me. So one day I thought, right, if that's what he thinks I am, I will be. The next time a bloke in the pub made a pass at me I said okay. And after I'd done it once there was no reason not to do it again, was there? The money came in handy. That's something else John isn't interested in. We could have sold the story to the newspapers for a fucking fortune, but oh no! That would have been "impure", wouldn't it?'

The flare of indignation died. She raised one shoulder in a shrug. 'I let blokes come around every now and again. Not many, because most of them are too frightened of John. But there are some who get a kick out of it. Sometimes I even kid myself it's me they want. You'd think I'd have learned by now. Even John was only after something he thought he saw in me, and now he doesn't even want that any more.'

She looked Ben up and down. He felt burned by the contempt he saw.

'But it doesn't matter, does it? I'm only a fucking whore. I should be used to selling myself.'

He pulled to mind an image of Jacob sitting beneath the suspended, mud-smeared engine, imagined it dropping. He tried to crush his conscience with it. 'Will you help me?'

Sandra stared dully at the photographs on the floor. She looked old and beaten. 'Do I have any choice?'

'We can keep whatever you say confidential. He doesn't have to know.'

'Just get out.'

He picked up his bag and coat. She was still standing among the photographs when he left. When he got into the car he realised he was still holding the tissue he'd used to staunch his cheek. The blood on it formed a Rorschach pattern of spots and swirls. He screwed it up and thrust it into his pocket without trying to see what it told him.

Chapter Nineteen

◆━━◦◦◦◦◦◦◦◦◦━━◆

Colin tried to kill himself in the same week that the social services agreed to hold a case conference about Jacob. Ben had presented them with the photographs of Kale's activities in the back garden, and told them of Sandra's willingness (if it could be called that) to verify that her husband was mentally ill and a threat to his son. That would have been enough to spark an investigation in itself, but his news that she had a past they had completely overlooked was like dropping a lighted match into a box of fireworks.

Ben told himself he had no choice. He was under no obligation to Sandra, and he couldn't afford to ignore anything that would strengthen his case. He tried to convince himself that it would eventually have been discovered anyway, that he was protecting her enough by keeping quiet about her more recent affairs.

It didn't make him feel any better.

Her request for confidentiality was agreed to by the local authority, although not happily. In spite of everything, Ben still felt they didn't believe that Kale was actually dangerous. He didn't know if this was a reluctance to accept that their original assessment had been wrong or simple miscalculation, but Carlisle in particular responded with the grudging compliance of a child that'd had its fingers smacked. By now there was no disguising the antipathy the social worker felt for him. He obviously regarded Ben as a troublemaker who was trying to split up the newly formed family. Ben hoped that wouldn't blind him to the risk Kale posed to Jacob.

He was trying to be realistic about what to expect. Even now Ann Usherwood insisted there was no chance of him getting Jacob back. That wasn't something the case conference would even consider. 'As I've said before, Mr Murray, a definite threshold of risk would have to be reached for them to even consider taking Jacob from his father, and this falls well short of that. They might put him on the Child Protection Register, and insist on close monitoring while his father's mental health is assessed, but that's probably all. I really think you should put anything else out of your mind.'

He couldn't, though. The feeling remained that it wouldn't be so simple. It was no longer just a matter of Jacob and Kale, now it was Ben and Kale as well. He couldn't see it being resolved in a reasonable way.

Kale wouldn't permit it.

He was still fretting over what might happen when Maggie called to tell him that Colin had fed a hosepipe from the exhaust into his new BMW, locked himself inside and turned on the engine.

In some ways it was more of a shock than when Sarah had died. That had been a fluke, a capricious trick of a random universe, devastating but no more so than if she'd been in a plane crash or struck by lightning. But Colin's attempted suicide seemed to contravene some undefined natural law. Ever since Ben had known him he had been the reliable, orderly one of the two of them. For him to try to kill himself was unthinkable.

But then so was him having an affair.

Ben had wanted to go to the hospital straightaway, but Maggie told him not to. Colin was out of danger, she'd said, and both she and the boys were there. 'He doesn't need anybody else.'

She had sounded cool and self-possessed, as if her husband were recovering from a bout of flu rather than a failed suicide attempt. Ben supposed it was shock, but when he called round to the house the evening after Colin had been discharged she greeted him with the same degree of control.

'You can't stay long. I don't want him to get tired,' she told him. Her smile was as unyielding as ceramic. He'd braced himself for tears, bewilderment or recrimination. Instead she exuded the self-satisfied confidence she normally assumed for her dinner parties.

He was still wondering at it as he followed her to the lounge. Colin was sitting in an armchair in front of the TV, but the sound was turned down so low he couldn't have been following what was on. He looked embarrassed when Maggie led Ben in.

'Look who's come to see you,' she announced, with a falseness that made Ben wince. She told them she would be in the kitchen if they wanted her, then left. The aftertaste of her presence hung in the air with her perfume, inhibiting conversation even more.

He sat on the edge of the settee. 'So how are you feeling?'

'Okay.'

Colin looked at his hands, the TV, and finally his hands again. His face was pale, thinner than the last time Ben had seen him. The enormity of what he'd tried to do stood between them. So did Ben's sense that he'd let him down. He felt he didn't know him any more.

'Do you want to talk about it?'

Colin switched his attention back to the TV. 'What is there to talk about? I tried to kill myself, I didn't ...' He shrugged, then broke out coughing. 'Sorry,' he said when the spasm had passed. 'Still a bit wheezy.'

'Why did you do it?' The question that had been pushing at Ben finally surfaced. 'Why didn't you fucking *say* something?'

'There was nothing to say. Jo finished with me.' Colin gave a wan smile. 'Another fucking cliché, eh?'

Ben found he was vetting all his questions and responses before voicing them. 'When?'

'Last week.'

The first thing he felt was relief that it had been a sudden thing; that he hadn't been so wrapped up in his own problems that he'd missed the signs. Then he felt ashamed for feeling that way. 'What happened?'

'She's been offered the chance to work for the record company's New York office. She's going next month, but she said it was better to finish now so there were no loose ends. End of story.'

'That's what made you ... you know ...'

'Try to kill myself? I suppose I didn't like thinking of myself as a "loose end".'

'Does Jo know?'

'I doubt it. Most people at work just think I'm ill. There's no reason for her to know anyway. I didn't do it to make her change her mind, or to spite her. I did it for me.'

The matter-of-fact way he spoke was unnerving. 'You're not going to try anything again, are you?'

Colin put his head back and stared at the ceiling. 'No, I don't think so,' he said, thoughtfully. 'To tell you the truth I can't even really remember how I felt when I did it. It might be the sedatives they've pumped into me, but it all seems a bit distant now. I can't imagine getting that worked up about anything at the moment. I just feel sort of hollow.'

Ben remembered how he'd felt after Sarah had died, and then again when Jacob had gone to live with Kale. But he'd never felt suicidal.

He wondered if that said anything about him.

'What about Maggie and the boys?' he asked, feeling obscurely cheated. 'How've they taken it?'

'Oh, okay. Maggie's been very good. Andrew doesn't really

understand what's going on, but I wish Scott hadn't found me.' He pursed his lips. 'Or, at least, I wish it had been someone else.'

Maggie had told Ben how their eldest son had gone into the garage and seen his father sitting in the locked car with the engine running. Ben didn't like the boy, but he wouldn't have wished that on him. 'What did she say about Jo?'

Colin glanced uneasily towards the door. 'She doesn't know about her.'

'Even now? She must have some idea!'

'She thinks it was pressure of work that got to me.' Colour had come back to Colin's face, but it only emphasised its shadows.

'So aren't you going to tell her?'

'What for? It's finished. There's no use upsetting her any more than she has been.'

Ben made no comment, but he was thinking about how Maggie had behaved. He wouldn't have called it upset.

'The doctor's signed me off work,' Colin continued, 'so I think we're going to go away somewhere in a week or two. Try and put all this behind us.' He didn't sound enthusiastic.

Before Ben could answer, the door opened and Maggie came in. The smile could have been on her face since she left.

'I think that's enough chat for one night. Don't want to tire him out, do we? Doctor's orders.'

She stood by the open door, waiting for Ben to leave. He looked at Colin, expecting an objection, but none came. Colin was looking down at his hands again.

Ben stood up. 'I'll be in touch. We'll go for a beer before you go away.'

Colin nodded, but without conviction, and Ben knew they wouldn't. Even if Colin wanted to, Maggie wouldn't permit it.

'He just needs rest,' she said, after she'd ushered Ben into the hallway. 'He's been doing too much lately, that's the problem. I'm going to make sure he has an easier time in future. No more working weekends and nights, and having to stay out with silly little bands till all hours.'

She opened the front door and turned to him. 'There's been too many things pulling at him lately, but that's over now. He needs to spend more time with his family. We're all he needs.'

Her smile was as bright and determined as a beauty queen's, and seeing it Ben realised that Colin was wrong. She knew. Not all the details, perhaps, not names and places, but enough.

And now she knew she'd won.

Footsteps sounded on the stairs. He looked around as Scott came down them. The boy regarded them sullenly, making no attempt to speak as he went past.

'Say hello to Ben, Scott,' Maggie said, but he didn't even slow. Her smile twitched as she watched him disappear down the hallway. 'He's still a little upset.'

Ben said goodnight and left. The door clicked shut behind him. He found he had tensed himself, as though the entire house would shatter like glass.

As he went back to his car he thought that a family could stay together and still be destroyed.

The case conference was scheduled for the following week. He'd finally begun to accept that he wasn't going to get Jacob back. Or, if not accept, at least realise that there was nothing he could do about it. He knew he had to come to terms with it and get on with his life. More than that, he had to try and *rebuild* one, because there wasn't much left of the life he'd had. But knowing that didn't make it any easier to do. He felt he was just treading water, waiting for the day of the conference to arrive.

He told himself things would be better afterwards.

The night before it was held he went to the launch party

of a new magazine with Zoe. He had tried to cry off, but she wouldn't listen. 'What are you going to do if not? Sit at home by yourself, watching telly and getting pissed while you worry about what's going to happen tomorrow?'

Actually, that had been almost exactly what he'd had in mind. 'No,' he said. 'Of course not.'

The party was at a cellar bar in Soho, a dark place of blues and purples that made everyone look cyanosed. He knew a lot of the people there, had either worked or drunk with them at similar occasions. Zoe, her hair red once more, stayed with him long enough to make sure he wasn't going to go straight home, and then disappeared into the crowd. Ben found himself talking to the magazine's picture editor, who seemed to presume he was there touting for work and obligingly offered him some. Then there was another photographer, an almost-friend he hadn't seen for over a year. Talk moved on to censorship, and Ben enmired himself in an argument with a writer, a vehement man with bad breath, over the responsibility of the artist. He was enjoying it until the writer called him a commercial photographer, as if that made him some sort of photographic hack whose views were invalid. Ben began to object, but realised he couldn't.

The man was right.

Everything that he did had a shelf-life. The fashion photographs were valid only for as long as the fashions they contained, and while some of his advertising work might lay claim to a sort of kitsch value, that was all. He was good at what he did, but what he did was nothing. It was disposable. And he had chosen to do it.

So what did that make him?

He had given up trying to achieve anything more than a technical competence because he'd believed that was ultimately all photography amounted to; a triumph of form over content, of craft over art. He wondered if the limitation hadn't been his, if he hadn't been blaming the camera because he'd had nothing to say. *And what about now?* He didn't know. Nothing sprang to mind, but the knowledge that he no longer even tried gave him an unexpected ache of loss. For some reason he thought of Kale, tirelessly arranging damaged pieces of metal in his search for a pattern.

Perhaps it wasn't so much what you had to say as trying to say it anyway that mattered.

All at once the drinks felt heavy in him. He was on the verge of becoming drunk, and he didn't want that. He put his glass down. The writer was still talking animatedly, taking Ben's silence for acquiescence. Ben excused himself and moved away. He looked around the room for Zoe's red hair, but the purple lighting made colours unrecognisable. He gave up and went out.

The night was cold and crisp. The street sparkled with the beginnings of a frost, not yet white but starring the dull concrete with pinpricks of light. Already the idea he'd felt on the verge of grasping was becoming less tangible. He tried to hold on to it, but then a cab drew up and the last remnants slipped away.

As he sat back in the taxi he was already thinking about what would happen at the case conference the next morning.

It was held in the main social services building of Kale's local authority. The room looked like an anonymous boardroom, with a long central table ringed by plastic chairs. Most of them were already taken when Ben arrived. Carlisle sat opposite him, speaking in low tones to someone whom Usherwood said was probably his manager. Next to them was the child protection co-ordinator, a grey-haired woman who would be chairing the meeting. There were several other people in the room, including a uniformed policewoman from a child protection unit, but Ben didn't know any of them.

The only people not there were John and Sandra Kale.

The grey-haired woman looked at her watch. 'I take it

Mr and Mrs Kale were notified what time to be here?' she asked Carlisle.

The social worker shifted uneasily in his seat. 'I spoke to them yesterday. They—'

He broke off as the door opened. The solicitor who had represented Kale before bustled in. He was red-faced and flustered. 'Sorry we're late,' he apologised. 'There was, ah, a bit of a hold-up.'

He didn't explain further and no one asked as first Sandra and then Kale himself entered. Sandra didn't look at anyone as she took her seat by the solicitor. She was, for her, conservatively dressed in a long-sleeved sweater and a skirt that came down to her knees. Kale wore the same creased suit Ben had seen him in before. He gazed unblinkingly around the room as he walked in.

When he saw Ben he stopped dead.

'Er, Mr Kale . . .' his solicitor said. Sandra was looking down at her lap. Kale stayed where he was for a moment longer, then went and sat down. He didn't take his eyes from Ben.

The grey-haired woman cleared her throat. 'I'd like to thank everyone for coming. My name's Andrea Rogers and I'll be chairing this conference. Rather than have separate meetings, both Mr and Mrs Kale and Mr Murray have agreed to attend together and to share information.'

She turned to the Kales. 'Ordinarily, I'd take a few minutes to have a word with you in private before we started, but as we're running late I'm afraid we'll have to move straight on.'

Sandra didn't lift her head at the implied censure. Kale continued to stare at Ben as the co-ordinator introduced the various welfare officers and professionals in the room. The last person she came to was a social worker from the local authority where Sandra Kale used to live.

Ben saw Sandra stiffen when he was introduced.

'Before we begin I'd like to stress that this isn't a legal hearing of any kind,' Rogers said. 'No one's on trial here.

The aim of this case conference is to consider various concerns which have been raised about Jacob's welfare, and to decide whether or not they provide grounds to put him on the Child Protection Register.'

Kale swivelled his head towards her. 'You're not taking him away.'

'No one's suggesting that, Mr Kale. But a complaint has been made, and we have a duty to examine it.'

She held his gaze calmly before turning back to her notes. 'The basis of complaint is with regards to Jacob's schooling and special needs. Also that some of your actions may have put him at physical risk, and may continue to do so. In addition we have to consider new information which has come to light about your wife that was overlooked by the local authority.'

Sandra seemed to shrink into herself. Ben felt the weight of Kale's stare shift back to him.

'Where is Jacob today?' Rogers asked.

'He's actually at school,' Kale's solicitor answered, throwing it up for approval. 'My client is now aware of the importance of his son's education, and has given me an undertaking that he will attend as normal in future.'

'I'm glad to hear it. But I'm afraid we still need to satisfy ourselves that the undertaking will be adhered to. And we also have to consider any additional action that may have to be taken to make up for such a long period of deprivation.'

'My client realises that, and—'

'He's not deprived of anything,' Kale said.

'I was speaking in an educational sense,' Rogers said. 'Jacob's autistic. He needs—'

'He's my son. I'm all he needs.'

'I know the background to this case, Mr Kale, and I do appreciate how difficult this must be for you, but allowances can only be made so far. We're here to try and decide—'

'There's nothing to decide.'

Rogers glanced at Kale's solicitor. 'Perhaps you can explain to your client that it's in his own interests to co-operate, Mr Barclay. He'll have a chance to give his views later, but right now there's nothing to be gained by obstruction.'

The solicitor anxiously leaned towards Kale and began whispering to him. There was a general shuffling of papers as everyone else pretended not to take any notice. Kale didn't speak but his jaw muscles were bunched tightly. Ben felt the policewoman looking at him. She gave him a cold stare when he smiled at her.

Finally Kale's solicitor sat back, but with the cautious air of a man willing a precarious structure to hold. He smiled unconvincingly at Rogers.

'Okay,' he said.

The professionals all had their say. An education welfare officer spoke first. He was a short, plump man with a stubbly beard. He described the excuses made by Sandra for Jacob's absence from school; that he was ill, he had a cold, a temperature, then told how he had recently visited the scrapyard and found Jacob sitting in a derelict car while his father used a cutting torch near by.

'He didn't appear to be ill, and there was certainly no reason I could see why he shouldn't be at school. When I asked Mr Kale why he wasn't, he refused to answer.' He glanced at Kale. 'In fact he didn't say anything at all. He continued working as if I wasn't there.'

Ben imagined Kale with a cutting torch in his hand and thought the man had got off lightly.

A child psychologist spoke next. She was a specialist in autism, and stressed the importance of special school-ing and mixing with other children. Depriving an autistic child of these was 'irresponsible', she said, and the way she avoided looking at Kale as she spoke was eloquence itself.

Kale sat through it all as if it were nothing to do with him.

The social worker from Sandra's old authority had a boyish face that was falling in on itself. Speaking with a faint stammer, he told them that she had been drunk on the night when her daughter was taken into care. Police had raided the council flat where she lived with her husband, intending to arrest him on drug charges, and found the baby girl dehydrated and half starved, and lying in her own urine and faeces.

Sandra kept her head down as he described the injuries that had been discovered when the child had been admitted to hospital, the evidence of broken bones partially healed, internal bruising, a fractured skull.

'The father admitted hitting her,' the social worker said. 'He said it was to shut her up. He blamed his wife, but only because she couldn't keep the child quiet. He didn't appear to think he'd done anything wrong. The little girl died in hospital three days later, from pneumonia. Wayne Carter was sentenced to three years for manslaughter, and another two for drug-related charges. Mrs Carter' – he inclined his head at Sandra, who had her hand shielding her eyes – 'was found guilty of neglect, but it was felt she'd been dominated and frightened of her husband. She was put on a year's probation. After that she moved out of the authority's jurisdiction.'

He closed his file. 'That's all.'

There was a choked noise from Sandra. Her shoulders heaved as she covered her face. Ben saw that her nails were raw. He stamped on the involuntary stirring of pity.

'Are you all right, Mrs Kale?' Rogers asked.

She nodded without lifting her head. Her hair bounced up and down. The dark roots looked sad and vulnerable against the bleached yellow.

'Would you like to take a break? We can—'

'Just get it over with.' Sandra wiped her eyes and lowered

her hands. Her face was red and blotchy. The solicitor handed her a tissue, which she took silently.

Kale watched her, impassive, then looked away. She might have been something he had never seen before.

Rogers turned to Carlisle. 'I think it's time we heard the social services' views, Mr Carlisle.'

The social worker drew a deep breath. 'Ah, well, to start with I think I should point out that although Mrs Kale – or Mrs Carter as she was then – failed to protect the child from its father, she had no direct involvement in her daughter's death. So while the, uh, breakdown in communication was unfortunate—'

'There was no breakdown,' the other social worker interrupted, calmly. 'We weren't approached. And it's all a matter of record anyway.'

'Even so, I'd like to make clear that—'

'Mr Carlisle,' Rogers interrupted, 'while I'm sure there will be questions to be answered as to why Mrs Kale's background was overlooked, that isn't the purpose of this conference. We're trying to assess what the present situation is and how to deal with it, not apportion blame or excuses.'

Carlisle seemed about to object, but the man Usherwood had identified as his manager put a restraining hand on his arm.

'Excuse us.'

They held a brief, murmured conversation. Carlisle straightened, reddening. He looked as though he had bitten on lemon rind. Ben felt a quiet chime of satisfaction.

As the social worker described the findings of their investigation, he could feel Kale staring at him, though. The weight of it was mesmeric. It required a physical effort to keep from looking back, but he didn't want to meet those eyes right then. He didn't even realise he was no longer listening to what was being said until the sound of his own name brought him around with a jerk.

'Would you like to talk us through these, Mr Murray?'

Ben looked at Rogers stupidly for a second. She was holding copies of the photographs he'd taken of Jacob and Kale. He glanced around and saw that so was everyone else. Or nearly everyone. Sandra was still half curled in her chair.

Kale's blank gaze was still fixed on him.

He felt scalded by it as he haltingly described what he'd seen going on in the garden.

'If you were worried why didn't you approach the authorities before you did?' Rogers asked at one point.

'There was no point. I'd already tried.' He looked at Carlisle. 'I knew no one would believe me.'

'And you didn't think it worthwhile to express your concerns to Mr Kale either?'

'He'd already warned what would happen if he saw me again,' Ben said. 'And when he did, he beat me up and shot his dog.'

There was a mild commotion at that, protests from Kale's solicitor, but Ben wasn't listening. He forced himself to meet Kale's stare across the table.

He saw his death in it.

They had to leave the room while the deliberations were being made. There was the choice of waiting either outside in the corridor or in an adjacent anteroom. Ben hung back until the Kales and their solicitor chose the anteroom, then went into the corridor. Usherwood came with him. She didn't offer any speculations, for which he was grateful. He fetched coffee from a vending machine, and they sat in silence.

Before they had left, Rogers had asked Kale if there was anything he would like to say. 'Either about anything you've heard so far, or if there's something you'd like to add before we come to any decisions about Jacob.'

He had turned and looked at her. 'Steven. His name's Steven.'

He didn't say anything else.

They were invited back into the conference room as Ben was on his third cup of coffee. He put the plastic cup under the bench and told himself that it was the caffeine that was making him shake as he stood up. The Kales were already sitting down as he and Usherwood entered. He took his seat, conscious that Kale was already staring at him. Sandra was still avoiding looking at anyone. Her eyes were red and swollen as she gnawed at the corner of her thumbnail.

Rogers waited until everyone had settled. 'We've discussed the situation and are ready to make recommendations for a care plan based on the information we've heard. While Mrs Kale's background has to be taken into account, we are prepared to accept that what happened twelve years ago does not necessarily have any bearing on her present family situation. There is no suggestion that Jacob' – she seemed to stress his name – 'has suffered or is likely to suffer any deliberate physical harm. However, because of his special needs it's felt that he may suffer *emotional* harm if he doesn't attend school, and this matter can't be ignored any longer. We feel that this risk is enough to warrant placing him on the Child Protection Register. In addition, he'll have to be assessed to see if any supplementary schooling or therapy are necessary to make up for the time he's lost.'

Ben felt disappointment settle on him as the implications sank in. Jacob was staying with Kale. Although he'd tried not to expect anything else, the confirmation was still bitter.

'Another issue that needs to be addressed,' Rogers went on, 'is the possibility of Jacob being injured either because of the unsafe environment created by the, ah, excessive quantity of scrap metal at his home, and also by some of your own actions, Mr Kale.'

There was the slightest trace of a frown on Kale's forehead, as if it was only now occurring to him what was going on. Rogers continued.

'Although we accept that he hasn't been physically harmed, and that there's no malicious intent on anyone's part, we nevertheless feel that it's in Jacob's best interests for the scrap metal to be removed. I'm sure that won't be too much of a problem, since you work at a scrapyard. If it is, then we can arrange its disposal for you.'

Kale was staring at her now.

'Do you understand what I've just said, Mr Kale?' she asked.

He was slowly shaking his head. 'You can't. I'm too close.'

There was an uneasy pause. Ben could almost see Rogers choosing her words. 'We're also going to suggest that you undergo an assessment by a mental health worker. I can—'

'Mental health worker?'

'I can assure you there's no stigma attached to this. But we do feel that it would be, ah, helpful in view of ... well, of certain aspects of your behaviour.'

When Kale didn't object she seemed to relax slightly. 'I suggest that we hold a review conference in three months' time, when we can hopefully—'

'No.'

The word dropped into the room like a bomb. Rogers spoke patiently. 'I understand how you feel, but—'

'You don't understand anything.'

Rogers turned to Kale's solicitor. 'Mr Barclay, would you advise your client that he doesn't really have a choice in this. Co-operation is in his own best interest.'

The solicitor nodded, but Kale spoke first. 'He's my boy. We don't need people interfering.'

Rogers sighed. 'Mr Kale, we're trying very hard to do the best thing for everyone. But our main concern is Jacob's welfare. Now, I'm sorry to have to be blunt, but we *are* going to interfere, as you put it, and it will be much easier for all of us if you work with us rather than against us. It needn't be a problem, but if you refuse to co-operate then we may have to consider further options. One of which would be to take Jacob away from you, and I'm sure you won't—'

'You're not taking him away!' There was a wildness in Kale's voice that hadn't been there before.

'I'm simply pointing out the alternatives. I'm not saying—'

'Nobody's taking him again!'

Now Carlisle spoke up. 'No one wants to do that, Mr Kale. All we're—'

'He's done this, hasn't he?' Kale turned his glare on Ben. 'Your bitch took him once and now you're trying to do the same.'

He spoke as if there were only the two of them in the room. Ben couldn't look away from the intensity in his eyes. There was hate, but also something he never thought he'd see in Kale, something like panic.

Carlisle was making a placatory gesture with his hands. 'Look, Mr Kale, I've been involved with you and Jacob from the start, and I can promise you that no one in this authority wants to take him away from you, or to split up your family in any way.' He shot a frigid glance at Ben. 'I understand how hard this must be, but we really are trying to help you. We're not acting on any one person's say-so. Our investigations show there are areas for concern, and your wife—'

He stopped dead. His eyes widened at the size of his blunder. Kale turned to him.

'What about my wife?'

Ben felt the sudden tension in the room. He was aware that Sandra was sitting very still, her head down.

Carlisle's face was crimson. 'Er, I was just about to say that, er . . .'

'What about my wife?'

Oh God, Ben thought.

Rogers tried to take charge again. 'We're getting away from the point here,' she said, but Kale's attention was on Sandra. 'What have you told them?'

'You're not helping yourself, Mr Kale,' Rogers snapped. 'This isn't achieving anything.'

Sandra didn't lift her head from her chest. 'Look at me,' Kale told her.

'Mr Kale, I must insist—'

'*Look at me!*'

Sandra shut her eyes. Kale stared at her, incredulous.

He backhanded her.

The sound of it was shockingly loud in the quiet room. Both she and the chair would have fallen if her knees hadn't struck the underside of the table. It shook with the force of it. As the chair banged down on all four legs Kale hit her again.

This time it knocked Sandra to the floor. The expressions of shock around the table were giving way to movement. The policewoman was first out of her seat. 'All right, that's enough—' she began, reaching to restrain Kale as he stood up. He jackknifed his elbow into her stomach and slammed the back of his fist into her face. She pitched into a set of steel filing cabinets and slid down it. Kale's solicitor said, 'For God's sake!' and put his hand on his client's forearm. Kale wrenched him out of his chair and slammed his head against the table top.

As the solicitor collapsed, Kale bent and lifted Sandra by the front of her sweater. He punched her twice, very quickly. By then other people were moving. Ben saw Carlisle clutch at his shoulder, saying, 'Please, Mr Kale—!' before Kale spun him into the wall and jerked his knee into his groin. The social worker doubled up and Kale turned back to where Sandra was trying to crawl away. The policewoman was speaking urgently into her radio, blood streaming from her nose as

Carlisle's manager grabbed Kale from behind. Kale stamped on his shin and threw him into the psychologist, who was half out of her seat. They both went sprawling. Rogers was yelling something into a telephone as the policewoman flung herself at Kale again. He batted her aside, then bent and pulled Sandra's head around by the hair.

Without knowing he was doing it, Ben stood up. The scrape of his chair made Kale turn.

They looked at each other across the table.

Kale let his wife drop and wrenched the table away. It screeched across the floor and crashed on to its side. Ben picked up his chair and threw it at Kale's legs. Kale staggered as it struck his crippled knee. He kicked it away and came on.

The door flew open. A security guard burst into the room, looked around and said, 'Christ!' Kale head-butted him as two more guards followed. Pivoting on his bad leg, Kale kicked one in the stomach and jammed the heel of his hand under the other's chin. The one he'd head-butted clutched him round the knees. Kale punched him on the back of his neck. The guard let go but the door swung open again and two policemen ran in. The room seemed full of uniforms as they swarmed over Kale. He struck out at them, grim and silent, but then his leg buckled and he went down. Even then he continued to fight, still without uttering a sound. Someone yelled for handcuffs, and it was only as they were wrestled on to him that he cried out.

'NO!' he bellowed. 'NO! YOU'RE NOT TAKING HIM! HE'S MY BOY!'

He bucked and thrashed as his arms were pinned behind his back. A security guard grunted as he was caught by a flailing leg. 'Right, let's get him out,' one of the policemen panted. Still struggling, Kale was half carried, half dragged towards the door.

'NO! *NO!*' His eyes locked on to Ben's as they bundled him into the corridor. 'HE'S MY BOY! *HE'S MY BOY!*'

The door swung shut behind them.

A quiet descended on the room. The psychologist was gently weeping as she nursed a broken wrist. People began picking themselves up, helping those who were still huddled with their injuries. One of the security guards lay on the floor in the recovery position, attended by Rogers. The policewoman, her own face bloodied, was cradling Kale's wife in her arms. Sandra was moving her head slowly from side to side, tears cutting tracks down her swollen cheeks. She looked at Ben from eyes that were almost puffed shut.

'Oh, God, what have I done?' she moaned.

He had no answer.

Chapter Twenty

━━━━◆◇◆◇◆━━━━

Ben finished arranging the flowers and stood up. The cheerful splash of colour looked out of place on the dead winter grass covering the grave. The old flowers were a limp and sodden mess. He bundled them in the paper the fresh ones had been wrapped in and put them on the ground to take away with him. His hands were icy from handling the wet stems. He put his gloves back on and hunched his shoulders. There was no wind but the cold penetrated his heavy coat and struck through the soles of his boots.

He'd felt a need to visit Sarah's grave. No, that wasn't quite right — he'd felt he *ought* to visit it. But now he had changed the flowers he was at a loss. There was another bunch already there, not yet wilted, so he knew her parents had been recently. He wondered if they felt any closer to their daughter when they stood over the ground where she was buried. He wished he did. He wanted to be able to talk to her, to tell her what had happened, but the idea of a graveside monologue, even a silent one, seemed theatrical and false. So he stood there, stamping his feet, not knowing why he was staying but unable to bring himself to leave.

A sense of oppression had persisted for the three days since Kale had gone berserk. He couldn't explain it. He knew he should have felt vindicated, that Kale couldn't have chosen a more blatant way of proving him right if he'd tried. But a feeling that what had happened was his fault, that he was somehow responsible, obstinately refused to be shaken. It wasn't helped by the suspicion that other people also held him to blame. He'd spoken to the policewoman after Sandra Kale had been led away to an ambulance. She was holding damp paper towels to her bloody nose, waiting to be attended to herself, and as Ben stood there unharmed he felt compelled to say something.

'The back-up got here pretty quickly.' She looked at him without comment over the top of the wet grey paper. Blood had turned it dark, soaking into it as if it were a litmus test for violence. 'The officers who were here,' he said, unsettled by her silence. 'It didn't take them long to respond.'

She took the paper towel away from her nose and examined it. 'They were on stand-by. The local authority request it if they think someone could become aggressive.'

Ben had been surprised. He'd thought that he'd been the only one who knew what Kale was capable of. 'So you thought he might get violent?'

She had put the paper towel back to her nose. The look she gave him over the top of it was unreadable.

'We were asked to provide it because of you.'

Kale had been charged and held in custody, and, with Sandra unfit and unwilling to look after his son, Jacob had been taken into care. Ben had been told he'd been placed with a foster family, one living near enough for him to attend his own school, but that was as much as anyone would say. His offer to take him had been brusquely refused. The social worker – not Carlisle, who was still recovering – pointed out that he hadn't yet applied for a residence order. Besides which Jacob hadn't been taken into care permanently. It was hoped that he would eventually be returned to his father.

Provided that Kale wasn't sent to prison, of course.

Ben told himself he should be pleased, but somehow he

couldn't manufacture any satisfaction. The memory of Kale being handcuffed and dragged out was too vivid. He felt he'd made things worse, not better.

He felt like he'd broken something

The day after the case conference he'd considered getting in touch with Sandra Kale. In the end, though, he hadn't. He couldn't imagine she would want to talk to him, and he wouldn't have known what to say anyway. 'Sorry' was pathetically inadequate when someone's life had been wrecked. Instead he'd burned all the photographs and negatives he had of her. It seemed an empty gesture, and as he watched the paper and cellulose flare and blacken he'd been seized by the urge to add to it. He'd fetched the telephoto lens and polarising filter and carried them outside to the fire. He'd thrown the filter on straightaway, but hesitated with the lens. It ran through his mind that it was an expensive piece of equipment. If he wanted to atone it would be better to sell it and send Sandra the money. He'd weighed the familiar heft of it in his hands, then tossed it into the flames.

A man with two children came to the next grave. Ben and the man nodded in acknowledgment, then pretended the other wasn't there. The children were subdued but their voices still cut through the cemetery's silence. With a last look at Sarah's grave, Ben picked up the dead flowers and walked away. He detoured towards a bin on his way out. It was full of other bunches that had been discarded. Broken stems protruded through its wire-mesh sides, and the once-bright petals of chrysanthemums, roses, and carnations were crushed and faded, turning to rot. He dropped his own on top, then paused. After a moment he went to the car for his camera.

He used a full film, photographing the bin from different angles. He would have gone on except that an elderly woman was watching him suspiciously. When she began walking over with an intent swing to her walking stick, he packed up and left.

As he drove away he was struck with his own morbidity. The symbolism of a rubbish bin of dead flowers in a cemetery, a graveyard within a graveyard, was so obvious as to be hackneyed. He'd be reading the death notices in the newspapers next. He tried to laugh at the thought, but the mood wasn't so easily broken. He knew he was waiting for something to happen, without knowing what. When he was a teenager he'd had recurring dreams that woke him in a blaze of terror, convinced he was on the verge of some unspecified calamity that he could never quite see. It was like that now. His rational mind insisted it was just anticlimax, that he was simply unsettled, but it lacked conviction.

Nothing had been resolved. In spite of everything this was only a lull, a hiatus. Everything else had been a prelude. Now that Kale's psyche had been stripped bare, the civilised skin of restraint and control finally shed, Ben couldn't begin to imagine what the man might do, or where he would stop.

He was frightened of finding out.

It was on the news two mornings later. He'd been to a match with Colin the evening before, a Spurs–Arsenal derby that Tottenham had lost miserably, and he was preoccupied with that as he made his breakfast. It was the first time they had been out since the attempted suicide. On the surface Colin seemed to be back to normal. He never mentioned what had happened, or the girl who had triggered it, and had gone back to work after a few days as though it had never happened. Even so, Ben got the impression that something was missing. It was as if a part of Colin had died back there in the car. Or perhaps before, when the girl finished with him. Talking to him now was like listening to music through a Dolby system. It was a muted, filtered version, all the brightness and crackle skimmed off.

Ben hoped it wouldn't be permanent.

The news was on the radio but he wasn't paying any attention to it. Colin and Maggie were due to go on holiday the following day, taking Scott and Andrew to Disneyland, and as the report of a woman's murder droned on in the background Ben was wondering if Colin's fragile psyche would be up to the sight of Maggie rubbing shoulders with Minnie Mouse. He was pouring milk on his cornflakes when Sandra Kale's name leapt out at him.

He jerked as if struck.

'... body was found in the garden of her house last night by a neighbour,' the newsreader was saying. 'It's thought she was beaten to death. Thirty-one-year-old Mrs Kale was the wife of John Kale, who last year made the headlines when he was reunited with his kidnapped son after six years. Police are looking to interview Mr Kale, who was released from police custody on bail yesterday, after assaulting social workers last week.'

The newsreader went on to the next story. Ben heard something dripping and saw that he was still holding the milk bottle at an angle. He put it down but made no attempt to stem the spreading white pool that was trickling off the edge of the work surface. He felt dizzy, then sick. Then both passed. He looked around the kitchen, seized with the need to do something, but without any idea of what. Numb, he sat down.

My fault. My fault.

He stood up again, unable to bear being still. He went to the phone and dialled Directory Inquiries for the number of the police station in Tunford. The policeman who answered didn't sound like the one he had seen after Kale had shot the dog. He gave Ben the number for the incident room. When he rang it a policewoman politely asked who he was and why he was calling. He tried to explain, but knew he wasn't making a very coherent job of it. He wasn't really sure himself. The policewoman said she would pass on his message and thanked him for getting in touch.

He hung up and stared into space. Then he wiped up the milk and went out. There was no reason for him to be at the studio so early, but he needed to get out of the house. He hadn't gone a mile before it occurred to him where he really wanted to go.

He turned around and headed for Tunford.

Colin called him on his mobile when he was on the motorway. 'Have you heard?'

Ben said he had. 'I'm on my way up there now.'

'To Tunford? Is there any point?'

'I don't know.' He did, though. He needed to know that Jacob was safe, to make sure that the police were protecting him. But he didn't want to discuss it, didn't even want to think about it, until he knew for sure. 'Will you phone San—' *Shit*. 'I mean Zoe. Ask her to cancel today's shoot. Tell her ... well, just tell her what's happened.' Zoe would be able to think of a better excuse than he could.

A heaviness grew in him the closer he drew to the town. It was a cold and bright morning. The sky was a clear, arctic blue. He passed familiar landmarks; this was the turn-off he always took; that was the road that led to the woods; there was the police station; the pub. It was all unchanged, bleak and battened down for winter. He could almost believe the news report was wrong.

Then he turned on to the Kales' street and saw the cluster of police vehicles and knew it wasn't. Neighbours stood watching from doorways or bunched in small groups. Some of them were being questioned by uniformed police officers. He drove past, stopped and got out. The Kales' front door was open. Yellow tape sealed off the path and garden. A large white trailer with a band of black checks running down its length was parked outside. Steps ran up to a door, and as Ben approached it opened and a policewoman emerged. She saw Ben and came towards him.

'Can I help you, sir?'

He tore his eyes from the sight of a man in plainclothes on his hands and knees in the Kales' hallway, examining something on the carpet.

'I need to speak to whoever's in charge.'

She greeted this with a stony lack of emotion. 'Can you tell me what it concerns?'

'It's about the murder.' It sounded ridiculously melodramatic.

The policewoman asked him his name and went back into the trailer. A moment later she re-emerged. 'Would you like to come in?'

Ben went up the steps. The inside of the van was like a miniature office. A middle-aged man in a grey suit was talking to a beefy constable with a clipboard. He turned to Ben as the constable went out.

'I'm Detective Inspector Norris. How can I help you, Mr Murray?' He had a flat Midlands accent.

'Have you found Kale?'

'We're looking for Mr Kale to help us with our enquiries,' Norris said, non-committally. 'The constable said you had some information relating to Mrs Kale's murder?'

Ben ignored this. 'He's going to go after his son.'

He knew it beyond any possibility of doubt. The certainty had hit him like a physical blow in the car. He broke into a sweat again now with the need to convince the policeman. 'The social services put his son in care last week—'

'Yes, we know.'

Ben faltered. 'His wife gave evidence against him. He found out and . . . and that's why he did this. He's going to try to get his son.'

'Has Mr Kale been in contact with you?'

'No, but—'

'Perhaps you could tell me exactly what your involvement is, then, sir?'

'I'm the boy's stepfather.'

The policeman took a moment to consider this. 'I see.'

'Look, I know Kale, I know what he's like. He isn't going to let anything come between him and his son.'

'I appreciate your concern, Mr Murray, but if the boy's in care Mr Kale isn't going to know where he is.'

'They're sending him to the same school. He's autistic, there aren't many special-needs schools about. Kale's going to go there—'

'Just a second.' Norris went over to a man in plainclothes. He spoke, too low for Ben to overhear. The other man nodded and picked up a telephone. The inspector came back. 'I've arranged for a car to be sent. We'll have someone outside all day.'

Ben felt relieved, but not entirely reassured. 'You know he's an ex-soldier?'

'We're aware of his background. Is there anything else you can think of that might help us?'

It was phrased as a dismissal. Ben couldn't think of anything. He looked out of the small window set in the side of the trailer. The Kales' house was visible through it. 'What happened?'

'I'm sorry, sir, we're not an information service. We're in the middle of a murder investigation, so—'

'For Christ's sake, it was me who got her to testify against him!'

He hadn't meant to shout. There was a silence in the trailer. Norris regarded him, then sat down. The background noise started up again. 'Kale was released on bail yesterday afternoon. We know from neighbours that he arrived here about five. There were sounds of an altercation — nothing new, apparently — then Kale was seen to leave and drive away at about five thirty. A man was walking a dog along a path at the back of the house at about eleven o'clock last night. He noticed the Kales' kitchen door was open. By the light from it he saw something lying in the garden. He thought it was a body, but it was difficult to see.' He shrugged. 'There's a lot of scrap metal back there.'

'I know,' Ben said.

Norris glanced at him but didn't comment. 'He called the local police station. They sent someone to investigate and found Sandra Kale. At least, they guessed it was her. Someone had dropped part of a car engine on her head. Are you all right, sir?'

Ben gave a nod. The news of what Kale had used to kill his wife had made the room seem to tilt. He didn't doubt what it was. He'd seen him lift it over Jacob on two occasions. He flinched at a vision of the heavy cylinder thudding into the ground.

'We're still waiting for the pathologist's report on whether she was already dead when her head was crushed,' the inspector continued. 'She'd been badly beaten as well. It's possible some of the injuries were post-mortem, but they probably came first. Either way, the time of death fits when Kale was here.'

'Didn't anybody warn her that Kale had been released?'

Norris seemed to hesitate fractionally. 'At the moment I can't answer that.'

'They didn't, did they? Nobody told her.'

'As I said, I don't have all the information yet.'

Whatever criticism Ben might have made caught in his throat when he remembered his own role in events. *If not for me she'd still be alive.* His anger collapsed, taking its energy with it. 'Will you let me know if anything happens?' He fished in his wallet for a card. 'You can get me any time on the mobile number.'

The inspector took the card but didn't say if he would get in touch or not. 'Thank you for your help, Mr Murray.'

Ben didn't take the hint. 'You will watch for him at the school, won't you?'

'It's taken care of.' Norris signalled to the policewoman Ben had spoken to earlier. 'Will you show Mr Murray out, please?'

After the warmth of the trailer it seemed colder than ever outside. He went back to his car, ignoring the curious stares of the neighbours. He told himself that the police knew what they were doing, that Jacob would be safe. There was nothing else he could do.

It never occurred to him to ask if the shotgun was still in the shed.

He drove along his old route to the hill overlooking the town. He parked in the same spot and climbed over the wall. The woods seemed dead beyond any hope of resurrection. He slipped and fell on the slick ground and rotting leaves as he made his way down through them. Mud smeared his coat and clogged the gash in his hand made by a broken root. He wadded a tissue against it.

The huddle of oak trees seemed smaller than he'd remembered, more barren and exposed. He found a Snickers wrapper twined in the brittle remains of the grass in the entrance to his den. There was no other evidence that he had ever been there. He picked it up and put it in his pocket.

The hillside running down to the houses looked as though it had been scoured with acid. A pale polythene canopy had bloomed in the Kales' back garden, screening the area inside the dark ring of scrap metal. Children were gathered around the fence at the bottom, trying to see in.

A branch snapped behind him. *Kale*, he thought, and spun round to see a policeman in a reflective yellow jacket tramping down the slope towards him. The policeman stopped a yard or two away.

'Having a good look, are we?'

Ben's heart was still thumping. 'Not really.'

The policeman's eyes were unfriendly. 'Mind telling me what you're doing?'

It must be something in the air up here, Ben thought. Or perhaps it's just me. 'Just walking.'

'That your car parked on the road up there?'

'If you're talking about a red Golf it is.'

'What's the registration?'

'I haven't a clue.'

'What's your name?'

Ben told him. The policeman spoke into his radio, still watching him. He seemed disappointed by the response from it.

'All right, go on.' He motioned with his thumb towards the road.

Bloody-mindedness made Ben say, 'You sure you don't want to arrest me?'

The policeman gave him a psychopath's stare. 'I'm not going to tell you again.'

Ben took a last look down the hill, then trudged back to his car.

He went back to the studio, even though the shoot had been cancelled. He'd unlocked and gone in before it occurred to him that perhaps he should be more careful. Kale had already killed his own wife, and Ben had no illusions about what would happen if he encountered him again. But he couldn't take the threat to himself seriously. He didn't doubt that Kale would kill him, given the chance, but he also knew what the man's first priority was.

Jacob.

He tried to reassure himself that there was nothing to worry about. Kale was only one man, and, with his limp, neither an inconspicuous nor a very mobile one. Ex-soldier or not, it was only a matter of time before he was caught. And then the entire question of who would have Jacob would be raised again, because no one could doubt now that Kale had forfeited the right to his son.

Except Ben couldn't quite make himself believe it would be so simple.

He busied himself with make-work jobs; checking his darkroom stocks, minor repairs; anything to keep himself occupied. He'd almost resorted to cleaning the studio when he remembered the film he'd shot at the cemetery.

He wasn't expecting anything from it but developing it gave him something to do. The first prints were enough to show that the film had been faulty. It happened occasionally. The exposure was out, the colours so smudged and without resolution that the flowers were completely unrecognisable. The wire mesh of the bin had become a blurred geometric pattern over abstract slashes of spectrum. He tossed them down in disgust. Then he looked at them again. He picked them up, turning them this way and that.

Actually, he thought, it was quite an interesting effect.

He printed the rest.

It was the ambiguity that appealed to him. It changed mundane objects into something at once less concrete yet more substantial. What should have been representational now only hinted at its nature, provoking a vague sense of familiarity that defied recognition. He was considering how to reproduce the effect intentionally when the phone rang.

He snatched it up on the second ring.

'Hello?' he said, breathless.

'Is that Mr Murray?'

He recognised the police inspector's voice. *Oh, God, please. Please have caught him.* 'Yes.'

The potential for good news remained for an instant longer, then it was shattered. 'I'm sorry,' the inspector began, and suddenly Ben didn't want to hear the rest.

'Kale forced his way into the school this afternoon,' the policeman's heavy voice continued, delivering all of it. 'He's got his son.'

*　　*　　*

It was on the TV. There were the school gates, the school itself a squat brick building behind them. There were crying children being led away by adults. There were eye-witness accounts, a police car with its rear end crumpled. There was a corroded bumper lying dented in the kerb, crystalline scatterings of glass.

The inspector had been apologetic. He'd had two officers stationed in a car right outside the main gates. They'd been warned how dangerous Kale was, told not to take any chances, to radio for assistance at the first sight of him.

But that hadn't been until the rust-coloured Escort flung itself around the corner in a squeal of tyres and rammed into their car. Before it had stopped rocking Kale had materialised with a shotgun and blasted the radio and dashboard into fragments. He'd smashed the gun butt into the nearest policeman's face, ordered the second one out and clubbed him unconscious as well.

Then he'd gone into the school, taken Jacob and driven away.

'We didn't know he was armed,' Norris said. 'If we had ...'

If you had, it wouldn't have made any difference. Somehow Kale would still have taken Jacob. Even as he added the forgotten shotgun to the list of blame he had to carry, Ben felt the inevitability of it, as though this was the way it had to be, that events were drawing together towards an unavoidable resolution whose shape he could almost make out, but was frightened to see. He'd barely heard the policeman's assurances that Kale would be caught, that the car had been damaged, that a crippled man and an autistic boy couldn't get far on foot. He was remembering how Kale had shot the bull terrier rather than let anyone else take it. *It's my dog.*

He's my boy.

He didn't think he'd ever felt so scared.

The phone rang constantly at first. It wore him down, the hope and fear that each ring provoked. But it was only people wanting to offer their support, asking if there was any news. He told everyone the same thing. Thank you, no there wasn't, he'd let them know. He asked them all not to phone again, explained he wanted to keep the line clear. Eventually the calls dwindled and stopped, leaving him alone.

That was just as bad.

It was impossible to sit still. He moved from room to room in the house, just to keep moving, to evade the panic that threatened to overtake him. He poured himself a drink, but left it after the first mouthful. It would only have been an artificial relief and he didn't want to feel dulled. The sandwich he made went uneaten.

It was a completely different feeling to when Sarah had died. Then it had been disbelief and numbness. Even when she was dying, as bad as that had been, he had known what was happening, had been there with her. Now he didn't know anything, not even if Jacob was alive or dead, his brains blown out like Kale's dog.

The only thing he was certain of was that Kale wouldn't give up his son again.

Colin called around later that evening. 'You haven't heard anything?' he asked as Ben let him in, but it wasn't really a question. They sat in the kitchen, drinking coffee, not really talking. 'Maggie sends her love,' Colin said at one point.

Ben nodded, not caring. A distant thought surfaced. 'Aren't you supposed to be going on holiday?'

'Not till tomorrow morning.'

'Have you packed?'

The inanity of it made them both smile. The moment quickly passed. 'Maggie'll do it.' Colin hesitated. 'Anyway, I've told her I might not be going.'

'Why not?'

'Come on, Ben.'

'There's no point missing your holiday.'

'I can manage without Donald Duck for a few more days.'

'I know, but—'

'Ben,' Colin said, quietly but firmly, 'I'm not going to go, okay? It's my decision. I've told Maggie I'll fly out to them as soon as all this is sorted. So long as the boys can go on the rides they won't even notice I'm not there. I'll make it up to them later, and Maggie ... Well, Maggie'll have to make do with my Gold Card.'

Ben looked at him, surprised even through the haze of anxiety. Colin shrugged. 'Something like this puts things in perspective.'

He didn't say any more, but the look on his face was more like the old, pre-suicide Colin. He stayed till quite late, until finally Ben told him to go home. After he'd gone Ben went into the lounge. He turned on the TV and sat down in front of it. He didn't realise he was tired, would have said he could never sleep, but at some point he slipped into a doze. He jerked awake on the settee, heart racing. The TV was showing a snow-filled screen. A soft hiss of static filled the room. The house was silent. He saw that it was after two o'clock. He went to the phone and lifted the receiver to make sure it was still working. While it was in his hand he considered calling Norris. But the inspector had promised to let him know if anything happened. He put down the receiver without dialling.

Where are they?

His mouth was dry. He went into the kitchen for a glass of water. Even that had to be forced down. He poured half of it away, and as he put the tumbler in the sink his hand caught the edge of the draining rack. The glass slipped from his fingers and smashed.

He mechanically bent down and began picking the pieces up. The smaller fragments were scattered across the kitchen floor. They reminded him of something. It hovered at the brink of recognition. He stared down at them, unaware that he'd stopped moving as it came to him. The shattered windscreen in the road. The damaged police car. The bumper from Kale's battered Escort. *Where would Kale go?*

'Oh, Jesus.'

He ran to the phone, dialled Norris's number. A police-woman answered. Ben's voice shook as he asked to speak to the inspector. His urgency must have convinced her. She told him to hold. Norris came on, sounding tired.

'They're at the scrapyard,' Ben said.

The drive to Tunford, the second in twenty-four hours, was both the fastest and the longest. The roads were empty and he kept his foot flat on the accelerator once he reached the motorway. The car rattled. He could feel the vibrations through the steering wheel as he appealed to a God he didn't believe in, offering deals, making promises. *Let him be all right. I'll believe. Take me instead.*

It fell into the empty air.

He hadn't told Norris he was going. He hadn't planned it himself. The inspector had promised to check out the scrapyard, but it had been impossible simply to sit and wait. He was certain that Kale had taken Jacob there. With Kale's own scrap collection out of bounds, there was nowhere else for him to go.

It was inevitable.

He resented having to slow down once he came off the motorway. The roads were unlit, and once he instinctively stabbed at the brake as something darted from a hedge in front of him. The flowing tail of a fox disappeared through a fence on the other side. He crashed the gears and accelerated again.

A police cordon blocked the road. Beyond it he could see the scrapyard's walls, illuminated by a forest of flashing lights.

Oh God. He wound down the window as a policeman came towards him.

'What's happening?'

'Sorry, sir, the road's blocked. You'll have to turn—'

'Have you caught Kale?'

'I'm sorry, sir, but you'll have to—'

'Tell Inspector Norris that Ben Murray needs to see him! Please, it's urgent!'

The policeman grudgingly went back to his car. He crouched down and picked up the radio handset. An age past before he straightened.

He waved Ben through.

Police cars and vans lined the road outside the scrapyard, canted at crazy angles. Two waiting ambulances stood amongst them. The flashing lights gave the scene a fairground appearance. He pulled in as soon as there was room and left the car without locking it. Uniformed police surrounded the yard's walls from behind the cover of their vehicles. Most of them carried guns. One of them saw him and hurried over. Ben pre-empted any questions by asking for Norris. The policeman regarded him suspiciously and told him to wait. Ben looked towards the yard's tall gates. They were closed, but parked in front of them was Kale's Ford Escort.

He felt sick.

The policeman came back and led him through the confusion to what could have been the same white trailer that had been outside the Kales' that morning. It seemed much longer ago than that. Norris stood by its steps, talking to a tall man in a bullet-proof vest. Their breath steamed in the cold air. He broke off when he saw Ben.

'Mr Murray, I don't think—'

'Are they in there? Is Jacob all right?'

Norris drew a breath as if he was going to argue, then let it out as a sigh. 'Kale's car's here, so we're assuming he is. We don't know any more than that. The owner's on his way with the key to the main gates.'

'Can't you go over the wall?'

The tall man broke in. 'It's topped with broken glass and barbed wire. I'm not sending anyone over that when there might be someone waiting with a shotgun on the other side.'

His scalp showed through his cropped blond hair. He didn't attempt to hide his antagonism at a civilian presence.

'This is Sergeant O'Donnell,' Norris said. 'He's in charge of the Tactical Firearms Unit. Now if you don't mind, we've got a lot to do, so—'

'If Kale's in there you might need me,' Ben said, quickly. 'I know him.'

'I don't think—'

'Please. I won't get in the way.'

Norris considered. 'I'll tell the superintendent you're here. He might want the negotiator to talk to you.'

He went up the steps into the trailer. The policeman called O'Donnell detached himself and walked away without another word. After a moment the trailer door opened and Norris beckoned Ben in.

The light inside was bright, the atmosphere foul with coffee and cigarettes. The small space seemed full of activity. A heavily built man with a moustache and bloodshot eyes was perched with one meaty thigh on the corner of a desk. A small cigar burned down between his thick nicotined fingers. The man next to him had sandy hair swept sideways to cover his bald scalp like a groundsheet at Wimbledon. Neither wore uniforms. Both looked tired and crumpled.

Norris said, 'Mr Murray, this is Detective Superintendent Bates and Detective Inspector Greene. Inspector Greene is our negotiator. He'll be handling communications with Kale. Assuming he's in there,' he added, dryly.

'He is,' Ben said.

The superintendent was the heavily built man. 'Let's hope

you're right,' he said, with the air of a man who didn't like being roused in the early hours. 'Ken, see where the bloody owner's got to, will you? He should be here by now.'

Norris quickly left. The man he'd introduced as the negotiator turned to Ben. 'What can you tell us about Kale?'

Ben tried to assemble his thoughts. 'Uh, he's ... he's unstable. Unbalanced. Violent, very fit, except for his leg. He got shot when he was in the army. In Northern Ireland.'

An irritable sigh from the superintendent stopped him. 'We're not interested in his CV. We want to know what his state of mind's like, so we know what we're dealing with.'

He ground out his cigar with an expression of barely concealed impatience. Ben tried again. 'He's obsessed with his son. Nothing else matters to him. I think ...' The words had to be forced. 'I think he'd kill both of them rather than let anyone take him away again.'

The negotiator nodded, calmly. 'What's your relationship with him like? Do you think he might listen to you?'

Ben felt them all looking at him. 'I'm the reason he's in there.'

He told them, as clearly as he could, his role in Kale's madness. 'So he's not going to chuck his gun out of the window at your say-so, then, is he?' the superintendent commented when he'd finished. Greene looked annoyed but made no comment. The trailer door opened and Norris put his head inside.

''Scuse me, sir. The owner's arrived.'

The superintendent heaved himself to his feet and went out. The negotiator gave Ben the first friendly smile he'd had all night. 'It'll be all right if you wait in here. We'll let you know if anything happens.'

'What happens now?' Ben asked, struck with a fresh fear at the prospect of action.

'When we've got the gates open we'll see what the situation is inside. If Kale and his son are in there, we'll establish a line of communication. Get him talking, find out what he wants, reassure him.'

Ben thought of the superintendent's impatience. 'You won't just rush straight in?'

Greene seemed to know what he was thinking. 'The last thing anybody wants is a confrontation. In most situations like this it's just a case of waiting them out.' He gave him another smile. 'Don't worry. We know what we're doing.'

So does Kale, Ben thought, but said nothing.

The negotiator left. Ben waited as long as he could stand it and then walked to the door. No one stopped him from leaving the trailer. He saw the senior police officers gathered by a car. The scrap dealer was with them, an overcoat thrown over his pyjamas. His stomach strained against them like a pregnant woman's. He looked confused and frightened as he answered their questions.

Finally, he was led away. O'Donnell, the sergeant in charge of the firearms team, went at a half-run to a group of policemen clustered behind a white Land Rover. The superintendent, the negotiator and Norris came back towards the trailer. Ben stood back, but none of them so much as glanced at where he stood in the shadows as they went inside.

Ben shivered and realised how cold he was. He looked down and saw he hadn't fastened his coat. He zipped it and turned up the collar. But his body had already lost too much of its heat for it to make any immediate difference. His skin felt icy and dead.

There was movement over by the gates. Two policemen in body armour ran towards them in a crouch. Others aimed guns at the top of the wall. The two men huddled over the lock, then the gates were swinging open. The Land Rover's engine growled to life. It pulled slowly up to the entrance and stopped. Its headlamps shone into the darkened scrapyard, but from where Ben was standing he couldn't see inside. Armed police disappeared through the gates, black figures briefly lit by the car's lights. Ben could hear the crackle of radios, make out snatches of words. After a moment the Land Rover drove slowly inside.

He couldn't bear it. He edged away from the trailer, all the time expecting someone to shout and stop him, but no one did. He didn't have to move far to see through the open gates.

Kale had been busy. The Land Rover had pulled up just inside the yard. Its headlamps and the beam from a spotlight on its roof lit the area inside the gates with a harsh, surreal white light. In it Ben could see that the drive leading to the office building had been blocked with wrecked cars. They had been piled on top of each other in an untidy heap three and four deep, crammed between the neater stacks on either side. The jib of the crane was visible above them. He could just make out the black shape of the office behind it.

The police who'd gone into the yard were making no attempt to climb the barricade. Nothing seemed to happen for a while. Then the trailer door opened and the negotiator came out. He would have walked past if Ben hadn't spoken.

'What's going on?'

Greene looked startled to see him. 'Go back to the trailer, please, Mr Murray. We haven't secured the area yet.'

'I won't go near the gates, I just want to know what's happening. Please, tell me if they've found anything!'

The negotiator appeared to reach a decision. 'Not yet. He's barricaded himself in, and we've been unable to reach him on the scrapyard's phone. He's either ignoring it or ... or he can't hear it.'

Ben noticed the hesitation and knew what it meant. His voice was unsteady as he asked, 'What are you going to do?'

'We'll have to try talking to him another way. Now, please, Mr Murray, if you don't go back to the command post I'll have to ask you to leave the area.'

His face was grim with concentration as he hurried away. Ben noticed for the first time that the man had put on a bullet-proof vest himself. He drifted back towards the trailer in token obedience, but couldn't bring himself to go back inside. He watched as Greene went through the gates to where O'Donnell stood in the shelter of one of the Land Rover's open doors. Other police were crouched by the barricade, facing the office building beyond. Ben saw Greene raise something to his mouth.

'JOHN KALE.'

Ben jumped as the amplified voice rolled across the night. The echo hung in the cold air, slowly diminishing. *Kale-ale-ale.*

'ARE YOU IN THERE, JOHN? THIS IS THE POLICE. NOBODY'S GOING TO HARM YOU. WE'D JUST LIKE TO TALK.'

Talk-alk-alk. The echo died away. There was no answer. The wrecked cars towered silently around them, broken and blind mechanical corpses. The negotiator tried again. Every now and then he would pause, waiting for some response, a sign of life, and then continue on a different tack, speaking in a steady, reassuring voice. The dark scrapyard absorbed his words, offering nothing in return. Ben hugged himself. *Please, God.*

Greene and O'Donnell conferred. Ben could see them talking on the radio, presumably to the superintendent in the trailer. He felt like screaming. As if in response the scrum by the car broke up. Two officers tentatively began to climb the barricade. Ben could hear the metallic scrape of their progress, the teetering of bonnet and roof under their weight. The wrecks were precariously balanced, but eventually the policemen reached the top.

The boom from the office was almost drowned out by a sound like hail hitting a tin roof. One of the policemen climbing the barricade cried out, and then both were tumbling down in a riot of confusion. The uppermost cars shifted in a screech of metal, then toppled off with an appalling crash. Ben saw the police scatter as the whole thing collapsed. There was chaos, people yelling, pounding footsteps, and over it all the shotgun cracked out again and again. Someone was shouting, '*Move, move, move!*', and through his shock Ben felt an utterly devastating relief, because Kale was still alive, and if Kale was alive then Jacob would be too.

'Thank God,' he said, not caring that he was crying. 'Thank God.'

But his relief turned to shame as he saw the figures running from the yard, carrying the injured to safety, not just the two men who'd been on the barricade but others who'd been caught by the falling wrecks. There were frantic calls for ambulances as they set the bloody, groaning or unconscious figures down away from the gates, shouts that someone was still trapped. One man's face was a gleaming black mask that reflected the lights from the police cars as he was dragged out. Ben watched as he was laid down, the protective vest that had proved useless stripped from him and used to support his head. There were sirens now as the ambulances drew up and the attendants leaped out. In the background he could hear Greene's voice through the loudhailer. Without realising he was doing it he began moving forwards, walking through the injured policemen with no fixed idea in his mind, only the urgent need to stop this from going further. Someone grabbed him, roughly.

'What the *fuck* do you think you're doing? Get back! Now!'

The policeman's face was contorted with anger and fear. Ben felt the man's spittle fleck his cheeks.

'I need to speak to Inspector Gr—'

'You fucking *deaf*? I said *move!*'

The policeman seized him, began pushing him away. He could see the negotiator standing behind the Land Rover's open door, framed against the fallen car hulks. 'Greene! Greene!' he yelled as he was propelled backwards. The negotiator turned and saw him, seemed to hesitate, then came towards them in a stooped, shuffling run. His face looked haggard.

'I told you to stay out of the way!'

'Let me talk to Kale!'

The negotiator jerked his head at the policeman still holding him. 'Take him back.'

'No, wait! Fucking get off me!' He tried to shrug off the policeman; failed. 'At least let me try!' he shouted to the negotiator's retreating back. 'He's not going to listen to you but he might me! For fuck's sake, will you *listen*?'

Greene halted, then signalled to the policeman. Ben felt himself released, but he could sense the policeman poised like a heeled guard dog to take hold of him again, eager to vent his outrage on someone. His breath in Ben's face was sour with frustration as the negotiator said, 'What would you say to him?'

'I don't know, offer to go in myself if he lets Jacob go.' The negotiator gave an emphatic shake of his head and turned away. 'All right, all right.' Ben rushed the words out. 'He wants his son. All this is because he thinks people are trying to take Jacob away. I'll say I won't even try to see him again, that he can have him. I can tell him that I'll never bother them again if he gives himself up.'

He stared at the man, willing him to agree. 'Please!'

The negotiator glanced towards the shambles in the scrapyard. He turned his back as he spoke into his radio. Ben heard the superintendent's gruff voice through a snap of static, but couldn't make out any words. Greene came back. He gave a terse nod.

'We're not going to let you speak to him. He's volatile enough as it is, and we don't want to risk doing anything that might provoke him into hurting himself or the boy. We've got to calm him down and get him talking to us, but you can stay near by in case he asks anything you can help with.'

He motioned for Ben to follow. 'Keep behind me.' They

went through the gates into the yard. Everything was suddenly much larger. The white lights and the smell of oil and metal lent it the surreal quality of an airport at night.

The sergeant gave him a hostile look as they reached the back of the Land Rover. 'Wait here,' the negotiator told Ben. 'He can't see to shoot over the cars, but I want you out of the way anyway. If I need you I'll let you know.'

Leaving him, Greene went to where O'Donnell stood behind the Land Rover's door. Sirens wailed outside the yard as the loaded ambulances raced away. Ben looked past the policemen to the office building, just visible above the jumble of wrecked cars. They still blocked the road but now it was in an untidy sprawl, as if they had been tipped out of a bucket. It looked like an adult version of the scrap pile in Kale's garden.

Facing the shadowy office across the top of the car door, the negotiator raised a loudhailer to his mouth.

'THIS IS IAN GREENE AGAIN, JOHN. WE'RE STILL HERE. NONE OF US ARE GOING ANYWHERE, SO WE MIGHT AS WELL TALK. I KNOW YOU'RE UPSET, BUT THIS ISN'T GOING TO DO ANYONE ANY GOOD. THINK ABOUT WHAT IT'S DOING TO—'

Ben lunged for his arm before he could finish the sentence. 'Don't say Jacob!' he said quickly as the negotiator furiously turned on him. 'Kale calls him Steven!'

The heat went from the negotiator's eyes. He motioned Ben to get back and put the loudhailer to his mouth again. He continued in the same measured tones, a reasonable man, offering reasonable alternatives. *It won't work.* The conviction gripped Ben with a cold certainty. Kale wouldn't listen to reason. He had his own insane agenda, and rational solutions didn't figure in it. They wouldn't be able to talk him into giving himself up, and if they eventually tried to rush him he would shoot Jacob, then himself.

Ben couldn't see any way out that didn't end in blood and death.

He was shivering uncontrollably. Greene was trying to convince Kale to answer the phone. He could have been talking to himself in an empty room for all the effect it had. The negotiator paused, then said, 'I'VE SPOKEN TO BEN MURRAY, JOHN. HE DOESN'T WANT THIS EITHER. HE SAYS HE DOESN'T WANT TO SPLIT YOU AND STEVEN UP. TALK TO US, JOHN. LET'S SEE IF WE CAN—'

The shout carried clearly from the office building. '*Is Murray there?*'

Ben tensed at the sound of Kale's voice. The negotiator hesitated. 'YES, HE'S HERE, JOHN. DO YOU WANT TO SPEAK TO HIM? PICK UP THE PHONE AND—'

'*Send him in.*'

'YOU KNOW I CAN'T DO THAT, BUT YOU CAN TALK TO—'

The blast of the shotgun made them all duck. This close, Ben could see the muzzle flash through the barricade. '*Send him in!*'

O'Donnell said, 'Shit!' Greene drew in a long breath. Ben reached him before he could use the loudhailer again.

'Let me go in!'

'I told you to stay back there!'

'Let me do as he says!'

The shotgun bellowed again. '*You've got five minutes.*'

Ben clutched at Greene's arm. 'Please! I might be able to talk to him! If not you don't know what he might do!'

The negotiator yanked his arm free. 'I know what he'll do if you go in. Get him out of here,' he told O'Donnell.

'He's got my son in there!' Ben shouted, realising for the first time that it was true. But the sergeant was already pulling him away, signalling to another policeman. 'Take him back to the command post.'

The policeman gripped his arm above the elbow and herded him through the gates. 'All right, I can walk, let go!' Ben said, but the policeman didn't loosen his hold as they went outside. The ambulances had gone, but discarded pieces of equipment and uniforms still littered the road like the detritus from a bloody street party. An armoured vest lay in the gutter like a run-over dog. A solitary boot stood upright, its leather glistening and wet. Here and there dark patches that weren't oil stained the frosted tarmac. Ben wondered how finding some old cuttings in a brass box could have led to this. He was shivering more than ever as they reached the white trailer.

'I'm going to be sick,' he said.

The policeman stood back as Ben leaned against a lamppost. His radio gave a hiss and a tinny voice squawked out. The policeman spoke into it, briskly, then put his hand on Ben's shoulder. 'You going to be all right?'

'Just give me a few minutes.'

'Go in there when you've got yourself sorted. Someone'll get you a cup of tea.'

Ben nodded thanks without looking up. The policeman left him outside the trailer and jogged back towards the scrapyard. Still bent over, Ben watched him disappear inside.

He straightened and looked around.

The activity of the police outside the scrapyard had subsided to a tense expectancy. They faced the gates from behind the protection of their cars and vans, waiting to see what Kale would do next. No one looked back as Ben approached them.

He tried not to think of what he was doing as he headed for an empty gap between two police cars, as if even the noise of his thoughts might attract attention. Greene's voice was blaring from the loudspeaker again, but he barely heard it. When he reached the gap he hesitated. The nearest police were only yards away. Doubt immediately began to batter at him. *Just do it.*

He carried on walking.

He was past the cars, moving out into the open space in front of the gates. He could see through them to the Land Rover, the tangle of wrecks. He was in plain view now. He quickened his pace praying for a few extra seconds of confusion, shoulders tensing with the expectation of the sudden challenge. He had gone less than half a dozen steps when it came.

It released him like a starting pistol. He sprinted for the gates as shouts and footsteps raced after him. Up ahead he saw O'Donnell and Greene turn, and veered around the other side of the Land Rover as the sergeant started moving to cut him off. His throat and chest hurt as he swerved away from another policeman, and then the tumbled barricade rose up in front of him.

He'd planned to go across where the fallen cars were lowest, but now there was no time to do anything but leap at the first wreck he came to. His foot skidded off an icy wing, but he grabbed on to something cold and sharp and hauled himself upward. There were yells from behind and below him now. A hand seized his ankle. He jerked his foot and kicked back. Someone said, 'Bastard!' and his foot was released. The car bodies were icy and rough. He clawed his way up on to the roof of one and jumped from it on to the next as it shifted beneath him. He closed his mind to their see sawing instability as he scrambled over them, hearing the clamour at his back as the police followed. He reached the top, shouting, '*It's Ben Murray, I'm coming over!*', and as he slipped and scrabbled down the other side there was a boom and a flash of light from the scrapyard office. *Oh, Jesus, the bastard!* he thought as he slipped and fell. He tried to turn it into a jump, pushing himself clear, and landed heavily on the broken concrete of the drive. He curled himself into a ball and wrapped his arms around his head as the shotgun crashed twice more, but the expected shock of pellets ripping into him didn't come. Above him it sounded as though handfuls of pebbles were being thrown against the cars. Someone screamed, '*Back! Back! Get down!,*' and for a few seconds he thought the entire barricade was coming over on top of him as it rocked and clattered under the policemen's retreat.

Then it went quiet.

He slowly uncurled. He was lying at the foot of a car canted over on its side. He looked up at it rearing above him and hurriedly moved from underneath. He felt bruised and scraped in any number of places, and his ankle protested when he put his weight on it, but other than that he was unhurt. He rubbed his arms to try to stop shaking, but he couldn't keep his teeth from chattering. 'Oh fuck,' he breathed. 'Oh fuck.' The memory of the shotgun explosions was still reverberating in his head. But they had been to drive the policemen back, not aimed at him.

Kale wanted him inside.

Greene's voice, unamplified, came from the other side of the barricade. 'Murray! *Murray!* Can you hear me?'

'I'm all right.' The words were an inaudible croak. He put more force into them. 'I'm all right!'

He could hear the negotiator's relief in his pause. 'Okay, just stay where you are. Get behind some cover if there's anything near by, but don't move away from the cars. Just stay put.'

Ben didn't answer. He looked down the drive to the darkened building. Slices of light from the police Land Rover shone through the barricade in fractured patterns, but none reached that far. It waited for him, impassive and silent. Ben started towards it.

'Murray? Mr Murray!' Greene's voice fell away. 'Look, don't be a bloody idiot ...!'

He kept walking. There was frost underfoot. It gave a minute, frictionless crunch with every step. The towers of lifeless cars on either side of him were coated with it. As the shattered patches of light from the Land Rover were left behind and his eyes adjusted, he could see the wrecks shining with a pale luminescence in the moonlight.

His hands were sore and frozen from his scramble over the barricade. The armed police already seemed a long way away. Greene began calling him through the loudhailer, telling him to go back, but even that seemed distant and unimportant, far less real than his footsteps on the icy concrete. It was between him and Kale now. As it always had been, he realised.

He remembered when he and Colin had come along this same drive. The scrapyard had figured in his thoughts so often since that he could hardly believe he'd only been there once. He wondered if he'd made a single right decision since then.

He wondered if he was making one now.

He felt exposed and alone as he approached the unlit building. He glanced uneasily at the square black hole of the first-floor window. That was where the shots had come from. It was wide open, but he couldn't see inside. He knew Kale would be watching, though. Sighting down the barrel.

He shivered under his bulky coat. He had no plan, no idea of what he would do when he reached the office. There was no chance of him overpowering the ex-soldier, and he didn't believe for a second that Kale might want to talk, that he could be persuaded to give himself up and let Jacob go. There was only one reason why he wanted Ben to go inside, and for a second Ben felt a heady disbelief as the nearness of his own death confronted him.

But there was nothing else to do.

God, I'm frightened. He was almost at the building now. Its shadow lay across his path like a hole in the ground. He walked into it, more conscious than ever of the open window above, resisting the impulse to hurry from beneath it. *Don't give him the satisfaction.*

He could see the ground-floor room where he and Colin had met the fat scrap dealer. Next to it was the open maw of the passageway. It was a solid block of darkness. Ben halted at its edge. At its far end, invisible, were the steps leading up to the first floor where Kale would be waiting. *And Jacob, please God.* There was a smell of damp brick. He felt in his pockets for matches. He hadn't any. He looked around him, putting off the moment when he would have to go into the blackness. There was a lightening in the sky to the east, and he realised with surprise that dawn couldn't be very far off. He stared at it for a long moment, then turned and entered the passageway.

He felt his way along by touch. It was impossible to see. His foot kicked something hard, and he skittered back before he identified it as the first step. He groped around until he found the wall, and a cold steel railing. Holding on to it, he started up, treading as softly as he could. The steps came to a small concrete landing, then turned back on themselves, still rising. He paused on it, out of breath. A small window was set high in the wall. It was almost obscured with dirt, but the steps here weren't quite so dark. He continued up. He was almost at the top when Kale moved out of the shadows.

Ben stopped. He couldn't see Kale's face, but he could make out the barrel of the shotgun aimed at his chest. He put out his hand in a desperate staying gesture, knowing it wouldn't do any good.

'Wait—' he said.

There was a roar of light.

Smoke from the shotgun blast hazed the air. His ears were still ringing as he swiftly reloaded, watching the photographer's body for any movement. The double impact of the twelve-bore shells had flung it down the steps, crumpling it against the back of the small landing. As his eyes adjusted from the muzzle flash, he made out the black splashes of blood on the walls and floor. He looked for a moment longer, making sure, then snapped the shotgun shut and went back into the office.

Keeping out of the direct line of the window, Kale crossed over and stood with his back against the wall to one side. He picked up the broken mirror tile he'd ripped from above the toilet sink and tilted it until he could see the barricade. The predictable bastards were starting to come over. He readied himself, then spun round and fired through the window, one barrel straight after the other this time, not both together as he had done with the photographer cunt. He ducked down, ignoring the pain in his knee, cracking the breech open and pumping in two fresh shells, slithering on his arse to the other side of the window, and then he was up and firing again.

He dropped back to the floor, his bad leg stuck out awkwardly in front of him. He reloaded with one hand while he had another look with the mirror. Shouts and yells, but the bastards had fucked off. The twelve-bore wasn't accurate at that range, probably not lethal, even with 'OO' buckshot cartridges which would put a four-inch hole through two-inch wood at ten feet, and blow photographer cunts practically in half at eight, but it had a good spread. He made sure none of them had dropped down on his side before he lowered the mirror.

Keeping well outside the perimeter of chairs, wastepaper bins and boxes he'd set up to mark the area where the police marksmen bastards could get a shot, he went over to the desk. It was tipped on its side in part of the room he knew would be out of any line of fire. Steven was curled behind it, eyes squeezed shut, hands over his ears, rocking backwards and forwards. Kale felt angry again for being made to use the shotgun. He stroked his son's head.

'Shh, it's all right. It's all right.'

'No bangs! No bangs!'

His son's hair felt soft and fine under his fingers. He pushed his hands gently down from his ears. Steven shook his head violently.

'No bangs!'

'Not many more.'

There were seven shells left. When he was down to two he would use them to make sure the bastards didn't separate him and his son again.

He stayed there for as long as he dared and then, skirting the area he'd marked out, he went back to the window to check with the mirror. The barricade was still clear. He hoped it had taken some of them out when it went down. He'd rigged it so it would collapse if anyone gave it so much as a sour look. It'd still slow them up long enough to do what he had to when they cottoned on that they couldn't talk him out. The telephone was ringing again downstairs, but he took no more notice of it than before. He returned to the desk. Steven's eyes were still shut but his rocking wasn't quite so violent. Kale lowered himself to the floor and put his arm across his shoulders. He unwrapped a stick of chewing gum, broke it in two and gave half to Steven, half to himself. The boy chewed without opening his eyes.

'They just don't give you any peace,' Kale said, looking down at him. 'There's no time. They can't just leave you alone.' He brushed a strand of hair from his son's face, then put his head back against the desk and looked at the paling sky through the window.

'We were almost there. I could feel it. I've been close before, but not like that. I was near to it in the desert, but I didn't realise, not then. Not until what happened to you and your mum. It was right in front of me, but I couldn't see it. There was so much ... *broken* ... it took your breath away. It was like that was how things were supposed to be, that was normal. But it was too soon. I wasn't ready. You've got to be tempered first. You've got to be nearly broken yourself. It purifies you, makes you see more clearly. You've got to go through that before you can see it's not all shit, there's no such thing as good or bad luck. Everything fits and works together, like a big machine. It's all part of the same thing, all part of the Pattern.'

He broke, off, tilting his head to listen. Outside, it had gone silent. He turned to Jacob again.

'There's a reason for it all, for everything,' he went on. 'That's what the Pattern is, it's the reason. You've just got to be able to see it, that's all. Scientists say everything's made out of the same stuff, all these little ... little *bits*. They think they've found out what the smallest bit is, but then they realise there's something smaller. So that means that you, me, this floor, that desk – everything – is all connected. And if it's all connected then what happens to one thing or person, even if it's on the other side of the world, it's still part of everything else. Part of *us*. It still affects us, even though we don't know it. There's all this ...'

He frowned, locking his splayed fingers together.

'... this *meshing* going on, all the time. Everything interlocks. So long as the Pattern's in sync it's okay. But sometimes you can go out of sync with it, and then—' He clenched his hands together in a double fist. 'Things break. Like those wrecks out there. Each one's sort of ... *frozen*.' He savoured the word. 'They're like recordings. The Pattern's there, in each bit of them, and if you could see it you could understand *why* things happen like they do, you could avoid the breaks. But you've got to know how to look.'

He stopped as the loudhailer started up again. He pushed himself across the floor to the window. The sky was lighter now. The wrecks in the yard were no longer just frost-covered shadows. Through the mirror he could see the bastards still weren't doing anything on the far side of the barricade. Just mouthing off.

He went back to the desk. Steven was rocking again. Kale held his son and rocked with him.

'When you came back it was a sign that I was getting close to seeing it. Things were falling back into place again, I was getting back into sync. Even the way you are is part of it. I didn't understand at first, but it is. You're locked in here—' He rubbed his son softly across his forehead. 'You see everything as a pattern. I'm trying to see one, and you're trying to get out of one.' His expression hardened.

'They wouldn't leave us alone, though. A bit more time, that's all we needed. Just a bit more time.'

He put his head back, tiredly, then snapped it round at new noise from the yard. Crouching awkwardly, he left the desk and went to check through the window with the mirror. There was movement. An engine was being revved. The cars in the barricade suddenly shuddered. As he watched, one of them slewed around and fell. He had a glimpse of a yellow mechanical arm and then the mirror exploded into fragments.

The belated report of the rifle came as the bullet chunked into the wall on the far side of the room. Kale counted to ten, ignoring the cuts from the glass, then fired one barrel blindly through the window. He dodged back before anyone could draw a line on him, moved to a different position and snapped off the second barrel.

He dropped to the floor, reaching for the shells. Five left. Three more for the bastards. A sound came from behind him. He slapped the breech closed with only one shell in it and spun round, bringing the gun to bear.

The photographer was in the doorway.

It had taken all the strength Ben had to crawl up the steps. He saw Kale aiming the shotgun at him for a second time but couldn't move. He'd no idea how long it had taken him to drag himself up there, how long he'd lain unconscious. He was slick with his own blood. He cradled what was left of his left hand in the crook of his right arm. Every now and again, without warning, the pain from it would whirr closer until he almost blacked out. It was the one he'd stretched out towards Kale. The shotgun blast had taken most of it away before smashing into him.

Through the ragged hole in his coat, the armoured vest that he'd picked up from the street outside was visible, its outer fabric shredded above his heart.

It had been damaged before he put it on, looked as though it had been struck by something when the barricade collapsed on the police. Ben had hidden it beneath his own coat so that if Kale did shoot him he wouldn't see it and blow his head off instead. It had stopped the blast from killing him, but his ribs felt as if they'd been crushed. Each breath seemed to tear something inside his chest. His vision was blurred, either from loss of blood or from cracking his head in the fall.

He clung to the door frame to keep from falling again now, and saw Jacob huddled behind an upturned desk. *Thank God.* Jacob's eyes were tightly closed. His face had the pinched, set expression he wore when he was upset or frightened. Ben knew the boy didn't realise he was there. He tried to say something to him but his voice wouldn't come. He looked back at Kale, noticing without really comprehending that the furniture and various objects had been arranged to form a loose square in front of the window. Standing outside it, Kale stared at him down the length of the shotgun barrel.

He lowered it and came towards him.

Ben saw the stock of the shotgun swinging into his face but couldn't avoid it. A light burst in his head, and a new pain spun into the others. He felt himself hit the floor, but only distantly. He opened his eyes and saw Kale's boots. He rolled over and looked up. Kale was a giant, towering above him. The shotgun butt was raised in slow motion. Ben watched, incuriously, for it to begin its descent.

'No, Daddy, no, Daddy, no, Daddy!'

The cry gradually penetrated the fog in his head. Kale was no longer looking down at him. Ben moved his head until he could see Jacob. The boy had his eyes open now, but they were darting about, looking at everything but Ben and Kale as he frantically rocked himself.

'*Nonono!*'

'It's all right,' Kale said, but the boy only rocked harder, chanting his denial. There was a huge grating of metal from the yard. Kale glanced uncertainly towards the window. A grey daylight was coming from it now. Ben began to drag himself towards Jacob. His hand shrieked, and so did he.

Kale looked from him to the window and back again.

Another huge clamour came from outside. Ben pushed himself along the floor with his feet. His hand left a giant slug-trail of blood. He saw Kale's face contort. The man pressed the heel of his fist against his forehead as if he were trying to crush it. He took a step forward.

'Get away from him!'

Ben shoved himself the rest of the way and pulled Jacob to him with his good arm. Jacob moaned and rocked, eyes shut again. Kale gripped the shotgun.

'I said get away!'

Ben stared up at Kale as he held their son. He wanted to speak but the effort to reach Jacob had taken the last of his strength. There was a rushing in his ears. His vision was breaking up. He struggled to keep his head upright as Kale raised the shotgun and levelled it at them.

The room lit up as the sun crested the scrapyard's wall. Kale winced at the sudden brightness. He looked out across the frosted tops of the cars as the light bounced and splintered from their uneven surface. Ben saw him frown.

Then his face cleared.

Still staring outside, he lowered the gun. Through the rushing in his ears, Ben heard him murmur, 'There ... It's there ...'

Like a man in a dream, Kale slowly turned back to them. He no longer seemed aware of Ben as he gazed down at Jacob. A screech of metal from outside made him glance at the window again. Going to the makeshift cordon of furniture, he moved aside a broken chair with the same deliberation he'd applied to rearranging his pieces of wreckage. He stood by the breach he'd made for a moment, letting the sunlight fall on his face.

Then, fixing his eyes on his son, he put the shotgun stock to his shoulder and stepped backwards through the gap.

The crash came immediately. Ben cringed, clutching Jacob to him, but there was no pain, no impact. After a moment he cautiously looked up.

Kale had been hurled sideways by the marksman's bullet. It had taken him through the chest. He lay twisted on the floor, one arm thrown above him, the other straight out in a parody of the exercises he performed in his garden. His eyes seemed to be staring at a point above Ben's head, at something behind and beyond him, and Ben felt an urge to turn and look. But his eyes were drawn to the blood soaking through Kale's sweat-shirt. He lay in a puddle of it. Streaks and splashes fanned out from him in dark whorls, hieroglyphs of an unknown language which changed and grew as their substance spread across the floor.

Jacob was keening. Ben pressed the boy's face into his shoulder to spare him the sight of his father's corpse. The rushing in his ears became very loud. He put his head back against the wall and saw an oblique strip of sunlight running over the ceiling. Motes of dust danced in it, spinning frenzied patterns. He tried to focus on them, and was still struggling to decipher their semaphored message as his vision faded away.

Chapter Twenty-One

———⋄◦⋄———

The wasp bumped against the window. The sun streamed in through the whole length of the west-facing wall, filling the studio with light. The next window along was open. Zoe went over and tried to cuff the wasp towards it with her hand. 'Go on, piss off.'

Its buzzing rose in pitch until it found the gap and flew out. 'Stupid things.'

'You should just squash them,' the girl said, unscrewing the cap from a bottle of mineral water. 'I always do.'

Zoe looked embarrassed. 'If it had been a fly I would have.'

Ben didn't say anything. He'd seen her usher out flies as well, but she did her best to keep her humanitarian tendencies strictly in the closet. He saw her glance at him as he struggled with the camera lens, but she made no offer to help. After a few false starts they'd established that he would manage by himself, no matter how long it took. Sometimes the shoots ran a little late, but so far no one had complained. The quality of his work wasn't affected.

Besides, he was becoming more adept. The prosthetic hand had been difficult at first, but he was growing used to it. It was his left, which he only used to hold and support anyway. Once you got over the shock of seeing the arrangement of metal rods, wires and plastic instead of flesh-and-bone fingers, there was an almost aesthetic beauty about the thing. It was just a matter of getting acclimatised. They'd told him at the prosthesis unit that there were other models he could have, some of them styled and coloured to look more realistic, but he wasn't sure if he wanted that. The blatant artifice of the present one seemed more honest. He'd begun making a photographic study of it, both on and off what was left of his maimed hand, experimenting with the effect he'd discovered with the dead flowers. He wasn't sure yet how well it would turn out, or if he would ever show it to anyone, but it was something he wanted to do. If nothing else it was good therapy. It forced him to accept what had happened.

He got the lens off and fitted another, aware of Zoe and the model trying not to watch. 'Five minutes and then we'll make a start on the last session, okay?' he said. He put the camera down and went over to where Jacob was sitting on the settee. 'Fancy anything to drink, Jake?'

Jacob shook his head, not looking up from the jigsaw puzzle spread out on the coffee table. For a change he was assembling this one face up. Ben held the prosthetic hand under his nose and moved its fingers. Jacob broke off what he was doing to study it.

Ben watched him. He would miss having him at the studio after half-term finished. He'd worried about how him being there during shoots would work out, but it had been fine. He thought Jacob had enjoyed it too, but it was sometimes difficult to tell.

The residency application had been approved while Ben was still in hospital. The adoption proceedings were still under way, and might take another year. But he'd been assured there would be no problem.

He wouldn't be entirely easy until then, though.

He tried to pick up a piece of jigsaw and succeeded at the fourth attempt. He held it out. Jacob took it, put it back with the rest of the jumbled-up pieces, and selected his own.

'Smartarse,' Ben said. 'I'll tell Grandma Paterson not to let you play on her chairlift this weekend.'

Jacob smiled briefly. His usual absent expression returned as he examined the prosthesis. It still fascinated him. He touched the steel rods and wires, lightly tracing their shapes. Ben manipulated them for him. The boy raised the hand to his face and looked through it. Kale's eyes stared out at Ben through the steel fingers.

'You about ready?' Zoe called.

Ben gently moved his hand away. 'Okay.'

Jacob went back to the puzzle.

*　　*　　*

WHERE THERE'S SMOKE

SIMON BECKETT

Imagine not knowing the father of your child. Not knowing his name. What he looks like. What sort of person he is. Although Kate Powell is desperate for a baby, that's something she can't accept. Single and independent, she likes to be in control of her own life. Even if, somehow, it has become empty and meaningless.

Then she meets a man who seems the answer to all her problems. But appearances can be dangerously deceptive. Soon Kate's life is out of her hands.

And out of control.

A selection of bestsellers from
Hodder and Stoughton

Where There's Smoke	0 340 68592 1	£16.99 ☐
Where There's Smoke	0 340 68593 X	£5.99 ☐

All Hodder & Stoughton books are available at your local bookshop or newsagent, or can be ordered direct from the publisher. Just tick the titles you want and fill in the form below. Prices and availability subject to change without notice.

Hodder & Stoughton Books, Cash Sales Department, Bookpoint, 39 Milton Park, Abingdon, OXON, OX14 4TD, UK. E-mail address: order@bookpoint.co.uk. If you have a credit card you may order by telephone – (01235) 400414.

Please enclose a cheque or postal order made payable to Bookpoint Ltd to the value of the cover price and allow the following for postage and packing:
UK & BFPO – £1.00 for the first book, 50p for the second book, and 30p for each additional book ordered up to a maximum charge of £3.00.
OVERSEAS & EIRE – £2.00 for the first book, £1.00 for the second book, and 50p for each additional book.

Name _____

Address _____

_____

_____

If you would prefer to pay by credit card, please complete:
Please debit my Visa/Access/Diner's Card/American Express (delete as applicable) card no:

Signature _____

Expiry Date _____

If you would NOT like to receive further information on our products please tick the box. ☐